Praise for *Green Corrosion*

———

"A colorful cast traverses this bleak but remarkably depicted world."

— Kirkus Reviews

Praise for *Servitude*

———

"Another home-run by one of the best authors in the business. Costi Gurgu is a genius."

— Robert J. Sawyer, Hugo Award-winning author of
The Oppenheimer Alternative

TITLES BY COSTI GURGU

Servitude

RecipeArium

The Lighthouse at the End of the World (RO only)

The Glass Plague (RO only)

GREEN CORROSION

Costi Gurgu

Kult Books

This is a work of fiction. All of the characters, organizations, and events portrayed in this novel are either products of the author's imagination or are used fictitiously.

CORROSION

www.costigurgu.com

A Kult Book
Published by KULT Books
Toronto, ON, Canada

ISBN (Trade Paperback): 978-1-7386593-0-2
ISBN (e-book): 978-1-7386593-1-9

Cover illustration by Luca Oleastri
Cover design by Superpixel Design
Book design by Superpixel Design
Printed in the United States of America

ACKNOWLEDGMENTS

———————

Many thanks to my wife, Vali, my first reader and supporter. Also, to my amazing editor, Marg Gilks. Her work on this novel is invaluable. And to Emanuel Grigoras whose support and enthusiasm helped me reach the publication stage.
Special thanks to Michael Haulica who encouraged me to turn my multi-awarded short story "Corrosion" into a novel.

I.

The Silkers

The sky was the color of moldy cheese. A upside-down, frothy swamp hanging so oppressively low, some of the decaying towers pricked its purulent belly.

Geo always felt sick after looking at the sky, but he inevitably looked every time he observed the Golden Tower, or the Silkers Tower, as people called it. The only high-rise structure in the city still in use. All the other high-rises had been abandoned long ago, after entire floors collapsed with the tenants inside. They rose, derelict, their windows clotted, in a ghostly jungle. The Silkers Tower, though…it supposedly had been consolidated and adapted to the new conditions. The golden structure gleamed like the only source of light in a city of eternal mist and green reflections.

Geo breathed deeply a few times to calm himself. The unwholesome effluvia of corroding bodies coiled through the air. He shut his eyes and ignored the fetid damp creeping through the rebreather. Then he looked around and felt a pleasant thrill, an ever-present fear, and lust, all at once in a bubbling, poisonous mixture. Lately, that had been the marinade his brain floated in.

He was part of the Silkers procession that had traversed the city from its port to their Golden Tower. Ninety Silkers soldiers had disembarked and took to the streets of the city to be next to their brothers in the most celebrated event of the year—the Water Passage.

The people of the city filled the streets, eager to glimpse

the glorious army. And Geo was at its head, in the lead. Next
to Prince Boris and his court, surrounded by Boris's elite guard
of Luna Warriors, atop the royal wheeled platform of rust-red
water-silk.

He was thrilled to be in such dangerous company. He lusted
for the kind of attention this display of power attracted. And the
fear was ever-present, fear of the Silkers' reality and their way
of life, their values and ever-shifting interests. Fear that today he
was at the center of their attention and tomorrow he might wake
up discarded. Fear of what being part of the Silker Court implied
and what not being part of it meant for Geo's clan.

The mayor and his Blue Officers watched the passing procession from the central balcony of the City Hall. It was supposed
to show the people that the procession was for him, for the ruler
of the city. But Geo knew that in reality it meant that the mayor
was not invited to be part of the procession and was not invited to watch the Water Passage Ritual, as he, Geo, was. Geo, the
prince's special guest. Last year Dinesh of the Bones Clan, who
had mysteriously vanished; this year, Geo. Prince Boris's special
guests and friends. The Silkers' ever-shifting political interests.

The City Hall was a two-storey building lined with waves
and waves of mortar to keep it from collapsing under the continuous attack of the water. It looked like a thick, monstrous candle,
the wax melted in ripples from years of burning. Its balcony was
the only thing moved forward so it remained on the outside,
overlooking the Mayor's Square and the Golden Tower. Prince
Boris said that they had decided to rehabilitate the Golden Tower
as a sign of respect for the City Hall. But Woodman the Elder,
Geo's grandfather and the leader of his people, had a different
opinion on the matter—that Prince Boris wanted to rub the
mayor's face in the fact that they had the knowledge to actually
convert an old structure to survive the vicissitudes of their times.
And that the Golden Tower of the Silkers looked a thousand
times more royal than the City Hall. And that all the people
could see it, because the two buildings faced each other.

The procession stopped in front of the Golden Tower. The
mayor waved formally and the prince nodded elegantly. The

crowd gathered in the Mayor's Square burst into cheers. The three detachments of the prince's three armies took their places around the royal platform and waited. The Luna Warriors secured the tower's entrance and took up position as a guard of honor.

Geo shuddered. He was about to enter the infamous tower for the first time. He was about to pull his clan into history. They were about to go public. Official. Known of. Dangerously exposed. Thrills and fear.

Luk was a slim young man barely touched by corrosion. His face was disfigured by a deep gouge on his left cheek where he'd sandpapered the corroded flesh away before it could spread its roots. It had left a mark but the flesh was clean under the pale skin. He wore a curious thing around his neck—a silver cross on a silver chain. Curious because, as Geo knew, Christianity was a forgotten religion. After more than two thousand years, Christianity, along with several other old religions, had been suddenly and completely erased from existence.

Luk's voice was cheerful and his attitude a balance between respect and lightheartedness. He wore his Pupa insignia with pride. He was one of Prince Boris's pups in training, ready to tear open the military school's cocoon and spread his wings. A future Silker officer.

"Here you are, sir," Luk said and pulled away a curtain covering the entrance. The young man entered the room first and held the curtain aside for Geo. His smile widened and his skin flushed pink. Geo entered a room with blue-papered walls and glassless windows framed by golden curtains. A small empty basin, an intricately sculpted bone chair, and… Geo stopped and stared in confusion.

A feminine body was waiting on the edge of the bed, barely covered and flawless, all voluptuous curves. Geo gulped instinctively. Her skin stretched unblemished and luminous, not the slightest sign of corrosion. Her face was hidden behind a very distinctive black textile mask, eyes invisible under opaque chitinous lenses, yet her mouth was exposed, her full lips a shiny blood red.

"May I present to you Lady L, sir," said Luk.

A golden emblem shone on the forehead of her mask. Geo focused on that and tried to remember his lessons. Prince Boris had a complex system for the ladies of his court, consisting of three main orders.

The Chimaera Order was more legend than reality. Geo's grandfather, Woodman the Elder, was of the opinion that they were the prince's secret guard. Any one of his court ladies could be a Chimaera—a lethal warrior assassin ready to defend Boris, or kill at his order.

The Morpho Order was the prince's intelligence bureau. No one had seen a Morpho and lived to tell of it. They worked undercover, spying, lying, infiltrating, spreading rumors—practically controlling the very reality of the world. Whatever reality they created through their cunning manipulations became the reality for all.

And finally, the Sun Glory Order, the members of which wore their emblem openly, were really the prince's harem—his lovers, the mothers of his children, his advisors, his entertainers. Anything he imagined, they performed. Rumor claimed that their lovemaking was the stuff of magic. Their sex skills were supernatural. A night with one of them would haunt you forever.

"Lady L." Geo recovered and inclined his head. "It's a pleasure."

"Of course it is." Her lips smiled.

"If you need me, sir, I'll be in Pupa Quarters, six floors up. Just tell the valet and he'll fetch me."

"Thanks, Luk. Was there anything in my agenda that you forgot to mention?"

"No, sir, I told you everything. The valet will be here to pick you up at six for the Passage ceremony."

"The valet, not you?"

"I'll go through the ritual tonight, sir. We can meet again in two days, after I've completed the Passage. Only then I'll be a Moth and we'll have to be reintroduced."

Luk was grinning. A child. Not that Geo was much older, but

sometimes it seemed that a couple of years made all the difference.

"I didn't know," said Geo. "I'm looking forward to meeting you as a Moth, young Pupa. Good luck to you!"

"Luck has nothing to do with it, sir. But thank you all the same. See you in two days. Lady," Luk inclined his head to the woman in Geo's bed and left.

"So." Geo looked again around the room and tried to swell his chest and look more imposing. "How can I help you, Lady L?"

"Not much, Mr. Ambassador," said Lady L, her lips still smiling, red and voluptuous. She reclined on her elbows and exposed even more shining skin. Weird fragrances rose like heat from her body. Heavy smells, strange and delicious.

"How do you find Lady L, Geo?"

Prince Boris's voice brought him back. He shivered and cleared his throat. "Boris?"

The prince laughed and slapped Geo's back. "She's something, isn't she?"

One or two? thought Geo. *One, minimum consequences.*

"Yes," Geo hurried to answer, hoping to put the subject to rest. He knew that Lady L was one of Boris's Butterflies and while he was confused by her presence in his room, he wanted to show Boris respect and deference. He couldn't spoil their relationship so close to signing a deal with the Silkers.

"Well, she's your host in the Silkers Tower," said Boris. "She'll be with you day and night, sharing her experience and knowledge with you."

"That's…"

"That's a Silkers tradition and I'd be honored if you accepted, my friend."

One or two? Deal with the consequences later.

"Of course I accept, Boris," said Geo without hesitation.

"I hope you'll be up to her standards." The prince broke into a huge grin. He was a booming barrel of energy and appetite for life. "I'm joking." He punched Geo on the shoulder.

Geo smiled. His visor plate was partially transparent, so unmasked people could see his face and feel that they were dealing with a human being and not a robot. He nodded and tried an even bigger smile, hoping it was visible to both Boris and Lady L.

"Or is he?" Lady L interjected.

Geo looked at her and hesitated.

The prince burst into explosive laughter. "I am, I am joking. But, my friend, life at court is very visible. There was a rumor that Dinesh Bones couldn't quite satisfy his host. His, uh…his reputation—or more accurately the Bones Clan's reputation—suffered immensely."

Prince Boris left the room and his Luna Warriors grouped around him.

Geo avoided looking at Lady L. What had all that been about?

"Relax, Mr. Ambassador, nobody forces you to satisfy me. I'm your host. We establish the boundaries together."

"That's good." Geo paced the room a bit to relax. Why was he so tense? Boris had proved to be nothing but a joyful, warm man. He turned to Lady L for elaboration.

"Yes, Dinesh's host was Lady V. She's quite the talker and she's always kissed Boris's ass."

"Ah," said Geo and sat on the bone chair. It was smooth and warm to the touch.

Lady L rose from the bed. She stepped closer, her opaque lenses fixed on his mask, her red lips parted slightly. The heavy fragrance that he'd sensed before was back again. He inhaled deeply and closed his eyes. It was intoxicating. He refrained from exhaling. From showing any sign of desire.

"I'll be with you every moment, here or wherever your diplomatic mission might take you. Ask me anything." She walked around him slowly, lightly touching his suit. "We'll share this room while you're the Silkers' guest."

She sighed a little bit and placed her palms on his shoulders. Geo saw her lips in his peripheral vision, close to his visor, her breath hot. Her scent found its way through his rebreather as if it weren't there. He felt calm and relaxed.

"Lady L—"

"You can call me Lena, Mr. Ambassador."

Geo sighed and realized only afterwards that he'd done so. He felt embarrassed, but still relaxed. She had that effect on him.

"What would you like me to do now, Mr. Ambassador?"

"Whatever you normally do," he heard himself saying and tried to focus and remember what his plan had been for the day.

Lena flowed back around his chair and went to the bed. "I'd like to rest now, Mr. Ambassador." She took off the cloth covering her breasts and threw it on the floor. Geo tried to look in a different direction, but she *tsked* and gently brought his head back around. "You needn't worry. I like when people are looking at me."

One or two? What would be one now? Geo stared at her dreamy breasts. She wasn't his first...why kid himself? She was his second and definitely the first one to look so ravishing. Could this be real? Could this really be happening to him? *One or...why waste time. Definitely one.*

"What would you like me to do, Lena?"

The woman's lips curved in a grin and her tongue slithered lazily over them. "What do you think, Mr. Ambassador?"

The Rain Hall was at least four levels below the Golden Tower. It was two floors high and spiked through with pillars—a stone forest with trees connecting the soil and the sky, dressed in luminescent green algae from the Ont Lake. Tatters of the famous gold silk, its undiluted threads that had made the Silkers empire, fluttered from the ceiling, spreading their musty aroma throughout the hall, imbuing people with dread and shivers. It was the silk of gods and monsters. It was the shield that protected the Silker warriors.

Bone logs were scattered among the stone trees. They were covered in moss and guarded by finely dressed Silker officers. Fat candles flickered, their flames shattering the darkness of the hall. The fragrance of melting wax mingled with the silk's miasma.

Prince Boris dominated the scene from a bone throne placed on a dais covered in gold silk. Geo sat on his left, two heads lower, and next to him sat Lena. Next to Lena were two Silker commanders in full regalia. On the prince's right were Commander Mort, the Luna Warriors commander, whom Geo had been introduced to earlier, and another commander who looked ancient and lethally corroded. He was a heavily sandpapered, shapeless lump of flesh with muscles like tightly knotted strings. His green eyes were the only things to possibly identify him as a human being. Geo knew the legend behind that lump of corroded flesh. Cephastix, the Antheraea Mare commander. The first sailor of the Gel Sea. The Kraken Killer. The Ghosts Puppeteer. The Dead Flesh Admiral. Geo avoided the Mare commander's eyes.

Twenty-seven boys entered the hall, scarred skin on their naked chests. Still young enough to be barely touched by corrosion. How could they submit themselves to such a barbarian ritual, Geo had wondered ceaselessly since he'd received the invitation to the ceremony. He knew in theory what the whole thing entailed and would have skipped it gladly, but...his clan's future depended on his so-called diplomacy. And diplomacy right now meant a strong stomach.

Prince Boris rose from his throne and the dim light in the hall grew even dimmer. A strange noise, a terrible, cruel sound filled the hall. Geo shivered and looked around in shock. He'd never heard it before and yet, it woke something inside him. As if it tapped an ancestral instinct, his skin under his envirosuit prickled, and icy fingers caressed his spine.

"Do you know what this is?" Boris's voice was sinister and solemn.

"Yes," whispered Geo. A tear rolled down his cheek inside his rebreather mask.

"Have you ever heard it before?"

"No," he murmured and then said louder, "No."

"Then how do you know?"

"It talks to me..."

"It. Talks. To. You."

"It touches something inside me..."

"So, the Woodman Clan can feel it too. You're not that different after all."

"No, we're not," said Geo before he could think about it. It seemed the right thing to say.

"Can you say its name?"

"Rain."

"Rain!" shouted Boris.

"*Rain,*" all the commanders repeated in unison.

"RAIN!" The hall reverberated with the collective voice of every living being under its ceiling.

"Water!" said Boris.

"WATER!" echoed the Silkers, their voices like thunder.

All twenty-seven boys knelt next to the bone logs and stretched their left arms along their surfaces, resting them on the soft moss. The officers raised huge battle-axes. Their metal shone darkly under the luminescent algae. The gentle, fluid sound of rain soothed Geo's heart.

The blades fell with a swish, like steel cutting through water. Severed arms rolled.

The rain stopped. Blood flowed down the logs. Water had turned to blood. Battle-axes rested. The Water Passage had taken its toll.

"Let's celebrate!" said Boris, grinning. A weird light glinted in his eyes.

Geo swallowed back vomit. He could not allow himself to show weakness in front of the Silkers Court. He stared at the blood flowing freely and remembered the sound of the rain—the calm, soothing sensation of flowing liquid. It melded with the fragrance of melting wax, the flicker of candlelight. When Boris repeated, close to his mask, "Let's celebrate," Geo managed to smile.

2.

The Water Passage

Painted in crimson and black and carpeted with moss wool, the torchlit dining hall was cavernous, full of smoke and stone tables and chairs. The line of clan representatives coming to offer their congratulations for the Pupas who would soon join the Silkers army was long and macabre. They were dressed in their best, covering what was still their regular body and exposing their corrosion: deep gouges of raw flesh, sandpapered cavities, shapeless lumps of what had once been arms, legs, shoulders, or chests. They wore the damage as if it were a mark of pride, like soldiers displaying their battle scars.

Lady L named each representative for Geo: "Ian of the Bathurst Clan, 6 percent of the city's territory, 340 strong; Hamid of the Transit Clan, owners of the transit rails, 1,022 strong…"

As a guest of honor, Geo dined at Boris's table. Tonight the prince reigned from the wooden throne gifted by the Woodman Clan. To his right were Lady Y, princess of the week, and Boris's four commanders; to his left sat Geo and Lady L, and the Silkers' Horn and Wasp. Boris's table was surrounded by two other curved tables populated by all his ladies and other court dignitaries that Geo had never seen. The guests sat at separate tables in the center of the hall, surrounding the round table of the mayor. All the people who counted in the city and therefore in the entire Ont Kingdom were there. And every one of them was staring at the wooden throne and whispering in awe. Not a single tree had survived the Black Rain Year anywhere in the kingdom. Wood was almost as expensive as gold silk.

More important to Geo, though, was that access to wood meant access to the most coveted resource of all—fresh, clean, liquid water. Now everyone knew that the Woodman Clan had it. Woodman the Elder had said that this reveal was a calculated risk. Well, in Geo's assessment, this risk calculation had assessed Geo as zero value. As in if it worked, they made it into the good life; if it didn't, then Geo was the only one they'd lose. The only aspect he couldn't fit into any calculation was the danger of him exposing the clan's location under torture. *"He must really trust your mettle, little brother,"* his brother, Alex, had said.

"Who are they?" Geo pointed to the four commanders. He knew they must be Boris's commanders, but had never seen them at such a close distance before.

"Forget about them," said Lady L.

"I'm a guest at the same table with them. I think it's just polite to know their names and say hello."

"If you get to say hello to them, it means you're already dead. You cannot meet them. It's Silkers etiquette, Mr. Ambassador." Lady L pointed toward the other guests in the hall and for the first time Geo noticed that not one guest, absolutely no one, was looking straight at the commanders. They were all avoiding that part of the table as if there was a void and it didn't exist.

"They, on the other hand," —Boris grinned at him and indicated the two men sitting next to Geo— "you must meet, because you're going to work with them from now on."

The other two men were the Horn and the Wasp, two important people in the Silkers' hierarchy, yet not as important and mysterious as the four commanders. Geo hadn't met them personally but had crossed paths with them several times. Geo smiled, nodded to the prince, and turned to the two men.

"That's Michael, the Silker Proboscis. He's your contact for all your Silker affairs. Whatever you want or need, he's there for you. *Everything*." Boris almost spelled out the last word. "And," he cut in before Geo could greet the Horn, "people call him the

Horn. He hates it. Could you guess why?"

Oh, shit! Geo could barely restrain his surprise. *"Never assume anything."* It had been one of the first lessons his grand-father had taught him. *"Always stay back and listen first, think it through, and then talk."* Well, the math behind all this was too complicated and the people around him were waiting for his answer now, not a minute later.

"I presume because a proboscis is a silent part of the moth and has a very specific function, and that is not to make music like a horn."

"What did I tell you?" laughed Boris with satisfaction. "Our man Geo is a well-read man. He is definitely not a Dinesh."

Everyone at the table laughed as if sharing an inside joke. Again with Dinesh, the vanished favorite from last year. Geo could only grin a bit wider, just to show that he shared their mirth, if not their joke.

The proboscis was a corpulent man missing both ears and half a face. His left arm had turned into a spidery thing, eight thorny legs quivering continuously on his clothing and nearby objects. Each leg ended in paws with eight claws. Instead of a hand, his right arm ended with an insectile head with eight human eyes and one wide, toothy mouth.

"And he is Jodi, our Silker Hymenoptera." The prince indicated the second man. "Also popularly known as the Wasp, a term he actually likes. He is my Commerce comptroller. The contract between us, Geo, was drafted by him and it will be supervised by him every step of the way. If you miss a payment, my hymenoptera will hunt you down."

Everyone laughed again, but Geo couldn't bring himself to grin wider anymore. "Gentlemen, it is an honor to make your acquaintance."

"Just remember that while I'm on your side," said the proboscis, "the Wasp just lies in wait to ambush you. That's his nature—nothing personal."

The hymenoptera was tall and thin and completely cocooned in black clothing. Geo generally found it difficult to tell a man's age because of all the missing parts and bits, but with this man it was difficult to even see his features. His face seemed perpetually shrouded in darkness within his hood.

"Now, Boris, you've placed me in a difficult position here," said Geo.

The prince cocked his head and regarded him with his "official" smile, one that Geo had come to know well. It wasn't Boris's honest smile when he was amused or warming to someone. It was the mask he offered to all of those approaching him on a diplomatic mission, or with a political request.

Too late now to tiptoe back on what's been said, thought Geo. "My grandfather wanted me to talk to you about something very...special."

Boris's table fell silent. As if a switch had been flipped, the entire hall fell silent and everyone's eyes fell on Geo.

"Discreetly," added Geo in a near whisper.

The prince raised his arms and servants entered the hall with trays of food. Music started pouring from speakers mounted on the walls. The guests returned to their business.

"It's their job to hear everything and advise me," said Boris, gesturing to the people at his table.

Geo nodded. In the beginning it had been only him and Boris, enjoying a drink, in a private talk, sharing a meal or a seasilk cigar—the special treatment. But one could consider this, too, "special" treatment. After all, the prince was sharing his table with Geo.

A servant placed a gold tray in front of the prince. Then others brought bigger trays loaded with smoking meats and vegetables for those at the tables to the prince's right and left. Nothing was placed in front of Geo. The servants all retreated and a little girl carried a covered bowl to Geo. Only after she'd placed the bowl in front of him did the others start eating.

"How's your food, Geo?" asked the prince.

It was the same as always, here in the city, for him. Grilled vegetables. So burned that there wasn't enough moisture to hold their molecular structure. Spiced with only dehydrated and roasted spices from the deep south. "It's exquisite, as always. Thank you for your hospitality."

"I'm so happy, Geo. So, what's the thing your grandfather wanted me to hear?"

"There's another Rain coming," Geo said, almost in a whisper.

Lady L turned to him, her dark mask expressing only indifference. Boris put down his fork. He nodded as if answering an internal dialogue. Geo was afraid to take his eyes from the prince and see the reactions of his proboscis and hymenoptera. Every little detail counted now.

"Leave," said Boris in a very low voice.

Everyone from his table rose and walked away in perfect silence. The rest of the guests looked around, uncertain and confused.

Geo got up. "You stay." The prince placed his hand over Geo's hand.

"Please, enjoy yourself," Boris encouraged his guests. "Music," he ordered, louder.

The music fell like a sound tornado over the hall. Geo sat back down, one chair closer to the prince.

"When?"

"We're still observing. But it should be sometime in the next month."

"Another Black Rain…"

"It will be different this time."

"How?"

"Are we negotiating?" said Geo, and felt horrible. The Woodman's Council wanted to profit from their scientific research, but this was something that shouldn't be negotiable. Or so Geo felt. They should save as many as possible. His grandfather felt the same.

"What do you want?"

He hesitated just enough for Boris to notice. It was a mistake on his part. Woodman the Elder had instilled in him the art of negotiation. One never goes in unprepared. You do your homework beforehand and once you're in, you know to the smallest detail what it is that your clan needs, wants, and will get. There is no margin of error in negotiation. It's not a time for calculations and hesitations.

The prince grinned and turned completely toward him. "I see. Interesting."

"They're not even human anymore. They're…" his grandfather had said once.

"Corrosives?" Geo had asked him.

"No need for that word. But the truth is, they're something else. They're different than us."

Geo knew that the Woodmans needed to come first. He knew that the clan's interests were more important than his desires and ideas. But…

"What is it that your clan wants?" asked the prince.

"A trade. Science for science. Data for data. We give you our research on weather, and you give us your research on the Gel Sea."

"And what do *you* want?"

"What do you intend to do with the knowledge you'll get from us?"

"What else, my friend? Prepare, of course."

"Will you share it with the mayor?"

"Why would I…" Boris looked at Geo, perplexed. Then he nodded, understanding. "The mayor is just an egotistic bastard. A religious zealot. He's a maggot in the City Hall Palace."

"There's about a month until the next Rain. *I* want the city prepared for impact and the people saved."

Boris burst into laughter, laughing so hard that for a moment Geo thought he was choking on something. The prince was a diminutive man, all bones and sinew, with a bald head and a narrow, mean face. His chin had been eaten away by corrosion. As for his left arm, the Silker's weapon, it had always been carefully covered, wrapped tightly, as if the prince was afraid of his own weapon. No one knew what was hidden under the wraps. No one dared ask. Legend had it that he'd slain an entire army with only his left arm in less than a minute. People kept speculating on what it could be, but Woodman the Elder said that it was only exactly that—a legend, a rumor far distant from the banal truth.

For a long time, the Woodman Clan had debated the truth

regarding the mutations generated by the gel water. Then Geo had seen the effects the gel water had on people with no access to liquid water; he'd seen the Children of the Nightmare Lord and the Children of the Dream Mother. He'd seen them all and then he'd met Boris.

"I'll tell you what, Geo. I'm going to give your clan what it wants. Then I'm going to make you a separate deal."

Geo leaned forward to be in a better position to hear the prince's soft voice. The music was overwhelming and the voices of the guests added to the cacophony. He didn't want to seem eager, but couldn't afford to ask the prince to repeat himself, either.

"If it were up to me, the city could go to hell. I'll do everything in my power to protect my people. But the city and its inhabitants are not my responsibility. And yet…" He paused as if he were still thinking it through. "And yet, I'm willing to protect the city as well if you accept the position of hyalophora in my clan."

"I apologize for my ignorance, Boris, but…"

"Don't apologize. You couldn't have known, as we've never had a hyalophora before. You'll be my science advisor. You'll be my liaison with the Woodmans, as well as with any other clan that pursues science."

Geo knew that if he answered hastily now, he could offend Boris. It was a generous offer. Holy Wood, it was an honor for Geo to be considered for this. Had he made such a good impression on the prince? He felt himself blush under the mask. Probably not. The Woodman Clan had made a very good impression on the prince, with their wood, and access to fresh liquid water, and their advanced science, and Boris only wanted direct, unrestricted access to all that. Not exactly direct control of the resources, but very close to that, if he controlled the most important man in the Woodman Clan. And yes, Geo knew that in a way he was the most important man of his clan. He was the only one with the proper training to deal with the outside world and now, after all this time, he had the right connections to help the clan successfully function in the outside world. He was the easiest man to lose as well, if need be. He was the only one who couldn't contribute directly to the clan's day-to-day survival. He didn't have any necessary skill to that end. The irony of being the Woodman ambassador.

"Aw, you're speechless. That's so beautiful to see," said Boris.

"I'm…I *am* speechless. This means so much to me in so many ways, you appreciating me that much, believing in me, in my knowledge and…I'm…"

"Quit stalling, Geo. What is it?"

The quick, real calculation was like that: to be Boris's *anything* meant to go through the Water Passage. The savage ritual he'd just witnessed. Not only his left arm would be chopped off; he'd have to try to grow in its stead some sort of weapon. If he failed, he'd become Boris's dog. But even worse than all this was the fact that he'd have to consume gel water and turn into a Corrosive. Become like the rest of them—a chunk of corroded flesh. And that was a *not in a million years* kind of solution for Geo.

"I am deeply honored by your offer, my prince," said Geo.

"So, are we agreed?"

"Unfortunately, my duties to my clan won't allow me to swear allegiance to you. I simply cannot abandon my clan."

"Now you understand," said Boris, still grinning.

He stared at Boris. There could be so many interpretations of what the prince had just said. Geo had thought he knew Boris well enough to build a strong and enduring relationship between him and his clan. And yet there were these moments when the man stepped sideways in such a nonchalant manner that one could neither prepare for it nor turn it in one's favor.

"An individual is only flesh and flesh is temporary. The clan is a bond and the bond is permanent. The clan is survival," Boris recited from the Silker Constitution. Again his face turned somber and sinister.

"So, your offer was only a test," said Geo.

"No." Boris's grin came back instantly, as if a light were switched on. "My offer still stands. If you pledge your water to me, I'll consider the city my clan and the Woodmans my family."

3.
The Varnish Tax

Magi's laugh was like raqls chirping when the sky was bright green at summer's peak. She was nothing like him or her mother. She was slender and so gracious in movement. She seemed more a dream-born child than the product of two ordinary Gelled. And her way of seeing the world made everything bearable for Stev. She made everything feel easier and kinder. There was always a sliver of hope when she was around.

"So, the spelling is: snake, scarero, and rat!" His wife ended that on a dramatic, higher note.

Magi burst into laughter. Again.

Stev beamed with happiness. Then he controlled his expression and frowned. "Yeah, yeah, we're a fa-fa-family of jok...ers." All to Magi's delight.

His wife, Sara, *was* a joker. She was the most carefree person he'd ever met. Short and plump, with a round and always smiling face, Sara was the embodiment of cheerfulness. Always flushed and seemingly short of breath, always saying funny, absurd things, always making faces and tickling Magi. Sara could be sober and businesslike. She just chose not to be. "Life is too short for seriousness," she told him every now and again. Especially when she was seeing him falling into his bouts of sadness. There had been times when he'd been utterly annoyed and jealous of her optimism and cheerfulness. But not since Magi had been born. Magi needed all the brightness in the world. He secretly hoped Magi would grow up at least half as shining and full of life as Sara.

"All right, you. You had your fun. Now, Magi, what's the f-f-first letter of the word?"

"Snake!" said Magi and exploded into laughter together with her mother.

"If it's a sssssss-snake," he hissed loudly, and made as if his hand were a snake, moving quickly to munch on Magi's tummy, "it needs to eat!"

Stev stopped and listened intently while Sara was kissing Magi's nape and tickling her. The room was full of laughter, but he could swear he'd heard someone knocking on the door. Yes, there it was. No pattern to the knocking, so it had to be either a client who didn't respect business hours, or something official. Not necessarily bad, since they were knocking and not breaking down the door.

Sara and Magi were still playing. Still smiling, Stev descended the stairs to the shop. He lit a lamp and approached the door, where the visitor had become quite frustrated and was knocking continuously. He also heard voices. So, not just one person. It must be something official. Who could it be, this late at night?

He opened the door. The street was in complete darkness and empty. The city was usually quiet at night. One could only hear the Nightmares prowling the streets.

His lamp shed light on two men. One short and fat, smiling kindly. And another one, even shorter, but skinny and wearing a grim expression. Doc and his assistant, Pi. Oh, right— Stev had completely forgotten about Doc's monthly visit to administer the varnish treatment to Sara.

"S-s-sorry. C'mon in."

"*S-s-sorry* doesn't cut it," said Pi, mocking his stutter. "When there's an appointment, you need to be ready."

"S-s-s-sorry," said Stev again, keeping the door wide open for the two men to enter.

"That's the only word you know?"

"Enough, Pi," Doc intervened.

"What?"

"That's enough. Leave him alone."

Pi got closer to Doc and whispered in his ear, "I asked you not to talk to me like that in front of our clients."

Doc breathed deeply and stepped back. The smile returned to his face. Stev had always noticed how sad Doc's smile was in comparison to Sara's. He looked from Doc to Pi, uncertain. Although Pi was a young man of barely twenty, maybe not even that, he'd always looked sick and dark. Stev had always imagined that Pi's sickness was coming from his heart. It showed on his face and in his eyes. Grim, dark, angry, ready to bite and spit. Ready to talk ugly and mean. How had the gentle doctor ended up with such an assistant?

"Stev, take me to Sara, please," said Doc.

He invited Doc upstairs. Pi made to follow, but Stev stepped in front of him. Stev was tall and bulky. He could look quite imposing if he wanted. But he'd realized very soon in his life that he'd get more out of it by smiling and talking, and negotiating, than bullying and inspiring fear. "S-s-sorry, only Doc allowed," said Stev.

"I'm Doc's assistant," Pi retorted angrily.

"Only D-Doc allowed."

"Wait here for me, please, Pi," said Doc.

Pi returned to the shop and looked around while again mocking Stev's stutter. Stev decided to ignore him. Nothing good would come out of him confronting Pi and eventually taking him down a notch. Peace was more important than pride.

"Hey, Doc. So good to see you," said Sara.

"Good evening, Sara. Sorry for the late hour, but I have more and more patients from one month to the next."

"No worries. We're not early sleepers. Stev, could you take Magi to her room, please?"

Stev nodded and took Magi's little hand to lead her out of their bedroom. The treatment was not pretty and Magi was too young to witness it. It would change her forever and Stev wanted to keep her innocent for as long as possible.

After the Black Rain, when everything liquid that was

water-based had solidified—or rather, become gelatinous—only a few liquid reserves had been left, deep underground, fed by subterranean rivers and lakes. People lucky enough to find such treasures kept their existence secret. Everyone else was forced to consume the gelled water and became Corrosives, people whose bodies were covered in a verdigris, their flesh gnawed at like ordinary metals are consumed by rust. Some tried to keep their bodies clean of the verdigris, but they ended up corroded skeletons, their flesh consumed faster than metal rusted.

In the beginning there were only a few infected groups, who begged the government to do something. Then the situation became dangerously widespread, slowed only by the discovery of what could best be described as an anticorrosive varnish. It protected for a while, then it had to be renewed. And it cost a fortune. Only the very wealthy, the biggest corporations, or the clans that bartered the varnish for total servitude could afford the stuff. It was rumored that the Blues were behind the anticorrosive varnish business, that it had funded their electoral campaign.

When he returned to their bedroom, Doc was injecting the treatment into the thick skin of Sara's breasts. Or whatever remained of them after being attacked by corrosion. Before meeting Stev, Sara had lived with her mother on the streets. She'd started rusting on her arms and breast. Too poor to afford the treatment, her mother appearing too old to be accepted as a servant by any clan and therefore given treatment in exchange for work, Sara had tried to keep the corrosion at bay by filing the flesh of her arms and breasts. But the verdigris kept coming back. It kept gnawing at her young flesh.

Stev had saved them. He'd taken in Sara and her mother. Sara's mother had been only thirty-two, but had been aged and worn by life on the streets—fighting off the Nightmares and the sewerer gangmembers, and lack of food, warmth, and proper hygiene. When Stev had finally offered her a home, she'd remained only a stick of flesh, constantly trembling. She hadn't survived the year. That was why Sara's cheerfulness seemed like a miracle to Stev.

He watched the procedure, forcing a smile for her benefit. He knew how much such a treatment hurt. But Sara bore it bravely, smiling back and making jokes. Doc answered her jokes with chuckles and humorous retorts.

Unlike Sara's mother, Doc was old in human years, but didn't show it. He'd invented the varnish treatment, so he'd had access to it from the beginning. Corrosion could wear you out in a matter of years, or it could keep you alive for decades past the age when a human being should normally lie down to rest.

Something fell and broke in the shop below. Doc looked up from the point where he'd inserted the syringe to Stev and grumbled, embarrassed, "What's he done now?"

Stev went down the stairs two steps at a time and entered the shop. Pi was stuffing his pockets with fairy mushrooms. The kind used for brewing beer and making drugs. Powerful drugs. Pi had broken into the storage room and now was helping himself. In front of Stev!

"Put it all b-b-back, Pi," said Stev, keeping his voice steady.

"B-b-back," Pi mocked him. Then he raised his arms as if in surrender and stepped back, out of the storage room, a wide grin stretching his face. That grin, with his mean look, made him look really ugly. *Ugly*. That was a word Stev didn't think of much, or even hear used much. What did that mean? Normally, he'd thought ugly was something so evilly distorted, one could not look at it. But right then, he could look straight into Pi's face, realize his meanness, his ugly behavior, his entire ugliness, and not step back. For a short moment, Stev felt something he hadn't felt in years, since he'd left the gang life behind and taken up baking. He felt Pi was like a worm and the need to crush him, to squash him under his sole, was overpowering.

"I asked you t-t-to put everything b-b-back, Pi," said Stev, watching the young man.

"What? Put back all the forbidden merchandise? The illegal drugs?"

"No d-drugs."

"I'm pretty sure fairy mushrooms are forbidden."

"Put it b-back!"

"Or what?"

"If it's illegal, you are not ab-bove the law."

"I am not above the law," confirmed Pi, still grinning. "I. Am. The. Law."

"Law means j-j-justice and what you're d-doing is not j-justice," said Stev, walking toward the young man.

"From my point of view, this is j-justice," said Pi mockingly, taking out a piece of mushroom and biting on it.

Stev slapped Pi's hand and the mushroom flew from his fingers. He grabbed Pi, lifted him in the air and turned him upside-down as easily as if he were just a doll. He started shaking him. All Pi had stolen started falling from his pockets onto the floor. Stev felt rage—the quantity of fairy mushrooms he'd just taken in front of him, shamelessly, as if he could just shake down Stev so easily, was worth his entire business. Beyond that, those fairy mushrooms were not Stev's property. They belonged to the mayor. Pi had stolen the mayor's property, placing Stev and his family in a very bad position with the ruler of their city. With the government. To think only of that crassness and the danger Pi had placed his family in without a second thought made Stev tremble with fury.

"What are you doing?" Doc was climbing down the stairs fast.

He was followed by Sara, who raised her voice and now he realized she'd been talking to him for some time: "Stev! Let him down. Let him down!"

Stev let Pi fall to the floor. He was still trembling with fury, but fought to regain control. Sara knelt next to Pi to help him up. She tried to straighten the boy's clothes, but Pi slapped her hand away and rose from the floor by himself.

"I'm so sorry, Pi," said Sara. "Please let me offer you a wicked bread, on the house." She grabbed a loaf from the counter and tried to push it into Pi's hands, but the boy slapped it away. The bread fell on the floor. When Sara bent to pick it up, he roughly pushed her down, staring at Stev as if daring him to act again.

Sara embraced Stev's legs to keep him in place. To stop him from acting again against Pi.

Doc put a hand on Pi's shoulder. "Stand down, boy."

Pi brushed off Doc's hand as roughly as he'd pushed Sara. Then he turned and confronted the old man. "What did I say about doing this stuff in front of clients?"

"Get out!" said Stev.

"Not before you pay my tax."

"It's the government tax," said Doc.

"Pay my tax now, you stuttering fool!"

From behind the counter, Stev lifted the wooden-mushroom flour bag and the bread bag he'd prepared as payment, per their usual agreement with the government, and threw them at Pi.

The young man let them fall on the floor and grinned. "Not enough, fool."

"What?" said Doc.

Sara rose from the floor and looked at Pi, bewildered. Stev stepped forward and Pi automatically took a step back. Then his face darkened with anger as he realized what he'd done. "The tax has doubled. You're short, you stupid rust."

"T-t-that's the tax we ag-greed on."

"Not anymore. If you want your woman to keep her tits, you pay the tax."

Stev stepped forward and almost grabbed Pi again, but Sara and Doc jumped to stop him. Doc bent and took the two bags with the payment from the floor. "Don't worry, Stev, you're good. You paid for the treatment."

"No, he didn't," Pi said, shaking.

"Yes, he did. Out!" Doc pushed him to the door.

"He owes the rest of the tax!" Pi yelled.

"He *paid* the tax," said Doc, exiting the shop.

"Here, take this." Sara offered Pi another bag of bread. "Please. That should do it."

Pi shoved her and she fell again. "No. He has to pay!"

Stev jumped and caught Sara before she could hit the floor. Doc closed the door. But Stev could still hear the young man yelling, "He has to pay! *He* has to pay!"

4.
Silk Tea

The night was deep and the city quiet. The sky looked like black mold, bubbling and boiling with fury. Never a good sight. Torono was a dark vastness of ruined concrete and barricaded windows. Here he was, three floors up in the Golden Tower, hosted in luxury and decadence while down there, the people of Torono lived in squalor, every day treading between life and death with no certainty, no hope. All that they could hope for was a night's dreamless sleep. That was the only thing that could give them the certainty of tomorrow.

"The tea is ready, Mr. Ambassador." Lady L's deep, warm voice made him shiver. She was like the night outside, a tempting darkness obscuring the terrible truth.

Geo turned and sighed. The overwhelming stench of rotten meat pervaded the room. Everything was mostly shadows and flickering candlelight. Moss-fragranced wax couldn't entirely cover the silk tea stench. Only the purest tea had such a strong aroma.

Lady L had shed most of her clothes and was now waiting for him, her honey skin barely covered. How could she still be so beautiful, with such perfect skin, if she drank the gel water; if she was one of the corrosion children? mused Geo, taking in the exotic tableau and being afraid that if he moved, the whole thing would only be an illusion and he'd discover the monstrous truth.

Lady L's head remained hidden under the helmet with the Sun Glory emblem etched on the forehead, and the black textile mask stretched over her face. Her eyes were invisible under the opaque chitin lenses but her mouth was still exposed, lips still blood red. Nothing could damage the lipstick or whatever it was that she applied. Her lips were perfection embodied, a scream for pleasure and lust. He exhaled hard and tried to focus on the entire scene, not only her skin and her lips.

Geo blinked. There were small golden speckles floating in the air around her. It might be a trick of the candlelight. Everything in the room was so foreign, so sophisticated to him, a simple boy from the Caves.

Lady L walked toward him, her movement sinuous. "Tired?"

"Just in awe of your beauty, Lena."

Her lips parted in a slight smile, revealing glowing white teeth and the tip of her soft tongue. "I'm just a fly in your web, Mr. Ambassador. No need to sweet talk me. I'm already trapped, my wings stuck, my belly exposed."

Geo shivered and fought not to show he was breathing heavily; to keep his voice from trembling. "What tea is that?"

"You already know it, Mr. Ambassador. Your filters aren't strong enough to block its smell. It's silk tea from the prince's special collection. Threads aged twenty years, laced with nunnehi pollen, brewed with fresh, liquid water from the prince's reserves."

He'd heard of the nunnehi pollen when he'd first been served the silk tea by Prince Boris himself, at the beginning of their friendship. The prince had explained then that nunnehi were the fairies of an extinct people called the Cherokee. The Cherokee had melted in the Green Rain like so many others. But in the end, after all sorts of beautiful stories and legends, Geo still hadn't found out what exactly a nunnehi was, what plant's pollen he'd ingested and gotten high on, so his brother Alex could estimate the danger he'd been exposed to.

"What's a nunnehi?" he asked.

"Better question—what's silk tea?".

He accepted the deflection and sat on the bed, inhaling the

tea's fragrance—as rich and promising as he remembered—as Lena poured the black liquid very slowly into two porcelain cups, rare treasures saved from the Black Rain. The tea had a viscous consistency, a bit thicker than he remembered.

"Silk tea is a communion with the dead. A dance with the spirits. A leap into the heavens before falling back to mud."

Her voice captivated him and before he realized it, she was kneeling in front of him, offering him a cup. He accepted and tentatively caressed her hand. That was when he remembered he was still wearing his full gear. She understood and started taking off his gloves. Her skin was so soft, so cool…so decadent. So addictive.

Lena threw his gloves toward the window and took off the cloth covering her breasts. She guided his hands to cup them and fondle them. "The spirits will visit us tonight, while I'll be your prey, flesh in your hands, life at your mercy," she whispered.

Geo drank a bit of tea and felt the liquid roll slowly down his throat. Slowly, like a drop of honey, taking its time, crystallizing with every inch it slid. He felt its burn and the spiciness of the nunnehi flooding his nose and his brain.

"Tonight, you're the barbarian ravishing the princess, Mr. Ambassador, and the princess will ravish you back." Lena's tongue licked his naked belly. He saw her full red lips leaving streams of pink light behind. Their touch sent electrical spikes into his body. He arched his back under her tongue's trail.

"Tonight" —Lena pulled him up— "you, my savage ambassador" —she let the last of her clothes fall, revealing everything underneath. Geo was ready to climax like he'd never climaxed in his entire short life —"tonight, my sweet beast." She knelt again and freed his belt with a single smooth gesture and his pants fell to his ankles. He felt cold air and wet lips and hot tongue, and the room crackled with electricity and colors. A leviathan red mouth full of spikes descended upon him from the rotting green ceiling and he felt swallowed. He discharged violently and a bright explosion engulfed his brain until he was no more.

The party's clamor stayed behind the shut bone doors of the Presidential Room. Boris preferred to do business in this room because it was the most claustrophobic one in the Golden Tower. He'd decorated it himself. Carefully, after studying dozens of important people's reactions to different stimuli. He'd never backed down from a show of force and power to impress, but he'd always been partial to intimately cowing his counterparts.

The prince invited the city's mayor to take a seat in front of the fireplace, where trembling black flames rose from a pile of smoldering cracked skulls. Trench algae burned unseen inside the skulls and released a suggestion of rot. Nothing too strong; barely registering on the senses, in fact. The mayor stared at the flames with visible curiosity. He sniffed a little bit and frowned. He was a small and wiry, skin on bones man. The top of his bald head shone with the flames' reflection. He wore big, shiny hearing aids, as his ears were completely gone.

"A drink, my friend?" Boris said into a shell to direct it toward the mayor. It made his voice sound whispered and somewhat windy.

The mayor startled and turned toward the prince, who stood next to the window, stirring drinks. The windowpanes were created especially like telescopic lenses, enlarging in this case the turbulent green sky. The purulent clouds seemed to boil directly on the window's glass. The mayor jumped from the chair and took a couple of steps backward. "I should head back," he said.

"Why such haste, Mayor?" said Boris and held out a drink to the man. It was a bubbling blood-red cocktail. Grayish smoke rose from the concoction.

"What's that?" said the mayor, keeping his hands to himself, as if reluctant to touch a poisonous object.

"Nightmare's Blood." Boris grinned. "Just a Silkers tradition."

"If it's tradition…" said the mayor and took the drink. He eyed the prince with uncertainty and a touch of fear.

"No drugging my guests. I swear." The prince crossed his heart and slid his big thumb over his throat as if cutting it. "Anyway, I'm alone here. Your man, Silver Star, is in this room with us, protecting you. So, if anything, I'm the one putting my life in your hands."

The man referred to was an officer wearing a tall helmet with a silver star on its front and horns protruding from its sides. He stood guard next to the room's only entrance, as silent and unmoving as a statue.

The mayor nodded and, breathing noisily, took the rest of the room in. The ceiling was high and completely invisible in the moving darkness that seemed to hang in the air below it. It looked like dark clouds boiling in a silent storm. The walls were gray and looked like something slimy was leaking on them. The only light was provided by the black flames, so there were no details, no clarity to what was moving down the walls. The mayor turned a small wheel on the hearing aid. There was a constant hiss, like dead air, suppurating into the room.

Boris's grin widened. "Please, drink. Enjoy. You'll like it. And then you can brag that you've been served by the prince himself."

Silver Star was suddenly next to the mayor. The man took the drink and sipped. He nodded approvingly, then handed it back to his master. The mayor tasted it, smiled to the prince, and suddenly erupted into a coughing fit. "Motheruster!" he said hoarsely and stomped his foot.

Boris laughed. "Strong stuff. For real men."

"He didn't even blink," said the mayor with some effort.

"I know, Silver is a killer," Boris sat on a bone throne that was a few heads higher than any of the chairs in the room. Its edges were all fangs and claws. There was only one spot where you could touch that throne without getting cut. "I don't know where you found him, but he's worth his weight in silk." Boris placed his drink on a small table next to the throne.

"So, Boris, what was so urgent that we had to talk tonight?" The mayor regarded the prince, his eyes both haunted and calculating. A touch of corrosion had taken a bit of flesh away from his right cheek. His almost nonexistent lips were stretched into a line, never smiling, never shifting in any way, no matter the subject under discussion.

"I'm bringing in a big transport of iron silk."

"I can't open my city to iron."

"I know. The Blues' manifesto stays strong in Torono. I uphold it with every fiber of my being."

The mayor studied the prince. Boris wore his ever-present trademark grin. He held the mayor's gaze calmly. "So your fight against drugs is as strong as ever," Boris said, "I'll give you two places where you can hit the drug gangs and your credit with the population will go through the roof."

"But?"

"But I need to bring this transport safely into the city," Boris replied. "I'm testing the market with a new variant of iron. Weaker, safer, more…water friendly."

"And I suppose that if it works and you can keep your customers alive longer, your drug empire will flourish and you'll be richer than ever." The mayor kept staring at Boris.

The mayor had no idea. He still held pre-corrosion values, like most people his age. Wealth didn't matter anymore. What would Boris do with money in the ruins of the new world? No. The only thing that still mattered was power. And with power came control. Never in the history of humankind had men been so close to godlike powers. To godlike control of the world itself. Boris's grin faded as he leaned in and said to mayor, "Do you remember what you desire, Mayor?"

The man didn't answer. His eyes shone with the reflections of the black flames. His breath came out long and hoarse.

"Well, Mayor, you're in luck. I can make it happen."

"How?"

"That's my problem. But I can deliver in a couple of days."

"Then your transport is safe, Boris."

"We have a deal," confirmed the prince.

"That we do."

5.
The Mayor's Blues

Beyond the noise of the rain lies silence.

I am alone, surrounded by hundreds of Silker warriors. Everybody is still; they don't even breathe. It's quiet. The silence, in the presence of the sick rain's rattle pouring from the loudspeakers, fills me with loneliness.

The candle flames tear the Initiation Hall from the darkness. The smell of wax and incense hangs in the air. Arms are stretched out on the logs; the Silker officers raise their hatchets, and zzzip! The red shadows of the chopped arms jump on the walls while the thick, stifling air absorbs the screams—the silk screams of the rain, the porous screams of the stones…

Panic assailed him with the memory, quickly followed by his mind lurching into full awareness. He was panting, his body trembling. As he struggled to get up, he noticed that the screams had stopped. *I was hallucinating!* Two words came back to him— silk tea! No, that can't be. *I've actually attended the Silkers' ritual. I've been there. But that was some hours ago. Holy Water, where am I?*

He sighed and the pain in his back made him groan; he felt like each of his bones had been crushed. Silk tea might give him hallucinations for days, but never physical pain. *Something happened. One moment I—where was I? The Water Passage Ritual. Then I retreated to my room and…* He blinked, but only inky darkness filled his vision. He realized he couldn't see; he could only make out a web of shadows. *What the sky's silk is happening to me?* He stared as hard as he could, and distinguished shapes approaching through the mist. His heart pounded.

The noise of the rain in the dream hadn't disappeared, only faded. *Swish, swish*—not rain. He touched the ground around him and felt cobblestones. He was lying in the street somewhere. He couldn't remember how he'd come to be there.

The swishing sound was getting closer.

He cursed and got to his feet. His whole body felt as if it were being torn. His heartbeat turned into a torrent that thundered in his temples and his mouth filled with the bitter taste of danger. He instinctively reached for the dagger tucked up his sleeve, but could not find it. His fear growing, he touched his chest, but his knuckle-duster was gone too. He couldn't find the knives in his boots. His sweat froze, feeling like icicles down his back. He was a naked piglet, squealing in front of the butcher.

A hand grabbed his ankle.

Geo thrashed and kicked madly, trying to crush the soft flesh of the sewerers attacking him. Then, in the midst of his hysteria, he froze. A sudden frenzy devoured the silence of his executioners. It sounded like a whole crowd had engaged the sewerers in bloody slaughter. And he was still blind! Desperation clogged his throat like cotton. He gagged.

Strong hands grabbed him and carried him into the light. Somebody sprayed something in his eyes. He screamed in sudden pain and fell. But in a few seconds the stinging in his eyes and the headache faded, and he started to distinguish shapes. Then, slowly, details.

Oh, Holy Wood, not them! he thought, smiling wide and friendly. He was in the middle of a Blue Patrol.

One of them, with a silver star on his metallic mask, bent over and offered him his hand to help him to his feet. He was a mountain of a man, still quite human in shape, with the uniform stretched tightly over his muscles and his helmet a different shape than those of ordinary Blue Patrollers. His was a more of a tall dome with horns all around, like a crown. "Mr. Ambassador, I'm so glad we found you in time!"

"What happened? Why am I here?" said Geo.

"I don't know, sir. We got a report and came to check it. Luckily for you."

"Thank you, Mr...."

"Everybody calls me Silver Star."

"Thank you, Mr. Silver Star. I appreciate your help."

"Now we have orders to escort you to the train station. Don't worry, we're right there." Silver Star moved purposefully to stand at Geo's shoulder and urged him forward. The Blue Patrol followed close behind.

People looked at them in wonder as they passed. Most averted their eyes. It said a lot about the mayor's regime.

Geo realized that during the night he'd been dumped under the air-road, right at the back of the train station. Very close to not only the train station, but to the Golden Tower. Which also made it close to the mayor's palace as well.

There were only three trains still working—northbound, eastbound, and westbound. Pretty basic. Geo would have to take the northbound train, but with the patrol at his back, he didn't feel comfortable actually showing them the direction of his clan's Caves. So he made a left from the station's waiting hall and walked to the eastbound platform. Then he felt Silver Star's fingers grabbing his arm and pulling him back quite aggressively.

The man smiled widely. "I'm sure you had a rough night and may be confused, but we're here to make sure you're getting on the right train to go home." Silver Star turned on his heel and walked to the northbound platform. Two Blue Patrollers pushed Geo from behind in the same direction.

Holy Water! They know. They had actually watched him and knew more about him than he'd assumed. And they wanted him back home. But why?

When the train arrived, Silver Star produced a cylinder with the mayor's seal on it. He handed it to Geo. "This is from the mayor to Woodman the Elder. Please, don't open it beforehand; give it to him directly."

Misshapen silhouettes move in slow motion in the flickering, yellowish light of the candles. The air is heavy with wax and incense, silence and sweat. An incredible, blood-curdling noise cuts like a cold blade through those waiting and sends a shudder through all of us.

"What's this?" I ask involuntarily.

"It rains," the Silkers Prince answers. "It rains," he hisses. "Have you never heard the rain?" His question pierces me, and I suddenly feel him, sinister and solemn. Yes, sinister and solemn like a headsman.

"I know the word…"

"This is the rain, Geo, the initiation mistress in the Water Trial," he whispers to me, revealing one of the great secrets of the Silkers.

"The rain," I repeat after him.

"Yes, the rain of water, the water of life…"

"…and corrosion."

"Don't you ever say that again—ever," Boris hisses in my ear.

Geo shivered, startled awake. The hallucination brought bitter vomit into his mouth.

The train panted over the moonlike surface of the wasteland. The green daylight was torn by veils of mist. He stared at the hypnotic barrens, land that had once been ripe and burgeoning with crops and seas of grass. Now it was the biggest desert in North America.

Must stay awake, he told himself, and tried to ignore the desert landscape, the pollution. *Must focus on my own problem—how did I come to be lying under the air-road, my pockets empty, my eyes blinded by iron silk? It can't be anything else—just iron silk has that kind of effect. I've tried other stuff, but never iron silk. Never! This is bad shit.*

Geo looked around. There was an ambient sound and smell he was so accustomed to that he hadn't paid attention to it before. The car was full of people from the small settlements north of Torono who had come to the city to sell their goods and were now going back with whatever they had traded them for. All were crowded in the ancient, creaky cars the Rails Clan was using, all from the times before the Black Rain—survivors of the deluge, rust, and rot.

How had he gotten into that much trouble? There were so

many aspects of this single question—location, missing time, drug use, political interests—that had put him in that situation. Who would benefit from this?

Let's see…after the Silkers Water Passage…no, no, much later. After the Ritual party when he'd been a guest at Prince Boris's table… no, no, even later than that. He'd retreated with Lady L to his room.

He closed his eyes and remembered vivid images of her red lips and heavy breasts. She'd served him silk tea laced with… nunnehi pollen. That could not be it. He'd tried that before and the effects were totally different from what had happened to him. So, what had happened?

He had no recollection of anything after Lady L, after Lena… he…they had…what? They had what? His body remembered the pleasure, his climax, and yet, his mind could not. What the fuck! How could he report that to Grandpa? Woodman the Elder would eviscerate him.

He tried to calm down so he could think of the next logical step: who could do that to him? Although he considered himself artistic, math had always been his forte. In a simple world, fact plus fact equals conclusion. The most plausible hypothesis was that Lena had drugged him with iron silk besides the silk tea and the nunnehi pollen. But why would she do it? She was supposed to be loyal to the Silkers, to Boris. And Geo was Boris's friend, ally, trade partner. Boris could have cut some pockets in his belly right at their first meeting. Geo had always been alone, vulnerable. It made no sense for the prince to wait until after declaring publicly that Geo was his most precious ally to fuck him over.

Who else could Lady L work for? The mayor, with his Blue fucks. Wasn't math beautiful! Was possible that the Silkers' Lady worked secretly for the Blues? How long could she do that undetected, especially when employing risky tactics like drugging their guests with iron? It still didn't add up. *What could the Blue fucks want from me?* If they knew who Geo was and knew of Woodman the Elder, they must have known the Woodman Clan business in the city, so why didn't they ask for anything? There must be higher stakes there, but what they might be was a mystery at the moment. The facts didn't add up, unless...unless they had heard him talking with Boris about the next Black Rain. But that would be too much to deal with. No, he wouldn't go there. Not yet.

What other angle was there? The political one.

The bitterest enemies of the networks peddling ecological drugs like iron silk were the mayor and his Blues Party. Ever since wresting power for themselves, they'd warred continuously against the drug lords. Before them, the governments were driven by classic ecological concepts: let's make the big guys reduce pollution, and then we can rebuild nature. Well, we tried not to pollute anymore, but we didn't cooperate with nature, we raped it—or as they said, adapted it.

Subtract the conventional governments and we get the Blues, the apparent solution to the mess they'd left. Their slogan—What if we could see the blue sky again?—struck a chord. People were tired of an eternally dirty green sky that hung over their heads like the scummy surface of a swamp. The Blues seemed clean and promising: "We're not guilty of the Universal Corrosion, we didn't trigger the desertification of our land, we didn't mutate the water and the beasts. We only want to salvage what's left. But differently—by understanding nature, protecting it and moving within its cycles, so that it will never again turn against us."

Their great electoral promise—the Adaptation of People to Nature Program—had started with the creation of the first tool-people. The first generation had been rudimentary. Yet, society had need of drill-people, pipe-people, coil-people, and much more evolved people that were still unattainable. The only true breakthrough had come two years after the program's inception, with the sewage-people, or the sewerers, the waste-cleaning beings without whom the cities' sanitation would be impossible, since water had turned to jelly during the Universal Corrosion and could no longer be used for cleaning purposes. Now the sewerers ate all the waste, all the slops—*And they were going to eat me earlier*—and expelled what their bodies couldn't use as urine, which drained easily through the old sewers.

What the Blues had not taken into account was that the new

environment acted upon people, as well. For each solved problem, ten unpredictable problems arose. If one added to this the deterioration of the adapted humans' characteristics caused by ecological drugs, it was simple to understand their bitterness and determination to stop drug trafficking. In theory, they wouldn't work with drug lords. In theory—but life was strange.

Geo realized he was being tailed. Obviously, he thought, they wanted to know where his clan was hiding. He rose, feigning sleepiness, and headed toward the car's exit. On his way out, he glanced surreptitiously at the tail as he passed the man's seat. The man had a cloth over his mask, trying to look like he was sleeping. *What your mother's silk are you hiding under that cloth, fucker?*

Geo found himself a comfy place to wait on the stairs that led to the upper level. It was darker there, but he was already getting used to it; he could make out the shapes of the travelers asleep on their baggage in the passage between the cars. By the musty stench, he guessed they were ground-cheese farmers. They were not a concern for him.

After a few seconds, the spy cautiously exited the car. While his eyes were still adjusting to the darkness, Geo jumped him. Two kicks to his face, an elbow in his stomach and another on his chin, then Geo pushed him down and sat on top of him. The farmers woke up and huddled together, frightened and silent. Ignoring them, he snatched the cloth from the spy's mask.

"Motherfucker!" Geo spat on his mask. "Is this our agreement?" The mask bore, on the left cheek near his ear, a red flower with hanging ribbons—the symbol of the Silkers.

From the corner of his eye Geo caught movement; he moved too, faster than the Silker, and crushed his hand under his heel. The spy screamed in pain. There were bits of fish and shiny scales all over the passage floor. A fish head, its gaping mouth full of fangs, stared at Geo with glassy eyes, and from under his heel poked the stump of the man's fish-hand. Bad choice. If it had been something more dangerous—a crocodile, for instance—Geo would have lost his heel. But this also told him that he was dealing with a Silker officer, one that had passed the

Water Trial. A tough and faithful warrior.

Geo punched him once more in his chest, then pulled him up. The Silker was wheezing from the punch to his solar plexus, and he clutched the door's bars as he tried to say something. It sounded like a snort. Geo planted a fist in his ribs and he let go of the bars with a loud groan.

As Geo opened the door and prepared to launch him through it, with supreme effort, the Silker shouted, "Help—wait! I must help you!"

Geo stopped at the last moment and looked at him. He kept him in the same precarious position, where the warrior could see the wasteland outside speeding past, and asked, "What did you say?"

He drew a deep breath, more a gasp, and wheezed, "Last night, Lady L reported that you'd been kidnapped. When we found you, you'd already been 'saved' by the Blues. So, I've been sent to observe and protect you."

"From whom?"

"I don't know…the ones who kidnapped you. And possibly the Blues too."

"Prove it."

"Let go of my right arm."

Geo released his arm and he reached toward one of his pockets.

"Hey—hey! Easy. I want to see your every move."

Moving slower, the Silker pulled out what looked like a rolled-up parchment. Geo took it and unrolled it. It was a bloody piece of skin, on which was written *On the order of Prince Boris*. Geo spat in disgust, then asked, "How do I know it's authentic?"

"Smell it. "

Geo inhaled and gagged. Vomit burned in his throat. Rotten meat. Silk tea stench.

"You know we're the only ones who keep the pure silk. Everything we sell is diluted to 17 percent. Only a pure silk could give you that." Panting and trembling in pain because of the position Geo was keeping him in, the Silker nodded toward the skin scroll.

Geo released him. "How could they kidnap me from the Golden Tower? I mean, directly, right from under your nose."

"It's not unheard of. Ambassador Dinesh before you suffered the same fate."

"Where is he now?"

"We never found him."

"And Lady L…"

"She alerted us."

"Why didn't they take her too?"

The Silker was obviously confused.

"She was with me when this happened."

"No, she wasn't, Your Excellency. She was in her room, coupled to her supply. She discovered your absence in the morning."

Her supply? What was he talking about? Geo had more hours of math in front of him. But for now, the chances of Silkers being behind this were down to 20 percent from 50. Suddenly the mayor rose to the royal eighty. And Lady L was apparently off the suspects list. Or was she?

"You're getting off at the next stop," Geo said and turned his back to the Silker.

"But my mission—"

"Really, man, look at your arm. Go and take care of that. Tell the prince I'll be back as soon as possible."

6.
Mushrooms

Mic liked to come and visit his friend Stev because his family was always cheerful and playful. Even when Mic made some of his bad jokes, Sara would still laugh and make him feel good. And she would always appreciate his fashion sense. People who were happy and indulging were very rare these days. And it was not that he was a happy man generally, but a good mood in people around him put him in a better mood, and those days felt good. So, when you saw someone like Sara in a dark mood, her face swollen from crying, eyes glazed by distant thoughts, mouth pouting, and sweet little Magi shying away from you and trembling in a corner as if in fear of a terrible thing, then something really bad had happened. Mic dreaded such situations.

He retracted his collaret and his elbowrets, trying to minimize them as much as possible. He'd entered their shop with his skin tracery expanded in full glory, grinning, and preparing his own jokes for Sara. He'd needed some shine on that gloomy day. But the air in the bakery was freezing and downright dreadful.

It was weirdly quiet. Mic shivered and his tracery rustled, too loud for the silence in the place. He knocked on Stev's office door. He heard a grumble and opened the door. "Was that a *yes*, or a *maybe*?"

"Mic." Stev acknowledged him and returned to his business.

"What's wrong, Stev?" Mic closed the door and sat down on

the chair in front of the desk. He ruffled his collaret again and struck a daring pose, exposing the delicate work for his friend's appreciation.

The baker sighed and looked at him. His expression was not merely serious, it was dark. Mic had seen Stev in his dark period when he was younger. He'd seen enough of the man's anger and violence to realize something very bad had happened here. Mic liked to keep in touch with his partners and always stay up to date with the latest developments. But coming here today had definitely been a bad choice. Mic didn't have time for bad moods and ugly business. He needed bright days and optimism. He'd worked on his tracery for so long, preparing for tonight's party with the barbers, that he'd longed for someone to notice it and offer a kind word of appreciation. But when people were so focused on their own issues, who gave a fucking rust about Mic?

"We're g-g-good, Mic."

"Glad to hear it! All right then, I won't bother you anymore, my friend." He got up and turned to the door.

"S-s-somebody broke into the s-s-storage."

Mic froze. The storage was the room where Stev kept his mushroom stock. Including, most importantly, the *fairy* ones. The most potent hallucinogens in the world. More powerful than silk. Stev was one of the few people who knew where to get them. And he was the best baker of such delicacies in the kingdom. Such things were illegal, but the mayor himself was Mic's biggest client and therefore Stev's. The client who made Blues turn a blind eye to Mic's illegal operations. Without the mayor, Mic would be just another small-time, terrified crook, always in hiding. And the mayor paid Mic in advance for a constant supply of fairy dust. That meant a constant supply of fairy mushrooms for Stev to bake. So, in the end, the fairy mushrooms in Stev's storage were the mayor's mushrooms, paid in full, in advance, and expected on schedule. Miss a deadline and the mayor would miss keeping his Blue boys away from Stev's business and family, and ultimately from Mic's business and family. A very small but vicious circle.

"Did they take the—"

"No, I c-c-caught him in t-time."

"Oh, good," Mic breathed with relief. "For a moment I was worried there, friend."

"But, he now kn-nows."

"Well, even if he tells the Blues, the mayor will protect us."

"This one's the p-p-prince's man."

"Ah, I see. All right, uhm…"

"He'll be b-b-back. With w-w-warriors."

Mic dropped back onto the chair, thinking. That was worrisome. To say the least. He knew that the prince and the mayor collaborated to a certain extent. But…this was forbidden stuff. Stuff declared illegal by everyone in power. Fairy dust could alter the brain chemistry further and turn the user into a monster. Officially, no one wanted mind-altering drugs like fairy dust and rusty silk on the market. And that's what made them so damn in-demand and expensive. And therein lay the crux of the problem—the prince was the official king of all silk products, including the drugs. So, fairy dust was the competition and under the guise of upholding the law, the prince was hunting down all fairy dust trafficking networks. And the mayor couldn't tell the prince to stop. The mayor had to play the part of upholding the law to its full extent, if the prince denounced anyone.

"Motheruster!"

"I need you to t-take the mushrooms from here."

"The delivery is in a week. Would you be able to deliver?"

"No."

"That's a *serious* problem, my friend. That will make you the target not only of the prince, but also of the mayor. So, we need solutions. Real solutions and quick ones."

"Speak to your father," said Stev.

"Bad idea. He hates me for doing this."

"Get everyone here t-t-today, for a v-v-visit. We'll deal with it. But now, t-t-take the mushrooms."

Mic sighed and rubbed his forehead. This was the worst day. It started with all the work on the collaret and the elbowrets, then it turned bad when he'd come here, and it seemed it would continue to get worse. Approaching his father about this business with Stev would only make it ugly. And what would turn it into the worst day ever would be coming here with his family and spending a few hours in a lame visit, playing nice, instead of meeting his girl. The sweet and mysterious Jana. He sighed again and nodded his compliance to Stev.

7.

Hope

Stev's office was that oasis of peace and solitude to Jon. Stev's wife, Sara, knew not to ever enter it and usually managed to keep their child out too. As for Jon's family, they were so busy with visiting the bakery that no one thought to intrude. Jon smiled and studied the accounting wall. Stev was a baker and a flour maker. He liked to keep a tight business. The man had a good head. And more importantly, he had a good heart. He was very much like a son to Jon.

"So, teacher, you call him M-M-Mod. You d-d-discovered another god. What's his s-s-story?" asked Stev as he brought two teacups to the table. He placed one in front of his guest and one at his place. Plucking a dried mush flower from a tin can on the table, he dropped it into Jon's cup and crushed it into dust with a spoon before sprinkling tarb bark dust on top. The hot water melted the bark dust to a yellow foam and the tea turned a deep rust red as it steeped. Stev knew how to prepare the best mush tea this side of Torono. Jon sighed with satisfaction and nodded.

"The question is not *what's his story*. The question is *why*."

Stev nodded, deep in thought. Jon knew that most of the stuff they discussed was flying over the young man's head. Stev had a family to provide for, several communities to feed with his bread, and the regular trips out of the city to keep his pantries full of raw materials for his flours. He was really more like a bak-

ery alchemist and one of the few reasons people still survived
in this day and age. But the man was patient and eager to learn.
He was the best candidate for Jon's successor. The next teacher.
Better than any of his two surviving sons. His first son, from
before the Black Rain, would have been a different story, but…
no use dwelling on the past. That had been the first philosophy
for Jon to discover and adopt. It had helped him survive the gel
years, adapt to the new reality of their bodies degrading after the
gelled water had ravaged them, and strive to become the head of
this wonderful community and guide them into making a decent
and civilized life for themselves.

Jon spoke in his teaching tone. "Let me tell you what I
discovered. Let me confide in you where thought and reason led
my mind after digging the Mother out of Her divine hiding. It is
actually beautiful in its destructive simplicity. It is all about the
metamorphosis. The ongoing process of metamorphosis. The Divine Mother doesn't stop after turning our flesh to rust, or turning us into monstrous creatures. She doesn't rest after we stop
eating or drinking, or drawing breath. She just…doesn't stop."

That was the essence of all his teachings. Of what life was
now for them, for the new people. The gelled water, or the Divine Mother, as he'd named it, never stopped gnawing at them
and transforming them into something else. Not the individual,
but the transformation of humanity from what they'd been before the Black Rain to whatever it was they would become a few
generations from now. No one could guess what that *something
else* was. Jon had two theories and both of them were grim.

His first theory was that the Divine Mother was purposeful.
That the gelled water was manipulating their very own genetic
information, taking and replacing bits. Now, if that manipulation
was done by man, they would certainly pursue a very concrete
goal. Like the Green Party before the present mayor's Blue Party
had done manipulating it and producing the sewer-people and
drill-people. But with the Mother, who could tell what Her goal
was? *Why* all this was happening was clear in the mythology
he'd started putting together. But to what end? No one could
know the mind of such an alien god. And yet, in his first theory

Jon dared to think that it might be for their punishment—to make humanity suffer and perish. After taking away from humanity's genetic information and diminishing humans as humans had done to their own world, the Mother would eventually transform the human genetic material to simpler and simpler forms, to the point where the intellect would vanish, and the consciousness would melt away, leaving humans simple crawling creatures, dwindling on the face of the Earth. The perfect punishment for the perfect destroyer that humans were.

Jon's second theory was that the Mother was blind and purposeless. Man's transformations were not the result of a punishing god, but rather merely the effect of a new evolutionary purpose and entropy. The Mother was blind, yet the genes were selfish and purposeful. They wanted to survive no matter what. Pure and simple. Consciousness had been an evolutionary accident in humans. As long as it had kept the genes alive, it had been suffered. But now, consciousness had proven dangerous for humanity's genes. It had created the ecological apocalypse that had brought the Black Rain and the gelled water. It had almost brought the extinction of humans themselves and with them, the extinction of their own genes. So, all the transformations humans had been suffering were actually prompted by their own genes to turn humans into a different creature, without consciousness and without the drive to destroy nature and in the process destroy themselves. Genes were working to take away humanity's intellect and consciousness. To take away the soul.

And that brought Jon to the crux of the problem—was there divinity? Before any of these he'd believed in one philosophical theory of his time, that consciousness was put in humans by God, so He'd have this very quick interface to find out what we were thinking about. If consciousness was God's doing, then the genes could not take it away. They shouldn't have the power, the divine authority to do it. But God...God as he'd been thought about by people before the Black Rain...that God didn't exist anymore. Very few still remembered Him.

So, either there was no divinity and everything was evolution and selfishness, or there was divinity and everything was crime and punishment. These were the two theories that wouldn't let Jon sleep at night. Either way, science could explain everything. Even the existence or absence of divinity.

But he couldn't tell his disciple that. He couldn't expose his community to that kind of truth. A scientific explanation was too much for poor Stev. Science had never brought humans hope. It had only brought clarification where there was doubt. It had only brought reason where there was just fear. But now, the poor corroded beings of this apocalyptical world needed hope, not reason. They needed purpose, not hard, cold explanations. They needed a new mythology. One that would keep them warm and content during their passage into the dark night of their minds.

"You see, Stev," said Jon, "our ongoing metamorphosis will eventually lead to a being quite different than what we are now. The Mother will see it through. So, the question is not what, but why."

"If the M-M-Mother will see it th-th-through, that means the M-Mother does all these transformations in our b-b-bodies."

Jon nodded approvingly. He sipped slowly and sighed. There were so very few things he could still enjoy after the Black Rain.

"So, if the M-M-M-mother does it all, who is this Mod that could also b-b-bring transformations in people?"

"Ah, that's a very good question. Semantics." Jon grinned and felt again the elation he used to feel when teaching his students before and one of them had the kind of inquiring mind that Stev had. The kind of mind that not just recorded the information, but made the necessary connections between different parts. And signaled where the presented information was not enough to illuminate the truth of the matter.

"All right, Stev, now pay attention to this—the Mother is omnipresent because She is the water in the world, everywhere, every moment, coursing not only through the land in rivers and lakes, but through our bodies as well. If you think of the process of transformation, Mod is Her acting agent. It is her *will*, if you want. He is an integral part of Her. Not a separate body, just a separate entity. Her will, His action."

"Just like how M-M-Mr. Ambassador is the agent of the C-C-Cave."

"Geo?" Jon faltered a second, then he brightened. "Yes. Yes! Exactly."

"But, I don't know…it's just…"

"What is it, Stev?"

"I don't t-t-trust Mr. Ambassador. His C-C-Cave sounds imaginary. Not reality."

Sometimes Jon wondered if a mythology wasn't a bit too much for the new people. Yet, it was his last act of kindness for humanity. So, better make it good. For them.

"What is trust?"

"T-t-trust is the feeling I have when Bart makes good on his p-p-promise," said Stev.

"Good, close enough. So, you trust Bart because he makes good on his promise. Correct?"

"Yes. B-Bart promised to bring me masha flour each seventh d-d-day of every week and he's doing exactly that."

"Good. Good. So, if Bart has gained your trust because for the last five years he's delivered you masha flour exactly *when* he promised, that means you can tell Bart all your family's secrets, no?"

"What? No!"

"Why not?"

"B-b-because while he is a trustworthy merchant, it doesn't mean he will not harm me if he knew m-m-my secrets."

"So, what is the difference?"

Stev pondered. He grimaced. "That's a tricky question."

"No, it's actually quite simple. What follows becomes tricky."

The door opened and Magi, Stev's five-year-old, ran in, laughing. "Da, Da, save me!" She jumped into his open arms.

Di, the girlfriend of one of Jon's sons, ran in after Magi, panting and red in the cheeks. "I'm so sorry, Mr. Jon. I'm so sorry, Mr. Stev. I tried to stop her but she's too quick."

Stev kissed his daughter's hair and put her down. "Now, Magi, what d-d-did I say about coming inside my office?"

"But, Di almost caught me and you had to save me! I'm your little princess!"

"All right, Magi, I saved you. Now go on, b-b-back in the shop."

The two girls ran back, giggling, and closed the door behind them. Stev chuckled and took a sip of tea. Jon breathed hard. Every moment of happiness had become a struggle for him. A struggle to keep his heart beating regularly, to keep breathing, to clear the dizziness from his eyes. But it was worth it. He'd never give up enjoying his family and friends even if it would leave him breathless. In a way that was it—love and happiness should leave you breathless.

"I'm sorry, t-t-teacher. I told her not to b-b-bother us. She knows the rules."

Jon waved his hand to show that he didn't care. In spite of the effort, he kept smiling. Despite all the hassles he felt good in his heart. "I'm afraid that we are close to the end of our visit today. If I want to leave you with something today, Stev, it's this: Mr. Ambassador is the agent of the Cave, which is very much a reality. I know the Cave is real because I've been there before the Black Rain. The Woodman Laboratories are very much a reality, like your shop is. So, if I've ever earned your trust, then you should trust me when I say that the Cave is real and the information Mr. Ambassador trades with us is real too."

Well, that was a stretch. He didn't have any way of checking the information Geo Woodman was trading with them. But somehow, he trusted the boy. He'd sensed an earnestness in him and the pain that comes from believing something with all your being and not managing to convince others of your belief. He intimately knew that Geo wanted to help them and even save them, if they needed that. Whether the boy could actually pull that off was an entirely different matter.

"If you trust me, Stev, trust Mr. Ambassador too."

"I will, teacher. I will make every effort to t-t-trust him."

Jon gulped the rest of the mush tea and rose with some effort. Pain in his bones, soreness in his muscles, and dizziness in his head—he'd grown too old for this savage world. But he needed to stay until the end of his mission. And that meant a few more years. At least. He knew it sounded greedy, but it wasn't. It was only hopeful. Hope that he would be able to make a difference.

"I'm sorry, t-t-teacher, but I need your help today."

"Mic's business?" Jon asked immediately. He'd known this would come up, and he dreaded the moment.

Stev nodded, his expression unhappy. The old man didn't consider Stev guilty of this. He'd been only one cog in his son's machinations, and Mic had taken advantage of Stev's love for Sara and his desire to slow down Sara's corrosion. Who wouldn't do anything for the people they loved? Even questionable things. No, if anyone was to be blame for this, it was Mic.

"Mic told me you need to bake some fairy dust in the next few days, but your bakery would almost surely be the object of a raid."

Stev nodded again. His face was flushed—with embarrassment, Jon guessed. Or a mixture of embarrassment and anger, if he knew anything about the man. The man who'd become his best friend and as dear as a son to him.

"I'll make room for your kitchen in my shop and you can come and work whenever you want, Stev."

"T-t-thank you!" said Stev, his voice trembling.

Jon hugged him and sighed. He'd never abandon his friend. Stev hugged him back and Jon sighed again and relaxed. It was all good. As long as he could take care of his people, his family, everything would be good.

8.
The Cave

The sky was a sickly green. The mountainous landscape was shrub green. The mountain peak was the only spot without color, just gray stone, dry moss, whistling wind full of twirling spores. Hesitating, Geo stared at the cracked stone at his feet. This trip had not gone as expected. This trip had gone bad. Really bad. He looked to the skies, void of the avian life that he'd seen in documentaries. No birds had flown here for decades. Ever since the Black Rain. Would this shit never end?

"Geo?" His brother's voice surprised him. He knew they could pick him up on their sensors, but he hadn't expected anyone to actually bother him. They always maintained tactical silence unless otherwise instructed. But his brother—well, for one, Alex was not security.

"I'm coming in," said Geo. He pressed the button in his suit and the rock under his feet shuddered slightly, then began descending slowly into the mountain's peak. The stone roof closed above him and white artificial light replaced the greenish nightmare. He stepped off the platform and took the two steps to the elevator's door.

A thousand meters lower, the elevator opened into utter darkness. Geo tapped the security code on his sleeve's pad. Two strong lights flooded the bridge crossing a bottomless chasm. A narrow metal bridge.

At the end of it, a tiny door opened into the mountain wall and Geo was finally home.

Beyond the dusty penthouse skylights, the greenish morning light disperses a moldy brown atmosphere. The initiated lie down on mattresses under the flood of liquid light. They gnash their teeth under their masks, experiencing an invisible, silent pain. Only their taut bodies show the suffering they endure. The left arms of each end in stumps, chopped close to the elbow. Shapes bud from the flesh of these stumps, yet unformed but casting amazing silhouettes reminiscent of predators and scavengers—vultures, carnivorous fish, rapacious reptiles, even octopuses. There are also some unsuccessful, meaningless shapes, buds with no specific function.

Boris makes a sign and his guards bend over these last ones and tenderly, smoothly pass the hatchets over their necks. They work quickly and efficiently, like butchers in an abattoir. There are gurgles, welling blood, some heads that are completely detached. At my feet, his neck split, a sixteen-year-old boy writhes uncontrollably. I remember he had a girlish voice and an immeasurable appetite for life. He's been my guide in the Golden Tower.

Boris turns to me and says proudly, "Behold my officers. The miracle of life through water. The water creates life through them now. Some of them can't manage to pass the nine thresholds of sleep, so we help them through. But the others become my officers, each chosen by the water, one by one." He shows me the head of a boar, its mouth agape, struggling to open bleary eyes. It springs from an arm that seems too fragile for its hairy enormity. I glance toward Boris's left hand, always gloved and hidden under his coat. He laughs and tells me, "You're smart and brave. When you decide, I'll make you my First Scientist. Don't you want to be my First Scientist? I'll make you my First Corrosive!" He throws his head back and guffaws.

Geo woke up gasping for air. His mouth was wide open, held in place within a frame that held his tongue down while a vacuum tube worked in his throat to clean the filter. He panted and his brother looked at him with a worried expression. "I'm sorry, little brother. I know."

Geo shook his head and closed his eyes. No, Alex didn't know. He would never know. He would never leave the Caves.

Alex looked to the floor. Geo knew that face—the guilt, the pain, the hunger. Alex was tall, athletic, intelligent, with excellent hand-eye coordination, perfect for the role of ambassador. And yet, the smaller, thinner, and unathletic Geo had been given the role since they were little children. And even growing up so obviously different hadn't changed Grandpa's choice. Instead of staying home and studying, Geo had been sent into the world to advance the Woodmans' interests. And Alex had become the scientist, despite his natural inclinations.

"Today it's taking longer, Geo. But if you care about your pretty face, be patient. The Silkers prepared your tea with gelled water this time. They didn't follow the protocol. You'll have to refrain altogether, next time you're there."

A deadly drowsiness flowed through Geo's veins and his head felt as though it was being pierced by a hundred nails. *I'm a damned magician frightened by his own magic. The gelled water, the water of life, and corrosion. Great Wood, why would the Blues want to pour gelled water down my throat?*

After the ecological disaster, humanity had fallen even further into the Universal Corrosion period. Everything liquid that had been water-based had solidified—or rather, had become gelatinous. There were only a few liquid reservoirs left, deep underground, fed by subterranean rivers and lakes. Like the one in Woodman's Cave. People lucky enough to find such treasures kept their existence secret. Everyone else had been forced to consume the gelled water and had become Corrosives, people whose bodies were covered in a verdigris, gnawed at like ordinary metals are consumed by rust. Some tried to keep their bodies clean of the rust, but they ended up corroded skeletons, their flesh consumed faster than metal.

The Silkers called the gelled water Life Water. Once you drank it, you were at its beck and call. It could keep you alive for as long as it wanted—ten years or three hundred—you couldn't die until it wanted you to. You could maim yourself, you could become a shapeless and corroded piece of flesh, yet it wouldn't allow you to die as long as you still had flesh on your bones. You could chop off your left hand and go through the terrible pain of the nine thresholds of sleep; just focus on it and imagine something, anything—a hammer, a woodpecker, a frog, or a bull—and something would grow back, but not another hand. If the pain was unbearable and you couldn't focus, you'd be left maimed.

"There you go, done. Theoretically, you're clean," his brother announced, waking him up with his forced cheerfulness. "Now we have to take a few scans. There's something off with you today."

Geo shook his head groggily. He was fed up with these games. He hated the ones he'd left in the Caves, because they got a home, children, a settled life. But no, he'd been trained, he'd been implanted with all sorts of expensive devices, he'd been educated since childhood for this. He already had a network, connections; he kept them alive in the world. *What rights do I have?*

Geo followed Alex to the scanning room. On the way he passed a mirror on the wall. The man looking back at him seemed too young, too fragile, but most of all, naked. He was used to seeing himself geared up all the time. Like the astronauts from the old times when doing space walks. Only these days, he was space walking in Torono. Or just the city, as people called it everywhere. The center of the damaged world. How quickly they'd fallen from an entire planet—no, fuck, from an entire solar system—to a single city and its surrounding barrens. Humans were inconsequential. Technology and science had made them gods and showered them in fortunes and then those same fortunes had turned them back into worms as fast as if you'd flipped a switch.

The scanning sarcophagus was humming silently, a droning that raised Geo's anxiety levels. He tried to shut his eyes and count until he fell asleep. Not a chance. The droning amplified all the past day's dread and brought back the nightmares. He opened his mouth and inhaled deeply. It was hard to breathe.

He heard Alex's voice nearby. "Shit!" His brother was not in his isolated partition anymore. He felt Alex take his left hand in his and squeeze. "Slow down, little brother. Breathe. You're having a panic attack. I'm here. I won't let go, all right? I'm here."

The droning noise had ceased, but Geo realized this only now. He was still squeezing Alex's hand. The weight on his chest had lifted and he was now breathing normally. Sweat had gathered in droplets on his nape and back.

"What the fuck happened out there?" Alex's tone was calm despite the words. Geo turned his head and anchored himself in those calm brown eyes. His older brother had always had older eyes. Not kind, or warm, just deeply inquisitive and wise. They made Geo feel that he was in safe hands. His brother would always know what to do.

"I honestly don't know yet. There are a lot of variables—"

"Drop the ambassador shit, Geo. You're talking to me. What. Happened?"

"I've been there, Alex. I've seen a Water Passage." Geo shook his head and shuddered. "It's brutal. It's nothing we could have imagined."

"So, Boris kept you there from the beginning to the end, as promised."

"I've been there beyond what we thought to be the end. The ending is still to be revealed. I was his guest at the reception after the ritual, then I spent the evening with one of his concubines—"

"You've spent an evening with a Sun Glory?"

Again the hunger in his brother's voice. The outside world thrilled, with its stories and legends that had shaped their childhood. The luminous and mysterious world from their imagination. The grim and deadly world of reality.

"Yes, that was sort of a gift from Boris."

"Is it as advertised?"

"And more, Alex. As delicious, but way more dangerous. I don't know how I'm going to handle this."

"Oh, you lucky bastard. What did she do? Was she too much for you?"

"What would that even mean, you shit?"

They both burst into laughter.

George sighed and closed his eyes. "I don't know what happened. One moment I was with Lena, the Sun Glory, the next I woke up in the street, blind, confused, drained of energy. Meat for the sewerers."

"Fuck, bro. What did the Sun Glory give you?"

"A silk tea laced with nunnehi pollen. That's it."

"Those don't create those kinds of effects."

"I know. I'm pretty sure I've been poisoned with iron silk."

"Shit. Shit, Geo. First gelled water and now iron silk. This is…"

"I know. This time they fucked me good. And I don't even know who it was."

"Well, let's resume the scanning and find out what the damage is."

9.
The Woodman Council

Woodman the Elder was a tall old man with a big white beard, bushy eyebrows, and a military bearing. His skin was pale and dusted heavily with freckles, and his smile was sad. Though terminally ill, he still dressed impeccably. *"We're in a cave, Grandpa! Why do you keep dressing like that?"* a teenage Geo had asked him during one of their training sessions. Of course that had turned into another puzzle for Geo to solve: *"People dress in a certain way for multiple reasons. Determining what the reason is will help you navigate the rough waters of corrosion diplomacy."*

"Something doesn't add up," said Woodman the Elder, placing the message from the city's mayor on the table. It wasn't a message so much as a straightforward expropriation order on national security grounds. He'd given them five days to leave the Caves and allow the mayor to take full ownership of them.

"It doesn't matter," said Samuel Hastie, the Chief of Security. "They don't know where we are, the boy stays put, we wait for this to blow over."

"There's something he doesn't tell us," growled Greg Rumi. He'd always had a manifest dislike for Geo. Over the years that dislike had soured and festered. Geo had never guessed what he'd done to make the old man hate him so much. For a while Geo had thought that if he was very respectful and kind to old Rumi, the man would see the light and move on. That had never happened.

"I know—the mayor didn't say 'please' in his order," said Geo innocently.

"Don't play smart ass with me, boy."

"Then don't—"

"George!" Woodman cut him short with an authority that Geo could never disobey.

"I'm sorry, sir. I know. He's old and senile and—"

"George, if you do not behave I'll have to remove you from this room. And that would be a shame, seeing as you're our ambassador and will have to untangle this mess for us. I'd like the council to work with you on this, not just give you orders."

"Bah, he's just not seasoned enough to do this job. I said this over and over. We put our lives in the hands of an immature mama's boy."

Geo cringed and had a flash of their last meeting before his departure on this ill-fated mission. It had happened in the same council meeting room.

"We want a bid on our information. Come back with offers and we'll choose the winner," Greg Rumi said, his tone magnanimous, as if he'd just given his daily instructions to one of his employees.

"We can't do that. We need to think of the people." Geo looked around the table to the rest of the council members. None of them acknowledged his plea in any way.

"They're not people," said Rumi coldly. "They're Corrosives."

"Grandpa, please," said Geo. "We need to do the right thing. Share the information and convince everyone that they have to take early measures and save as many as possible. We don't want the Black Rain fatalities again. And on our conscience this time."

For a brief moment there was silence around the table. Woodman the Elder shook his head and sighed in disappointment. "It's been voted. The decision is made. There's nothing I can do, George."

"But Grandpa, this should be bigger than a vote in the council!"

"You have your order, boy," barked Rumi with satisfaction. "Just follow it like the good boy your momma thinks you are."

Back in the present boardroom, Geo turned his head to Woodman the Elder. The old man signaled for Geo to keep his cool.

"Greg, why don't you tell us why you think George is hiding something. I would very much appreciate every statement and accusation to be substantiated, not just thrown out to provoke and see what it turns into." Woodman the Elder smiled at Rumi.

"He hesitated every time he answered questions regarding his time in the Golden Tower. He took long seconds to answer almost every question. To think it through and select what to tell us and what to hide from us."

"He's tired and still reeling from a very bad experience, Greg," said Woodman. He leaned on the table as if encouraging Rumi to go on.

"Our procedure requires that he answer every question without thinking it through. So we can have the natural, instinctive answers, without his processing and selection. That's how we can make our decisions the right way and protect the company. He's deliberately working us like we are his contacts from Exterior."

"George, is there something you want to tell us?" Woodman turned and asked Geo as serenely as he'd talked to Rumi.

Geo exhaled and let go of his bitterness against Rumi. He had enough problems without adding the angry Chief of Science to them. As always, he'd have to accept his attitude as he accepted any other facts. "I'm not hiding anything from the council, sir. There are, though, dozens of details I didn't include in my report, as time is not on our side now, the way I see it."

"What kind of details?" said Woodman the Elder, motioning to Rumi to keep quiet.

"I cannot yet find the words to express the horrors I've seen. I am unable to paint for you the gut-wrenching reality of what the Exterior is now. Maybe someday we'll have time for me to report that nonessential information and not the pressing issues that threaten our existence. But that day is not today."

Rumi snorted dismissively. "Mama's boy, as I said."

Geo rose from his chair and suddenly the entire room's chemistry changed. Hastie rose as well, ready to pounce on Geo, his muscles taut, his eyes following his every move. Geo smiled, pleased that he could create such a reaction in a room full of adult men. But immediately nausea overwhelmed his pleasure. He could sense something wasn't adding up, as Woodman the Elder said. He'd made sure he hadn't been followed. He was 99.99 percent sure no one had seen him coming to the Caves. And yet...what could the mayor's game be?

"See his face?"` said Rumi. "Even now he's thinking before speaking."

"I'm done with the report," said Geo. "Take what you want from it. But I think Grandpa is right—there's something wrong about all this and I'd be more responsive to Mr. Rumi's polite requests if I could wrap my head around what happened in the city and why the mayor thinks this expropriation order could work. If I knew what his game is. But my answering your every question in a certain amount of time to make you feel in control will not actually put you in control. And my priority now is to think this through and solve it. So, gentlemen—a pleasure, as always."

Geo left the room without waiting for any dismissal. This was the first time he'd dared defy the council, but he'd had enough of their corporate bullshit. Now was not the time to play political games. Now was the time to act. And what scared him the most was that he didn't know how to act.

"This is not over," Rumi called as he left. "You will answer for your mistakes."

"That's enough, Gr—" Woodman clutched at his chest and fell.

Bree slowed down when she heard voices drifting toward her from ahead. No one was supposed to be in the labs today. She considered going in, slamming the door, and surprising the intruders, giving them a scare. Probably it was another prank by Alex's friends to catch him off guard. Alex and his dumb friends. Always getting into trouble. Careless and frivolous. Yeah, that was a good idea. Catch them in the act and then call security. A couple of days in the chill cells would do them good. The labs were not a playground. These were not safe areas.

She scanned her security pass and the door hissed open. The voices grew louder, but they didn't come from the labs. They came from her grandfather's office. Weird. Her grandfather was supposed to be in the council, debriefing Geo. She moved forward carefully to eavesdrop.

"Giving that thug a wooden throne was our biggest mistake. Now they know we have a big source of fresh water."

A woman's voice, strong Hispanic accent. Probably Maria Lopez, the CFO. The other voice was her grandfather's—Greg Rumi.

"Acknowledging to the world that we exist was our biggest mistake. We are self-sufficient. We don't need the Exterior. They need us. And now that we are exposed, they'll come to get it."

"And are we prepared to fight them off, as Woodman said?"

"No, we're not, Maria. We are certainly not. And that's why that stupid kid, that joke of an ambassador, should have been kept at home. Locked in a cell, if possible. He's done too much damage as it is."

"Well…"

"We don't have the luxury of uncertainty anymore, Maria. You heard the mayor's message."

"I know, but he doesn't know where we are yet. We're still safe."

"Are we?"

"What? Do you know something I don't?"

"I know that Geo is as dumb as they come. He says they haven't followed him, but—really now. Are we to trust him after the mess he's made?"

"No, you're right. Geo is a liability."

"The whole Woodman family is a liability. They took it too far now. I don't care that they're the owners. That was before. Now is now. I won't put my family in jeopardy to protect their ego. They don't own us."

"No, they don't. They're just survivors, like the rest of us."

"You know what we need."

"Yes, I do. I just hoped it wouldn't come to this."

"Well, it came. And now we have to prepare—"

Bree knocked on the door to Rumi's office. She could not let them get too far with this nonsense. Her grandfather should not say the words.

"I'll send the report to you, Mrs. Lopez," said Rumi and then raised his voice. "Enter."

Bree opened the door, allowed Maria Lopez to exit the office, then watched her as she left the laboratories. *Now* there was no one else in the labs but her grandpa and her. His wrinkled face had frozen a long time ago in a bitter expression of disappointment and anger. In school, Alex used to joke that they had been awarded a chemistry prof with a bitter core and an extra side of wrinkles. She didn't know much about her grandfather's youth, or life in general, for that matter. She didn't know what had made him that way, or if he'd been like that from the beginning. But judging from her mother's perspective, he couldn't possibly have been like this from the beginning. Her mother was cheerful and playful, always finding reasons to laugh and joke and play tricks on those around her. Her mother was like happiness incarnate.

"Do you need something, Bree?"

"What was that, Grandpa?"

"What was what? Be more specific. I don't have all day."

"'The whole Woodman family is a liability. They took it too far now.'"

"You were not supposed to hear that."

"Weren't you supposed to be in the council? Debriefing Geo Woodman?"

"None of this is your business. Don't you have a job to do?"

"This is my job. Keeping the Cave together. *You're* pushing it too far now, Grandpa."

"How dare you, you little snot! Get the hell out of my office!"

Bree didn't move. She squared her shoulders and looked him in the eye. It had been years since she was afraid of her grandfather. Lately it had been just a matter of respect and politics. But now, he'd just lost her respect. He'd never been anything else but a bully. "You are *not* moving against the Woodmans," she said.

"*You* are not telling me what to do. If you don't mind your own business, you'll get sent back to the kitchen. Next to your momma."

Bree felt it like a punch. She had no idea of any history between her mother and her grandfather. But that had sounded like there was something, and that she wouldn't like discovering what it was.

"You may think this is about you and that you can order me around, but this is beyond you, old man. Geo has sacrificed everything to this stupid mission, to us, and you'd better start giving him the respect and support he deserves."

"I'm doing this for the safety of everyone in this Cave. But you, you stupid, hormonal girl, think this is about you and your feelings. Always carrying the flag for gutless Geo."

"How dare you!"

"Don't interrupt me! Everything is about you and your feelings, like your momma. Geo *is* a liability and he has brought us to the brink of destruction. *Your* feelings don't come before our survival. You will do what I tell you to do."

"No, Grandpa. This time you will do what I tell you to do."

"This is your last warning, girl. Forget Geo. Alex is your future. Mind your place. And when things start happening, wait next to your momma for them to pass. Then you can return to your labs like a little good soldier."

"No, this is *your* last warning, Grandpa. You're not making any wrong moves. Because I'll be watching you and I'll be one step ahead of you."

She turned and left the office without giving him any chance to reply. She'd—what would she do? *Because I'll be watching you…*

That was as lame as they come. She had stayed away from politics. And especially from her family's confrontations. She'd always preferred to leave whenever there had been a conflict between her parents, or between her parents and her grandfather. She couldn't handle conflict. She'd always preferred running over confrontation.

Because I'll be watching you. If that was the best she could do against her grandfather, she might as well have handed him a written approval of his behavior. Greg Rumi had always been strong headed and yes, a bully. A smart one also. Not the same as Alex's dumb friends. Her grandpa was one of those bullies who always got away with their abuses.

Bree stopped and looked around. No, she wasn't going to go home and see her mother. She wouldn't be able not to ask. Not to open that can of worms. She...

There were noises from the medical labs. Someone was still there. She might as well make herself useful and try to forget all of it. For now. For now, because she had to do something about it.

10.
Old Spirits

Jon forced himself to look. Always. It took strength to see his wife's pain, but it was important to witness it and support her. Mar was a mere thirty-six. Jon knew this because he still counted, despite the fact that water children didn't count years. They considered themselves ageless, just like water. But Mar was thirty-six and by pre-Gelled Period criteria she was still young, although by Gelled standards she was quite old. Yet, considering he was fifty-nine (that was ancient in Gelled terms), she was really young. And yes, that was another thing—he was probably among the very few water children to still compare pre-Gelled standards with contemporary ones. And surely the last one to still use the term "contemporary." And only in his thoughts.

Doc inserted the syringe's needle under Mar's skin for the tenth time, next to her left knee. Corrosion had started eating at her flesh on both legs a decade ago. They had been in a good situation, so he'd been able to pay for the treatment right away. That slowed down the rusting effect, but didn't stop it. It had probably given her a couple of decades of walking on her own legs before she'd need a wheelchair. Jon had been deeply worried about what she'd do after his death. He'd never hoped to live past forty, let alone past fifty. But now he was more relaxed—his eldest son, Ton, had taken over their shop, and while the boy was not half as smart as his mother, he was hard-working and dutiful. He'd be able to take care of Mar in Jon's absence. As for his younger son, Mic, well, that was another story and truthfully another worry.

To cover the entire corroded area, Doc needed to do some fifty injections with the latest varnish formula. That was a small fortune. But for the last few years, Doc had managed to take them off the official lists and had offered Mar the treatment for free. Which was a relief, considering the expense of Jon's expanding family—his sons' girlfriends, maybe soon to be wives. Four people who right now were barely touched by corrosion, but in a few years, they would need treatment as well, so the payment would very quickly become unbearable.

Mar was a tall, beautiful woman. She'd always had that femme fatale look about her. Obviously, Jon was the only one who still knew what "femme fatale" meant. Oh, maybe Doc too. Doc had been a student at UofT before the Gelled Period. Right when Jon had started teaching philosophy there. They'd met at the time, then lost touch during the events of the brutal Transition Period. And then fate brought them back together when Doc reemerged as the inventor of the varnish treatment and unfortunately had to accept as patron the Bathurst Clan. And Jon had been the prominent figure of the clan's school, charged with teaching the basics to all the chiefs' children—but forbidden to spread education to the masses.

Mar groaned in pain. Her first groan. She could hold it up to around fifteen injections, then she'd start groaning. But then she'd manage to shed no tears until Doc was out of their bedroom. She'd always kept up a tough image for everyone. Jon had been the only one who'd seen her pain and fear. Everybody else thought of her as the Stone Lady. The fearless woman with a will of stone and water principles. Not the beautiful and sensitive princess he'd grown to love more dearly than life itself.

Jon could see the varnish solution spreading under Mar's ebony skin like a milky-white spiderweb, spreading its threads slowly and connecting with the other injection points, creating a protective web directly on her flesh. Penetrating the upper layers of flesh, it actively isolated the corroded areas so they wouldn't spread. For a while. For as long as the varnish was in place, before the flesh ate at it, slowly but surely. It had to be built that way so the organism could accept it and as a result consume it and make it part of its life cycle. That was the most they could do. There was no healing treatment to combat corrosion. Just an extension on the flesh warranty.

Ton placed a plate of honey cookies on the table. They were Mar's signature dessert, and a constant in their lives. Jon had always thought of those cookies as a sort of the glue between his family members and between his family and their friends. Everybody had eaten Mar's cookies and had come to expect them while visiting there. Doc took one and bit off a good chunk with obvious pleasure. Doc had said repeatedly that he loved those cookies.

Jon realized that he was the last of Doc's links to the past, to another life he still dreamt about. Which was why Jon knew that while Doc was a good man and possibly his best friend, he was not a reliable resource for his resistance movement. He'd kept all his plans and moves secret and as far as Doc knew, Jon was the retired shopkeeper of the Universal Store and the husband of beautiful Mar, the girl that Doc had courted ardently before she'd chosen Jon. The woman that still held Doc's heart, from the look in his eyes every time he'd treated Mar.

"Let me see your neck, Jon," said Doc, dragging his chair close to Jon's.

Ton helped his father take off the cloth he wrapped around his neck to protect it from the oppressive humidity. Then he averted his eyes and left the room without a word. Another good man, thought Jon. Yet another one unreliable for his resistance. And even for continuing Jon's legacy. That was why Jon had preferred Stev as his successor rather than any of his sons. Ton was too sensitive and compromising, while Mic was too narcissistic and superficial, the type that would always cut corners to achieve his selfish goals faster.

"This doesn't look good, Jon. You're reaching the point where you'll lose your ability to speak."

"I still know how to write." Jon smiled. His voice was low and rusty. One would have to listen closely to hear him.

"I'm glad you still know that, because it will help you a lot when you'll also lose your esophagus. Then you won't be able to eat and…" Doc gulped and began cleaning the rust from Jon's neck. Jon knew that Doc was feeling Jon's failing health more deeply because of their friendship and especially because of the prospect of years of solitude after Jon's passing. But at the same time, Doc was not an actual physician with actual training and experience with losing patients. He had a PhD in chemistry and took care of everyone with the varnish treatment because the varnish was his baby. Not because he was their doctor.

"I need a little bit more time," said Jon. "I'll start the treatment as soon as possible."

He didn't have the resources to carry on treatment now that he was so close to one of his resistance's objectives. He'd devoted his life to opposing the corrupt power of the government in order to make a future for his people. For his children. For his family and his friends. Only after paying his dues for that could he finally pay something toward his own treatment.

Ton came back into the room, head lowered as if he didn't want somebody to see where he was looking. Sometimes he was still a child, thought Jon, feeling the warmth rising in his chest.

"Da, there's someone spying on us."

Doc looked at Ton in confusion. Jon raised his eyebrows. How could someone spy on them in their own home? He instinctively looked toward the windows. Pi was there, staring at them, making no effort to hide his actions. He was not spying; he was observing them. The little runt was a creep.

"Shit!" said Doc.

"Thank you, Ton. That creep is our concern. Get back to your work as if nothing happened." Then Jon turned to his friend, one eyebrow raised.

"The little shit spies on me to see if I give the treatment to my friends without payments. He never dared do something like this before. But since the mayor enlisted him in the ranks of his tax officials he's become a burden. A real pain in the ass."

Jon laughed at that. It was Doc's turn to look confused.

"Remember when that used to be a real affliction?"

"What?"

"Pain in the ass."

Doc looked bewildered for a second, then started laughing as well. That was a bad memory and not laughable at all, but the two of them were probably the last people in the world to still remember that and be able to place it in a *contemporary* context to realize the irony of their situation. The modern children of water were not afflicted by any disease. They didn't have any of the past's problems, like diabetes, hepatitis, cancer, or any of the old illnesses. Yet they were all, without exception, afflicted with the corrosion. That was the only thing still making them suffer and eventually killing them. Jon would give anything to have some hemorrhoids giving him trouble, and no corrosion eating at his flesh.

"I'm too old for this shit," said Doc, panting after the laugh.

Jon rose from his chair and went to his desk. He opened a drawer and took out a small hemp bag. He opened it, searched inside with his fingers, then took out a tiny gold nugget. "Do you think this covers it?"

"What?"

"Mar's treatment. Is this enough?"

"Jon, Mar's treatment is free. I would never take payment from you!"

"I know, my friend. I know that. But now you've got to cover your ass, or that Pi will turn into a real hemorrhoid and give you more pain than it's worth."

"I don't know, Jon. You're my friend and I have the right to visit with you."

"Yes, but we don't know if he actually saw you give Mar the treatment. We need to make sure you're safe if we want your help in the future."

Doc sighed. "As I said, I'm too old for this shit."

Jon placed the nugget in Doc's palm and closed it gently. He smiled and led his friend to the door. "My friend, Stev, told me of the trouble you had there with Pi."

"Yeah, as I said, Pi has become a pain in the ass since he's been put on the mayor's payroll."

"Should Stev be worried?"

"No. Pi has an ugly character, but he's not bold enough to pursue revenge. He'll be petty with Stev in the future, but nothing more. He's just too cowardly to do anything else. Especially against somebody as imposing as Stev."

"All right then, I'll tell Stev to relax."

Doc smiled in his turn. He shook Jon's hand and shuffled away. The world had started to grow small on them and they felt it more with each passing year. That was why Jon had to spend his entire fortune on the next move of his resistance. He had to leave this world a better world for his loved ones.

"Da, the creep is back."

Jon startled and looked over his shoulder at Ton. The boy seemed amused. The creep? He rose with a grunt and a sigh. Arthritis was a thing of the past. Yet, once it infiltrated an organism, corrosion started solidifying flesh and rusting joints as if they were metal mechanisms. Jon had once joked with Doc that he also needed to discover grease for bones and tendons. The older he'd gotten the more seriously he'd started thinking of injecting oil into his joints. At one point, Doc had to make him swear he'd never do such a thing. Apparently Doc had done a lot of research and experiments and oil-injection was not a thing.

"What are you…"

"The creep is at the door, asking to talk to you."

"I don't know…"

"The guy who was spying on us earlier," said Ton.

Jon stiffened. Now he made the connection—the creep was Pi, Doc's assistant. What could he possibly want with him? Maybe he'd been hasty in giving Doc the gold nugget.

Ton led his father into the shop, where Pi was checking the merchandise under the watchful eyes of Di, Ton's girlfriend. The young man lifted a cooking stone and studied it closely. Then he carelessly let it fall back.

Ton stepped forward to take care of the situation, but Jon put his hand on the boy's arm and held him back. "Are you looking for something in particular?" Jon asked, his voice forceful.

"What?" said Pi, looking at the old man.

"How can we help you?" said Jon.

"Can't hear you, old man. You have to speak louder."

Ton shook off his father's hand and moved forward, stopping in front of the diminutive man who stood with his chest puffed out, almost daring Ton to manhandle him. "He asked you if we can help you," growled Ton.

"I—"

Ton silenced Pi with an imperious gesture. "I didn't finish. *He* asked you that, but *I'm* asking you to leave."

"Not before I get what I'm owed," said Pi with an ugly grin.

"The only thing you're owed is a kick in the ass," said Ton, his voice quivering with anger.

Jon knew that when his son got that tremor in his voice, things were going to get ugly. Ton was not a wise young man, nor a calculating one. He was impulsive and governed by his feelings. And while he was not brutal, he could easily resort to verbal and sometimes even physical violence when pushed too far. And too far for Ton was practically still easygoing for Jon.

"What my son means, mr. Pi, is that you must state your business while you're on our property."

"Still can't hear you, old man. Really, you two are the worst businessmen."

"Ton, offer our customer a rest," said Jon.

Ton looked back at his father, his eyebrows raised in confusion. Offering a rest was a code for Jon and his boys when playing the ancient and nearly forgotten game of football. It meant to force the players on the other team to the ground.

The boy grabbed Pi by the scruff of his neck and yanked him forward, then tripped him. Pi fell to his hands and knees, and Ton placed his knee on Pi's back, forcing him to stay down. Pi grunted in pain, then screamed in fear.

"Mr. Pi," said Jon, "now that you've accepted my offer to rest, you're also closer to me, so you can finally hear me talking."

"Let me go, you stinking old fool! You don't know who you're dealing with!"

"I can't *let* you go, since I'm not forcing you to visit my store, or sit down in front of me. But since you wanted to talk business, here I am."

"I can't understand a word of what you're saying, you stupid, stupid old fool. But I bet that when they cut slices of flesh out of you and your sons, you'll know to talk louder and clearer!"

"Ton, our guest is still too far from me. Push him closer, please."

Ton hesitated for a second. Then he shrugged and drove his knee hard into Pi's back, pushing him toward Jon. So close, in fact, that now his father was looking into Pi's eyes from a mere handspan away.

"Can you understand me now, Mr. Pi?"

"Gel you!"

"All right. I take it you can understand me now. I have two witnesses here who can certify that I was a polite host to you, offering you a rest and a kind word for your trouble. So, we can continue with formalities and polite chit-chat, or we can get down to business."

"Tell your worm to take his knee from my back," grumbled Pi.

"But that's not a knee. That's the chair's backrest. I'm sorry my hospitality is not up to your standards, but that's all I can offer you right now."

Pi tried to shake himself free of Ton, but the boy took pleasure in pinning him down harder. Di watched in amusement. She was taking care of a customer who was scanning the shelves nervously.

"I'm here to collect the varnish tax," said Pi with a lot of venom.

"Don't you work for Doc? You should be up to date with everything," said Jon.

"I don't work for Doc. I work for the mayor. And I go with Doc to his patients to collect the tax."

"All right. No worries. I paid Doc the tax."

"No, you didn't."

"Why do you say that?"

"Because I'm the one supposed to collect the tax. If Doc wanted to collect the tax he would've taken me with him. But he didn't. He came alone. That means he wanted to cheat the mayor of his tax."

"Right. Mr. Pi, I find it exhausting to repeat myself. Doc got the payment. There was no need for your presence here. Now, if—"

"He shouldn't do it," Pi spat. "I'm the tax collector. Doc is not allowed to collect it."

"Well, as far as I'm concerned you are Doc's employee, even if you ultimately work for the mayor. And you are not welcome on my property. Even when and *if* Doc's coming with a treatment. Next time I catch you stepping inside my property, I won't be so hospitable. Am I clear?"

"I am an official tax collector. You cannot refuse me access to your property!"

"I can and I'm doing it. As an *official* tax collector, you should know the law. Ignorance may get you killed. Ton, please escort Mr. Pi off our property."

Ton grabbed Pi, lifted him as if he weighed no more than a child, and walked him to the door. Then he shoved him into the street and shut the door behind him. Jon watched through the shop window as Pi stumbled and fell. Street children jumped on him, trying to empty his pockets. It took him a good thirty seconds to get the children off him and stand. He looked back to the shop but couldn't do a thing, so he had to leave.

"Are we in trouble, Da?" asked Ton.

"Yes, we probably are, son."

"Then why do it, Da?"

Jon sighed. He was tired. He wanted to speak to his son about the philosophical approach to autocratic governments, but knew that Ton might mishandle the information and adopt dangerous behavior. The safest route with his son was the simplest one. "Sometimes, people in a position of power may feel invincible and start abusing their position based on the effect that fear has on regular people. There's a fine line between small abuses and crime. Because yes, governments can commit crimes if left unchecked. Do you understand what I'm saying, Ton?"

"I do," said Di when Ton took longer to answer. "You're absolutely right, Mr. Jon. I've seen it happening."

"Yes, your father's death. I remember." Jon turned to his son, who was still having trouble processing his father's words. Jon knew that it wasn't the words he couldn't understand. It was what those words meant. His son had been born into a world of dictatorship and hardship. Freedom was a strange notion to him. As well as accountability when it came to those people serving the dictatorship. It just wasn't something that occurred in his reality, and therefore he found it hard to grasp.

"You're a godsend, Di. Please, take care of my son. I wouldn't want him getting the wrong idea and starting to do something we'd all regret."

"Have no worry, Mr. Jon. I'm here."

Jon began climbing down the steps to their apartment, step after painful step. It would take a while. *Are we in trouble, Da?* That would haunt him for a while, because while he was confident the world needed his resistance movement, he'd never wanted to put his family in danger. And if his innocent and quite naïve son had asked that, it meant that the reality had become even more dangerous. He had to…he didn't know what. What could he do to keep them safe?

11.
The Nightmare Lord

The red building looked like a dead hand with a dozen torn fingers rising into the sky. The Black Rain had eaten at it brick by brick. The mayor said that this had been the seat of power before the corrosion. Silver was too young to know things like that. He'd been born after the Rain. For him, this was what it was. The palpable reality. He couldn't understand the fear old people wore over their hearts like a shield, their melancholy for things that couldn't have and shouldn't have existed. Ah, that was the name of the damn plant that crept over the ruins—*melancholia strangulosa*. He loved scientific names. He could throw them around and impress his troops. They were also known simply as stranglers. The vines strangled the red building and were known to have a taste for human flesh. This was the place where the Nightmare had last been spotted.

Ah, and gargoyles. Silver couldn't understand gargoyles. Those deformed, grotesque little men. And the name—garrgls. What were they supposed to do? Gargle rain water? Apparently it didn't do them any good with the last Rain. Most of them were melted and gnawed into even more grotesque shapes. Why would people sculpt those little monsters into the body of a building? Weren't there enough monsters in the world as it was? Why would you add your own monsters? Liquid people. With their dark and twisted minds.

"Movement to your left," Mantis, the lieutenant of his elite squad, whispered to him.

Silver turned his binoculars to the left corner of the ruins. Thorn bushes had covered the black road like a dense miniature forest. Nothing moved in the bushes. The day was still as unflinching stone. Humid air filled his nostrils like damn creeping gel.

There!

A black shadow moved through the strangler greenery in the shaded corners of the tortured old building. This was Silver's favorite playground—the most haunted area of the city. People had been avoiding it for decades. If you valued your flesh, you didn't want to trespass on the stranglers' fields.

Silver tapped his fingers on the stone next to his head. A white snake wriggled from behind the squad and stopped next to Silver. It was twice as long as a human, its thick body ringed in light gray and white. Its head was humanoid, its monstrous feminine face wearing a sad expression. It stopped and looked down.

"It's there, Worm. We found it."

Worm whimpered, keeping its head down.

"I need you to go on the other side of the ruins, behind the bushes. Wait there for my signal. When given, it's yours. Got it?"

Worm shook and a pair of fluffy white wings erupted from its body, like a wool cape. Its upper body rose slowly from the ground. Silver growled and his lips drew back into an almost inexistent line. Worm shivered and convulsed in pain. It fell back to the ground.

"I asked you something."

"Mmm," Worm murmured and sighed, its face twisted in pain.

"Good. *Now* you can go," Silver said and looked away, disgusted.

The snake rose again, faster. It silently took flight. In a matter of seconds it was high above and executing the directions Silver had given it.

Silver looked back at his elite squad. Eight men, all tough

killing machines. His warriors didn't flinch, didn't tear up, didn't sweat. They were cold as stone. Every one of them owed his life to Silver. He didn't know about honor, but fear and debt worked fine for him. All the crap the old people used to say about honor and oaths sounded to him like words meant to bring them peace of mind, not something palpable, real. His was the real world. The old people's was just a dream. And mind you, not a realistic one, either.

Silver watched the area through his binoculars. The Nightmare kept to the darker areas. It was moving lethargically, as if waiting for— He looked around for signs of movement. Nothing. Everything else was still. Perfectly still. That was not good and actually made the hunt even more exciting.

Silver felt the ping in his mind—Worm was in position. He rose and began running as close to the ground as possible. His warriors followed. Humidity and heat assaulted him savagely, but the thrill of the hunt made Silver invulnerable. He could walk through fire and not feel a damn thing if on the other side was the target he'd tracked.

They reached the corner of the ruins and stuck close to the stone wall. Nightmares were usually careless, but when cornered they were the most dangerous predator of their world. Well, after Silver. He grinned at the thought.

They wanted to get as close as possible before it sensed them. Silver risked a look around the corner, watching the monster for a couple of seconds before ducking back. He shivered with the thrill of the hunt. The Nightmare was a tattered black veil of ethereal flesh, fluttering under its nervous system impulses. He had never seen anything like it. He'd heard of ethereal flesh, but never actually seen it. He'd thought of it more like a metaphor than an actual reality. Oh, the thought of coming back into the city with his trophy; the horror on people's faces!

He looked back to his warriors, breathing heavily with excitement. They were watching him. Anxious, trembling with expectations, slavering for the coming clash. His squad. His killers. He nodded slowly—yes, the sources had been right. Yes, they were hunting an ethereal. Yes, they'd be heroes! All this was implied in that simple nod.

He felt Worm's ping in his mind. The regular ping signaling to Silver that the creature was in place and awaiting the attack order.

Silver pulled the mace from his hip clip with his left hand and drew the sword from the sheath on his back with his right hand. The mace was almost as big as the sword, with rusty nails sticking out of its wicked head. He heard the metallic scrape of weapons being drawn behind him. This was the moment.

He murmured, "This is for you, my Nightmare Lord. We'll return this Nightmare to you." Then he straightened and told his warriors, "Master your flesh."

His men repeated after him, "Master your flesh!"

They rounded the corner running and yelling, weapons high. The Nightmare froze for a fraction of a second. But instead of attacking, it rose higher with a single waving motion. Silver leaped, slicing at it with his sword. The monster was beyond his reach. He landed on his feet, most of his warriors landing behind him after also leaping to attack the Nightmare. One of them took out a slingshot, pulled the band back forcefully, and released. The projectile tore through the ethereal flesh.

The Nightmare wailed. It rose even higher and expanded its body until it covered the sky like a tattered black veil. Darkness fell over them, turning the green daylight into night. In the center of the dark veil, the monster's nervous system gleamed bright blue. They all hesitated for a moment. They'd all seen the eleven movies of the gone age, when the sky had apparently been free of the green charge and people could see the stars— tiny, glowing dots of light adorning an indigo night sky. Bedtime stories.

Silver noticed one of his warriors sliding to the ground and into meditation stance. His flesh rippled on his bones. His body was trying to transform, but his mind resisted. The Nightmare was trying to release the warrior's flesh to the will of the Nightmare Lord. *Master your flesh, brother!* thought Silver and yelled savagely, "Shoot it down!" The three slingers in the squad stretched their slingshots.

A groan turned Silver around in time to see the chest of one of his warriors exploding in a rain of blood. The man gurgled blood and fell. A diamond viper continued its flight through his chest right into the brick wall of the ruins. The squad turned after the snake, slingshots shooting and swords poised. But Silver knew the snakes' strategy. While you followed the first predator, the rest of the pack took away their prey. And indeed, a swarm of vipers was pulling away the body of the fallen warrior while his men were moving in the opposite direction.

Silver ran and sliced with his sword and smashed with his mace, but there were too many snakes. He stopped, looking with disgust at the three reptiles he'd managed to kill. The body of the dead warrior vanished into the ground in the blink of an eye. That was what the Nightmare had been doing. It was posing as a lure for the snakes. They were attracted by movement and heat.

Screams and curses jolted his attention from the snakes. The monster hovered above them, and had taken advantage of the snakes' ambush to rub against three of his warriors before being driven back by their swords and spears to its position in the air, out of their reach. The three men writhed in pain. Their skin was raw, red and blistering where the Nightmare had touched them, as if their flesh was boiling.

Silver bent over the first fallen warrior and swiftly thrust his sword into the man's heart. His writhing stopped. His body fell still. His flesh slid from his bones like lava over rocks. His lieutenant did the same to the second one and nodded to one the men to end the pain of the third fallen warrior. For a couple of moments, all was quiet. Quiet, dark, and star-speckled. Then the darkness moved.

Silver twisted, jumped, and sliced through the ethereal flesh of the Nightmare just as it was preparing to slide over him. He landed and rolled as far away as possible from the Nightmare's tatters.

"Slingshots!" he ordered.

The two remaining warriors carrying slingshots pulled them and released. Two projectiles tore through the night veil. The Nightmare's wail shook the ruined building's foundations. A cloud of red dust rose from the wall of bricks.

The monster put distance between it and them, gaining speed rapidly.

Worm! Silver thought and began running after the Nightmare. His squad followed.

Worm rose suddenly in front of the Nightmare and unfurled its silvery-white wings to their full size, two giant spiderwebs stretching outward like a sticky wall. The Nightmare slammed into them and stuck. It tried to get away but the more it fought, the more tangled into the web it became. Worm closed its wings slowly, trapping the Nightmare's ethereal flesh in an unbreakable silk cage.

Silver Star stopped running and closed the distance with a casual stroll. He sheathed his sword on his back and slid the mace back into its clip on his hip. Reaching the tangled ball of silk and ethereal flesh, he studied it for a few seconds. *Lord, it's beautiful!*

The Nightmare's head was that of a young girl with gray skin and eyes set in deep hollows. What remained of its lips was ragged pink flesh, pulled back in a snarl to expose thin, needle-like teeth.

"What shall I name you, my child?" said Silver.

The monster growled and spat a gob of black and red phlegm. Silver twisted aside, avoiding its touch by the width of a finger. The ground where it landed burned and hissed, steaming subtly.

"Hmm, feisty little one. I'll take good care of you, don't worry. You'll wish you'd controlled your flesh when the Nightmare Lord has taken hold of your soul. But you'll learn. You'll see."

He straightened and focused his thoughts on his creature. Worm twisted as if under electric shock. Then its whole body writhed and contracted, and its face contorted in terrible pain and horror. No sound exited its gaping mouth. Silver had taught it not to make noise. The more it writhed, the more it crushed the Nightmare. The monster's wails were piercing. Almost unbearable.

Eventually Silver exhaled, satisfied. Worm fell to the ground, trembling. The Nightmare was finally silent.

Silver turned to his warriors. All were armed to the teeth, trained and fit. No remorse, no feelings, no hesitation. None thought as deeply as Silver. They all knew his depth. And the new Nightmare would learn it too.

12.
Woodman the Elder

Geo startled. He opened his eyes and saw that Woodman the Elder had placed a freckled and wrinkled hand over his. The old man smiled warmly. He was out of danger for now, the doctor had said. But something had to change in his lifestyle. Geo wanted so much to tell him to step down from his position as CEO of Woodman Enterprises, yet now…

"Did you eat, Geo? You've been on the run for almost twenty-four hours."

"Alex brought me something, Grandpa. I'm good. How do you feel?"

"Like a newborn," said Woodman and grinned widely. Then he looked down and sighed. "I'm sorry."

"What for?"

"I'm sorry I asked you to be point man. I threw you out into the Exterior without considering what this would do to you."

"I may not be immune yet, but I'm getting there, Grandpa. Don't worry about me."

"That is why you were my choice for ambassador and not your brother, who was the obvious choice for everyone else."

Geo cocked his head in wonder. He didn't understand. It was the first time the old man had talked about this. About why he made that choice despite overwhelming criticism and how it affected his popularity. He'd lost all of his former allies and risked everything for this. At the time it had been considered suicidal to his career.

"Your brother is brave and has good instincts and reflexes. He's physically fit, mentally fit—everything necessary for the Exterior…except for one thing."

"What's that, Grandpa?"

"It's fear, my boy. And—"

"So I'm a coward!"

"Fear and cowardice are not the same."

"Then I don't understand."

"Do you know what the definition of a hero is?"

"No," Geo said and sighed heavily. He leaned over his grandfather to hear him better. Since his mother's death, his grandfather had been the only one to praise and encourage Geo, the only adult in his life to show concern and affection. He needed that now.

"A hero is a narcissist with dreams of grandeur. They instinctively know that doing a public service will position them in a special place of favor and public appreciation. So they do the deeds without any consideration for safety, the future, or any value system. They act out of a desire to be rewarded only."

Geo swallowed his words and disappointment. His grandfather was looking frail and ill despite what the doctor had said. Geo's opinion burned inside him and he wanted to speak, but chose not to; he wanted to give the old man a chance at recovery. There would be a better time later for this philosophical discussion.

"Fear makes you think, and ponder, and calculate. It doesn't make you jump to every occasion. It makes you rational. And we need rational decisions every step of the way if we are to ever leave our Cave."

Woodman lifted the respirator and drew a deep breath. He took a few seconds to regain his strength. Geo took his grandfather's hand in his and waited patiently. Woodman could not leave them just now. They needed him more than ever. They— Geo felt ashamed. They may not need him, but he, George, still needed him. He still needed his grandpa's solid, kind presence in his life.

"But more important than fear, the thing that you have—and not many of us do—the thing that makes you so special—"

"Grandpa!" Alex burst into the room and ran to the bed to hug the old man. Behind him, a girl hung back in the doorway. Bree Rumi. Alex's shadow. They were together most of the time. Not only during working hours, as colleagues working on the same research project in the labs, but almost everywhere else outside working hours.

Geo smiled. Bree would probably be Alex's wife in the future and if not, his brother's best friend and companion. He knew that no matter what happened to him out in the Exterior, his brother would never be alone.

"We have some troubling news, Grandpa," said Alex.

"Then don't upset him. Let's go outside and talk about it." Geo rose from his chair and took Alex's arm.

"No, I want to hear it. As long as I draw breath, this will be my job." Woodman took Alex's other arm and kept him sitting on the bed's edge. "Sit, George."

"You don't worry, Grandpa. You rest; we'll deal with every-thing," said Geo, still standing.

"I said sit. And you, young man, speak."

"The blood results and the scan interpretations have come back. Geo was not only contaminated with gelled water, he also breathed the air directly, and there's a foreign agent in his blood."

Geo felt the blood leave his face. He swallowed hard but stayed silent. Shit! Shit, shit, shit! How many things had they done to him and he'd just taken it all in utter ignorance. How stupid could he be? That was probably what his grandpa wanted to say made him special—stupidity. That was what had set him apart from Alex.

"Do we know what that foreign agent is?" asked Woodman.

"We haven't seen it before. We're still running some tests. We'll know more soon."

"Take a guess."

Alex sighed and visibly searched for words. For the first

time, Geo could see his brother was scared. What could scare his *brave* brother? Had Geo been poisoned and he was going to die? What could possibly be—

"We don't want to take a guess, Mr. Woodman," said Bree.

"We need to know what's going on inside him."

"And we're working on that. You'll have our report this evening. But right now, we need to…try and clean his gut."

"Is he…" Woodman paused to inhale from his ventilator. "Is he in any danger?"

"Sorry, it's too early to tell." Bree's voice held a faint tremor. "But if you don't need him anymore, we'd like to take him with us to the labs."

"Sure, go. Now."

"I'm sorry, Grandpa." Geo shook his head. "I let you down. I'm not ambassador material."

"Don't, George. Just let them take care of you."

"We'll take care of him, but you have to rest now, Grandpa," said Alex.

"You listen to me, Alex. George is your charge. Don't let anything happen to him. You hear me?"

"Always."

13.
Blue

"So, tell me, what did you do now?" Bree looked at him seriously, almost frowning. "Oh, don't make that face! I need to know for scientific purposes."

"All right, madam scientist, you'll have to be more specific with your questions."

She wore a white lab coat, yet still looked willowy while all other scientists looked bulky. She was always cheerful and full of energy, as if her grandfather, the dark and morose Greg Rumi had had nothing to do with her genetic material. Where he seemed like he was always plotting to assassinate someone, she was a light and luminous feather, floating on a gentle breeze through the laboratories.

"I honestly don't know, Bree." He managed to maintain a slight smile. "I don't know when what happened."

"Were you always on drugs?"

"What? No!"

"Then tell me what happened during the time you were not under the influence until the moment you lost it."

"And that's the problem—I can only tell you what I saw and what I thought happened. But if so many things were given to me without my knowledge, it could have happened anytime. Before or after *I lost it*."

Bree stepped forward and took his hands in hers. She looked

him in the eyes. "Hey, hey, don't fret. We're on top of it. You're safe. Nothing bad has happened yet."

"I drank gelled water!" he almost screamed, then took several deep breaths. In, out, in, out.

"Your nightmares…" she remembered, and hugged him. "I'm sorry."

He let her hug him. He still didn't know how to react to women's kindness. He felt awkward. He had no idea if he was supposed to reciprocate or just wait for it to pass. It wasn't bad. It was actually quite relaxing to be hugged and held protectively.

Bree took a step back and talked to him as if he were a child, enunciating slowly. "It happened, your nightmare happened, but nothing bad came out of it. We cleaned you out thoroughly. There's no danger. See? Your nightmare was nothing but a bad dream with no consequences."

"Hey, what's going on here? You making moves on my girlfriend?" Alex's cheerfulness sounded forced. He'd probably heard what they were talking about.

Geo felt better. The two people he trusted most in the world were there for him. And they had saved him so many times, he owed them more than he'd ever be able to repay.

Bree took a step back. She giggled.

"If you don't marry her quick, next time I'm back I'll propose," said Geo.

"So, what did you do out there?" Alex looked troubled.

Geo watched them both. He'd gotten them worried. Maybe he was guilty of being stupid and careless, but thinking back, he couldn't find one step where—well, that was always debatable.

"I was in the Silk Parade with Prince Boris. Nothing happened there. Then the Water Passage Ritual. That was horrible, but nothing happened there, either. No drinks, no food, no drugs, no touching, nothing."

"Then?"

"Then it was the dinner after the Water ritual. A party for everyone of importance in the Exterior. Many people there, all Corrosives. All controlling something in the kingdom. And Boris unveiled our gift to him there and presented me to the world."

"Oh, shit," murmured Alex.

"Yeah, I felt the same."

"Then why do it?"

"Grandpa wanted it. He wants us publicly in the Exterior. He wants us to get more involved in Exterior politics."

"Father opposed it, but he was outvoted," Bree remembered. "I know that he is terrified of this move Woodman the Elder forced on the council."

"Not for my sake, I bet," said Geo, trying to lighten the mood a bit.

"No, you're right there. He still sees you as an ignorant brat with no real qualifications to be sent to the Exterior in the name of the Woodman Corporation."

"All right, but nothing happened then, right?"

"A lot happened then. I was only a curiosity for them until that moment. A second later I became the main point of interest for the whole party. I think Boris did it on purpose. He wanted me to see the dangers to my—to us, as they really are."

"What dangers?" Alex sat down and looked from Geo to Bree and back.

"Every power in the kingdom now knows we have access to liquid water. Everyone wants that water now. Who will act on it depends on the political maneuvers Boris will force on us."

Alex paled and stood. It was obvious he wanted to leave the lab, as if suddenly in a hurry to find something, but he stopped.

"What is it, Alex?" Bree turned him to face her.

"Well, now we have the results for the strange substance."

"And?"

"What Geo just said puts everything in a different light."

"Alex." Bree pulled him back when he turned again to flee.

"It's not good, Bree."

"Hey, you're talking about me," said Geo. "I think you could at least look at me and be honest, for fuck's sake!"

"Grandpa needs to be here and hear it too."

"He will hear it after I hear it, Alex."

Alex looked around. There was no one else in Bree's lab. Just them. No surveillance camera. Hopefully no one was listening in.

"All the preliminary tests indicate that it is some sort of tracking agent. For lack of a better word, your bowels were coated with a special paint that can be tracked with the right technology."

"Shit!"

"Oh, god!" Bree sank into a chair. For the first time, Geo saw her expressing fear. She looked confused.

Geo remembered the encounter with Silver Star. So smug, so condescending. And instead of thinking things through, Geo had allowed himself to be manipulated. He had run home. *Stupid and weak. Mama's boy, indeed.*

"They didn't need to follow me on the train to find out where I live. They had a smarter solution. And now they know."

"Yes. Now they probably know where we are." Alex was a man of action. He couldn't remain confused or undecided for long. And ten seconds was long for him. "But we still have the upper hand."

"How?" said Bree.

"Because we know and they can't surprise us. But we need to talk to Grandpa. He will know what to do."

"We need to tell the council. They must have a plan for this kind of scenario." Bree was recovering as well. Only Geo still felt small and betrayed, a puppet that had served an invisible master and now was thrown out in the cold.

The moment Boris revealed the throne, my fate was sealed. And I didn't have a backup plan in place. I was not prepared for this contingency. "If the council has a plan for this, then they are giant assholes!" said Geo.

"Yeah," said Bree.

"Why?" Alex again looked confused.

"Because they didn't tell me about this possibility. They didn't prepare me for the possible scenarios if Boris publicly revealed the source of his wood. They left me exposed and liable to make mistakes."

"Is it possible they wanted this to happen?" mused Alex. "That they wanted to see who would dare confront us; to know who their enemies are?"

Geo didn't believe that. He felt weak and there was a terrible pain in his chest. He had difficulty breathing. He put his hand on his chest and turned his back to them. This was too much. He'd made some terrible mistakes and couldn't be sure which one had started this. His biggest mistake was obviously Lena. He'd been drilled over and over that he was never, under any circumstances, to engage in sex with Corrosives. That had been one of the three commandments. The second one. And he just— He had to, hadn't he? He had to play into Boris's hand to maintain a lucrative relationship with the Silkers. He had to...

"Are you all right?" Bree's cold hand pressed against his forehead, as she were checking for a fever. He was on the floor behind the lab's central table, still fighting to breathe and calm down his chest pain.

"Geo?" Alex was on his other side, looking distraught.

"If they wanted to test the waters, they don't know how big a mistake that was. They don't know what they're up against."

"I know they should've consulted with you before, but..." said Alex.

"I'll be all right. Give me a couple of minutes," Geo whispered. They nodded and gave him some space.

Geo closed his eyes. He remembered the terrible song of the rain he'd heard during the ritual. He avoided thinking of the red spilling all over, just focused on the sound. The terrifying, soothing sound of water falling from the sky. The miracle. Clear, liquid water, pouring down on them from a blue sky. Just like in the movies. He focused on that color. Blue. Blue was good. Blue was life. He'd had sex with Lena. He'd done the unforgivable. He allowed the blue to swallow him. The pain turned to pressure. The suffocation turned to mere effort. Blue was good. Lena's curves swam through the blue ocean of the sky. He just had to follow her. Swimming was relaxing. Lena the Sea Cat. It sounded right. Blue was good.

"Your mission is over. You stay put, here in the Cave. We prepare. *If* they come, they'll regret it. And make no mistake, gentlemen, we are at war."

Woodman the Elder sounded firm and confident. The council was silent. They looked at him reproachfully. Greg Rumi's face was dark and hateful. Geo knew he was to blame.

"Understood?" Woodman asked him.

"Yes, sir," Geo replied and looked down at the table to avoid the eyes of the council.

14.
Gray

The barren expanse lulled Geo into a doze. It was so easy to slip into numbness and forget everything and everyone. People were at the end of the gelling world and still clinging to it. It would be so easy to just let go. To rest.

The train shook on the tracks. Geo started and opened his eyes. Same shitty reality. Same poor, corroded people traveling from their cheese farms or rat nurseries to the city for stupid trading, to bring back home some useless tool or comforting drugs. All were fighting to survive. That was all it was to be living in the Exterior—survival. Unless you were Prince Boris or the mayor. Then it was about how you could screw up other people's lives.

He hated politics. Despite the fact that it was very much like math and he loved math, politics was not about abstract concepts and theories. Politics was about real life and real people. Nothing abstract about taxes, protection, or food. Or most of all about water. But he was the ambassador for the Woodman Clan in the Exterior and everything was politics now. Politics and survival. And he hated it all. He could take living geared up for weeks, eating only his dried-up Cave food, not touching anyone, even posing all the time for everyone as the fearless Woodman ambassador. But watching the jockeying and scheming to take advantage of every weakness of the Woodmans, and trying to prevent any action being taken against his clan, that was…

Holy gel! He'd been fed gelled water, iron silk, and a freaking tracking agent. Three completely distinct things. Three things that led in three different directions. That was what was missing from the equation. That was what even Woodman the Elder was saying—that something wasn't adding up. There was not one, but two, possibly three parties that had taken action against him and sabotaged his mission. The Woodmans were confronting several enemies at the same time. He'd made the best decision, leaving the Caves despite direct orders. He had to solve this pile of shit before the stench could reach his clan.

Those who had given him the tracking agent clearly wanted to locate the Caves. They were after a fresh water source. Liquid water. There was this urban myth that if you resumed drinking liquid water, you could reverse the corrosion. It had no scientific basis and the Woodmans had proven it wrong. Geo had tried to tell that to everyone who would listen, but hoping for success against all odds was always a bad plan.

What about the iron silk? Possibly these two were connected. They may have given him iron silk to render him unconscious in order to feed him the tracking agent. That sounded logical. The more important question was, how did they do that? Where was the breach in his and Boris's security? As for the gelled water, was that agent supposed to work only with gelled water? Because if it was, then he was back to square one with only one enemy. Yet, even in this promising scenario, the question remained: *when* had they poisoned, drugged, and tagged him?

Torono became visible on the horizon on his side of the train, dark gray against the emerald green of the gelled sea and the purulent green of the sky. With its broken spires and damaged towers, it looked like abandoned ruins, although it teemed with life. Its population lived in its bowels rather than in its towers and high-rises. Geo had seen pictures of the city before the Black Rain; it had looked much different. This was the monster that had always lurked inside the bright city's bowels before the Rain.

As the train drew closer, he could distinguish the glow of the Golden Tower. Its silhouette was the only sign of prosperity and even life in the city. Say all you want of Prince Boris, he was a visionary and a civilized force in the kingdom. Geo both feared and admired the man. He felt drawn to and repulsed by Boris at the same time.

He needed a real plan now. So that going against the clan's decision to stay home and wait wouldn't turn into a stupid, even more damaging move. He'd been careless and this mess was his. He needed to—to what?

He'd go directly to the mayor and discuss the entire situation with him, rationally. The mayor was a former businessman, so he'd listen to reason and profit. Although, math. If the mayor was indeed the one after the Woodmans' water, what could Geo give him that was more valuable than the Cave itself with its clean water reservoir?

A woman sat down next to him. She was heavily corroded and covered her destroyed body with tattered canvas. The smell alone— Geo pushed himself up. The woman laid her fingerless hand on his shoulder and pushed him back into his seat. *What the gel?*

"Boris sends his best," she said in a hoarse, barely intelligible voice. Her larynges were also quite corroded, judging by the sound of her voice.

"What?"

"You deaf?"

"Boris?"

"As in the prince, Ambassador."

"Who are you?"

"Not important. Boris expected you back by now, so he sent me to warn you."

Geo clicked from his math-oriented problem-solving frame of mind into real-life crisis mode and straightened his back. His left hand moved to his pocket and slid into his brass knuckles.

"The mayor declared you *persona non grata*, and ordered your arrest on sight. They also put a bounty on your head."

"Wow, you actually said the Latin words right. I'm impressed." Geo grinned, trying to appear nonchalant and in control.

"Wow, you're actually a dick, as everybody says." The woman took her hand from his shoulder and lowered it to her lap.

Geo held his breath. She had a Silkers' butterfly tattoo on her wrist. She was one of Boris's Butterflies. Shit!

"I'm sorry," Geo said. "I had no idea who you were and why I should trust you. Especially after my last trip into the city. Now I see—and suffice it to say, I trust Boris."

"Good, Ambassador. Boris's advice: leave the train before your station. They'll be waiting for you."

The woman rose and trudged away from him. Geo scanned the train car and sighed—no one had paid them any attention. He turned to watch the Corrosive Butterfly leave and frowned. He rose and looked at all seats behind him. She was nowhere in sight and couldn't have moved that fast. A short, thin man opened the door between the cars and exited. No one else.

Entering the city proper, the train slowed down. Girders and rubble lay everywhere. Rusted metal rebar showed between the brambles growing amidst the desolation. People followed the progress of the train from the ruins.

Geo jumped from the train's steps and rolled down the slope. He came to a stop in a thorny bush and grunted in pain. He'd not had much training in escaping a moving train. Who would have thought…

He looked around, fully alert, and noticed some shapes running through the ruins toward him. Scavengers. Cannibals. That was not a good development. He turned and ran in the opposite direction. He had to make it to the Woodmans' base camp in Torono. Or at least find the prince. Boris would help him. And Lena. She'd raised the alarm when he'd been kidnapped. They would know what should be done.

The tallest ruin in Torono loomed over the tracks and the train station. It was a listing, skeletal metal tower. The mayor's main source of metal. The Blues' crest fluttered above the mine entrance. The Golden Tower was a short distance behind it. And the Woodman Clan's base camp was another short walk eastward from the Golden Tower. The metal shells of former vehicles and other machines from before the Black Rain stood between him and safety. He would have to avoid the station and all other places where Blues might be patrolling. Instead of the direct route to his clan's base camp, he'd have to take the very long, scenic route.

The scavengers were almost on him. They were moving faster, as this was their territory and they knew every trap to avoid and route to take. Geo skidded on gravel and grabbed a rebar rod to keep himself from sliding all the way down to the tracks. He pulled himself up and up, and one last step brought him to the eroded concrete platform that was his target. Then he screamed and backed to the edge of the platform. He heard the scavengers laughing and whooping savagely nearby.

A Nightmare was lurking on the concrete platform, cutting off Geo's way out. Unless he wanted to jump back toward the tracks and face the scavengers directly. The Nightmare was purulent gray and shapeless, with dozens of yellow eyes sliding down its surface and following his every move from any position and direction. Its mouth was wide open, crowded with stone teeth and three tongues like three tentacles, snapping moistly toward him, trying to grab him. The stench alone was enough to render someone unconscious. Geo switched off the sensorial access.

He took another step back, balancing dangerously close to the edge while frantically searching for something in his suit pockets that could help him against the monster. The scavengers were climbing the gravel slide behind him. He kicked one of the attackers who tried to push himself up onto the platform, then another one, but they were too many and too fast.

He slid his brass knuckles onto his fingers, pulled out his barbed mace, and started swinging furiously left and right. Not much choice there—either get consumed by the Nightmare or get eaten by the cannibal scavengers.

He put one down with his skull smashed to pulp, another with half his teeth flying. After kicking one between the legs, he half turned, but someone caught his left arm from behind and

held him as another punched him in the stomach. A sixth assailant grabbed his mace hand and bit down on his wrist. Luckily
his suit was armored and a bite meant nothing to Geo.

Howling in pain, the one holding his left arm suddenly
released it. The other two stopped and looked beyond him with
terrified eyes. He only needed that fraction of a second to smash
the fifth one's face with the mace. He turned in time to see the
assailant behind him pulled into a monstrous mouth by its three
tentacle-like tongues.

Geo didn't hesitate. He ran straight toward the monster,
grabbed at its flesh, and used it as an anchor while balancing on
the platform's edge. Then he jumped to the other side, behind
the Nightmare, and started running, never looking back. He
didn't care if the scavengers followed him. He was close to
the inhabited area, where the Blues patrolled, and his hunters
wouldn't dare venture there in the middle of the day. Not for a
hunt.

Reaching the ruins of a row of brick houses, he stopped
and caught his breath. The street in front of the ruins was full of
people. A Blue Patrol crossed the road. Geo slumped down in the
shade, concealed behind a concrete pillar. He had to find something to cover his suit, or he'd be easy prey for the Blues. Especially if there was a bounty on his head. He needed something
gray. To blend in. Yeah, gray would be good.

15.

Corruption

"This is the one," said Pi, pointing toward Stev's bakery.

The Luna officer nodded to his warriors. They advanced as one and entered the bakery.

"Why didn't you break down their door?" Pi was annoyed at the silence and smoothness of the Luna Warriors' actions. He'd imagined a big show of breaking down the door, tearing through Stev's shop and house, dragging his entire family into the street, and publicly shaming them. He wanted to torture them, but if the Luna officer needed to do the torturing, he'd be content with just witnessing it.

The officer ignored him and followed his warriors. The customers drew back from their path and ran along the walls to exit the shop. The warriors spread throughout the shop to ensure they could see everything.

"Where are the drugs?" the officer asked Pi.

"First, restrain them." He pointed to Sara and Magi. "Don't let them get away."

The officer turned and stared down at him. Pi smiled. "There." He pointed toward the storage room.

"Open it," the officer said to Sara.

"Oh, come on! Just break down the door!"

Sara nodded. She looked scared. Magi huddled behind her. They both walked quickly toward the storage room and the woman fumbled with a bundle of keys. Her hands were trembling and the keys fell to the floor. She picked them up, panting in fear. They fell again.

"Mommy?" Magi asked her in a frightened voice.

"Oh, motheruster!" Pi walked over to them. He grabbed the child and pulled her away from Sara.

"Magi!" cried Sara, reaching for her.

"Open the door." The officer stepped between Sara and her child.

Sara turned to the door, drew in a deep, quavering breath, and thrust the right key into the storage room's lock. She twisted left twice and pulled the door open.

The officer stepped into the storage room. Pi let go of Magi and looked into the room from the threshold. It was a cube with different types of mushrooms drying on the walls, sacks of algae flour, bags of spices, and bowls of fermenting yeast. The heavy smell, combined with the humidity, hit Pi like a wet fist.

The officer touched and smelled some of the mushrooms. But Pi knew already that the *fairy* mushrooms were not there anymore. He could recognize them anywhere. They were the only ones with blue iridescence. He stepped back and looked around the shop. No place to hide it here, but there was an entire house above them. Hundreds of places to hide—well, from what he'd seen last time, quite a considerable amount of fairy mushrooms. But only a fool would still keep the stash in the house, knowing the law would come for them. So, where else?

"Any more ideas?" the officer asked him in an irritated tone.

Where else? Pi was frantic. Stev and his shitty family shouldn't get away, after what Stev had done to him.

"Out," the officer ordered his warriors.

"Wait." Pi grabbed his arm. The officer stopped and stared at him hard.

"Sorry, I didn't mean to—but they had it. It must be with their friends!" He brightened, realizing that the two most annoying people were friends. The mushrooms must be hidden with that old shit, Jon.

"You're lucky you're a taxman," said the officer. "But this is your first strike."

"No, no, I'm telling you, it must be hidden with their friends. And I know who they are!"

"If I hear one more word, it will be strike two," the officer warned him.

"But—"

"Strike two. Now, do you want to check the friends? If the drugs aren't there, it will be strike three and your death sentence, taxman."

Pi considered. He wanted so much to take them to Jon, but… what if? There was a very small chance the drugs would not be there. But what if?

"Good choice," said the officer and left.

"Get out!" Sara shrieked.

Behind her, the little girl had started crying. So fucking annoying! The bitch would continue to get her tits treatment, while he would have to suffer in silence as Doc gave it to her. For practically free! The amount they were paying now was ridiculously low. Doc and his fucking friends!

Pi pushed Sara away and grabbed Magi by the scruff of the neck. The woman somehow regained her balance and was on him, screaming and yelping like a bitch in heat.

He smashed Magi's head onto a table and let the unconscious child fall to the floor. Sara's scream was so fucking beastly. Pi knew why he hated them all. Snatching a wet rope full of mushrooms from the storage room wall, he whipped Sara with it. The woman grunted in pain as she covered the child protectively with her body.

Pi lashed her again and again and again, until his arms felt leaden and he gasped for air. Physical effort was murder in this humidity.

The woman lay in a puddle of blood, still covering the unconscious child.

Hmm, according to the law, it was also considered murder to harm another human being in such a way that you aggravated their corrosive condition. He bent, curious, and noticed how the edges of the wounds on Sara's back had already started taking on the definitive rusty tint. It could just be the blood, but better not to risk it. This should be enough. Stev's family had paid his debt to Pi.

The man stepped over the two bodies and walked slowly to the exit, trying to regain his breath. He grabbed the doorknob and hesitated, looking back at Sara's bloody body. No, he decided, it wasn't enough. Pi was the Law. This wasn't enough. He wanted to make Stev suffer. Like, *really* suffer.

He opened the door and stepped into the street.

"Hey, man," a voice said, startling him from his thoughts. Pi turned and saw a face he recognized—it was that small-time drug dealer. The one working for the mayor. He grimaced with disgust and walked away.

"What the fuck! Help!" he heard from inside the bakery.

Pi grinned with satisfaction. *Let them be afraid. No one messes with the Law and gets away without paying.*

16.
Base Camp

Geo surveyed the structure from a distance. People were milling in front of it. No one dared getting closer, or—god forbid—entering it. Corrosives were highly superstitious people. Even Boris had shown signs of it.

The structure had been called St. Lawrence before the Black Rain. It was written in big letters on its frontispiece. Geo had no idea why. St. Lawrence was the patron of poor people. It had probably been a building where poor people were fed. But now the Corrosives called Saint Lawrence the Rat King, the patron saint of rats. Especially since his former building had become infested with dog-size rats. Rats were considered holy in the new kingdom, so the former St. Lawrence building had become the temple of the Rat King.

Geo used to say that the Woodmans knew better. They still held on to the old science and things like super-large rats didn't compel them to consider them deities. But a couple of years spent inside the Corrosive society had turned Geo into a skeptic. The difference between what the old science said was possible and what the new reality showed was actually possible had grown greater and greater. Woodmans didn't know better. They knew squat. And they made decisions based on squat, instead of on the intelligence he had given them. People like Rumi were stuck in the past and failed to understand and adapt to the new reality. And if truth be told, they hadn't understood the former reality. The one they had broken with the same old attitude— what can we invent to save Earth from climate change? A better battery? Maybe a better farming approach? And then Nature had said, "Yeah, no." And the Black Rain had come.

Grandpa Woodman was the only one trusting him but apparently he wasn't enough anymore. He'd grown old and isolated. And an ancient Rumi in power would eventually prove fatal for the Woodman Clan. He failed to see that now there were new laws of physics and chemistry. What he'd once known as science was old news and unless he augmented that science with the new reality, he was doomed to fail once again.

At the back of the building stretched the Rats Field, another avoided area. Corrosives would throw food there and leave immediately. Toronions were pragmatic people: feed the gods to keep them away. They prayed to the Rat King and held holy any rat, but there had been many people attacked and even eaten by the Corrosives' disgusting new gods.

Geo activated his ultrasonic emitter, waited a few seconds, then opened the back door into the Rat King Temple. The gigantic rats scattered in front of him, hissing and squeaking angrily, their claws scratching the floor. Several tried to resist the ultrasound and confront him. He amplified the emitter and even the bravest of the rats scampered away in agony.

He walked carefully through darkness. The ground level was a huge hall full of broken furniture and rusted structures. Dense nets of spider webs covered at least half the space. Huge insects and even a rat or two hung in the sticky traps.

When he'd decided to use this place, Geo had traced the exact route he was supposed to follow to reach the best location inside the building for the clan's hideout, or base camp, as he liked to call it. The route that wouldn't disturb the rats' nests and wouldn't lead into a spider web. After two years of using the place, he knew every step to follow without even thinking.

Geo had decided that this big hall must have been some sort of market. Probably a market for the poor. There were still the remains of fridges and shelves on the walls, where merchants had probably displayed their goods. He'd fantasized many times what exotic foods they had eaten before the Rain. He'd seen torn pieces of cans and plastic packaging, with words like mackerel and salmon and prosciutto, and he could sense how the former world had been a lot richer in—everything. He had only his grandparents to blame for losing that wealth. But who would that serve? Well, it would serve them now in the upcoming confrontation between the old world and the new one, if the mayor had his way. Geo had to somehow divert the mayor's attention from them, and then he'd have to change things in the Cave. He didn't know how, but...

He finally reached the door of his hideout. It was in a room at the back of one the former stores. The room was kept free of giant rats or insects with a carefully maintained network of sonic emitters. In the back wall of the room was a very thick, heavy door that initially could have been locked only from outside with a long handle. It opened to a refrigerated room. He'd replaced the mechanical lock with an electronic one that now used his clan's chip to open from both outside and inside. The chip was implanted under the skin of his right forearm.

Geo scanned his forearm and the lock clicked open. He pulled the big handle and opened the door wide enough for him to slip inside. The light had come on automatically when he'd unlocked the door. He entered and closed the door behind him.

The room was quite big. Two walls were full of ancient weapons—firearms. The kind for which the Corrosives had completely lost the technology, to the point where they now considered them a myth. There were also grenades, gas masks, oxygen tanks, and other military paraphernalia meant to help Geo survive another Black Rain, an attack by a small army, or a very dangerous road trip across the barren country.

Another wall was entirely covered in shelves filled with cans of food. In a corner there was a stack of liquid water reservoirs, enough for him to survive half a year, if necessary. Or to conduct his diplomatic missions for several months and continuously replace his isolation suit's water reserve. A mattress rested against the fourth wall. Next to it were books, new clothes, and a table and chair. A terminal on top of the table was always on, ready to receive communications from the Cave.

The entire hideout reeked of ancient, outdated technology, but ironically enough, that technology was what kept him alive for so long in the alien world of the Corrosives.

Geo took off his helmet and breathed deeply. He'd connected the hermetically-sealed room to the outside air and mounted a few filters to clean the dense Exterior air that was too rich for his lungs. He could seal the room from the inside and breathe and live in there for months. Unless the Exteriors found out how to cut his air supply.

He opened a UV station and inserted his helmet, then his gloves and closed the door. Then he pressed ON.

Stripping off his entire suit, he lay on the mattress and closed his eyes. He was so tired. His breath grew steadier and he kept his eyes closed. Yet, no sleep came. Eventually he opened his eyes and looked at the pale ceiling. Yes, he was tired, but not physically tired. He was just tired of going against the current with his clan. Tired of fighting their fight against their will.

A steady flow of air came in through the vent and lazily moved a piece of paper pinned to the shelves—the map of the city before the Rain. The city's grid hadn't changed much. It was just that its flesh had rusted and turned to dust. He rose and took the map over to the table, next to the terminal.

Woodman the Elder had marked the Golden Tower before Geo had left on his first mission. The Silkers' headquarters had been a beacon of light for a long time. A landmark of human ingenuity and perseverance. Across the Mayor's Square was a building that had hosted a bank before the mayor took it for his seat of power. According to the map, the entire area was atop the Dark Path, the underground city. Pre-Corrosion it was called simply the Path, but nowadays it was a very dark district of the city, with it being underground and no sunlight reaching it, ever. There was no electricity available in the city, and Geo preferred to avoid this subject as, like liquid water, it was a source of envy and greed.

He drank some water and opened a can of fruit. He ate slowly while staring at the map. The mayor's building was practically the same as before, only a little bit more ruined and decrepit. It had had a gate to the Path, and Geo had heard that now the gate was barricaded. The mayor didn't want his subjects to invade his palace in the night and cut his throat while he slept.

Of course, Geo could instigate some sort of revolt and keep the mayor busy. So busy he would have to postpone his claims over the Woodman Caves. But the key here was postpone. It would be only a temporary solution and it would also result in numerous deaths, as the mayor's Blues were a bloodthirsty army. Not numerous, but well trained and armed.

Diplomacy was probably out of the question. People like the mayor wouldn't trade the bird in hand for the promise of one in the bush. Geo had nothing more valuable to offer the mayor in exchange for peace. The slaughter and casualties as a result of his decisions would not persuade him to stop and ponder. To negotiate. As long as it wasn't his life in the balance, the mayor had no problem throwing other people's lives away.

He could go and talk to Boris. Boris had a bigger army than the mayor and wielded more power. But what could Geo give Boris in exchange for starting a civil war? Ah, right, the prince had asked for Geo's loyalty. He'd asked for Geo's water. Well, he would not have that. Geo was uncorrupted and he would stay that way.

He exhaled and nodded. He had no other solution. The last solution was the only one. He'd have to prepare, he'd have to plan everything in detail, and the chances of success were very low. But it was better than the alternative. "Master your flesh" was the Corrosives' creed. *I'd rather my flesh have no mind of its own. I prefer to keep my flesh clean.*

It was decided, then. He'd better start planning.

17.
Corrosion

The door was open, but Doc knocked on the doorframe before entering. Jon and Stev turned toward him and stared in horror at Doc's disheveled appearance. Doc tried to smile as he searched for words. Jon realized that if he felt this horrible even before hearing what must be bad news, Stev must feel ten times worse.

"How are you holding up, son?"

"I d-d-don't know what th-that means."

"Oh, sorry," muttered Doc.

Jon rose from his chair, trying to conceal a grunt of pain, and moved to stand next to Stev. He was only as tall as Stev's chest, so trying to physically comfort the big man by putting an arm around his shoulders or something similar was impossible.

"So?" asked Stev in a harsh voice.

"Doc, give it to us straight," said Jon in an effort to sweeten Stev's harshness.

"I'm sorry, Stev, but it's bad news."

"So it's corrosion," said Jon.

"That's the first point, yes."

"How m-m-many points there are?"

"All right," Doc sighed and tried again to smile. "All right, Stev. Sara has a new area of corrosion. It's larger than her first area. And it's advancing rapidly, due to the trauma inflicted."

"I see," grumbled Stev. He breathed with ease. "We can deal

with that. We'll have to add it to the monthly treatment."

"I'd be happy to do just that. Only…"

"Only?" Jon interjected before Stev could.

"I'm afraid that with the new treatment, your costs will triple. If it was just me, I'd give you a break. But—you know."

"Pi," grunted Stev and his face contorted in anger.

"Well, he's just doing his job, gentlemen."

"No, no, Doc, let's stop here." Jon stepped in front of Stev and tried to push Doc back.

"Pi has put my Sara in this situation!" Stev's anger could barely be contained.

"What? No, you must be mistaken."

"My son saw him, Doc. Mic was here when Pi left the shop after…"

"Oh, god, no!" Doc stepped back, horrified.

"So, you can imagine—"

"Yeah, no, you're right. I'm sorry, Stev. Pi will never come back here. I swear."

The three men stood in silence for a few seconds. Jon had so many thoughts crossing his mind at once that he felt dizzy. He realized that they weren't only thoughts, but feelings too. It was like a high traffic alert between his brain and his guts.

"He'd better not," said Stev, panting as if winded.

"So, Doc, how much would that be?" said Jon, smiling at Doc to relax him.

"It's six credits—in merchandise or whatever. I'm sorry, but the area is huge and the corrosion's—"

Jon stopped him. "Got it, got it. I'll talk to you later about this. Now, tell me what we can do to slow down the spread until the treatment."

"Well, that's the least of your worries." Doc walked past Jon and faced Stev. "Sara was in a lot of pain, so I gave her some sedatives and she'll probably slide into sleep in the next hour or so."

"That's good," said Jon. "Thank you, Doc."

Stev nodded approvingly. But Doc wasn't finished. He was looking at Jon like a teacher regarding a slow kid. *Shit!* Jon realized what it was.

"We need to go to Sara now, Stev," Jon said and went out the office door as fast as he could.

"Why? What's wrong?" Stev followed.

"You need to keep her from falling asleep until the sedatives wear off. Or she'll be in danger of turning into a Nightmare," Doc yelled at them from the office.

Mic, Di, and Jon's wife, Mara, watched them with every expression from horror to fear crossing their faces. Fortunately, no one else was in the shop. Stev had closed for the day and Jon's family had come to help in any way they could. Jon's older son, Ton, had stayed behind to manage their store.

"Don't let Doc leave," Jon yelled to his family. "I need a word with him."

Sara smiled widely at Stev. He bent and kissed her forehead.

"You see, Tiny, nothing to worry about," she said and caressed his big hand. Then she pulled him down to her and whispered in his ear, "I'm worried about Magi. She won't talk to me."

Stev's little daughter sat on the floor with knees gathered to her mouth. Exactly as they'd left her when Doc was here, Jon remembered. The kid was traumatized. She'd never known violence, let alone the horrible violence applied to her mother. Jon redirected Stev back to his wife and said, "It's all right, I'll take care of Magi. You two just talk."

"Talk! Stev talks an average of twenty words per day!" Sara burst into laughter—joyful, careless laughter, as if back to her old self. Clearly, the sedative was working. "But it's all right. I'm talking for the both of us."

Jon picked Magi up. She was like a doll. No reaction, no sign of any life. He took her downstairs to his wife. "Can you please take care of her? Things might go wrong up there."

"Sure, sure, sure. Here, sweet little thing. Let's sit here." Mara sat down behind the counter and gathered Magi in a tight hug. She kissed her hair, then she began singing a lullaby in a hushed voice.

"Doc, you need to start treating Sara right away. I will pay for her. And please, don't bring Pi back to this street. Not even close to us."

"But Pa, you said—" Mic began.

"I know what I said, but I've lived a long and full life, Mic. I'm so proud of both my boys. I love my life, my love, my family. I'm good. I don't need treatment."

Mara's voice trembled as she continued singing to Magi. Jon turned and saw her looking at him. Big tears slid down her cheeks. He knew she wouldn't stop him. Not because she didn't think he should take the treatment for himself, but because she loved him. He smiled at her and blew her a kiss. She smiled back, sad and happy at the same time.

"Jon!" Stev sounded scared.

Jon quickly climbed up the stairs.

"I'll kill that waterfucker!" Mic growled.

"No one's killing anyone." Jon called, his voice calm and didactic.

He finally got upstairs. Stev was holding Sara carefully, trying to avoid touching her raw back, his left arm supporting her neck and his right hand caressing her face. Sara had her eyes half closed, a very tired smile on her face.

"Just let me rest a bit, love," she whispered to Stev.

"No, no, no, you mustn't."

Sara's head slid over to rest on Stev's shoulder.

"Teacher?" Stev's voice was imploring. He caressed Sara's head, but didn't have the strength to force her to stay awake anymore.

"Oooh, that is so beautiful!" Her voice was suddenly full and vibrant.

Jon came closer and watched her face. Sara was flushed, sweaty, her gorgeous hair stuck to her face and scalp. Her eyes stared somewhere up near the ceiling. Jon looked there; the ceiling was cracked and grayed by time's passing. It certainly was nice in a somber way, but nowhere near *beautiful*.

"That's amazing! How didn't I see it before?"

Jon waved a hand in front of Sara's eyes, but she kept staring, unwavering. His hand was not there for her anymore. Or, apparently, the ceiling. She was looking at something beyond it all. He carefully bent over and looked into her eyes. Her pupils were so large they had swallowed the irises. He saw only two completely black pools. Flashes of color crossed the pools like the meteorite shower he remembered seeing once. A shower of stars, was the popular expression. Something was happening to Sara, some sort of metamorphosis, but into neither a Nightmare nor a Dream.

"They're calling to me. They're showing me the ways. It is so easy to—oh," she whimpered, "I don't know the word. When ships go over water…"

"Navigate," whispered Jon.

"Yes." Her face brightened and her smile reappeared. "It's so easy to navigate the skies."

"Teacher?" Stev murmured. Jon saw tears in his eyes—fat tears, for the first time in the big, man's eyes.

"Shush, my boy. Shush, now. She's happy."

Jon wanted to turn away, but Sara's change was mesmer- izing. Her face was beautiful, her expression beatific. Jon cried silently next to Stev. He didn't know what was going on. He had no idea how to help her. But somehow, he felt at peace. Sad, but at peace.

18.
Red

The overall wrap he'd found in the forgotten market inside the Rat King's temple covered Geo from head to toes, but stank to high heaven. He didn't care to know what had been transported in that textile wrap. He just wanted to walk anonymously through the city, which the dirty rag allowed him to do. And when people wanted something from him, it allowed him to become somewhat visible, in a way that would still keep people away from him. He was sort of memorable, but in a bad way. Not like with people seeing his hi-tech suit and remembering him because of it. Stench was the perfect way to be memorable in a *keep away* sort of fashion.

He'd penetrated the Golden Tower through a back entrance he'd known about from Boris, back in the days when the prince had secretly showed him the night life of the city. Back in the days when Geo had felt that everything was within his reach. He'd just had to extend his hand and every desired fruit would just fall into his open palm. That was another one of Boris's powers—to offer you the world with a smile and no warning of consequences.

Geo checked the corridor. No one paid him any attention. The Golden Tower was practically a vertical city with thousands of people living inside, from the prince down to the cleaning crews. All sorts and shapes. It was crowded and bustling with people doing their jobs. One could rarely see anyone just sitting idly. And guards patrolled only the ground floor. Once you passed them, it was understood you belonged there, in the tower.

He produced the key to his room and inserted it in the keyhole. It was one of the very few rooms equipped with a key lock on a very select floor. Yet no one cared that the dirty man tried one of the select doors. The door screeched as he pushed it slowly open and stepped inside. For a few seconds he forgot to breathe.

Something moved under the red sheet on the bed. Geo automatically produced his cudgel and fell into a fighting stance. The sheet slid down to reveal a naked woman. Holy gel, it was Lena! Geo breathed more easily. The woman slithered down from the bed and prepared to fight. He stared, mesmerized by her shapeliness. She was beautiful. After all the horrors—

Lena moved lightning fast and kicked him in the chest, then followed the movement and jumped on him. With a smooth twist she brought him down and sat on him, ready to punch his faceplate. Nothing bad could happen to him, as the faceplate was very strong and made to endure a lot more than punches. But he worried she might get hurt. And why would she—oh, yes, he was costumed in that stinking rag.

"It's me!" he said, struggling to sound confident.

The woman hesitated. He pulled away the gray tatters covering his head and revealed his helmet. He knew she could see his face now. She watched him for a couple of seconds, her expression lost under her black mask and the huge lenses covering her eyes. She got up and pulled him after her. He tried to hug her, but she pushed him back.

"You stink, Mr. Ambassador!"

The room's ceiling was a night blue sky covered in a web of cracks filled with gold paint. It was beautiful in a corrosive way. The new aesthetics. Beautified dereliction. The candles' flames shivered in the cold evening draft. The web of cracks seemed to move in tandem.

"Gel for your thoughts," said Lena in a hushed voice.

Geo grinned. He turned and took her in—black mask covering her entire face, save for her always red, full lips. Her perfect body. Her irresistible curves. It was like…it was like she emanated something to entice and hold men. Yet he liked the danger of the game. Danger and sex always made a good pair.

"I think I'm falling in love—with this world. With the corrosion."

Her revealing mouth shifted from surprised to cunning smile. "You almost had me there, for a second."

"I feel more relaxed than I've felt in days. Thank you…"

"I'm here to serve at the pleasure of Mr. Ambassador."

"Oh, all right, then. It's good to fully understand what that service entails."

Lena caressed his face around his breathing mouthpiece. "You're such a teenager sometimes. I wonder how old you are, really."

"Can't you tell?"

"No, we—we *Gelled* don't have the same way of growing old as you do. So no, I can't tell."

"Then let me tell you. I'm too young to be bothered and too old to accept anything without a proper explanation." She chuckled. He grinned and felt happy. He didn't know why, exactly.

Geo pushed himself up in the bed. He leaned against the headboard and arranged the pillow at his back. He ran his fingers through Lena's curly brown hair, so soft and shiny, like living silk. He'd wondered why her hair was so strange. So beautiful. He'd never seen the like.

"Let me prepare some tea," she said and rose from the bed in a single slithering move. He sighed at the sight of her full naked glory and swallowed hard.

"Uh, I…"

She turned and he assumed she was watching him with worry, given the shape of her mouth. He could not see her eyes. He'd never seen her eyes. He'd assumed she had big, gorgeous eyes.

Brown, possibly. Deep, soft brown. Doe eyes.

"No, thank you. After the last incident, I prefer to take a break from this world's delights."

"What actually happened, Mr. Ambassador?" She sat back on the bed and placed a hand on his thigh.

"I woke up in the street, drugged, confused, my mind foggy, unable to judge clearly and make the right decisions."

"That must have been frightening for you."

"What part?"

"Not having control."

"Yes, that too."

"You know that the silk tea doesn't have those effects. The purity of what we serve our friends, what I served you here, is absolute."

"I know, Lena. I have no doubt you gave me the best."

"Than what makes you hesitant now?"

"I—it's hard to explain."

"Try me."

She was always so balanced. Her voice neutral, no tremor, no emotion. Always analyzing, deciding, choosing. Geo wished he could be as good as her. He knew that was her job as Boris's guests' envoy. She had to know what the prince's guests felt, needed, desired, and how to keep them happy. He'd seen her gestures of tenderness toward him and could only hope they indicated some feelings for him. He needed that. He needed someone to care for him and be in his corner. Or his life in this beautiful but cruel world would be—well, he didn't have the word for that.

"My clan is in danger. My clan's survival depends on me and my choices in the next twenty-four hours. I cannot bring more harm to them by indulging in pleasures that can wait."

Her mouth parted in a smile, revealing white, perfect teeth. "I think you don't trust me. Not anymore. I lost your trust and I became useless in my role as your companion in the Silkers Clan."

Why would she smile saying that? *"People smile to hide their discomfort or to hide their true feelings,"* Woodman the Elder had said once. It was during a lesson in interpreting facial expressions to help Geo manage a negotiation.

Lena felt hurt and hid her true feelings behind that smile. That was one possible interpretation. The most plausible one. Or—or she feared she could lose her position near Geo. Which was a lot less plausible. She wasn't actually going to lose anything in the Silkers Clan. She'd keep the same rank and benefits. Or at least that's what Geo thought he'd understood about the Silkers' structure and functioning. He didn't know of any of the prince's wives that could lose anything, short of being accused of betrayal. Then the story would change. Dramatically.

And that was where math was good. The second hypothesis was struggling to resist the winds of logic. It was based purely on Geo's desire for Lena to care for him. And that didn't stand up. But what if that was the truth and he'd risk losing his only ally in this world?

"I'm sorry we've reached this point, Mr. Ambassador. I'll tell His Highness I've become useless in this position. But no worries, you'll be given a new guide."

"No, Lena. I didn't…"

She waited. Probably looking at him.

"Look, I'm just trying to explain to you that it has nothing to do with you. For all I know, you're the one who saved my relationship with the Silkers. You told them that I'd been abducted and they found me. They saw that I was the victim of a plot, not an active participant in the mayor's machinations."

"Oh?"

"The mayor's strongman, Silver Star, played the role of rescuer only to see me sent straight home with a message for my clan's chief. The mayor wants our Caves. He wants to take my home."

"I see. Now it's becoming clearer."

Geo exhaled slowly. It felt good to have someone to talk to. How much could he say to her, though? He trusted the Silkers, and especially Lena, but some of the Woodmans' problems were theirs alone. And yet, this was not a secret worth keeping. This would be quite public, quite soon. So why not trust Lena completely and let her help him? Wasn't she there exactly for that purpose?

"See, Lena, they had a way to track me to the Cave. Now they know where we live. And they threatened they'd come to take it by force if necessary. I can't let that happen."

"What did Woodman the Elder decide?"

"To dig in and fight," said Geo and cursed mentally for not being able to see her reaction. He wanted to know if she was on his side or not.

"Then why are you here, Mr. Ambassador?"

"Because it is…"

—it is my fault that they discovered us. Because it is my fault that we are in this horrible situation. And I need to fix it without anyone from the clan paying for my mistakes.

Lena tipped her head to her right as if listening to something. But her mouth said it pretty clearly—she wanted to hear Geo's reasons.

Because I need to prove to them I'm not a mama's boy. He looked down and sighed.

"Isn't the ambassador's role to listen to their chief and act on his orders?"

"In my opinion, Woodman the Elder is wrong here. The council may have had a role in that too. He's increasingly relying on them. And there's Rumi, who's bitter and spreads poison every time there's something important—"

"Rumi?"

"The CSO, one of the clan's heads. It's a bit complicated. Not more than here, with the Silkers and their castes and hierarchy, but different."

"All right, what did this Rumi want?"

"To fight. And then to melt back into the background. The Exterior doesn't need to know we exist, is what he says every time."

Lena stayed silent and unmoving. Barely breathing. Her sculpted, shiny breasts moved in slow rhythm with her breath, so slowly that they almost seemed a statue's chest. Her skin was smooth and unblemished—surreal, in a world of corrosion of the flesh.

After what felt like eternity, her lips parted. "To a certain extent, it seems he and Woodman the Elder were agreeing."

"Yes."

"Then why are you here?"

"Their decision means war. I know I can avoid war. I have to do all in my power to avoid war. And if I fail, then they'll have their war the way they wanted it. For me it's a simple calculation."

Lena smiled.

"I know that I don't look as manly to you now, but that is the truth and it is more important to me than—"

Her index finger touched her lips. "Sshhh…"

Geo shut up. Lena's smile widened. It was a wonderful smile. Full and warm.

"You look more appetizing to me than ever, Mr. Ambassador. I don't love war either. And I love a man who fights against war."

He felt a warmth coursing through his veins. He felt an erection coming. He was oscillating between embarrassment and rising desire.

"We're here now in the Corrosion Age because men had thought that war should drive the economy and innovation. Because they waged an eternal war against each other to see their profits grow and grow." She stroked his manhood while talking.

"But for me, war is the old men's way. Now is the time for a change. For diplomacy and subterfuge. Now it's time for forceful peace. For us, the new people." Lena bent over his body, kissing and licking.

"Then I need your help," said Geo, breathing hard.

"Anything."

"I need to know where to find the mayor in the next ten hours. Alone and willing to talk, even if…" he smiled "…forcefully pushed to do so."

19.
Blue

The lightbulb gave enough light to disperse the eternal night in the market fridge turned Woodman Base Camp. But not nearly enough to read or see details on a map. Paper—that was another thing humanity had lost during the Corrosion Age. The Woodmans hoarded it with lust and greed, then rediscovered the manufacturing process so they could produce it as a luxury gift for worthy partners on the Exterior. So far Prince Boris had been the only one worthy. Obviously, the criteria for who was worthy and who was not had been the object of countless nights of debate.

The map occupied the entire tabletop and was covered in plastic sheeting, another relic from a long-gone age. Plastic had once littered the entire world. Melted and transformed by the Black Rain, it had turned into one of the deadliest traps for everything living. The Corrosives called it the AnJie. The Woodman scientists had tried to discover what exactly had changed in its chemical composition after the Rain. What was giving it a life of its own, the power to move without external forces pushing it, the hunger to strangle flesh and suck the fat out of it, and how fat fed the ever-hungry AnJie. They'd had no success so far. Luckily for them, the plastic untouched by the Rain had kept its original composition and characteristics. So they kept using it, though sparingly in the Exterior. They were almost like those historical explorers trying to keep certain technologies away from the natives of distant islands.

According to Lena's intelligence, the mayor slept someplace other than his palace: across the street, in a bunker he'd built inside the former underground city known as the Path. He'd disrupted the passage through the Path with his Thousand Year Shelter, as it was known in the mayor's inner circle. Everyone with a shred of real power had bought a place inside his bunker in case of another Black Rain. It must be some bunker, to be able to shelter the number of people Lena was talking about for even a month, let alone the one thousand years advertised in its name. But, as always, dictators liked to talk in absolutes and superlatives, to emphasize their power and better control the masses and their competition.

Geo spat to the side and gnashed his teeth. Now that bastard was trying to upgrade his bunker to the Woodmans' Cave. He was trying to expand his domain at the expense of Geo's clan's livelihood. No one believed nowadays in another Black Rain. That had been a once in an age event, not likely to repeat for several centuries. The mayor and his party kept telling the masses that they now lived clean, not polluting their environment, adapting to the new conditions with blue technologies. No way the disaster was going to strike them twice. And yet, the mayor wanted their Cave, their fresh water supply. Their lives. Because he thought it was within his power.

The map Geo had viewed showed the Path as it had been before the Black Rain. He recalled Lena's mental drawing and visualized it over his ancient map. Yeah, the mayor's bunker had taken over several stores that before had sold goods in the Path. It wasn't as big as what he'd presented to his investors when he'd sold them survival space there, but still quite impressive.

He took the map out of its plastic cover and used a pencil to draw in the area where the bunker was supposed to be. He tried to scale it, to calculate what distance he'd have to cover to find the bastard. Lena couldn't get information on the interior plans. Rooms, halls, corners, guards—nothing from inside. Apparently the mayor had managed to keep it all secret. Based on her expe-

rience with the mayor's palace, she'd guessed the bunker probably had a gaudy interior. Lots of heavily decorated rooms, with
all sorts of unnecessary objects stolen from the city's buildings
crowding the space, meant to impress and subdue the powerful.

The light flash of a silent alarm startled Geo. Someone trying
to breach the HQ's perimeter had triggered it. For gelling sake,
this was the King Rat Temple! No Corrosive would dare disturb its peace and confront the thousands of mutant rats inside.
Unless…

He gulped and turned off the light and attached the helmet
to his suit. It automatically switched on and enabled night vision. Grabbing the map, he shoved it inside the suit and zipped
it up, then crammed a bag of water and a few meat strips in
the suit's pockets. Slipping the knuckle-duster on his left-hand
fingers, he took out his cudgel and exited the room as quietly as
possible. If he was going against the mayor's elite squad, against
Silver Star's men, he was in big trouble. And frankly, they would
be the only ones daring enough and crazy enough to trespass on
the holy grounds. He had no chance in an open confrontation.
He had to hide his room, lock the door, and vanish.

It was quiet. Only the *tic-tic* of the rats' claws on the concrete
floor and metal counters. Darkness filled every corner. The living
city was far from the temple. The ruins surrounding it were filled
with rodents and Nightmares. Geo switched on the rat-repellent
device. He needed a clear path to the back door out of this building. The rats scampered in a cacophony of claws, scratching over
the floors and walls. He tiptoed around counters and broken
glass. He knew his way around with his eyes closed.

Then he heard the voices. Not many, but loud enough to
wake the entire building. Silver Star's men were getting careless
if they thought they could come after him and treat the whole
thing like a Sunday walk. He reached the easternmost corner
and stuck to the wall, waiting to see where the voices were going. There weren't many. Perhaps only two voices, engaged in a
conversation.

Geo cranked up the volume to his receptors. Some static,
loud rat squeaks, the groans of an old building, and yes, two

voices. Distinct voices. One man, one—Geo froze. What was that? He was high, but he simply could not hallucinate that voice. He listened closer. Both voices were from his home, his retreat when fear or nausea hit too hard in the outside world. He felt a tear rolling down his cheek and swore. He didn't need tears inside his helmet. Trickling tears disrupted focus. He had to stay focused now. Especially now.

"Well, it looks exactly as dreary as I imagined it. Even the stench."

"It looks like his pictures. It's already creepy. You don't need to add to it."

"Oh, baby, you're creeped out?"

"By you, asshole. God, I didn't know you're such an—"

"Asshole?"

"Yeah!"

Alex laughed and Bree's laughter followed. Nervous laughter, of people on edge, trying desperately to hold on and not slip into the abyss.

"What the fuck!"

They both startled and almost retreated. Hard, rasping breathing along with static filled Geo's ears. He stood in front of them, looking from one to the other, still trying to understand what he was seeing, still trying to believe it was not a hallucination.

"Geo?"

"What the fuck!" said Geo, a quiver in his voice.

They walked toward him, laughing again, this time with real relief. Bree hugged him and Alex patted his back.

"So, these are the famous Woodman headquarters," said Alex.

Geo kept looking at their faces, controlling his breathing. Controlling his impulses. Home had come there, to him. Into that hell. Into the Exterior's purulent reality.

He turned and walked back to his fridge-turned-room. Pulling away the camouflage, he unlocked the door. He pushed it and it opened with an infernal screech. Geo grimaced in annoyance. Everything was so loud—the door, their voices, the rats, even the Nightmares in the surrounding ruins.

Inside he decoupled the helmet and took it off. A rush of cold air kissed his face. The noise level dropped considerably. Oh yes, he realized, he'd forgotten to turn down the volume in the helmet. This was better. He exhaled heavily and collapsed onto the mattress.

Alex was inspecting the room, the objects in it. He was taking everything in like it was an anticipated experience and he wanted to remember it before going back to his life. Bree stared at Geo, studying him silently. She sat down next to him on the mattress.

"What did you do?" murmured Geo.

"Man, this is awesome!" said Alex.

"What did you do?"

"This was the most interesting thing I've done in a very long time!"

"What the fuck did you do, Alex?"

"What?"

"Why are you here?"

"Why are *you* here, bro? You've been ordered to stand down in the Cave. Wait for your friend the mayor to come to us. What are *you* doing here?"

"I'm saving you, that's what I'm doing," said Geo.

"You're not saving anyone but yourself."

"What!"

"You heard me. Your guilt was so great that you couldn't bear it. You ran away, thinking you have to take them on all by yourself to redeem yourself."

Geo stood up and confronted his brother. Bree rose as well.

"I don't need to redeem myself, *bro*."

"I know. You don't."

Geo looked at him, confused. He'd been so wound up by the possible stealth attack of Silver Star's elite squad that now, when the adrenaline was dwindling, he somehow felt drained and slow.

"Are you high?" Bree said. She shone a light in his eyes. He looked away, mumbling a bit, then felt shame, although he didn't know why he should be ashamed. That was his life now.

Thrust upon him by the Cave. By them. For them.

He pushed away her light. Moving to the table, he pulled the map from inside his suit and slammed it on the table.

"You shouldn't be here. You put yourselves and me in grave danger. You put Bree in terrible, terrible danger."

"He didn't put me in anything. I chose to come here."

"What am I going to do with you? I have big plans for to-night and now…"

"We're here to help, bro."

"How can you help me?"

"Really?"

"He's high. I don't know how much, or if we can…"

"I'm high, yes. Just a bit. The price for getting results here. And that brought me the solution to our problem. Tonight, I'll deal with it. You stay here and tomorrow you're going back and report to the fucking council that I solved their problem. That they don't need to concern themselves anymore with the Exterior."

"Is that what it is? My father?"

"Bree, I don't think that Geo—"

"Yes, Bree. It's your father. He erodes the clan's foundations with every little word he utters. He'll be our undoing in no time."

He felt like a weight had lifted off his chest. Yet he felt shitty for raising his voice at Bree. She'd always been there for him. She was not the enemy. But, wasn't that the unwritten law of humanity—children bear their father's cross?

"Listen, Geo—"

But Bree stopped Alex before he could address his brother. She remained silent, though. She nodded and sat back on the mattress. The two brothers stared at her, each afraid to talk.

"Yes, it's your business that you're high. As long as you can function, I don't care."

Geo flinched. It hurt to hear her saying that. The three of them had always been there for each other. The three of them against the world, as he put it every time.

"You left because it hurt to see internal political fighting getting the better of us. Our parents and grandparents had failed us once again."

They'd never talked about this. But he'd felt it countless times. They'd had the Black Rain because of their elders' failure. And now the same elders made the rules and shaped the new world, as if nothing had changed. As if their petty goals were everything in the world. As if the world gave a fuck about them.

"And we left for the same reason. We have to make it right before they make it worse than it already is. Yes, Alex and I are not savvy in matters of the Exterior, but you're here and that's what counts. And we know stuff you don't. Together, we'll make it right."

Alex patted him on the back again and nodded. "We're here, brother. You'd better take advantage of that."

"Honestly, I'm not comfortable with the level of risk and the percentage of possible failure," said Bree.

"Honestly, we don't have much of a choice," said Geo. "In less than five hours, the mayor's people will leave for the Cave. And then it will be out of our hands."

"Understood." Alex nodded.

"You're not worried at all?" Bree looked at Alex with curiosity.

"No. I trust my brother. He's been here for years. He knows this world better than us. If he's confident we can do it, then we can do it."

"Actually, I think he said that we don't have much choice, not that we'll do it because we can do it."

"Guys, guys. This is something you cannot do here, in the Exterior."

"What?" Bree turned to him.

"You don't have the luxury to chat and go back and forth on subjects. Here you need to act. Think fast, decide faster, act lightning fast."

"Whew, that sounded like something in one of those action movies," said Alex, laughing.

Geo sighed. He couldn't figure out how he'd been able to say all that with a straight face. He was a fraud. He was anything but fast. He was the worst action man. Always thinking and planning, and then rethinking and recalculating odds. But he had to act as if he could in front of them if he was going to keep their morale up.

"All right," said Geo, trying to not think too much about how big a fraud he was. "All right, everybody knows their role?"

Bree and Alex nodded.

"Have you managed to get a clear picture of the map? If necessary, do we know where all the exit points and escape routes are?"

"Done and done," said Alex

"Well then," said Geo, checking the time.

"Let's do it, bro!"

They went to the weapons wall and armed themselves. "You remember your training, Alex?"

"In what?"

"This kind of weaponry" —Geo pointed to the pistols they took— "can never, ever fall into the hands of Corrosives."

"Got that."

"Practice locating the auto-destruct button."

"No worries, bro. I got it." Alex armed himself, checked his suit, and went out of the room to stretch.

"He's a hothead," said Bree.

"It's just the adrenaline before the action," replied Geo, trying to sound confident.

"I worry about him."

"I'll look out for him. Don't worry."

"All right. And I'll look out for both of you."

"Us against the world," Geo said and looked her in the eye.

"Always," Bree replied and smiled. For the first time since they'd arrived.

"Put your helmet on, stay zipped all the time, and shoot everything that moves that isn't us."

"Just the mayor's people."

He stopped her. "No, Bree. Everything that moves. There are

things that will eat you alive before you can blink. Promise me—
everything that moves."

"I promise. Let's —"

Her radio emitted a scrambled noise and then they could
hear Rumi's distorted voice: "I know you went to the Exterior for
him. Come back at once, Bree. Don't be stupid."

Bree touched her radio, but Geo shook his head and stopped
her hand.

"If you don't answer my messages in one hour, I'm bringing
Woodman down, locking him up, and preparing a mission to go
after you."

"You won't do any of those things," said Bree.

"I swear to god, Bree. You have one hour to report that
you've taken a train back to the Cave. As for that dumbass
George, he can stay out there. If he comes back I'll lock him up
and he'll never see the light of day again. You hear me, Bree?"

20.
The Night Hunter

The Woodman brothers walked in front, covered in tatters that made them look as if they belonged. Or so they thought. The city was quiet. Bree didn't know if it was a particularly quiet night, or if the city was usually like this at night. Quiet and empty. If she didn't know better, she could think the city was devoid of life, just empty shells of steel and glass and bricks and concrete, ruins on top of ruins, no lights, no noise, no movement. Not even a gust of wind.

She had thought the city to be something else. She'd seen Geo's pictures, but the reality was always different. It was impressive in terms of scale, or magnitude. Yet, that was something to praise their ancestors, the actual builders, for. Not the Corrosives. It was also desolate. Oppressive. Like a bad reminder of the "good old days."

Bree was supposed to protect their back, so they could focus only on the target. She watched the surroundings as carefully as possible, but she realized that it was difficult for her to assess danger in this world. It wasn't her world. She had no reference. Her Cave experience meant nothing here. She now understood why Geo had been so shocked and so angry to see them there. He had to care for them now too, instead of focusing on the mission.

They were talking, sharing, missing each other. She'd not

seen brothers care for each other as much as the Woodmans. So different, yet so close. They postured, like all boys—hugs were just for special occasions, kisses only if something very dramatic had taken place. They could spend weeks in a confined space and not touch each other. Touches of any kind were for women. Men were tough, brave, distant, meant to protect and serve. Geo, though…Geo was different. He talked, he shared his thoughts, he liked to listen and touch the people around him. She'd imagined how hard it was for him to spend months away from home. Always suited up, always in isolation, always careful what to share with others and what to hide. How to present facts in such a way that the Woodmans would always seem strong and important. Untouchable. She'd realized that Geo's short vacations back in the Cave were his chances to be human, trusting, and cared for. Loved by others who asked for nothing in return. That was why her grandfather's attacks on Geo always felt so unjust and mean. That was why Bree felt closer to the Woodman boys than to her family.

She startled and whimpered. Geo immediately turned, cudgel raised, ready to react to anything that had upset her. Alex was a second slower. He'd always had better instincts and faster reactions than his brother, but not enough training and experience.

They followed her finger and watched an almost transparent veil fluttering in the air as if—but there was no wind. Not the slightest puff. And that white, shiny veil flew and fluttered as if caught in a very strong wind. It had an iridescent quality, like a network of tiny bright lights were caught in it. And—Bree shivered. It could not be! Music, more an impression than an actual sound, floated inside her head. A sad choir of feminine voices. Something from the dusked ages. So tragic that she felt her heart crying.

"Switch off the sound!" Bree heard Geo and looked at him, transfixed. Everything was so beautiful and tragic, it made no sense to go on.

Alex was jumping and sort of dancing around in a savage ritual. Geo managed to catch his brother's shoulders, brought him down, and kicked his leg behind the knee, forcing Alex to fall on his knees. Geo touched Alex's helmet, then immediately turned to her.

She was already walking, entranced, toward the source of the sadness. He grabbed her. She felt surprised by his brutality. He touched her helmet and the music stopped as abruptly as if cut with a knife. She felt angry and overwhelmed. Geo was staring at her through the two transparent faceplates. A heavy burden lifted from her heart and she finally managed to sigh. She felt as if she hadn't been able to breathe in a long time and now, finally, air could get through her constricted respiratory system.

Geo waved his hand at them and ran toward the broken entrance of a building. There was no door anymore and the wall around the entrance was smashed as if forced open with an explosion. Once inside, Geo switched on his audio. Bree did the same.

"What the fuck was that?" Alex's voice was trembling with excitement. His eyes glittered. He was grinning from ear to ear. Really! Bree felt an impulse to swear and kick Alex.

"That was a metas," said Geo.

"*That* was a metas? Holy gel, bro! That was incredible!"

"We almost screwed up there," said Geo.

"What? It was just a little dance."

"And a little death walk," said Bree.

"Bree?"

"People hear different things. That's why music is forbidden here, in the Exterior," said Geo. "It's not like the music we know from the Cave. Here, somehow, it works directly with brain chemistry. Or at least the music of the Nightmares and the metas."

"The children of the Dream Mother and the Nightmare Lord," said Alex reverently.

"All right, shitheads. Let's get back to our mission." Bree tried to keep the irritation out of her voice. She didn't know what upset her so much. The fact that she'd fallen prey to the metas or the fact that while Alex was dancing like a happy goat, she'd felt depressed? She'd felt—suicidal.

"Well, we're here," said Geo, keeping his voice low.

"What do you mean, we're here?"

Bree only saw a colossal space, as tall as the cathedral in their Cave but without limits. It stretched beyond what her night vision could help her distinguish in darkness. That was the *interior* of one of those mammoth buildings Geo kept talking about. One of those she'd seen from a distance when she'd arrived with the train. She felt overwhelmed. Everything was so monstrously big, so threatening, so…useless. What had made the ancients create so many monstrosities?

"Remember the map?"

"Yeah," said Alex.

"This is the big hall where we start. There are dwellings on the right side, so we don't go near that side. We keep to the left. The guards should be posted right after that big arch."

"Yeah, yeah, I remember the plans. Let's go," said Alex.

Geo looked at her with concern in his eyes. "Bree?"

"I'm good, Geo. Let's do it."

She took out her pistol and nodded to the two brothers. She was ready. They had to do this. They'd been mostly a problem for Geo on their way here, but now it was serious. Now it was real.

They advanced through the dark space slowly and steadily. She kept watch at their back, looking toward the dwellings. No movement. The nighttime was really a dead time in the city. Who'd have thought.

They gave the stairs to the underground a wide berth. A couple of shadows moved there, showing that the guards were exactly where Geo's source had told him they should be. So far, it had been good intel.

What source offered intel only if you got drugged? It was not that she didn't believe Geo. But it may be that he had a twisted vision of the world. He'd lived for so long alone in this dark world, that his way of seeing things may be different than theirs. Geo somehow had one foot in the Cave world and the other foot in the Corrosives' world. His mind was a hybrid of the two worlds. He didn't belong to either.

They reached the end of the cavernous hall and began

following another wall, far from the stairs. They'd passed six guards. So far so good. A few more steps and Geo stopped them. A huge hole in the ground was covered with fabric. They went around it and came face to face with a column. It was so thick one needed at least twenty people to encircle it. Everything was intimidatingly big. A few steps farther, they encountered the second column. It was partially collapsed. Then the fourth and finally the fifth. That was their target.

The columns had several metallic doors in them. The intel said *they lead to metallic cages*. Geo had translated that to be elevators like what they had in the Cave. Nothing strange about that. Except for people who had never actually seen an elevator working.

Geo had told them that according to his source, these elevators and their shafts were untouched—not used. So that was their way in—through something people avoided. Something that had become invisible in day-to-day life.

The men pushed a metal bar between the doors of the first elevator, right at the far end of the column, as far as possible from the guards. They forced the doors open millimeter by millimeter so as not to make the slightest noise. Bree watched their six, as they'd heard Sam Hastie saying to his men. They'd discussed what that could mean and concluded that it had to do with the hours on a clock. So the hours were used to indicate which direction to watch. Although "watch my six" was the only thing they'd ever heard Hastie say. Six o'clock seemed to be a very important position for security forces.

The doors opened with a faint whining and they stared into the blackness of the elevator shaft. The car was one floor lower, covered in dust and spiderwebs. A metal ladder was attached to the wall to their right. Alex signaled for them to wait. Gripping Geo's hand as an anchor, he leaned inside the shaft. One big step over and he placed his left foot on the ladder. He grabbed the ladder with his left hand and let go of Geo. Somehow he managed to keep his grip while he turned upside-down, head toward the elevator car and his legs up, feet anchored in between the metal rungs of the ladder. Bree gaped. She'd known he was quite athletic, but this was something beyond what the term meant to her.

He extended his arms down to the elevator car and grabbed the handle of the trapdoor on top of the car. He grunted as he tried to open it. It didn't budge. Again he tried. Again no result. Bree looked to the side. There wasn't enough room on the side to climb down. And anyway, there wouldn't be any way out then. They had to get inside the cabin if they wanted to penetrate the mayor's bunker.

Bree gasped as, without warning, Geo jumped and caught the thick cable attached to the car. The movement caused a little clanging, but not too loud. He slid down the cable and stepped lightly onto the car's top. He caught the handle and pulled. He strained for a few seconds with no result. The mechanism was rusted shut.

Bree jumped as Geo had done and caught the cable. She lowered herself hand over hand until she too was standing on the car's top. She fished from the toolbelt on her hip a tiny bottle with a pointed nozzle. Waving back the men sweating in their efforts, she bent over the handle. Saw the space where it was supposed to move from left to right. Introduced the nozzle of the bottle and squeezed gently in three different places. She then took out her knife and worked a little bit inside the handle mechanism, forcing it with the tip of the knife. Something moved slightly. She squeezed her little bottle some more where she'd felt the mechanism giving way. Then she stepped back and invited them to try again. *Boys*, she thought with love and smiled. She loved them both. She always had. They were so damn brilliant, both of them, and so dumb sometimes. So cute in their manly brawling with every little obstacle.

They opened the hatch and looked inside. It was dusty and stale smelling. No one had touched the car in decades. One by one they slid inside. Using the same metal bar, they forced the doors open again, so slowly it seemed an almost hypnotic act. Eventually the doors gave and slid to their end. There was a bit of light from a couple of torches. No one moved as far as they could see.

Bree exited last. They were in a large space. A stone wall on the right looked freshly built. They were inside the bunker. Wow! Geo's source had delivered! Thank Wood for that!

The plan was simple. Once inside, they were to go down a hallway from this large room, go left at the first intersection, then curve right and they should be in the mayor's apartments. According to the source there were no guards inside, as the bunker was closed to everybody. The only people living inside were the mayor and Silver Star and his elite squad, and they were there only during the night. No need for staff for food or anything else. The mercenaries were housed in a different wing of the bunker, so they shouldn't bump into them accidentally. The mayor wanted his peace and quiet in his side of the bunker, which was very good for the Woodmans.

Geo turned and stopped her. She held up her palms as if asking him *what*? He pointed to the elevator and then to his eyes and then all around. Bree was tempted to play dumb and pretend not to understand. She wanted a bigger part in this than just standing guard. Instead she sighed and nodded. She backtracked and entered the elevator car. Closing the doors halfway hid her from view from any angle. She took out her pistol and mounted the silencer. She was ready to cover their backs. To secure their retreat. At any cost—even revealing firearms to Corrosives.

Geo watched Bree retreating inside the elevator's car and exhaled. He didn't need to watch over her now. Yeah, his brother was in amazing shape but that didn't mean that he was ready for field duty. That he would survive in the Exterior. *Hah, who am I kidding. I can't be honest even with myself.* His brother was ten times the man he was. He was so proud to have this mission with Alex. So excited. So relieved and happy that his envy was insignificant in comparison.

Alex was waiting for Geo in the middle of the room. He scanned the room one more time. He felt a little bit odd about all this. Yeah, he got it—no guards inside. Yet this was not the mayor's style. This was strictly a military bunker, not palatial. The

mayor was a pompous bastard. He liked his lights and velvets
and silks. He liked painted walls and lots of the old artwork to
adorn his walls.

Geo stopped and amplified his audio receptor. Whispers.
Nightmares or Corrosives? Wait, the bunker was supposed to be
empty. No people, no whispers. Geo switched his visuals to heat
scanning. The walls were full. The walls—it was a trap!

"Alex! No—"

There was a *whoosh* and then a *thunk* and he saw Alex leaning back, a spear piercing his body, the point stuck in the floor
behind him. The walls opened and men stepped out with spears
and harpoon guns. They wore the mayor's uniform. Men raised
their weapons.

Alex's head was tipped back, blood foaming at his mouth.
He was alive.

Geo turned in a half circle, his cudgel deflecting the weapons
that came at him. He lunged and struck two knees in a quick
succession. The soldiers fell with grunts of pain. Another preparing to push his spear into Geo's chest stumbled back and fell
with a dark hole in his temple. Drawing his blades as he went,
Geo pushed his way through the last two soldiers and as he
passed them he extended the blades in each hand. They crumpled, holding their intestines in their hands.

Alex's body now lay on the floor, pierced multiple times
by the soldiers doing their duty and butchering the fallen. Geo
cried out in despair. He thrust the blades back into their sheaths
and took out his cudgel and mace. But before he could move, a
sudden commotion made him freeze. A new band of mercenaries
forced their way through the main doors, leaving corpses behind
them. The new band wore Silkers colors and Hyalo Warriors
insignia. They overran the mayor's men in a matter of seconds.

Geo went to Alex's side. He was long dead, butchered
in such a way that only his upper torso still hung above the
ground, impaled on the spear. His head was a step away, his
beautiful face twisted in a horrific rictus. Geo sobbed and looked
for Alex's belt in the bloody mess. He took it and mounted it
above his own. Then he checked Alex's pockets for any incrim-

inating evidence. He took everything that he could find, filling his pockets and suit.

"Sir, we need to move," a young officer said next to his ear.

Geo startled and scowled at him. "We have to take him," he said, gesturing at Alex's remains.

"Sorry, can't do. And we need to move now or we won't leave this place alive."

Geo looked toward the elevator. He distinguished Bree's face in the darkness. Or he thought he did. He signaled for her to stay hidden. Then he turned to the officer. "All right, then. Let's go."

Arrows whistled through the air and two of the Hyalo Warriors grunted in surprise. One fell writhing to the floor, pierced by three arrows. The second one had one in his arm and one in his shield. They all turned and started running from the room. Arrows whistled overhead like birds preying on them. As one, the warriors turned, shields up under the rain of arrows. Then the second rank rose behind the front line and blew through their blowguns. Their pursuers retreated immediately behind the stone wall.

Then an alarm filled the night air. It was a first for Geo. He'd never heard anything similar before. "What the fuck is that?" he said.

"The city is under attack. The Night Hunter is here," murmured the officer, looking Geo in the eye.

21.
Ex Nihilo Nihil Fit

Bree watched them carefully. She'd switched the night vision off, as the torches threw sufficient light into the room for her to distinguish Alex and Geo's movements. It would all be over in less than ten minutes. From what she'd heard from Geo, the mayor was a craven opportunist. Those kinds of people were the easiest to deal with. With the right push and the right promise, you got yourself a deal in no time at all.

Something was wrong. Geo had stopped in the middle of the foyer, while Alex was advancing toward their target. Geo looked around, carefully scanning all the corners of the room. He then turned to Alex. "Alex! No—"

That noise! The wet swishing noise of—she gagged, but kept herself from throwing up. The noise of ripped flesh. She looked to the scene in the foyer like it was a scene from a movie. Not her reality, but something she was watching from afar, on a screen, not involving her.

Alex was pierced by a huge spear that had entered through his chest and exited through his shoulder blade, impaling him to the floor. His head was tipped back, and there was bloody foam at his mouth—it must have pierced his lungs. And his eyes— oh, GOD! Alex! Alex was—Alex was— She scrambled over the elevator's floor, wanting to get out. Then she saw the swarm of Corrosives surrounding the brothers. Hacking at them, slaughtering their way through them.

Huge beasts, vaguely humanoid, their bodies disfigured by masses of red, crude flesh bulging unnaturally here and there, were dressed in patchworks of blue cloth that were stretched over muscles and protruding bones. Their expressions were savage and animalistic. Saliva sprayed from lipless, toothless mouths—mere slits on what once had been their faces. Horror pinned Bree to the elevator's floor. It was a scene from a nightmare.

One of the beasts chopped off Alex's head. It rolled in a rush of blood on the cement floor. Yet another beast raised his spear above Geo. Bree shot without thinking. "*One shot, one down,*" as her grandfather used to say during her training. The monster jerked back and fell dead. Then Geo rose and swiftly rushed through two beasts, leaving them both behind him, holding their intestines in their arms. Surprise replaced the hunger on their faces.

Bree turned, undid her helmet, bent, and vomited in one corner of the elevator. Her body convulsed in shock as she fell to her knees, one hand braced against the elevator wall. She panted hard, heard Geo's scream, and threw up again. Feeling as if she'd just brought up her lungs and stomach along with its contents, she remained on her knees, panting and sobbing, unable to rise from that soiled corner.

When a new wave of deathly noise washed over the foyer, seeming to eradicate everything before it, Bree focused on the great effort of rising. She felt exhausted. Peering through the crack between the doors, she saw new warriors, as hideous and monstrous as the others, only dressed differently, moving methodically through the room and killing with efficiency. The deathly ballet of these last beasts contrasted so much with the savage chaos of the first ones that she watched them, mesmerized. What was going on? She felt that a lot had happened in the span of two minutes and she couldn't understand any of it. She felt so out of sync and out of place that she just fought to keep breathing while the scene unfurled in front of her.

Geo approached Alex's body. Her breath came out like a

roll of barbed wire. He took his brother's belt and started going
through his pockets methodically, emptying them of anything
the Corrosives might get their hands on. He was following the
rule book to the letter. His face was ravaged, he looked almost as
disfigured as the Corrosives, yet he worked with short, precise
movements. She understood—this second wave of Corrosives
were friendlies. She wanted to come out and go shake Geo out of
his senseless trance, but then he looked at her. He signaled her to
stay, to hide. Don't follow. He was as sane as ever despite what
had just happened. He was— Alex's open eyes were staring at
her. Empty, frightened, lifeless. She stepped back, put both hands
on the doors, and pushed, closing the doors as if nothing had
happened.

   She woke up with a sigh. Her head hurt terribly. There was
a bad smell in the elevator. Vomit. She remembered vomiting.
She gagged and realized her helmet was on the floor. She'd been
exposed to the corrosive air for a while. She looked at the time
and couldn't comprehend what it meant. She had to remember
the night before, what time they'd left the Woodman HQ and
make some calculations. She'd been unconscious for some six
hours. Shit, it was the middle of the day. The streets would be
full of Corrosives. The thought gave her pause. She remembered
the beasts from last night's attack, hacking and slashing the
defenseless body of Alex. His head rolling on the floor. His eyes
staring at her.
   She had to move. She had to get back to the HQ before the
mayor realized they had penetrated his bunker and discovered
her inside the elevator. It was unbelievable that they hadn't yet.
   Where was she? She remembered the way into the building.
It was just a fifteen-minute walk to the HQ building. The short-
est walk into Death's embrace. She sighed again and moved.

   She used the primitive facilities in the HQ to clean and
disinfect her suit and then she cleaned herself. Her scientist's

penchant for preparation took over and she did a few tests on herself, then went through an entire decontamination protocol. While waiting for Geo, she found the box of food and forced herself to eat a can of meat. She almost threw up again, but managed to get through it. Then she found a distorted bottle with something brownish inside. *"They have the strongest liquor in the Exterior. Made of fermented mushrooms and herbs. It's disgusting, but sooo good! It tastes of garbage and mud. The first time you try it, you can barely hold it down. Then you learn not to smell it or hold it in your mouth longer than necessary."* Geo used to tell them stories about his first adventures in the Exterior. Then slowly, slowly, he stopped. Apparently there was nothing else pleasant and funny to tell them. Slowly he'd turned into that guy between worlds. That stranger who still shared a history with them, but not the present.

Bree uncorked the bottle and smelled it. She gagged. Horrible. Maybe this wasn't meant to be drank. Or maybe this wasn't meant to be smelled, but drank. She took a swig from the bottle and following Geo's advice, swallowing immediately. It burned her throat so painfully that it took her mind of reality. She drank again and belched. It was a horrible, horrible drink. But soooo good for forgetting. She put the bottle to her mouth and drank for a few long seconds. Then she stopped, retched, and fought to keep her balance. It was hard to stand.

She rejected the image of Alex's decapitated head. She had to forget that somehow. Tears found their way down her cheeks and chin, dropping onto her chest like fat droplets of warm, salty rain. She just let go of anything and cried. Waiting for Geo.

Bree woke up later, her head feeling overlarge and heavy. Her eyes were so puffy they could barely open. She felt thirsty and a little bit nauseous. Checking the time, she saw that she'd slept ten hours. Enough to clear her head. Shit! She didn't have time for sleep. She had to do something. Wait—Geo was not back yet.

Geo was missing. At the thought of losing him too, she felt close to losing it. No, she had to stay in control. She…

Actually, she realized, Geo was not missing. This was his world. He was out there doing his thing. She was missing. She was missing from the Cave. From her family. She'd left without a word, without a warning. She just now realized how stupid and childish she and Alex had been. Their ego. They had just been stupid and thinking only of themselves. Not even that—Alex would still be alive, if he'd been thinking of himself. His safety. They had behaved like idiotic, hot-blooded teenagers, thrill-seekers looking for adventure. Not thinking of—not thinking. Geo had tried to warn them. He'd been angry at them exactly for this, but they couldn't see it. They thought they were better. Stupid, stupid, stupid.

Bree walked the length of the giant freezer turned headquarters/operations base. It was too small for her nervousness. She needed more space to walk, to run, but that would mean putting on the suit and she wasn't ready to wear it again.

She saw a steel bar suspended above her head in one corner, as if meant for training. She jumped and caught it with both hands, then pulled herself up to chin the bar, and back down. And up and down. That was some good pain there. She burned off her anger and dropped down to the floor, breathing deeply in and out.

Geo had come up with this plan to save the Cave from war based on intel from his source in the Silkers Clan. *His* source. From the smell of it, a woman. And Geo seemed to trust her and get high with her. No, not a woman. A Corrosive female. They were nothing else but beasts. Bloodthirsty animals.

Cunning, too. It had been a death trap. His source had sent Geo to his death. And for that Alex had died. *It had been a trap.* Yeah, she'd realized immediately, seeing Geo pondering and scanning the bunker foyer, but only now she recognized it. They had walked right into a trap of Geo's doing. His source, his intel, his plan. He was supposed to protect them and he walked them right into it. He'd killed his brother. Goddamnit, he'd killed Alex.

She started running through the freezer, banging its walls with her fists until they were bloody. Kicking whatever stood in her way. She felt consumed by rage. She would smash Geo's face if she saw him right now. She would just punch and kick and punch.

Eventually she dropped down on the mattress with a grunt, panting. The rage had dwindled into frustration. They had walked right down into a trap. Yes, down in the bunker Geo had realized immediately, but Alex...Alex had been so inexperienced, so avid for adventure, he couldn't have realized anything. And he had taken the lead. He hadn't waited for Geo, as the plan had been. He'd been too eager to prove himself. And he'd paid the price for it. Geo had experience. Yes, he was not as athletic as Alex, but he— Bree remembered Geo always weighing things, always thinking a long time before speaking or doing anything. Now she saw it. Now she saw why Woodman the Elder had chosen Geo and not the obvious choice, Alex. Because he needed somebody who wouldn't lunge forward headfirst without balancing facts and evidence. Geo was the calculating one. *"He's just a scared little boy. A momma's boy!"* her grandfather, Greg Rumi, had told her when they'd sent Geo on his mission to the Exterior. He'd always had only discontent for this decision.

Now Geo was missing, taken somewhere by those Corrosives who had supposedly saved him. He'd signaled her to stay hidden, though, so he didn't trust them. His allies, and he didn't trust them. So much had happened and she'd slept through the day, and they'd missed the deadline. The Cave was probably under attack right now. And she was here. Alex was dead. And she was here, unable to warn them or help them in any way. She was useless.

It was Geo's fault, because he'd chosen to trust such a traitorous source. Or maybe the Corrosives were too cunning, too smart even for Geo. And they hadn't seen it. He'd come back double-crossed—no, triple-crossed, drugged, blinded, poisoned with gelled water, and still they hadn't learned their lesson. They thought they could make it better by trusting the same people who had made a joke of Geo once.

She had to do something or she'd go crazy in that freezer. She rose and walked to the door. There was a scientific reason for wearing her suit and helmet, but she wanted so much to just get out and run. She turned and stepped over to her suit, draped over the back of the only chair.

She noticed a bag at the foot of the chair. Alex's bag. Bree lifted it reverently. Taking a deep breath, she sat on the chair and opened the bag. Some provisions, a map, and Alex's journal. His big, thick, science journal. His research. What? She opened it and a piece of paper fell out of it.

Bro, you know I love you. So, no matter what happens, it's on me. I wanted to be in the Exterior for once. If something happens, here's my research on Dreams and Nightmares. Here's the science behind it. It's more important than we give it credit for. It will help you navigate better the Corrosive gelled waters of the Exterior. Stay safe and smart.

Bree closed the journal and pressed the note to her chest. *Oh, Alex, what have you done?* Where was Geo now when she needed him? She had to find him before something terrible happened to Geo, too.

22.
Fish Eye

"We are under attack. The Night Hunter is here," murmured the officer, staring at Geo.

Geo looked back and saw that Silver Star's men had closed and locked the doors to the mayor's bunker. Hearing the alarm, they'd decided to cease their pursuit.

The warriors entered a formation immediately. The officer indicated to Geo the glass doors into the building. Glass doors in a glass wall. Vestiges from a dead age. The warriors began running in formation and Geo was forced to go with them, as they had surrounded him in their protective wall.

The alarm stopped.

A growl shook the building like a shockwave, rising into an incredible, earthshaking roar. They all froze right before opening the doors. Geo dialed down his exterior audio.

The roar dropped to a growl.

"What's a Night Hunter?" asked Geo.

"Esox," said the Hyalo officer, nodding toward the glass wall.

Up the street there was a spot of sky darker than the rest. A spot moving quickly, its movements looking more like swimming than flying.

"The Golden Tower is right there," said Geo, pointing to the building across the boulevard. "Let's run."

"No."

"What do you mean, no? It's just there. We can make it."

"If it catches our scent then it will hunt us and the Golden Tower won't stand a chance against it."

The officer retreated and his squad followed, trying to move without making noise. They reached the stairs to the underground city. One of the warriors grunted, scared. They all looked back. The Night Hunter was there, looking at them through the glass wall with huge, dead eyes. Its head was the size of a locomotive, its snout so long that he could not see it entirely. It opened its snout and rows of hundreds of sharp teeth shone in the moonlight. Holy Gel!

Growling, the monster pressed its eye to the glass. The orb moved quickly, scanning them. The terrible shockwave of its growling disturbed Geo more than its physical appearance. *It's a fish,* Geo realized. *It's just a fish—*

The roar cracked the glass wall into an abstract spider web. The monster pulverized it into a cloud of glass particles, then reappeared with its snout in the opening. It passed through in an explosion of glass.

Hands pulled Geo. He saw the warriors running down the steps to the underground city. He followed in a rush of adrenaline that made him forget Alex and Bree; made him forget the Woodman Clan's future.

He jumped the last five steps as he felt the Hunter's mouth snapping behind him with a wet slap. He hit the floor, rolled, and rose, looking back. The terrible fish had its snout stuck in the stairwell. The concrete in the floor above had cracked around the edges from the force with which it had struck.

"Don't look back, just run!" yelled the Hyalo officer, pulling Geo after him.

Geo ran after the Hyalo Warriors. Adrenaline told him to run, but his mind told him that the monster wouldn't be able to break through the thick floor of the building. So he looked back—just in time to see the Night Hunter rematerializing as smoke inside the cavernous underground hall. And becoming solid, smoke turning into green-gray flesh, sharp teeth, and gills, undulating body. Geo turned and ran faster than he thought possible.

The warriors knew their way through the underground city. They passed the gates into the mayor's bunker. He heard a loud bang and saw the bunker's gates buckle, almost completely destroyed. Arrows flew from inside the bunker toward the monstrous fish. But it just dissolved into smoke and reappeared inside the bunker, in the midst of Silver Star's men. Terrified screams filled the night. The Hyalo squad didn't stop to watch the destruction.

Geo ran mechanically, numb with fatigue. The adrenaline had dissipated and though his muscles were too well trained to give out, his mind was dull. He only saw darkness around him. He heard the warriors' rhythmic breathing and footsteps, and just followed.

23.
The Wood That Doesn't Break

They were three levels below the Golden Tower. Geo only now realized that he hadn't paid attention to the how they'd gotten under the tower and how they got so deep under the city. *Some crappy spy I make for the Woodmans. Damn Rumi was right all along. Mama's boy. Good for nothing.* He sobbed and stopped in fear just as the warriors looked at him. They were all in formation along a wall in the room where they had brought him. Waiting. This was not a good time to show weakness. This was not the moment to let the events of the night get to him. Not in front of these warriors. Not when Boris was bound to find out from them that he'd cracked.

The room was some sort of a bedroom, like the ones above, but without windows. It looked like the bedroom of an officer, not a guest—a simple bed, small table and chair, empty gray walls, cement floor. And a glass of water on the table. It had that viscous look of gelled water boiled to turn it liquid. Only it didn't stay liquid for long.

The squad stood at attention. The prince had entered the room, followed by his own guard.

"Sir!" The Hyalo officer saluted.

"How many?" said the prince.

"Only one, sir."

"I see you're missing two, Lieutenant."

"The other one is at the infirmary. Lightly wounded. Sir."

"Good job, Lieutenant. Dismissed."

"Sir!"

The officer turned and exited the room. The warriors followed him, their movement brisk.

"You wait outside," said the prince to his guard.

Geo attempted to turn his face into something friendly. It required a lot of effort not to think of Alex. A lot of effort not to think of the war he'd brought upon the Woodmans. But after all this, to also smile like a real ambassador, that was the real torture. Not that he didn't deserve it. He deserved a lot worse than that.

"Well?" The prince was serious. For the first time in a long time.

"Thank you," said Geo and continued smiling as if this had been only one of their nights out.

"Of course. We're friends."

Geo nodded. He had several things he'd like to clarify, but needed to do so in a *diplomatic* way. So Boris's generosity would not dry up instantly.

"But you owe me one man, friend," added Boris.

"What do you mean?"

"One of my men is dead to save you. You owe me his life."

"I just gifted you a wooden throne worth half this tower. Isn't that enough?"

"So crass, my friend. Is this the way to talk about a man's life?"

Alex's life. What was he doing there? What was the sense in all that death if no goal had been achieved? And life went on, with everyone carrying their tragedies through the mud like careless assholes. Life didn't care. The world didn't care. Tragedies were personal. And so Boris didn't care either.

Geo rose from the chair. He always felt that when broaching an important topic, he needed to stand tall. If not to dominate his opponent, at least to establish eye contact on a level line. "I walked into a trap down there."

"So I heard."

"I wonder, how did the mayor know I'd come for him?"

"That's a good line of inquiry, Geo."

"Where is Lena?"

"Why?"

"Last night I asked Lena where I could find the mayor and she went and asked you. Only the three of us knew of my plan."

"The three of us and the man you were with in the mayor's bunker. The dead man."

"How do you…"

"Oh, I know everything that moves in this city even before it has a will to move, Geo. I thought you already knew that."

Boris relaxed on the bed. He was smiling again. He looked up at Geo, waiting. He'd obviously placed himself in a subordinate position to Geo. Nothing was random with the prince. Geo knew that. The prince wanted Geo to feel like he was in a superior position and then catch him on the wrong foot. Geo realized that Boris had never been his real friend. It had always been a cat and mouse game with him. And he'd dropped his guard so many times, giving Boris the upper hand, and more insight into the Woodmans than he should have had.

"The dead man was my brother."

"That was Alex…" said Boris and rose. "I'm sorry, Geo."

"Yeah."

"All right then, your debt is forgiven. You should have come to me, Geo."

"Lena went to you."

"Exactly. Lena. The information for her had been general knowledge—that's where the mayor's bedroom is."

"What?"

"I had a meeting with the mayor last night. Lena didn't know about it. And why should she? But if you had come to me and asked me personally for my help, I would have delivered the bastard into your arms last night. Problem solved. Brother alive. War avoided."

Geo stared at Boris and for an entire minute he just put all his dwindling will into not punching the prince. It wouldn't be very diplomatic. Not to mention that he was practically in Boris's powers now, in his basement. Eventually Geo exhaled, long and loudly.

"So, no love lost with your brother."

"Why do you say that?"

"No tears, no struggle. Everything's good."

Geo wondered if he really was incapable of showing emotion, or if Boris was playing a different game now.

"Not all families are blue skies and water," he said in a neutral tone.

"Well, that makes it easier for us then."

No point in standing. The prince had made it pretty clear. Geo sat on the chair, pulling it a little bit farther away from the prince. "How's that, Boris?"

"Because this means you will not act out irrationally when hearing what's happening. You'll be rational and calculated, and make the best decisions."

Geo felt the impulse to rise again, but refrained.

"The mayor has impaled your brother's skull in front of his palace, which will make it in front of mine too. He has man-speakers on every corner of the city, announcing a reward for your head."

The prince yawned with a bored air. He stretched out on the bed. Geo tried to receive the bad news as if it was about somebody else, not about Alex. Not about himself. He tried to detach himself from the news and keep calm. Judge. Rationalize.

"You mentioned the war. What do you know of that?"

"There will be one. Just not now. Your incursion into the mayor's territory has delayed his plans. He first wants to catch you and make an example out of you for his losses last night. Then he'll rally his troops and march over to your Cave. No mercy is the latest slogan in the mayor's camp."

Geo stared wide-eyed at Boris. He couldn't believe his luck. He'd delayed the mayor. He could—he could what?

"Don't be so modest, my friend. Your adventure last night killed twenty-one of his warriors and demolished his bunker. Out of the twenty-one, three are from Silver Star's elite squad. Which makes it even more painful for him. That's why he'll postpone the invasion until he gets you. You've become the most famous man in the city. Or infamous, depending on which side of the fence you're on."

"That's good news. Thank you."

"I don't see it that way. It's only a delay, unless you choose what's right for your clan."

Geo relaxed and closed his eyes. They were entering the second part of their negotiation. All now depended on how calm and composed Geo could stay while Boris was trying to play him. He heard Woodman the Elder's voice in his mind: *"You're not George Woodman when in a negotiation. You're an entity of iron will and persuasion. You know your advantages and your needs. Ask thrice the price and offer a quarter of what you can offer. Then do the math. All it is is an exercise in mathematics. No feelings, no personal stakes."*

"What if what they're asking for is personal?" he'd asked the old man.

"Nothing is personal if we don't want to make it personal. The wood doesn't break if we don't bend it. Keep it straight in your mind and you'll be all right."

"I'm listening," said Geo.

"Be my hyalophora, my science advisor, and I will protect you and your clan."

"You're asking me to take a big leap."

"What other choice does your clan have?"

And that was it. Boris had laid out his card and played Geo into a corner. *What other choice?* That alone made Geo seethe with anger.

"Have you thought of my information about the next Rain?"

"Yes. That was very useful. Thank you. It proves you mean well. It proves your good faith."

"If you organize a saving operation for the kingdom's population, I can offer you ways of combating future rains."

"Is this the Woodman's request? I can hardly see any advantage for your clan."

"My clan wants unlimited access to your studies."

"You haven't even mentioned that. Is that wise?"

"I have my reasons," said Geo.

"All right, I can give you a monthly report on our studies for unlimited access to the Woodman research."

"Your monthly report for our monthly report, plus my monthly visit to your research center."

"But Geo, as my hyalophora you'll be able to visit my research center daily and share all that information with the Woodman Clan."

"I *will* be your hyalophora while keeping my current condition. And I *will* give you full access to Woodman research for saving as many lives as possible. We need a plan by this time next week."

Boris grinned. He rose from the bed and stretched. His bones cracked. He looked more whole than most of the Corrosives. Geo had often wondered what his secret was, to stay in such good shape where most couldn't last a decade.

"Geo, my friend, let me be clear with you. Me saving the kingdom is not your business. You cannot negotiate that. Honestly, the lives of half of those living here right now are not worth saving. And anyway, I really don't care if they survive or not. I believe in survival of the fittest. And right now, I'm the fittest and the rest of them are the chaff. All that matters are my Silkers. That's all. So, I really, really don't want to hear one more time about saving the kingdom."

"But, your survival depends on the lives of that chaff that provides you with food, and ore, and so many other things. You cannot survive on your own."

"That's the mayor's role. He's the ruler of our little kingdom. When he fails to protect his subjects, I'll be the obvious choice as his replacement. No one will say anything then. No more elections. Just succession. *My* succession."

So that's all there was. Political interests. For Boris, the lives of hundreds of thousands was not worth more than a political maneuver against his opponent. The prince was a visionary without perspective. A sociopath with no interest in the future of humanity.

"Oh, come on, Geo, the Woodmans have no clout in the

kingdom. You may have precious resources, but no power. Your clan *is* a resource. That's all. So, better get in line and cooperate with who matters. Care for your own."

"And by care for them you mean that I should become a…"

"What? You want to say *Corrosive*? Yes, I know what you call us. I know how you Woodmans see us. I know the terror that roils in your guts when thinking you may become one of us. But frankly, Geo, what *other* choice do you have?"

"And what if I don't pass your water ritual? What if I fail to become a Silker? What happens then with my clan?"

"You won't fail."

"You can't possibly know that."

"I do. You. Won't. Fail. Trust me."

Trust you. I needed good intelligence on my enemy and you gave me outdated info. Not false, but not the important stuff. Not the vital info. I can't accuse you of lying to me. You scored one. But I can't thank you for helping me. That's a minus. Those cancel each other out. You're on zero on the trust issue, my "ally."

The prince stared at Geo, his eyes dark, intense. Waiting. Impatient.

My brother died because of your schemes. I give you minus ten. My clan is on the brink of war because of you. Another minus ten. None of this is your personal business, so you don't care. Plus one, twice. That's a two. You're still in the negative, "ally."

"All right, Geo. I'll make it simple for you. The mayor is out for your head. I'll give you asylum until tonight at nine. When it gets dark and you can hide, you're on your own. The Golden Tower and all the other Silker establishments will become forbidden to you. My protection will cease."

My clan is in danger and you're using that to blackmail us. Minus ten. You're minus thirty to plus two so far.

"Tonight at nine, you have two choices. One, run for your life. Two, swear fealty to me and your enemies will become my enemies. And I'll add a bonus for you—I'll kill the mayor myself. Just so you can see and feel what it's like to be under my protection."

The prince left. Geo stared at the closed door, unable to think. Two choices. The first one, a certain quick death. The second one, a terrible, delayed death. Boris had just asked him to choose his method of death.

24.
Transcendental Rust

He couldn't raise his arm once again. His whole body was trembling with effort and suffering. He had to do it, to reach the end of it. But he was exhausted. And once again he scowled at his impotence. His uselessness. He needed to gather his strength, both physical and mental, and finish the job.

What could Mar possibly see in him? That had become more of a philosophical question lately, rather than one dealing with the day-to-day reality. As in what had women seen in their men throughout history? And who knew better than him, that the reflection changed from century to century, sometimes even from generation to generation? Obviously, that vision should have been radically changed after traumatic events such as the Black Rain and the corrosion. But tonight, the distorted image reflected in the small shard of mirror the tables on him and dropped the philosophical approach for the concrete one—what could she possibly see in that deformed, corroded, reduced beyond recognition chunk of flesh?

Jon's face had suffered the most—almost gone, a disgusting, sunken-in parody of a face below the cranium. The nose had long ago been reduced to a dark hole. His eyes were but two craters on his troubled headscape. If the eyes were the windows into a person's soul, then Jon must have had an abyss for a soul. As for his mouth, that had become more a muzzle than anything, with his teeth visible in his collapsing face. His entire bald head was the cranium of a cursed and deeply punished monster. And all on the fragile, stick-thin neck that had remained after a lifetime of sandpapering the rust. His usual garment nowadays was a turtleneck that hid not only the hideous neck, but also the metallic frame still holding his head above his shoulders.

Maybe a higher purpose could take these questions away. He'd been through hell and back and was still consumed by this trivial nonsense. And yet, what could she see in him? He was fragile and old, and disfigured. Worthless. What—

"What's wrong with you?"

Yes, that could be another question. *Everything* was the answer. Everything hurt the wrong way. Everything went wrong with his friends. Everything went wrong with his life…

"How could you do that to yourself?"

Oh, Mar was here. The love of his life had actually asked the right question. He turned and saw her eyes turning white, as they did now that there were no tears to shed. When all the liquid in their bodies was gel and their tear ducts had become useless. Like him.

He knew what she was referring to. He turned to face her, hiding his back from her. He wished he could hide his face from her, but he couldn't hide his face and his back at the same time. So he cupped her face in his palms and caressed her. His beautiful angel. Her skin, the color of pure chocolate, had remained smooth and delicate. Dark, shiny silk. Rich and deep. Like her honey eyes.

"Jon, why?"

"It's something…complicated, gorgeous," he murmured.

"This could mean the end of you."

"Or the beginning," he said and smiled despite the unbearable pain he felt. He was almost there.

"What are you trying to do, love? Let me help you."

"Then take this." He handed her the whip. "One more time and it's done."

"Jon!"

"I promise you I don't intend to harm myself for the sake of it. When I'm where I should be, you'll understand."

Mar looked at the improvised whip with horror. She couldn't comprehend what was going on. Wounds were the only Achilles' heel for Corrosives. No viruses or bacteria could harm them anymore. No more arthritis, flu, or cancer. But open the skin and the flesh would start immediately to corrode. And corrosion was the death of them all.

"I can't." She dropped the whip.

"Then you'd want to leave the room for this next step."

"Jon, please reconsider. You've already caused more damage than your body can take. Let me call Doc."

"Not yet, gorgeous."

"But—Jon, I can't just watch you kill yourself."

"I'm not. You have to trust me."

"And you have to trust *me*, and tell me what's going on." Mar placed her palm over his hand, still caressing her face.

Why do you still care about me? was the first thing on his lips, but he knew better than that. Could he tell her? She was the smartest person he'd ever known, but his experiment needed her to make a leap of faith. To hope beyond hope that he'd succeed and his death wouldn't be in vain. If he was right, then the new people of Earth wouldn't need a new religion to ease their passage into oblivion. No, they would need a new science to give them a new purpose. To help them escape the clutch of Earth's nature. To escape her vengeance and pursue a new dream.

Mar would certainly understand that. But would she accept it? Such a strange feeling—to feel again like a teenager confronted by his mother and not sure if his young and juvenile desires could be understood by the wiser but out-of-touch parent.

"Jon?" Her voice had that slight touch of hope. Not his hope. But her own—that he could be reasoned with and made to step down. To listen to her love. How could she possibly still love him, after all his failings both as a man and as a husband?

"My gorgeous," he said and caressed her hair. "I—do you remember the stories of the realms?"

"What?"

"The realms of the sky?"

"Urban legends."

"Yes, beautiful," he acknowledged. "Based on the ravings of a few mad ones."

"What about them?" Her expression had become severe and her voice stern. So, he'd lost her already. That was as far as her trust would go.

"Nothing, beautiful. Would you please make me a tea?"

"Don't you dare! Don't you dare treat me like one of your disciples. Why did you do this?" She touched his back and he flinched.

"Because now I have proof of their existence. And I *need* to see them for myself. I *need* to find a reason. A purpose!"

"If you have proof, you don't need to see them for yourself. You *already* have proof!"

"I'm sorry, gorgeous," he murmured and retrieved the whip from the floor faster than she could react.

"No, Jon! I—"

But he found the strength to whip his back one more time. Then he shuddered and collapsed.

Mar grabbed the whip from his hand and threw it across the room. She took his face tenderly. Then she turned him halfway, so his bloody back wouldn't rest on the floor. "Tooon!" She yelled. "Ton!"

Jon heard the hurried steps of his first son. Now he could let them take care of him while he waited for the miracle to happen. And if not, well, he at least had tried.

"Mom? Dad!"

"Go get Doc. Now!"

Ton, his dutiful son, ran away. Jon sighed with the lack of strength to scream in pain, and let himself slide into unconsciousness.

25.
Of Monsters and Men

Bree walked carefully through the abandoned market, now turned derelict Rat King Temple, as Geo had told her after establishing their operations center there. Bree had wondered why the Rat King and not the Rat President or Rat Premier? They had been the last labels of power in the land. Probably they hadn't been used for as long as king or queen, so hadn't gained a memorable place in the collective consciousness.

Anyway, she had to be careful how she exited the operations center / temple, as doing it wrong would certainly be considered sacrilege in the eyes of the Corrosives. Although it was quite effective for the Woodmans' invisibility in the city. What did they had used to say before the Black Rain? The Devil's biggest accomplishment was to convince people he didn't exist.

Rats the size of large dogs scampered in the shadows, moving away from her ultrasound transmitter. She knew the technology worked, that she was out of danger. But just seeing those huge rodents with fangs the size of her arm raised an irrational fear inside her. How long was this tech going to protect her from them? What if—the *what if*s were the most dangerous thoughts in the head of a traveler through the world of corrosion.

She shuddered and left her fears behind. As instructed, she went out through the back door, directly into the Fields of Rats. The pest-controlled area between the central part of the city and

the lakeshore. A wild, overgrown field of weeds and thorny
bushes covered what looked like sports fields between brick ruins. So, that's what humanity's future looked like. She was now
all by herself, without a specific purpose for her walk, without a
third-party point of view. She could now feel the world as it was.
She could now filter and process the reality without guidance.
She was now an explorer as she'd dreamed of being her whole
life, yet she didn't feel the excitement anymore. Alex was dead
and Geo was—somewhere, not needing her. She was alone in
this.

She was alone and yet surrounded by life. She could hear
the bustle and hustle from the living city of Torono sprawling
behind the temple. That was something else. She should not give
in to bad thoughts and depression. If she wanted to survive in
the city, she needed her positive energy. Her will to comprehend
and adapt.

In front of the temple building was a bustling commercial
street of stores and outdoor stalls. Merchandise fluttered in the
wind and rotted on the tables. Produce and livestock, fruits and
herbs, textiles, even stone art and furniture. And people. Everything was so weird, so—alien. But most of all, the people made
Bree halt and stare.

All shapes and colors. And color didn't mean race, as she
was used to hearing in the Caves. It meant level of rust. And
shape meant depth of corrosion. These people were not in
the shape of humans anymore. Most of them were just lumps
of flesh with excrescences. Many had taken fantastic shapes.
Dreams or Metas, as they were called here, and Nightmares in
evolution. The corrosion's metamorphosis. Alex had been fascinated by it and had tried to decode it. She really had to read his
notes to see how far he'd dug. He'd been right—Geo needed this
science on metamorphosis if he was to knowledgeably navigate
this world. But this—this was no longer her world. This was no
longer humans' world. This was an alien world. The only thing
they had in common was their history. Nothing else.

Several Corrosives approached, studying her curiously. As
they were alien-looking to her, with her suit and helmet, she

was probably just as alien to them. Not only that, but the most striking feature for them must be her proportions, her perfectly human form, she realized with horror. That had been a mistake. She shouldn't be out here without a guide and without protection. She was the outsider here and they were the natives. This was their home and she was an invader to them.

Bree stepped back. They followed. More and more Corrosives were staring at her. She turned and walked hastily down the street. She realized that was not a good idea, as they could take it she was afraid and they might attack her because of that. But she was afraid and didn't want to test what would happen if she was too slow.

She turned left down the first street, moving down the road between derelict buildings under the eyes of Corrosives watching her from broken windows. The ones following stopped at the corner, following her with their eyes, standing with their leathery wings, their arthropod mandibles, their chitinous multiple jointed legs, and their corroded stumps.

Rounding the corner, Bree started running. She ran for about two minutes, then she saw an escape. She dropped beneath the street through a smashed concrete wall, plunging onto a subterranean floor. She hid behind a column and waited. There was no sound of following footsteps. She continued waiting. No steps, no shouts, no mob following the new Frankenstein monster. She appeared to be safe. For now.

It wasn't as dark as it was supposed to be in a subterranean space. There were a few small windows at street level, allowing the outside light to spread its festering green under the street. The subterranean floor was littered with garbage. Mostly parts of former cars. What the Corrosives didn't need, they'd left behind. She couldn't stay here. This was a...cemetery. Of a dead world.

Bree climbed back up onto the street. It was empty, as it was on the southern outskirts of the city, along the train tracks. Where the cannibals lived, if she remembered correctly what Geo had told them. At the time, everything seemed like chapters from a fantasy novel, meant to impress them. Geo was one of the most well-read young men in the Caves. And she'd thought he'd just been messing with them, trying to show off. But now, being here, she could see that everything was true. Geo had told them the story of his life in a light tone, laughing and joking, and letting them believe he was messing with them. How had he done it? Alone, unprotected, all by himself. He'd known he was the only one here. When life hit hard, he couldn't turn to them and cry, or ask for help. He had to stand back up and survive. How had he done it?

Where to now? In front of her she could see the ruins of the tall buildings of the city. All of it home to Corrosives. Behind her, the King Rat Temple, with its Fields of Rats keeping the Corrosives away. She would have to skirt the market's edge for about two blocks. But it was the only way back. And if she couldn't go through that, how was she supposed to delve even deeper into the city?

She inhaled deeply, preparing to run. Closed her eyes. Why? Why run? They followed her, but didn't seem intent on attacking her. They were probably used to seeing the same protective suit when seeing Geo. She probably wasn't completely alien. She walked back the way she came.

The market had returned to its usual hustling activity. Corrosives were trading, eating, drinking. Like a normal market scene she'd seen in movies. One of them, by the look of his garments well-off, nodded to her. Familiar, friendly. She nodded back. People turned and looked. Curious. Not threatening. She nodded to them and they nodded back. Bree felt a knot of nerves slipping down from her chest, releasing the adrenaline. She smiled with relief.

Moving without fear brought out the sour smell of her sweat. She imagined, if she were to walk unhindered by her protective suit through this market, what smells could she perceive. The sweat, pheromones, and spices of the surrounding biomass. That would be something. And then she felt alone again. If she was to take off her helmet, she'd be dead in a matter of hours. They called it humidity. But as she'd seen in the laboratory, the air in the world right now was meant to help the Corrosives survive, not her kind. Not regular humans. The air was so dense that it was like she was walking through soup. If she were to breathe that in, she'd fill her lungs with gelled water and drown. The same humidity helped the Corrosives keep their bodies from petrifying too fast, like marine sponges taken out of the water. But it brought them corrosion. It was all a bargain with Nature. She gave them life and took their longevity. It was a balance.

"There he is! There's the spy!"

Bree turned and saw a Corrosive dressed in some sort of armor. He was pointing at her. People turned and looked at her, doubt in their eyes. Shit! They thought she was Geo, because they wore the same kind of envirosuit.

"Get him! He's right there! Get him!" Armored soldiers detached themselves from the shadows and ran toward her.

26.
Alex's Spear

The door was unlocked and opened. A guard entered with a tray and placed it on the table. He'd brought a glass water and a bowl of porridge, or whatever passed as porridge for Corrosives. The water was unclear and had that subtle viscosity of boiled gelled water.

"Hardly a meal for an ambassador, is it?" said Geo.

The guard retreated as if he hadn't heard him. As if Geo didn't exist. Of course, it wasn't the guard's fault. He got orders. The door closed and was locked. Ha! Boris was making sure he didn't leave before he could give his answer. So, protected guest, or prisoner?

Somehow, after his talk with the prince, Geo had felt better. Although the entire situation reeked to high heaven, the fact that the mayor hadn't yet marched against the Woodmans made everything seemed better. Of course it wasn't better—he still had to choose between two deaths and if he chose the wrong one, his clan would still be attacked. *And that's how the subconscious works,* he thought and smiled.

Boris had sent him gelled water and food prepared with gelled water, although he knew Geo didn't need sustenance as long as he wore the suit. Geo eating and drinking it meant he'd taken up the prince's offer.

So, what were his choices? Mathematically speaking, the first equation was to try and pick the lock, incapacitate the guard, and run away. There was a 50 percent chance he'd make it outside the building. Straight to the Rat King Temple, pick—oh shit, Bree. She'd have to be there. But for how long? If he didn't return soon, she'd probably venture out, looking for him. Or maybe try to return home. But that was only wishful thinking. He'd been away for half a day and she was all alone in this strange world. Yet, he couldn't tell Boris. He had to keep Bree secret. An absolute secret. And rely on her beautiful mind. Rely on the fact that she was smart enough to find a way to survive.

So, in the first equation, he'd go to the temple, get Bree, and go home. Prepare for war. This time against the mayor and the prince. He'd explain to the council what he'd done and why, and the council…would crucify him. Especially Rumi. And they would find out about Alex…

Something nagged him about Alex's death. Of course it did—his brother had just died; how was he supposed to just forget it and—no, this wasn't healthy. He needed to think and decide, damn it!

Second equation—he'd wait for the deadline, say no to Boris to his face and again, go to the temple, get Bree, and go home. The problem here was that deep down, Geo knew that Boris wouldn't just let him go. He'd make a show of releasing him, and then Geo was sure that the Blue warriors would just wait for him in front of the Golden Tower door. He didn't have any proof that Boris had a hand in this, but the trap set for them in the mayor's bunker was too obvious.

And the third equation—he'd accept Boris's offer. He'd drink the gelled water, swear loyalty, watch the prince kill the mayor, and become the Silkers' hyalophora. Happy ending. Everybody goes home and lives happily ever after. Yeah, right. So many unknowns in this scenario. What would ensure that after eliminating the mayor, Boris wouldn't go against the Woodmans himself? And what could Geo do in that situation, assuming he was not Geo anymore because he'd gone through the Water Passage Ritual.

Three main equations in a system. Each were only the begin-

ning, presenting different variants to the situation. Each reeked
of rotten choices. And Bree was still alone, and Alex's head
was still impaled in the Front Square. His brother's head—this
seemed absurd and surreal. The worst nightmare had come to
pass and he couldn't do anything to make it right. To return it to
a previous moment. He saw the moment—the spear penetrating
Alex's chest and impaling him to the floor. Geo shuddered. He
fought for breath.

He rose and looked around, panting with effort and pain. He
leaned against the wall and squeezed his eyes shut. The spear
had burst forth from the corridor's darkness and went straight
through Alex as through he were a mud doll. Their suits were
made to withstand bullets traveling at a velocity far superior to
that of a spear, and yet—

What the fuck had happened back there?

"Get him!"

Bree turned and ran. People watched her, startled. Heavy
footsteps behind her told her that the Blue warriors were following her. At speed. And by the sound of it, she realized, dressed
in this suit, she was slower than them. She wouldn't last long.
She'd be caught and killed. Like Alex.

At the end of the building, a Corrosive was signaling her, inviting her in. Without thinking, she dove into his shop. He closed
the door behind her and locked it, then barred it by pushing a
metal rod through two rings on either side of the door. He then
turned and smiled at her.

His face looked like a sand crater with two sad, sunken eyes
and a mouth stretching almost from ear to ear as the corrosion
had expanded and he'd rubbed it away. "You're not him," he
said. "But, you must be of the same clan. Come, we must hurry."

The door made an awful noise as the Blue soldiers tried to
open it. They began thumping on it forcefully. It would eventually give way.

Bree followed her savior inside the building. They passed
through several rooms and finally passed through a door out

into a huge hall. It was enveloped in darkness and covered with dust. But she could still distinguish the tall murals under the grime, the hanging candelabra and the marble that made the floor. This had been an important building back in the day, in pre-corrosion times.

They crossed the grand hall and he slipped through a hidden door secreted in a wall. She went through and they were now inside a smaller room full of equipment. Antiquated, dusty, dead. But still, every wall was covered in screens, and in front of them keyboards and panels filled with buttons. A surveillance room, quite similar to what she'd seen employed for security in the Cave.

The Corrosive went to the back of this room and opened another door onto a corridor. They were inside the guts of the big building towering over the Corrosives' market. At the end of the corridor he opened a heavy metal door, looked outside, then nodded, satisfied. "You can go now. You're safe."

"That was your store. They know now," Bree said, her voice trembling.

"I must take everything from the store and move into a new location. Plenty of space in the city."

"Thank you! You risked your life for me."

"This is nothing. Geo did the same for me and my friends. Many times. My friend's son is alive today because of him."

Bree swallowed the knot in her throat. Geo had saved this man. There were Corrosives that would help them, the outsiders, against their own government. "My name is Bree," she said.

"I'm Stev. But now hurry—you must go." He pushed her out the door.

She nodded. "Thank you!" She turned and ran.

Geo knocked on the door. On the other side, the guard unlocked the door and opened it to look at him questioningly.

"Call the prince. I have an answer for him."

The man left without even closing the door. Geo could just walk away now. He could walk away without attacking Boris's men and turning the prince from an ally into an enemy. But the world wasn't that simple. He had to act the ambassador and put his clan's interests first. Even if someone like Bree's grandfather wouldn't see it that way.

Boris arrived followed by his own personal Hyalo guard. He was dressed in his finest silks and carried a glass of water in his left hand. His right hand—covered completely, as always, with black leather—was in a huge fist. It looked freakishly big for his slim body.

Geo picked up the glass of gelled water from the table and raised it in a salute to Boris. The prince raised his own glass, grinned, and they both drank the water.

"Welcome home, Geo," said Boris.

He signaled his guard to come forward. "Tell Actias Luna Commander I need two of his warriors to join me for a mission." The Hyalo guard bowed and left.

"I need to be there with you," said Geo.

"Of course, my friend. You'll be there and witness the mayor's demise. We both need to be there to be part of the regime change. Tonight, we'll make history."

"And as promised, you will dispatch the tyrant," said Geo.

Boris stared at him for a couple of seconds. Then his grin widened. "I'm always hands-on, Geo. I will make history and you'll be my witness. Then we're going to the swearing ceremony and you'll swear you and your clan's fealty to me, in front of the entire court."

"Sounds like a plan, my prince."

27.
The Beauty and Horror

The mayor's bunker had been cleaned up and repairs of what the Night Hunter had damaged were in full process. The damages were extensive and so were the repairs. The mayor had taken the opportunity to enlarge the structure and even begin some decoration of the foyer.

Dozens of torches lit the foyer. Geo stopped a step behind Boris. The princely honor guard of Hyalo Warriors arrayed themselves behind him. The mayor stood opposite them, with Silver Star next to him, his helmet obscuring his face, as always. His elite squad was lined up along a wall to the mayor's right.

Silver Star held Alex's head impaled on a rusty metallic rod between him and the mayor. Geo looked down from the wide, sightless eyes, gaping mouth, and blood-matted hair and struggled to keep standing and not drop on his knees right there and then. He'd never felt so much pain and hatred in his life. Somehow, he hadn't felt hatred for the mayor, who'd been an abstract figure for him until now, but for the brute guarding the mayor. The one who'd tricked Geo into going back home so he could track him. He'd started all this. The tall, muscular, rugged Silver Star, hiding like Geo under his helmet. Although Geo could sense the grin behind the metallic plate, and see the cockiness in his posture. How Geo wanted to see justice done to him! He would love to personally take off Star's helmet and gouge out his eyes after Boris was done with the mayor. He was sure the prince would allow Geo this small reward.

"Always a pleasure, Your Grace." The mayor's voice was high and pretentious.

"Likewise, Mr. Mayor," said Boris.

"I see that you brought me the perpetrator." The mayor pointed to Geo.

"That depends on our negotiation," said Boris, chuckling.

Geo stared at the floor, trying to not show too much of his struggle in his posture. He was 99 percent sure Boris was playing a part, talking about negotiations, and that eventually he'd keep his promise to Geo. Yet, there was always that one percent.

"Do you know who this character is?" The mayor asked, pointing to Alex's head.

Geo stared at the man in disbelief. Was this some sort of sick game?

"Oh, my dear Mayor. That is Alex Woodman's head. The heir of the Woodman Clan. You just declared war on them."

"Oh, fuck!"

"Yeah, that's what happens when you kill a clan's heir."

"Why was this Alex Woodman in my bunker?"

"You know how young people are," said Boris, grinning.

Geo felt like he was in a surreal world. Nothing made sense. This dialogue was not what he'd imagined. Plus it didn't have any connection with what had recently happened.

"I'm not sure I follow. I was told that the Woodman ambassador had attacked my bunker and I offered a substantial reward for bringing him to me. I had no idea that the ambassador was joined by the heir of his clan. Can the ambassador offer some clarification?"

"That heir was my brother!" Geo yelled at the mayor.

"What!"

"And we were here to talk to you about your ultimatum."

"What ultimatum?"

"Silver!" said Boris and nodded to Silver Star.

The mayor's captain pivoted on his right foot, raising the rod with the impaled head, obviously intending to use it as a weapon against his master. The mayor stepped back and at the same time, a detachment of thirty crossbowmen stepped out from the walls and pointed their lethal weapons at everyone, Silver Star and his squad included.

"I suspected foul play, Your Grace, and I knew that Silver works for you. I've known it for a while. So now we can truly start our negotiations." The mayor's voice had climbed even higher. He sounded like an excited child.

"The beauty and the horror," enunciated Boris.

The mayor looked at the prince as if he were mad. "What?"

But Geo observed that Silver Star, his squad, and the Hyalo Warriors dropped to the ground as if on cue. He dropped too as Boris took the glove from his right hand. Everyone on the ground covered their heads. Geo copied them.

Then silence. No one spoke for a while. Not the mayor, not the prince. Utter silence.

"We're done here," Geo heard Boris say, cheerful and re-laxed.

Geo uncovered his head and looked around. Everyone was rising. Boris extended his hand and he took it. "What just—"

The mayor was frozen in mid-turn, his face twisted in hor-ror. His skin looked glassy. The crossbowmen behind him were in similar positions—unmoving, silent, all life gone from their faces.

Silver Star hit the mayor with the metal rod. Alex's head went through the mayor's torso and completed a half rotation, pulverizing the unmoving body into billions of tiny fragments, as if it had been a glass statue. The body of a living man, a min-ute ago flesh and bones, had been turned into—glass. Fragile, lifeless glass. What could do that?

And Silver Star was the one delivering justice for Geo with the head of Alex. With the head of his victim. The double sword of Boris's promise.

The row of crossbowmen stood like statues, awaiting their own demise at the hands of Silver's squad. Geo shuddered.

The dining hall-turned-throne room felt even more cavernous, now that it was not festively arranged for official dinners,
nor so densely populated. Boris sat on his wooden throne at the
far end of the space. He was dressed splendidly in full regalia.
He even had a scepter in his left hand, a thing that Geo hadn't
noticed before. It looked vaguely like a bouquet—moss, leaves,
and flowers—and quite out of place in the somber throne room.
And his right hand was again gloved, carefully wrapped in gold
and black leather. Lady Y was still on a chair at his right, enjoying the main stage. Her time as princess of the week would end
in two days.

Boris's court sat around the throne on regular chairs. Commanders, bureaucrats, warriors, and nobles, all sinister and
monstrous figures. Even the princely wives, covered almost
entirely in fine water silks, waited in his shadow, tools ready to
be used by the prince's left hand. The Silkers' Wasp sat closest to
the throne among the courtiers. He stared at Geo with a hungry
expression.

Lady L—Lena—was the only one standing, two steps to the
right of the throne. Her face unmasked, her lips quivering, her
porcelain skin shining in the torchlight.

Geo kept his face blank. He couldn't allow the courtiers, or
Boris, for that matter, to see his feelings. To see his torment and
horror. He advanced to the throne and bowed. Turned to Lady
Y and bowed again. Raising his head, he noticed a figure in the
shadows, right next to the dais. He instantly recognized Silver
Star, leaning against the wall and petting two huge mastiffs with
black, distorted bodies and immense heads on thick and muscular necks. Their bloodshot eyes focused on Geo's every move,
their tongues lolling from slavering mouths garnished with
sharp fangs.

"Mr. Ambassador," said Boris, inviting him to come closer to
the dais.

"Your Grace," said Geo, fighting to control the tremor in his
voice.

"I have an announcement for everyone to hear. Today we
celebrate the Woodman ambassador's decision to join the Silkers

Court. He will become the Silkers' Hyalophora in two days' time."

"Hear, hear!" shouted the men.

"Drinks for everybody!" said the prince.

Servants entered the hall with trays filled with glasses. Other servants followed with bottles of wine. Dandelion wine, by the look of it. Geo shook free of his torpor, surprised that, given the present situation, he still could think of the kind of wine and other such frivolous stuff.

The prince rose and everyone followed suit. The princesses received smaller glasses that the servants filled with water. The men gathered around the prince and raised their glasses, filled with the golden liquid.

"To the Woodman Ambassador!" said Boris.

"Hail!" They tapped their glasses against their neighbor's and drank.

"To the new Hyalophora—may his service be long and successful!"

"Hail!"

"To the eternal reign of the Silkers!"

"Hail!"

"To Prince Boris!" shouted Geo and everyone joined him.

"My friend," said Boris, approaching him.

"Your Grace."

"How do you feel?"

"Confident."

"Good. That's what I want to hear. But how do you feel, really?"

Geo measured the prince and decided what to do. He'd already promised, he was in Boris's power, his brother was dead, and his brother's fiancé was all alone in a savage world. What else could go wrong? So, the math dictated that he share some truth, if not the whole truth.

"Angry, frustrated, in mourning."

"As expected," said Boris and shook his head. His eyes reflected Geo's feelings. Sadness and compassion shone in them.

How did he do this? wondered Geo.

The prince took another glass of wine from a tray and pushed it into Geo's hand. He signaled Lena to come over.

"My friend, I want you to process all these feelings and mourn as expected. I also want you to put your affairs in order before committing to the new position in my court. That's why I gave you two days before the ritual. When you return to the court, you'll no longer be the Woodman Ambassador, but my liege with them." Geo nodded silently. The prince grinned. "And for these two days, Lady L will still be your companion in my court. So, my friend, please grieve and prepare."

28.
Wamo

The Games Hall had been a storage facility before the corrosion. That's how Jon figured it. Because it was huge, filled with empty shelves, and completely devoid of any decoration. Simply a utilitarian space used to satisfy the hundreds of thousands of customers from the time before. When people were like grass blades, filling the world to its brim. Before the Black Rain wiped out three quarters of the global population, and the subsequent famine and pandemics had taken care of half of the survivors. And then lots of the remaining survivors hadn't actually adapted well enough to the ecological transformations triggered by the gelled water.

Jon sighed and took a seat on the top row of benches. He'd always liked watching matches of Wamo. Even in the beginning, when it had seemed so crude and brutal. But he guessed that gelled water changed people in the most intimate ways. Not only their bodies, but their minds as well. They were certainly different from what they'd been before. They just didn't know it anymore.

People were the product of their environment. Blue eyes or brown eyes, white or black skin, peaceful or warlike, matriarchal or patriarchal. All traits were triggered by the world in which people lived. The Neolithic Cucuteni matriarchal society evolved in a peaceful and bountiful Europe. They were great artists and engineers and knew absolutely nothing of war. When the Indo-Europeans flooded Europe with their warmongering habits, they practically wiped out the Cucuteni and established a patriarchal society. Environment forged people into a balanced, but static society. When in contact with *others* and with *otherness*, adaptability was not environmental anymore, but cultural.

Roars erupted from the watching public. The game of Wamo was afoot. The two teams faced each other from the distant edges of the playing area. Each defended a gate into the opposite bordering walls. They were called the *hungry mouths*. Because behind the walls were heaps of swarming sewerers baited there with rats' blood and organs. Once enough of them had arrived at the mouths, they were sprinkled with paint. The two colors always played were red and green. The Red Team would paint their sewerers in red and the Green Team in green. At the beginning of the game, the red sewerers were behind the red gate. But as the game advanced and the commotion and the smell of blood brought the sewerers to a frenzy, they moved all around and under the playing area.

There were holes in the floor through which a sewerer could insert their hand and grab an ankle or a foot. There were gaps in the mouths' bars through which a sewerer could penetrate inside the game area and attack the savory morsels that the players were. The male sewerers were big and strong. Stronger than normal people. Female sewerers were lithe and fast. Faster than normal people. Faster and rapacious. They could sever a jugular or an artery with their claws in a fraction of a second. When they had created the sewerers, the Greens had thought they needed to give them some advantage over the nasty and hungry monstrous creatures of the underground below the city. They hadn't thought they'd ever lose control over them. But as the transition from the Green to the Blues had been swift and bloody, the knowledge had been lost and now the sewerers were their own people. Useful as ever for the smooth functioning of the sewage system of the city, but independent and ferocious nonetheless.

On the mouths' walls there were seven baskets, high above the reach of anyone. One would need a strong arm and perfect aim to throw anything inside a basket. Each team had six players, two of which were called *throwers*. They were supposed to mark each basket. Two players were *backenders*, responsible for defending their sewerers. And two were *severers*. They were responsible for providing the throwers with severed sewerers' heads to throw into the baskets. Fill the seven baskets with seven heads and you'd win the game.

The game had been invented by a former mayor of Torono. They'd needed a solution for the worrisome growth in the population of sewerers. Initially he'd tried a hunting season, but that brought too severe a cull of them and the city had suffered. Eventually, that brilliant mayor had thought of a solution that provided a bonus—periodical entertainment for the masses and the necessary number of sewerers culled.

Jon's sons, Mic and Ton, were both playing for the Green Team. They had been playing professionally for a few years now. Quite skillfully, Jon thought, although they were not as talented as others on the Silkers' team. They were the real killers. They were in for the long game. His sons probably had a couple more years of playing, then they'd need to retire before they became too slow or too careful for the game. Wamo was a game of speed, perfect reflexes, and unwavering ferociousness. Something that warriors like the Silkers cultivated, while the sons of a shopkeeper could only maintain it in their youth.

The Green Team was the market team and it played against the Red Team, which was the Gatherers team. This was a game of pride. One guild against another. When clans played against each other it was a game of territory. But right then, that was the friendliest game one could hope to watch.

The Reds attacked. The Green backenders controlled their mouth. The Green severers tried to interfere in the Red advance, but could only delay them for a couple of seconds. The Red throwers slammed into the Green backenders while their severers passed the Red's defense line and jumped on the Green mouth's bars, blades in hand. Several sewerers grabbed at them, pulling them onto the bars, closer to their hungry mouths. One of the severers slashed panicky at the hands keeping him against the bars, then fell backward. There was a wet portion on his belly. Clothes in tatters, red spot expanding, damaged flesh exposed, he grimaced in pain and stayed down. But his team-mate howled savagely as he jumped down from the gate's bars and raised a severed sewerer's head covered in black paint in triumph.

The Green hurried toward the victorious Red. With one Red down, their team was playing now with five players. The game concentrated in the center of the playing field, as the Reds passed the head from one to the other, trying to avoid being caught by the Greens. Suddenly, a desperate scream stopped everyone in their tracks. The entire Game Hall looked down to the Green mouth. The downed Red player had been caught by two sewerers near the first hole in the floor. He was trying to get away, but didn't have the necessary strength to escape, and the sewerers were pulling him slowly but surely over the hole's edge toward their fangs. By the look of the pulling arms, they were two female sewerers. But the long and muscular arm of a male shot out of the hole and thrust his claws deep into the Red player's chest, making him scream in despair and pain.

Ton ran back to the Green part of the field. For several long seconds no one else followed. Then, the Red severer threw the bloody head to one of his throwers and started running back, and everyone else followed suit.

The Red player had managed to turn and keep his head out of the hole, but the lower part of his body was already inside. Ton jumped and his blade sliced through the clawed arm har-pooning the Red player in the chest. He cut it clean with only one slicing move. Then he threw the blade away and grabbed the Red player under his armpits and began pulling him back up onto the field. When all the other players grabbed him it was an easy job to bring him back. The entire Games Hall roared in continuous excitement.

The Red player's legs were bloody with bites. They pulled him out of the field and onto a bench, in the arms of the carrier. The carrier would take him into the cold room, give him a sed-ative, and put him on ice to help keep the rot away for a longer period, giving him a chance to work through the sleep thresholds and rebuild his legs. Such was the life of a Wamo player.

Jon felt the excitement taking over. Rationally, he still wondered how this grotesquerie could excite him. But on a visceral level, his mind was now flooded with adrenaline and endorphins and he felt rejuvenated. They were the children of the corrosion and that was how they functioned.

"Good game, Jon?"

Stev's kind voice was a total contrast to the savagery taking place in the field. Jon smiled and relaxed. "Pretty good. One Red out in a bloodbath."

"In the first round!" wondered Stev.

"I'm hungry," said Jon. "Do you have any bread?"

Stev grinned like a little boy and took from one of his pockets a dark brown bun. "Glazed seeded mush."

That was his specialty. He was the only baker to have that and while his competition had tried to replicate it, no one had succeeded so far. Jon salivated instantly. The crunchy exterior hiding the gooey dough at its core was one delicacy that gave Jon's life meaning. Or so announced loudly at every party, to the happiness of Stev and his family.

"Oh Stev, you divine baker."

"I saw something, Jon," said Stev and looked furtively around.

"No one can hear us here. Everyone's screaming and caught up in the game."

"I heard that the mayor is dead."

Jon stared at the playing field and didn't say anything. That was serious. If the mayor was dead, could they assume that the Blues' reign was over? Was this the moment to move?

"And…" Stev hesitated.

What could be more important than the mayor being dead? Probably who killed him. That would be an indication of what direction the power would flow.

"And I…"

Uh-oh. That sounded personal. Stev had involved himself in something.

"What did you do, Stev?"

"I I I... I thought it was Geo, but it wasn't him."

"Geo is in the prince's care now. What are you talking about?"

"S S S Silver Star's men were hunting somebody in a suit like Geo's. Identical."

Jon stared at his apprentice. The man was dead serious and scared.

"I thought it was G G Geo and as we'd discussed, that we should always help him because we trust him, I helped him escape. But it wasn't Geo."

Jon kept silent. His mind was racing, trying to recall everything he'd discussed with Geo, their plans to help the people of Torono. Everything he knew of the politics in the city. Could this other man from Geo's clan be the mayor's killer? If that was true, they were in deep trouble. Especially with Stev helping the assassin.

"It was a Liquid woman. Bree. She, she, she said her name is Bree."

"Did she kill the mayor, you think?"

"No!" Stev was visibly puzzled by this assumption.

Jon breathed easier. They were not involved in any conspiracy to kill the head of the government. And yet. And yet, there was another one from Geo's clan in the city and he hadn't known. Either this second liquid had been here a while, but no one had noticed and Geo had hid her, or she was a recent arrival and Geo didn't know about her or hadn't had the chance to introduce her to Jon, because Geo had been through so much lately too.

Then everything clicked into place. The "spy," as Silver Star had called the dead one, was a Liquid as well, and Silver had set everything up so that one Liquid would torture and kill the other one. But probably, the risen dead hadn't come alone.

Jon sighed. Everything had suddenly become very complicated and dangerous. So many things had happened so fast, it was very difficult to distinguish one from the other and give them meaning.

"Stev," said Jon.

"Yes."

"The woman is our secret. You hear me?"

"Yes, J J Jon."

"No one and I mean *no one* must hear that a Liquid woman wanders our streets. We need to keep it a secret until we find out more about her."

"Do we still trust Geo?" asked Stev. He wore the same expression he did when he thought he was smart and played a good hand.

"For now, Stev. For now, he's still our ally."

"I'd be curious to find out who the liquid woman is."

"That should be our priority."

In the game, the Reds were down to four players, but led with one head. Three of his baskets held heads, while only two of the Greens' baskets were filled. His boys were not in top form. He'd have to train them more. Perhaps some new strategy. If they were so weak against the Gatherers, what would they do against the Blues? For the next scheduled match was Market against Blues. And that would not be a peaceful game like this one.

29.
Grief

Geo exhaled a few times and dropped down onto the bed, exhausted but happy. Lena rolled over and went straight to the washbowl in the corner. It was always filled with clean, boiled gelled water, a lump of soap and a towel on the side. She began washing vigorously, from under the mask all the way down to her feet, with practiced movements, quick and thorough. He watched her and discovered for the first time that this habit of hers bothered him. It had always bothered him, but his mind had always been somewhere else, not focused enough to question and dissect. But now, with everything that had happened, he couldn't stop thinking of only the bad things. The worst. And right now, the worst was that Lena was his for two more nights only. After which, she'd be forbidden to him forever.

"Do I stink?" he asked and rose on the bed, arranging both pillows under his back to prop him up.

"Why would you say that, Mr. Ambassador?"

"You're always *running* to the washbowl to clean up after me."

"Maybe you don't know, being so young, but I have to make sure you don't leave me pregnant."

"By washing your chest?"

Lena stopped, looked down at the water, and sighed. She picked up the towel and dried herself. "I would rather not talk about this, if Mr. Ambassador is kind enough. It's only about my past, no connection whatsoever with Mr. Ambassador."

Geo got up and dressed. For the first time he'd undressed completely. Any precaution was futile, now that he'd drunk the gelled water. Almost twenty-four hours had passed since that first glass, followed by several others. There was no turning back now. He was a Corrosive now. Like the rest of them. Like Lena.

"I'm sorry, Lena. I didn't mean to upset you."

"No worries, Mr. Ambassador. Everyone has their own little birds chirping away in their brains. Sooner or later we all have to confront our birdies."

"We say demons…"

"Yeah, I know. I prefer birdies."

Geo walked to the table. The boy servicing their room had left a tray of dry pastries and a bottle of dandelion wine. Same vintage as the one served at the party earlier. Average wine. Not bad, but not superior. Right on the level of Geo's deserved role and importance. No longer the Woodman Ambassador, but the Silkers' liaison with the Woodmans. No longer a Woodman, but a Silker. Boris had turned everything 180 degrees on Geo, in a matter of hours.

He picked up a pastry. It looked similar to what he knew as Greek pastries in the Cave, yet he bet they had nothing else in common. Like the Silkers and the Woodmans. No, actually they were very much alike. They were all full of ambition and passion. All wanted the same things—for their clan and their family to survive, and to survive better than their neighbors. All shared feelings as old as humanity.

"What is it, Mr. Ambassador?"

"Could you call me by name tonight, please, Lena?"

Geo walked to the door. He opened it and startled. One of the infernal mastiffs from the party was guarding his door. The dog watched Geo with its small, bloodshot eyes. Its muzzle was slightly open and saliva dripped to the floor.

"I thought you liked it when we call each other by our titles."

"What's this doing here?" said Geo, opening the door wide so Lena could see it.

"I don't know. It is peculiar indeed."

The mastiff entered the room slowly, probably taking the opening of the door as an invitation.

"Is this supposed to happen?" asked Geo.

"Never seen one wandering the palace without a warrior. So no, I think this isn't supposed to happen. I'll call the guards."

"No, wait." Geo stopped her, closed the door, and sat on a chair, pulling at the dog's leash to bring it closer.

A silver chain was wrapped tight around its thick neck. Geo felt along the chain and found it—a silver cross. The same one he'd seen only six days ago. The day of the Water Passage Ritual. "What's this doing here?" he said.

"I don't know what that is, Geo."

"This is the cross that young boy was wearing the day we met."

"What young boy?"

"The one serving me. Something with L—Lukas. That's it, Lukas. He was a Pupa and was preparing for his Water Passage."

"Oh, I see."

"What, Lena? What do you see?"

"Lukas…uhm. This will be hard. I thought you knew."

"Obviously, I don't know."

"The Water Passage is a very difficult process. Only half of those trying succeed. Only the best minds with the strongest wills. You're going through one of these two days from now and you should've known and prepared. Instead of spending your time with me, you should prepare for the ritual."

"You avoided answering."

"Because it's not my job to prepare you."

"And yet, here we are. Just the two of us and since nobody else gives a shit about my fate, I'd really like to know what's going on."

"I will put you in contact with a teacher."

"I don't want a teacher. I want you."

"If you fail because I—"

"I won't fail. Boris promised me that there's no chance in hell that I could fail."

"Oh. I see."

"Oh, there's more now. I can see that. I'm in over my head, is that it?"

"Let's start with something simple—this dog is Lukas. Or was Lukas. And now it is something else."

Bree put down Alex's notebook. He'd always been a man's man. The leader type, energetic, athletic, loved rough sports. She'd never given him much credit for his scientific prowess. Yes, he'd taken his exams with good marks, but had never shown any inclination for research. He hadn't seemed patient enough, or interested enough. Yet this notebook showed her a different Alex. A better version that she hadn't had the chance to know. Tears rolled down her face. She didn't know why she felt so guilty for his death. He'd convinced her to come, not the other way around. If anything, she'd tempered his enthusiasm a bit. Not enough, though…

She picked up the notebook and opened it again to the first page: *The gelled water's influence on the human psyche and physical body is a matter of great controversy.* When she first read that statement, she'd laughed. It seemed like a good joke, considering that the number of scientists in the Cave was twenty-three. There was no chance of a "great controversy" on a single subject between twenty-three scientists from twelve different fields. A few pages later she'd discovered what he'd really meant and that had changed greatly her perspective on what or who Alex was.

The Sudbury Water Laboratories have generated two theories on this subject. All theoretically, mind you, and based on the scientific understanding we had at the moment the Black Rain happened. Our colleagues from Frankfurt have a different theory (that would be the third one) based on present practical research. They had managed to study three live specimens before their communication went silent.

The fact that there were other science centers out there still doing research and trying to pursue scientific goals didn't surprise her. But that some and not *all* Cave scientists were in touch with these labs and the communication was kept secret from their own colleagues, like her—she was supposed to be their leading physicist for god's sake! How many of the twenty-three scientists in the Cave knew of these communications? Why wasn't she inside the circle of trust? Why was Alex? Because he'd been a Woodman. That's why.

She closed the notebook, keeping a finger in it to mark the page she was on. On the cover there was a red stamp—*Top Secret*. She'd thought it was only Alex's sense of humor. But now she could see the truth behind it. The stamp was real, not a drawing. The Cave labs actually had a top-secret stamp! And somehow, this wasn't Woodman the Elder's style. Her grandfather, on the other hand, was the chief of the laboratories. This secret business had his stink all over it. But for him to trust Alex before his own grandchild was what really hurt. And Alex was supposed to be her fiancé and—god damn it! That's why her grandfather pushed Alex so hard in front of the council and wanted to remove Geo. That's why Woodman the Elder had kept Alex home and sent Geo to the Exterior instead.

This controversy is born of the belief that these monsters are created from human bodies by the gelled water. This is almost a scientific heresy. Much like it was with the possibility of the existence of the gel state for water.

Bree closed her eyes and remembered Woodman the Elder's exposition on corrosion—or Professor Woodman, as they called him back then, in university. The university amphitheater had been one of the first structures built in the Cave before the Black Rain. Woodman the Elder had built for the long run, not just for immediate survival.

"My dear colleagues…" Woodman the Elder had treated them as equals from their first day of school. Hearing him speak had made her the scientist she was today.

"My dear colleagues, the Black Rain has put in front of us one of the biggest mysteries humanity has encountered. The Black Rain has brought into our world gelled water on a global scale. Something that the science community had always considered impossible and later on of no importance. If you asked any twentieth century scientists about the four states of water, they'd correct you by stating that there are only three states. In the early twenty-first century, Elmer Fuchs, a physical chemist at Graz University of Technology in Austria, conducted experiments into water properties and had successfully simulated for a whole forty-five minutes what we today call gelled water. Unfortunately for all of us, the experiment was considered of only theoretical importance and therefore not worthy of a budget for future studies. This is the Frankenstein experiment of our times, ladies and gentlemen. One that we will study in depth and try to extract as many secrets from as we can, so we can reach the stage where we'd be able to control it."

The mastiff formerly known as Lukas sat quietly in the room, dripping saliva on the carpet while watching Geo and Lena eat and talk. Seven trays of food, from cold to steaming hot, occupied the center of the table. Geo found himself eating ravenously. He hadn't realized how hungry he was. More than that, he was finally able to taste all of those dishes he'd seen Boris and his people eat and never been allowed to even smell them.

"I—wow, I didn't imagine that—what is this?"

"*Snail a la moule-feuille,*" said Leni.

"Yeah, so I didn't imagine that snails would taste like this. I mean, wow, what a delicious treat!"

Lena laughed and since it was such a rare treat to hear and see her laughing, Geo stared at her. He was not able to see her eyes to know if she was laughing with her eyes too, but he imagined that. He imagined she had emerald eyes with long, luscious lashes. They would go so well with that mouth of hers. For now, he only watched her lips parting and indulged in the sound of her laugh.

She said, her voice still shaking a bit with laughter, "Well, the last part of the name may hide the secret behind its…deliciousness."

"I don't know French, but that sounds acutely gourmet."

"Yes, acutely is the key word here."

Geo rose and held his palms out, shouting, "Oh, oh, oh, I

know—*Nouveau Gourmet!*"

She leaned her head against the table, shaking with laughter.

"Well, my compliments to the chef."

"I think I've never heard that outside a movie," said Lena, breathing heavily.

"What am I going to do without you?" Geo sat back again and took her right hand in his. He rubbed his fingers against her skin. It was so soft and smooth, like nothing had ever touched Lena. No sun, no wind, no water—no corrosion.

"You'll become the hyalophora." Lena nodded and smiled.

"Yes, but without you."

"There will be others in your life then. Just wait."

"I don't want others. I want you."

"You shouldn't talk like that, Mr. Ambassador."

"I shouldn't, shouldn't I?"

He petted the monstrous mastiff: "I'm sorry, my friend. I'm sorry we didn't get a chance to talk more." The beast looked at him from under heavy, wrinkled brows. It sniffed Geo's hand, leaving it wet.

"What if I ask Boris for—"

"No, don't say it." Lena placed her palm on his lips. "Once you say it, you'll think it and it's better that some things remain unspoken."

"Well, I thought that I'd have to think it first to say it."

"Not like that. Thoughts impregnate your brain once they're spoken. And they can materialize afterwards. It's very important that you control your thoughts and never, ever speak something that you don't want to record in your brain."

"But if it's true…"

"You never know what is true and what is not. Just…"

"What?"

"Just don't make it true," she said.

"And yet, I know that I love you."

Lena laughed again, this time bitter and mockingly. Geo shivered when he realized how much her laugh hurt.

"No, Mr. Ambassador, you're just afraid."

"I don't understand."

"You feel alone and need someone on your side. Love can make you feel safe and not alone anymore. But in the end, we're all alone. And you mustn't speak out of fear."

"It's not fear, I know that this world is more beautiful with you in it. You're all the color in the world."

"No, I'm just its stain."

"Why do you speak like that?" said Geo, looking away.

"Because you said the key word here—beautiful. Everything revolving around that word is infatuation. Nothing deep. Nothing else."

"I'm not infatuated with you," Geo said and realized how defensive he sounded. How much like a teenager. Not like the ambassador of his clan talking to the wife of the head of state. The wife of his clan's future king. One of the wives, actually, but it shouldn't matter.

"I'm sorry," he said.

"It's all in the past."

"Good."

"We should prepare you for the ritual. You need to have a very clear mind and a very focused intention."

"There are two things that I hate leaving behind and that clouds my mind right now."

"You need to purge your mind of them."

"I'll have to take a walk soon to deal with one. But the other one is something I have no control over."

"Tell me," said Lena.

"Silver Star killed my brother. He walks with my brother's head impaled on the tip of a spear. He does that to—I don't know, to challenge me?"

"Silver is a very disturbed individual, Mr. Ambassador. Not even His Highness can control him completely."

"I don't know. Silver was His Highness's spy inside the mayor's forces for years. That speaks to his ability to obey and follow through with an order."

"You're right," said Lena. "But there's more to Silver than you know, and he is not your goal. He is so far out of your reach that you should just ignore him. Completely. He doesn't exist."

"As Torono doesn't exist?"

"I'm sorry?"

"I warned His Highness of a future disaster that will fall on his kingdom and told him that he can prevent the utter destruction that will follow, and His Highness doesn't care. As I shouldn't care that Silver just killed my brother in cold blood and now he's parading his head for all to see."

Lena covered his mouth. She stared at him silently. The mastiff rose and put its huge head in Geo's hands. Even with its mouth closed, its fangs still protruded like knives. Geo was startled by this. The teeth seemed utterly ferocious and not exactly like those of a dog, and yet it behaved like a dog, and it looked at him with so much intelligence that he had to wonder if there were thoughts still forming behind those eyes. If its brain had retained any of the man's potential.

The woman rose.

"Lena?"

She turned and exited the room without a word.

30.
The Operation Center

So, bro, in the next pages you'll get to what biochemistry and molecular biology is behind every and any human metamorphosis sparked by the new properties of the gelled water. I hope you remember Grandpa's lectures on gelled water. His theories and research are the stepping stones to understanding the corrosion's changes. But to really control the metamorphosis process, you need to understand what happens in the brain after the gelled water has started its changes of our neurochemistry.

You may sneer at the word "control," but after researching and yes, I'm not ashamed to admit, experimenting on several subjects, we concluded that the metamorphosis is triggered by the subject's own will and depends largely on their mental prowess, strength to focus, and—this will sound like alchemy—it strongly depends on the subject's culture and imagination. Don't close the notebook, read on and you'll understand what I meant.

"Goddammit, Alex!" Bree closed her eyes but they remained dry. She'd grieved enough for her fiancé. A stranger, apparently. She was starting to understand why he'd done most things, but she couldn't comprehend his mistrust in her. She felt that it was probably her grandfather's mistrust in her, as it had been in her mother. But Alex—Alex was supposed to know her better.

And experiments on Corrosives? They were not human anymore, but still conscious beings. Not just damn lab rats. There should be a line one should not cross.

A red revolving light replaced the white light of the operation center. That was a silent alarm. Someone had tripped the alarms. Someone was trespassing into the operation center's safety perimeter. The enemy was inside the—what had Geo called it? The King Rat Temple? So, what about the rats? Weren't they supposed to be the first line of defense?

Bree put the notebook down and looked around for weapons. She still had the firearm Geo had given her. Should she dress in her isolation suit? Dammit, she didn't know the protocol for such a situation. *All right, calm down, it shouldn't be such a difficult task.* She just needed a clear mind and perspective.

So, the refrigeration unit the operation center was in could be locked from inside and should resist any attempts of attack with the primitive weapons the Corrosives employed. Geo had made sure that the unit was fed with air through a system that was difficult to find. So she could lock herself inside and survive for—she looked around and saw the provisions. Well, for some time. She could survive inside for at least a week, if necessary.

Bree sighed in relief and leaned on the table in the corner. No need to use the firearm or confront in any way the Corrosives who had breached the perimeter. She'd only fired a weapon at a living thing once, and that was to save Geo. She didn't know if she could actually harm anyone else, human or Corrosive, if not in a similar situation. Just the thought of any weapon hitting living flesh, leaving behind a wound, triggering the suffering in the eyes of anyone—she retched and had to breathe deeply several times to settle her stomach.

That was it, then—stay put, don't make noises, don't let them know she was in there. Wait for the danger to pass. She sighed. Where was Geo? What had happened to him? Bree recalled Geo surrounded by the warriors in red, being taken away from that death trap of the underground bunker. He'd looked angry and ready to fight, only not against the red warriors. That should be a good sign. He was alive. He must be alive. Bree couldn't imagine living in the city all by herself. That had been a dreadful moment, when she'd realized she didn't know her way back to the Cave. She'd relied on Alex to lead the way here and get back. She hadn't thought even for a second that something would happen to any of them, as if it were one of those summer trips along the subterranean rivers under the Cave. And here she was now—no Alex, no Geo, no way back to the Cave. She wouldn't be able to live like that.

The first lock turned. Bree stood, alert. The second lock turned. Bree saw herself lifting the firearm and pointing it at the door as it opened and she had to fire. Corrosives crowded the entrance and her first bullets did some damage before she was overwhelmed by the attackers.

The third locking mechanism attached to the middle of the door clicked in the normal progression and unlocked the massive door of the refrigeration unit. And Bree realized she was still there, on the floor, with Alex's notebook in her hands. Her defensive actions had happened only in her mind. As the door opened she rose slowly, prepared for what might come.

A suited man stood in the entrance, helmet under arm. Bree sobbed uncontrollably and ran to him. Geo let go of the helmet and received her with open arms. She hugged him and cried into his shoulder, her body shaking. He hugged her back, holding her tight.

"I'm sorry I couldn't come earlier. I wish I could…" Geo said, his cheeks burning.

"I've known you since we were suckling babes, Geo. So, what are you not telling me?" Bree watched him carefully.

The last couple of days must have been so intense, filled with tragedies and discoveries for her, that Geo didn't know if there was anything that could surprise her anymore. And yet… How much could he tell her? He pulled away and paced the room. It wasn't that any of what happened and was going to happen should be kept secret from her. But how much could she take and still be herself? The cheerful, kind Bree he'd known his whole life. On his way back, he'd realized how much he needed her. The real, insightful, brilliant Bree, not a traumatized, depressed version of her. He knew he was selfish, but he really needed someone close in his corner. Someone who cared about him without any strings attached. Someone he could trust completely with his own life and the fate of his clan. That couldn't be anyone else but Bree. Not even Alex had had that place in his life.

"You're scaring me, Geo. What's going on?"

Geo sat down at the table and took Bree's hand in his. He squeezed it. "No, no, don't worry. It's not that…"

"What? Just tell me."

"Remember when I told you that I left the Cave against the council's order?"

"Yeah."

"I did it so I could save the Woodmans. So I could save the Cave."

Bree nodded. Geo smiled and let go of her hand. "Well, an opportunity presented itself and I took it. The Cave is safe. We will rest tonight and tomorrow I'll put you on a train and send you home. You can tell them that the danger is gone."

He could not risk her. He'd decided she'd go back to the Cave and to her own sweet self.

"Gone? What changed?"

"The mayor is dead."

Bree looked at him for a long minute. She stated, deadpan, "You killed him."

"No, although I wish I was the one."

"Then who did?"

"Boris, the Silkers' prince. He killed the mayor and assumed power over Torono. He's now the de facto ruler of the kingdom."

"Then let's go back to the Cave together. You can tell the council what went down."

"I have unfinished business here, Bree. I can't leave."

Bree stood up and paced. She moved toward her suit, but changed her mind. She looked back at Geo, then turned. "What was the price?"

"It doesn't matter now. The price was paid and service rendered. The Cave is secure. And you're going back tomorrow to tell them that."

The room was suddenly smaller to Geo than it had ever felt. Too small for both of them. Too small for all the secrets and plans he'd kept from the council, and Woodman the Elder, and Boris. Lena knew most of his secrets and she'd be taken from him the next day.

Bree dropped onto the mattress and sighed. She propped her back against the wall and smiled at him. "I'm staying."

"No."

"Sorry, I made up my mind."

"It's too dangerous for you. You have to go back."

"It's too dangerous for you too, and yet you've been out here for years. You're not alone anymore. Now you have me."

"*You feel alone and need someone on your side. But in the end, we're all alone.*" Geo could see those plump red lips moving and saying those words. He could not see her eyes. Bree talked with her mouth as much as she talked with her eyes. He realized that he'd always relied on people's eyes to see what they were feeling. If they lied or not. Lady L's eyes had always been hidden. But she'd always helped him. He loved her!

"I don't need anyone," he said and gulped as he heard the uncertainty in his own voice.

"I need you," said Bree quietly.

You feel alone and need someone on your side. But in the end, we're all alone.

31.

Chemistry

The sight of a nervous and commanding Bree was so out of character that Geo just couldn't express his own anger and frustration properly. Somehow the last couple of days had taken so much from him that he was not far from falling into hysterical laughter. That's how comical Bree's outrage looked to him. And yet, he knew she was at her limit too—maybe even farther gone than him. This was his last thread of rational thought and it was telling him he had to preserve Bree at all costs. He had to stop pushing before she stepped over the edge.

Bree scrambled to her feet. "I don't care about saving everybody. All I care about, right now, is saving you!" she almost yelled at him.

"How can you say that?"

"How can I not? You just don't see it!"

"What?"

"If you don't survive, they have no one to care about them. You need to survive first!"

"They have you!" Geo was now standing, shouting face to face with her.

Bree dropped onto one of the chairs. She was breathing hard. She sounded exhausted. "I'm not enough."

"How can you say that?" Geo knelt in front of her and took her hands in his. He searched her eyes.

"You've read Alex's journal. I wasn't enough for him. I wasn't enough for my grandfather. He always tried *to put me in my place*. In the kitchen with my mother. And now I just know it. I've seen you, I know you have a life here, you have people who care about you. People who have replaced us, your friends and family from the Cave."

"Oh, Bree. That's just not true."

"It doesn't matter if you believe it or not. I can see it. But I've decided to stay and in time, who knows, maybe I'll just become enough."

Geo felt tired. He had no energy left to fight her anymore. If she knew how displaced he felt all the time. He was continuously traveling between two worlds, never belonging. He was, as that ancient writer said it, a stranger in a strange land. But she was—he needed her more than ever now and at the same time he feared for her safety every moment she was in the Exterior.

"Now," she said with a big sigh, "I need you to survive this and so does the world. If you want to save everybody, you have to survive. I won't do it alone. I don't have what it takes. I don't care about this world, about the Exterior as you do. I only care about our world, the Cave. But I'll do it together with you. I'll fight for the Exterior as well, if you fight alongside me."

"You realize that I am now a Corrosive. I don't know how this will transform me. If I'll still be me afterwards."

"I'll be here to…observe," she added with a smile. "I'm a scientist. This is our opportunity to document this phenomenon."

"All right." He smiled too. "We'll do it for science."

"That's good. Now, Alex had the closest observation of what's going on during this metamorphosis—"

"From what you've told me, my brother was a real Dr. Mengele."

"Yeah, I understand your reticence. But we don't have the time to indulge in the luxury of ignoring his research and tracing his steps in a more humane manner. Right now, his research is all we have. And this is a matter of life and death with a ticking clock over our heads. So, Alex's studies."

"What's wrong, Geo? Too tired?"

"Thoughts impregnate your brain once they're spoken. And they can materialize afterwards. It's very important you control your thoughts and never, ever speak something that you don't want to record in your brain."

The same red, luscious lips had said that and only now had he begun making the connections. What if Lena loved him? What if she got upset because he'd said words that, as she'd stated, had been recorded in their brains, and later on Boris could—

"Geo?"

"So, what you're saying is that through gelled water, thoughts can…materialize?"

"Not exactly materialize, but gain a certain consistency that would make them permanent in your brain. A reality beyond the physical reality."

"Thoughts impregnate your brain once they're spoken. And they can materialize afterwards. That's what Lady L told me yesterday. I thought it was a figure of speech, but now…"

"Lady L—your guide at Prince Boris's court?"

"Yes."

"Why would she tell you that?"

"What do you mean?"

"Why would she warn you of something that clearly the prince controls? Why would she betray Boris?" Bree leaned forward, getting in his face.

Because she was afraid that with my feelings for her, my brain would betray her when…when I go through the Water Passage Ritual and Boris is manipulating my brain chemicals. Aloud he said, "At the time I thought it was just something to make her sound interesting and mysterious, but now—now I can see…"

"What?" Bree watched him carefully. He could feel her doubt. It was palpable, like sandpaper rubbing on a wood surface. Soft and smooth on one hand, yet abrasive and deadly on the other. How could he sense so much?

"If Alex was correct and a state of extreme pain, like that caused by chopping off my right hand would induce, opens up my mind to external and internal factors that are independent to my will and consciousness, then Boris or some of his people may have the power or the skill to manipulate my brain chemicals in order to make me undergo metamorphosis in whatever way they want."

"Wait, I don't—how did you get from what Alex said to all that?"

"When I was first a guest in the Golden Tower, a boy named Lukas served as my—let's say butler. He wore a very particular cross on a silver chain. It was a Greek Christian cross. Not the usual Latin one more commonly worn at one time."

Bree sat across the table from him. They hadn't slept in more than twenty-four hours, but she didn't show how tired she must be. She seemed electrified by their science session, assimilating as much as possible from the conversation.

"Later on, celebrating the death of the mayor, I saw two mastiffs—no, two chimeras, sort of mastiffs crossed with some-thing else. Something fantastic. They looked like mythical crea-tures, not normal dogs. One of them followed me to my cham-ber. And I discovered the creature was wearing Lukas's cross. That's when Lady L acknowledged that the mastiff was Lukas."

"What?"

"She explained to me that those novices that are too weak to go through the nine thresholds of pain and metamorphosis are manipulated by Boris and turned into beasts that are ferocious and loyal to him."

"Was Lady L with you in your chamber when this beast came?" Bree asked him in a neutral tone.

That's what she's taken from this story? "The important part, which you seem to be oblivious to in your scientific astuteness, is that she actually revealed to me, with that apparently innocent information about a dog, something very important regarding Boris."

"Oh, yeah. No, the scientist has caught that. And yes, that is the most important discovery for us—Lady L has betrayed her prince for you." Bree was deadpan serious.

"What? No, that was not—"

"I'm just messing with you, man!" Bree burst into laughter and punched his shoulder.

"Oh, for a moment I thought I was hallucinating," he said, chuckling.

"Nothing wrong with open-eyed hallucinations after more than twenty-four hours without sleep."

They laughed and laughed as if they'd just heard the best joke ever. Yup, they were reaching their limit for sleeplessness.

"The important thing is that we need to discover how to screen your mind against Boris's manipulation. I'm not so much afraid of what being a Corrosive means as I am of what being a creature created by Boris means." Bree was suddenly serious.

Geo nodded. "That's what I'm afraid of too. I need to do this. I need to become one of them and still keep my mind. I need to be able to continue my work for the Cave and—and for the rest of the world when no one cares about it."

"Get some sleep and I'll continue to study Alex's notebook. When I find what we need, I'll wake you up."

"You have to sleep too."

"I'll sleep after. Right now, all I need is some coffee."

32.
The Death March

Geo pointed to the wall. Another of his signs was there—a four-point star. Bree remembered Geo's list of seven signs. This was the second type of star. The first one had been the three-point star with a circle inside. This one meant—she saw the list clear in her mind—source of light. An electric torch or a gas torch. She followed the direction indicated by the largest points on the star and saw the cracks in the wall paint. There was the hiding place.

Bree was blown away by Geo's extensive network in the city: people, places, resources. She hadn't taken him for the hard-working type. He'd always seemed the dreamer kind, prone to thoughtful speculation and not very practical. Yet here in the big capital of the kingdom, he'd been working like crazy to turn the city into a friendly territory. Or friendlier.

The signs on the walls were actually an innovation of his— shapes carved into concrete or brick walls and planted with rust lichen. The carvings were so deep that the lichens were not going to grow over the edges, thus always displaying the shapes of Geo's seven signs for food and water, light, weapons, friends, hiding places, passages to the underworld, and danger zones. The signs were so discreet that if you didn't look for them, you'd never guess what they were. From a distance they looked like rust traces from a bygone era.

He'd downloaded into her armored containment suit's system a virtual map of Torono he'd created, which he said was 60 percent accurate. That and the knowledge of the signs system would ensure her relative safety in the city while he was away. He'd agreed to keep her there with him, though reluctantly, as he was still reeling from losing his brother. She'd had time to mourn and begin the healing process. Plus, reading Alex's notebook had been an eye-opener for her. She didn't know the Alex that had written in the notebook. Apparently, she hadn't known him and his research at all. And the fact that he'd been part of her grandpa's inner circle, working against Woodman the Elder and everything she'd believed in, had been another decisive factor in speeding her recovery process.

But Geo hadn't had the time to mourn properly. He'd been hit by a chain of events and revelations that had shaken his world view and turned his life around almost 360 degrees. He'd probably put the death of his brother in a drawer in his brain, closed it, and waited for a better time to open the drawer and process the whole thing.

"Now, I'm going to introduce you to a number of friends who would not hesitate to help you if that need arises," said Geo.

"Like the one with the bakery in the market?"

"Holy shit!" He looked at her with awe, something she hadn't seen since they finished university. When they were younger, she'd felt special every time he'd looked at her like that. She didn't know what words of wisdom were causing that awe in him, but it warmed her now in a way that brought tears to her eyes.

"I…" She struggled to say something, but all her willpower went into not hugging him right there.

"You've met Stev! How? I mean, it's one thing to see him in the market and another thing to meet him. Wow! Just wow!"

"Hey, it—" She stopped abruptly and frowned. There was a strange noise, coming closer. She realized she'd heard it for some time, very faintly, but it was growing louder as it got closer.

Geo froze and focused. Suddenly his eyes went wide.

"What's that?" she asked with a feeling of dread.

"That's…that's a mass of people. They, uh, I think it was called a *protest*."

"What?" She couldn't recognize the term in the context he'd placed it.

"It's when a lot of people have something to protest against, I think you can say. Usually against those in power, the rulers. Or so I've read; that was before the Rain."

Bree tried to wrap her head around that. It was a strange concept. She tried to imagine the people in the Cave protesting against the council. How or why? The Exterior was a strange world.

"Never seen one in person. Let's see what it's all about." Geo led the way back to the main street, where the clamor was definitely originating.

Geo stopped at the corner of Market Street and Black Street. He saw the merchants hurriedly gathering their products and closing their stands and shops. Women pulled children from the street inside buildings. He could sense the anxiety rising from the City Market. He'd never felt so intense. Something was wrong with him.

Coming along Main Street, passing the Golden Tower, a procession of hundreds of people walked slowly behind a—Geo's heart stopped. He looked down to the cracked pavement. The crowd was chanting something. He looked to his right, to Bree. She hadn't noticed yet; she was still watching everything with big eyes, her mouth parted slightly—her scientist's curiosity in action. He looked back to his feet, then up again to the crowd. He heard Bree gasp. She'd seen it too.

The crowd followed a headless body as it walked with small but heavy steps down the road. It carried its head tucked under its right arm. It was dressed in Alex's containment suit with the Woodman's logo on its chest. The head was Alex's head. Somehow, his beheaded brother walked. His corpse led a procession of hundreds of Corrosives. They chanted something ominous, like a deeply vibrating *humm*. Geo felt that humming noise vibrating through his body, shaking his organs, almost dislocating the flesh from his bones. There were so many wrong things here.

Bree cried out. She crumpled to the pavement in front of the procession. Her face showed such a deep level of horror that Geo could feel it immediately himself, as if he'd just tuned in to her soul. A second cry, and he sensed the danger immediately. He lifted his head and looked left and saw Silver Star on the opposite side of the street, watching them. He was moving his fingers as if playing a piano. Then Silver's fingers stopped and Geo felt nausea flooding him. Alex's corpse had stopped as well, like it was a marionette on threads.

Silver Star pointed at them with his left hand and Geo noticed several of his elite squad turning their heads toward him and Bree. He felt the danger emanating from them even before they decided to come after them.

Geo pulled Bree from the ground and ran down Black Street, pushing her in front of him. There it was, twenty steps before them—the escape hole in the wall he'd just shown Bree before coming to the intersection.

"Go back into the wall," he yelled at her, hoping she could hear him through the fog flooding her mind. He could actually *see* the fog that—he stopped and *tasted* the frisson of danger that washed over him. Turning his head, he saw the concrete chunk flying after them; it hit him almost instantly. The impact sent him flying through the air to land like a piece of meat in front of Bree. That second split into three parts—seeing Bree finally notice him in the air; hitting the ground and Bree jumping in front of him, trying to pull him back up; and finally, crumpling into himself as he struck the ground and everything went black.

33.
The Death Trial

It was hot, and humid, and suffocating, and noisy. He felt like he was bleeding from his ears. Nails thrust deep into his head. Everything was hurting so much. Geo opened his eyes. All fell quiet.

Geo realized he was tied to a concrete pillar, a breath away from his brother's corpse. The stench was unbearable. Alex's skin was green and here and there, ruptured by fungus. His head had been stitched back onto his shoulders. Worms crawled out of his nose and black flies erupted from his mouth. His eyes were almost entirely white, bubbling in a sort of effervescence. Staring at him.

Alex moved suddenly, leaning forward as if wanting to get closer to his brother and smell him. Geo reeled back, then bent his head forward and threw up. All around him, the place echoed with cries and shouts. He looked around and saw that he was tied to the execution pillar in front of City Hall, and a mass of people crowded the space and watched the whole thing with excitement. He noticed Silver Star in the central balcony of City Hall. Right where the mayor had been sitting when Geo had come to the Golden Tower with the Silkers Procession not even a week ago. And yet, a lifetime ago.

Geo averted his eyes from Alex's corpse. He closed them and tried to calm down. There was no use in panicking. He needed to think in the language of his old friend—math.

First, Silver Star had caught him—Geo sighed. Silver had caught him during the procession led by his dead brother. That was a mighty important point, because—and here the first equation would turn into a system: a) Geo didn't know he was the subject of a hunt; b) Silver Star acted aggressively and prompted Geo's reaction to run; and c) where was Boris in all this? After all, this execution was taking place in front of the Golden Tower. Boris should be aware of it.

Which brought Geo to the second equation turned into another system: a) Prince Boris was supposed to be the new mayor. Only the mayor had the power to order executions, so Geo's execution must come from Boris; b) yet Silver Star presided over the execution from the mayoral balcony, not Boris, which was odd, as the mayor should preside over each and every public execution; and c) somehow, Silver had made all this about Alex and Geo, and he had no idea what the charges could be. Although it was pretty obvious there would be no charges and no trial. Only a public lynching.

Which brought Geo to the third equation—Silver Star was capable of manipulating corpses. What sort of sick talent was this? Could this be Silver's secret weapon? Was he a…what was the word? A necromancer? Or was this just one of the side skills some Corrosives developed? No inclusion in the wider system here. Just a mystery.

What had happened to Bree? Suddenly Geo tensed. He looked around frantically, but couldn't see her in the crowd, or under guard with Silver's people. Luckily, she wasn't there to see him being tortured and savagely killed.

As soon as he acknowledged the crowd, its noise crashed against his brain like a tsunami. He groaned and vomited again, then drew a deep breath with some effort, the air gurgling down his throat, more like liquid than gas. That was when he realized he was out of his suit and helmet, for the first time fully exposed to the corrosive climate. A climate that he knew could kill a regular human who relied on liquid water.

That meant the gelled water had started to change his DNA.

He was more or less adapted to this new climactic reality. Probably closer to less, from the pain in his lungs, his head, and his muscles, but who knew, maybe this was the normal adaptation process. There was no one who could advise him and guide him through his changes. Not that it would matter in the end. Because he could feel it—the end was near.

Alex suddenly snapped at him, trying to bite off his cheek. Geo instinctively withdrew, hitting his head on the concrete pillar behind him. Alex snapped again, and Geo had to lean to the side as far as his restraints allow. Dammit!

"Torono!" Silver Star boomed through a bullhorn. The crowd replied loudly.

"What you see in front of you are two liquid brothers who will fight each other and *eat* each other for your entertainment! The one tied to the Pillar of Shame is a spy. A liquid human who came into our midst, earned our trust, and stole our secrets. Then mounted an attack on the very foundations of our city! Our livelihood! He and his liquid clan would like nothing more than to just terminate you and replace you."

The crowd booed and tried to break through the chain of warriors guarding the stage and rip Geo apart with their bare hands. Alex took advantage of the distraction to bite Geo's jaw, tearing off a strip of skin and splashing blood in a crimson rain. Geo thrashed and managed to kick Alex off the stage. The crowd went mad, lunging for the liquid blood.

"The other one is his brother. Now he's my necro-warrior, my liquid eater. His name is Judgement. He will regain his human strength through eating his brother. That's a liquid custom that brought down upon the liquid humans the wrath of the gods, and led to their extermination. Their extermination allowed *us* to rise up onto the world stage. And now the inbred remnant of the liquid species tries to take the world back from *us*!"

His last "us" reverberated above the square for a long time, turning the crowd into a pack of ferocious, crazed predators.

Alex clambered back onto the stage and approached Geo again. He thrust his nails into his brother's shoulder and began to slowly peel back his skin, leaving a moist, bright red track behind. Geo screamed in pain. He felt dazed. He felt on fire. He felt exposed to everything around him, all the elements, all the hate and the madness, all the bloodlust. It felt like a claw scraping down his throat.

"By mayoral order, cease this right now!"

The voice was deep and resonating. Through blurry eyes, Geo noticed that a detachment of Hyalo Warriors stopped right outside the square, behind the crowd. Their commander, a brawny individual with a tremendous snake undulating at the end of his left arm, was talking through a bullhorn, like Silver Star.

"TORONO!" Silver raised his voice.

The crowd yelled in response. Alex tore the first sliver of skin with a wet sound and bit through it hungrily. He was masticating slowly, as his jaw was slightly loose.

"I said, cease this right now! Disperse!" the Hyalo officer yelled again through his bullhorn.

Geo saw Silver make a sign to his officers and his warriors withdrew from around the stage, leaving the crowd free to do whatever they wanted. Oh, so he won't get cannibalized by his own brother. He'd get ripped to pieces by a frantic crowd of Corrosives.

"This is your last warning!"

"TORONO!" Silver's voice was hoarse.

The crowd went berserk and invaded the stage. The first line of attackers jerked, pierced by arrows, and fell back. The second line hesitated for a second, but still climbed onto the stage, and fell back under the rain of arrows. One of the arrows went through Alex's skull like puncturing cheese, but that didn't slow him down. His brother let go of the slice of skin he was munching and extended his arm toward Geo's raw shoulder. Another arrow went through Alex's outstretched hand and took it with it as it embedded itself in the concrete pillar behind Geo.

The corpse fell forward on Geo, gurgling and growling. Opening his mouth, he bit into Geo's chest. The pain was reaching unbearable levels. The sound of fighting, the corpse's stench, the hate and fear swirling around him like a tornado wiping the square clean of humanity—everything swept over Geo like a wave washing him from the land into the deep sea. He choked and fought for air. That came in the form of gelled humidity and filled his throat and lungs to bursting. The end was not darkness and silence engulfing him peacefully, but bright explosions of light and shrill screams of agony.

"Is there anything you want to tell me?"

Mayoral Prince Boris sat on his wooden throne, looking down on Silver Star. A couple of Silver's elite squad were there, right behind him. Lady S sat on a simple metal chair on Boris's right side. Other than that, the throne hall was empty.

"Nah," said Silver. "You're a busy man. Wouldn't want to waste your precious time."

"No, no, no, don't worry. Waste away, Silver."

Boris was smiling widely. He exhaled, satisfied, and lounged on his throne like a beast after gorging on warm flesh.

"All right, ask away."

"Hmm…you know, Silver, one might say you want to avoid telling me what weighs on your conscience."

"Absolutely nothing, Mr. Mayor, sir. I have a clear, healthy conscience. One might say it is at its lightest peak. In terms of weight."

"Is it, now?" Boris's smile slid into a dangerous grin.

Silver Star turned to leave.

"I didn't say you can leave."

"You didn't…" Silver stood with his back to Boris.

"Did you carry out an execution in the City Square?"

"Yes, I did."

"Was there a mayoral order for an execution?"

"The execution was carried out on my order," said Silver, turning back to face the mayor.

Boris stared at him silently, solemnly. Lady S had been unmoved all this time. Yet now, she leaned forward, watching Silver's helmet like a snake ready to pounce on an unwary prey.

"Oh, come on, little brother. You've proven yourself weak. I had to step up and right these wron—"

In a single fluid motion, Lady S expelled a storm of green gas. The two elite squads inhaled some of it and dropped to the floor, dead. That had happened between one beat and another. On the third beat, the gas cloud hung all around Silver's helmet.

"You see, brother? Your warriors mean nothing to me. If you were not my brother— Anyone else would be dead by now— publicly executed, so the people would know where I stand."

"I had to…" groaned Silver.

"Oh, spare me your xenophobia, Silver. I expect you to keep it in check. My will takes priority. Every. Single. Time."

Boris rose and stretched, his expression bored. He stepped down from the dais and walked to the window: "Come here."

"Tell your witch to release me," said Silver in a muffled voice.

"Rein. In. Your. Xenophobia."

"*Please*, Mr. Mayor, ask your *consort* to release me."

"Lady S, that's enough. Thank you."

The gas around Silver's helmet dissipated. He didn't move for a few seconds. Lady S sat back in her chair, elegantly poised and watching him intently. Boris remained with his back to him, staring out the window. Eventually, Silver moved slowly to the window. He looked out, following Boris's direction.

There were now ten concrete pillars mounted in a circle in the City Square. Ten men were bound to the pillars, all wearing a big silver star on his chest that was not part of their uniform. Boris had wanted to make it clearer for the crowd, who he was executing. In the center of the circle there was a pyre. And Alex's corpse was tied to the stake in the middle of the pyre.

"No! You wouldn't dare!" said Silver.

"I told you, your warriors mean nothing to me. And when they act against my will, they commit treason."

The crowd was larger than it had been in the morning. It looked like half the city was there to witness the new mayor's retribution. It was louder than earlier, but more peaceful. That the place was full of the mayor's warriors was certainly a factor.

One of his officers was making a declaration from the stage behind the circle of execution pillars. The public punctuated his words with cheers.

Boris opened the window. They were on the second level of the building, lower than the mayoral balcony in the City Hall Palace. But that placed Boris closer to the people. He raised a hand and everyone turned to see him. Their new master.

Silver stepped back, but behind him, Lady S pushed him back into place on the mayor's left, visible to the public. This was Boris's political statement for the city: there were not any opposing political forces in place anymore. Silver Star, the former mayor's muscle, had been subdued and attached to the new mayor's apparatus. And his warriors were paying now for their leader's error in judgement.

"People of Torono! Enjoy the free quality entertainment I've put together for you today!" Boris raised his voice in the silence that had fallen over the City Square. "But…" He grabbed Silver's arm and pulled him forward, bringing him up next to him in the window frame. He placed his left hand on Silver's nape and pushed his head down, so the man would look cowed and contrite. "But there's a moral to my entertainment. There's always something to learn from my acts."

Silence ruled in the square. Everybody knew Silver Star and was afraid of his reign of terror. Everybody knew that when you see the silver star on a uniform, you stay indoors. You bow your head and pray they do not see you. That they don't even know you exist. So now, seeing the most feared man in the kingdom cowed by the new mayor drew mixed feelings—people were relieved because the reign of terror had possibly reached an end, yet the head of that terror was still alive, apparently pardoned by the new ruler. Could that be the beginning of a new reign of an even worse terror?

"And the lesson today, my dear people, is that no one, and I stress this—*no one*—has the power to do whatever they want in *my* city. If the mighty warrior that Silver Star is has taken the law into his own hands and has thought of delivering justice without asking for permission, then Silver Star and his hands must pay for their error. For their *treason!*"

Boris thrust a dagger through Silver's right hand, resting on the windowsill, and stuck it there. Lady S grabbed Silver's left hand and forced it onto the sill too. Boris thrust a second dagger into his left hand and stuck it to the sill as well. Silver screamed in pain and surprise. He tried to move, but Boris kept him there, for all the people to witness his justice.

"LET. THERE. BE. JUSTICE!" Boris roared and raised his hands above his head.

Seven flaming arrows flew and hit the pyre, lighting it instantly. Alex's corpse straightened on the stake and tried to climb higher. The flames grew and engulfed the entire pyre, licking the corpse's legs. The crowd kept its silence. When the flames reached Alex's torso, it turned its head toward the green sky and released a high-pitched shrill. Thick smoke rose from the pyre and filled the square with a sickly sweet stench.

A path cleared through the crowd in the square. A line of one hundred Hyalo Warriors walked into the square, swords out. The officer leading them stopped next to the first warrior of the elite Silver Squad and cut him with his sword. Not too deep, not too much, just enough to draw blood. Then he moved to the next one and the first Hyalo Warrior behind him replaced him. Now they both cut their victims and moved forward. It looked like it was going to be a very long afternoon for everyone involved, as the Silkers' army had surrounded the square and kept everyone inside, to bear witness to the new the mayor's justice to the end.

34.
Humanity Clause

Bree checked every detail again and again. She was far from forming habits in this new world, so she had to be careful. And with Geo not coming back last night after he'd been caught, she needed to constantly do something to keep her mind preoccupied and the worry at bay. She knew that after the mayor had been dispatched, Geo had no other enemies in Torono, but still— that guy with the silver star on his helmet seemed quite decisively against Geo. There were still so many things she didn't know about what was going on in the Exterior.

She had to find Geo. He could be bleeding out in an alley somewhere, and— He'd specifically told her not come looking for him, no matter what. She had to remain a secret for her own sake, and to act like Geo's secret weapon of some sort—like the Cave Clan's secret weapon. She liked that idea at first, but now… how could she be their secret weapon if he ended up dead somehow, and she hadn't lifted a finger to help him?

She donned her helmet and locked it. Level of oxygen—full. Filters—full capacity. Scrubbers—optimal. Battery—100 percent. All displays functional. Sensors still working—74 percent. Good enough. But was it good enough? If she was looking for him and revealed herself to any of these armed factions, that would be bad enough. Not good at all. But if she didn't look for him and she found out a week later that he was dead and she could have saved him if she—ugh! She hated going in circles with her mind. In the lab, life was so simple. No thoughts of the Exterior, or life and death situations, or Geo. Back there, she'd thought of Geo often enough, but normal life just helped her move forward. And that was it—she had to move forward.

Bree decided to follow Geo's plan of mapping the territory and coming up with a way to save the people of—to save the Corrosives. Woodman Corp was safe enough. Her people were perfectly safe, tucked away in their Cave. If nothing else, at least she could help Geo with his plan. And while doing that, maybe she'd bump into him and bring him home safe. Lots of safes in her mind, she noticed.

She observed the neighborhood from the corner of the Rat King Temple. It seemed quiet, despite the market nearby. In fact, the market looked deserted. There was some sort of background noise she hadn't yet defined. Almost like the voices and movements of a mass of people. What the…

A Corrosive was waving at her from across the street. Shit! She wanted to retreat, then realized he was waving from the slightly opened door she had escaped through two days ago. With the help of one of the Corrosives. The one that knew Geo.

She checked the surroundings again. Nobody around. Weird. She crossed the street and recognized him: the man with the face like a porous sponge, with a wide mouth that seemed to always be smiling.

He beckoned her inside, then closed the door behind them. It was dark for a second, then light flamed as he lit torches. Bree startled when she discovered the dark had hidden several other Corrosives. She stepped back, ready to defend herself. She wished she had a way to flee, but the sponge-face was behind her, blocking the door. Now she wished she'd known better than to just accept the invitation on a whim.

"Good morning, my name is Mic and—oh." Bree swung at him.

Mic avoided her swing easily and stuck to the door with his

hands up in the air, in the universal sign of capitulation. "I'm sorry if we frightened you! We mean you no harm!"

"Oh no, dear, we come in peace!" a feminine voice said and Bree turned around to see an elderly Corrosive smiling kindly and walking slowly toward her. Her voice sounded old. The only thing identifying her as feminine were what Bree could only guess were the shapes of breasts under her robe of woven grass. That and maybe the facial features that one could still distinguish on a very worn, heavily sandpapered face.

Bree waited, still ready to fight, taking a stance she'd seen Alex fall into when preparing to practice with his friends. She so regretted now not taking any combat classes. She'd always thought she'd be just a lab nerd, an interior kind of dweller. No need for fighting skills.

"I am Momma Mar," said the old woman, patting her chest. "This is my husband, Jon." She pointed to another elderly Corrosive who stepped into the light. Jon nodded at her and smiled. He looked like a wrinkled candle, as if his skeleton had shrunk and then left him with an oversized skin. He too wore clothes woven from grass.

"And I am Mic," said sponge-face again. "I am their youngest."

He looked kind of young, although Bree couldn't yet understand the degrees of destruction gelled water caused to Corrosives' appearance. Well, on Corrosives' flesh, actually, if she remembered the science behind it.

"My name is Ton, and I'm Mic's brother," the weirdest of the Corrosives said in a hushed tone. Bree's eyes grew big at the sight of him—he had created some sort of decoration from his own corroded skin. "And you know Stev."

As she turned to see Stev, a wave of noise washed over them from outside. They all jumped and look to each other with troubled eyes.

The first to recover was the mother. "Well, we are the shopkeepers. That's how everyone knows us."

"I…" Bree hesitated. They looked scary with their wounds and gnawed flesh and compromised skin, but under all that disfigurement their eyes shone brightly. Their eyes smiled. Their eyes were warm. Their smiles seemed genuine, even if horribly skewed. "I'm sorry, you startled me when you all came out of the dark. I…"

"No worries, dear," Momma Mar held out her hand—a palm with only three stumps for fingers. "We should've known better."

"It's just that we don't want to draw attention," added Jon. His voice was hoarse and very low, and Bree noticed only now that he was missing part of his throat.

"My name is Bree." She looked quickly from Jon's throat to Momma Mar.

"Welcome to our home, Bree. Geo told us about you."

"Oh," Bree said, the sound escaping as she wondered when Geo had time to tell them about her.

"He told us there's a big secret that your clan unveiled and it may concern us. Torono. And that under the Humanity Clause, he's obliged to help us. To save us."

"Humanity Clause? Geo told you that?"

"Yes, he explained to us what it means and what it entails on his part."

"You're very well-spoken, Momma Mar," said Bree.

"Well, as a teacher I have to be. Otherwise what example would I give to the children I instruct?"

Bree was left mouth agape. She hadn't even realized that the Corrosives had schools, or any sort of education in place. She'd always imagined them as ruins dwellers, just a tad above the beasts in the field. She'd imagined they still maintained some rudiment of language, some semblance of rational thought, but nothing more. Although, to be fair, Geo had always spoken of them as if they were the Woodmans' equals. Everyone had thought it was just Geo trying to impress them.

So, if they were as smart as the Woodmans, what did they think of her now?

"We discovered some uncharted catacombs. The access is obstructed, but if you can tell us if they'd be good for our purpose, then we can get people to work on that."

Catacombs? Bree looked from Jon to Mic. Why would Geo be interested in—oh!

"I see you're surprised," said Jon. "Didn't Geo tell you?"

"No, he didn't," admitted Bree.

"So you don't know why we're doing this."

"Oh, I have quite a good idea why. He just didn't tell me…"

"That he was doing it for us," Jon finished her sentence.

She knew that Geo had taken the problem to the council, but her grandfather had quashed it. The council had not been interested in saving the people of Torono. Except Woodman the Elder. Geo was so much like him. But the Woodman Corp had no interest whatsoever in saving the Corrosives. After all, the Corrosives were not humans anymore—or that was the official line.

"Yes," she said and looked down, ashamed.

"So, can *you* help us?"

They looked monstrous, but they were only two elderly adults and two teenagers. The last two, second generation Corrosives, had been born less human—and yet, was that the thing? If you're shaped differently, you're less human?

"She won't, Dad. We need Geo, and now he's—"

"And now he's what?" Bree touched a Corrosive for the first time. She put her hand on Mic's shoulder.

"You won't help us, so—" Mic said, almost crying.

"Mic," Jon's voice was reproachful. "She has no duty to us. Don't blame her."

"What's going on, Jon?" asked Bree, sensing that their dad may be inclined to help her.

Mic turned and strutted away. Jon looked at her and his eyes were sad. "Geo is being executed in the City Square today."

"What!"

"By now, he's probably dead already. I'm sorry."

Bree stepped back. She was here with these Corrosives while Geo was EXECUTED? How was that possible!

She turned to flee.

"Wait! Bree!" Momma Mar yelled after her.

But she didn't care about anything anymore. She ran. Tears streamed down her face under the protective plate. Desperation tightened her chest. He was dying out there, in the city, in the middle of these monstrous people, and she wasn't with him. He was dying all alone.

She stopped running and screamed as loud as she could. Her frustration exploded under her helmet. Geo wanted to save the people of this city and yet they were killing him right now. He'd left behind his own family, his own flesh and blood, to save them. He'd seen his brother killed in front of his eyes while trying to save *them*! And what were they doing in exchange for all his sacrifices? They were *executing* him! So barbaric and primitive, so monstrous. They were all monsters! All of them! Starting with her grandfather and the council!

"Let me take you there," she heard Mic say. His voice was riddled with guilt.

She looked to him. He was crying. His lips trembled. His sponge-like face sucked up his gelled tears greedily. "Please, let me take you there."

35.
The Ritual

They carried him on their hands, above their heads, keeping him away from all those hands that wanted to rip him to pieces. They left behind Alex's shrieks and the howling of the hate-filled crowd. The sky was swamp green, scratched with rotting purple streaks. He was ready. Geo was now ready to die. He'd saved the Cave. He'd saved Woodman the Elder and Bree, and—he'd lost Alex. He lost—he failed Torono's people. All those poor survivors that no one cared about. That no one needed. Geo sighed. He'd tried. He'd tried. The sky was so, so green. He'd never seen the blue sky he'd seen in the movies. The sun. The stars. The clouds—like, real clouds, the white, fluffy things from the pictures, not the mushy, purulent ones hanging over them now.

He fell. They caught him right before he hit the ground. Haters attacked and the mighty Hyalo Warriors defended his body valiantly. Because that's what it was, wasn't it—just his body. He was already dead, perhaps. He was probably like his brother—waking up from death as a hungry corpse. The Woodman brothers will eat up the world.

The pain in his head was so sharp—

He woke up coughing, fighting for breath. His throat felt like sandpaper. They held his head so he could breathe easier and put a glass to his lips. He swallowed the water—sweet and thick. He remembered the last image of the sky as he'd seen it when transported here to this bed, and imagined he was drinking green water from that sky. Well, in a way he was, even if the water was brought from somewhere in the ground.

He tried to smile at so easily sliding into a nonsensical train of thought, then groaned—his lips hurt when parted too much. They were chapped and bloody. A wound on his face.

A familiar voice called to him. He opened his eyes, only now realizing he'd kept them closed. It hurt. The light hurt. His chest hurt when inhaling air. Or exhaling. His head hurt when trying to focus on only one thing. So much pain.

"Can you hear me, Geo?"

Ah, Lena's voice. He opened his eyes again and there she was. As enticing and intense as always. He'd like to just kiss those red lips. But his lips brought him pain.

"It's all right, love. Don't talk. I'm so happy to see you back among the living."

Ah, shit. He'd thought he'd died and was finally free. He remembered something about—Alex. His brother…his mouth, biting him, ripping his flesh away in a rotten hunger.

"No, don't cry," Lena dabbed his eyes with a soft cloth. "Doctor!"

He cringed at her high voice. "My—brother…" he croaked.

"I'm so sorry, Geo," Lena said, caressing his hair.

"No…" he tried again.

She came closer to hear him. He swallowed and just said it: "Is he—finally—dead?"

Lena's mask stared at him for a few long seconds, then she nodded, her red lips arching downward in a pained expression. That was all the confirmation he needed. He exhaled and slipped into unconsciousness.

He woke up again to darkness. It was so cold. He remembered it being summer and really very hot, but he was freezing. Sweat froze in icy droplets on his skin. He shuddered and tried to find the source of that annoying noise. When he turned his head to his right, he realized it was his teeth chattering in his mouth.

There was a torch burning on the opposite wall, quite far from his bed. It deepened the darkness in the corners. There was someone sitting in a chair next to his bed. A hunched figure, sleeping. An old Corrosive woman, her chin propped against her chest.

Geo felt better. Most of the pain was gone. He only felt stiff and very cold. Very, very cold. It was dark. How long had he been asleep? Well, it seemed he was in his room in the Golden Tower. Boris had brought him here after saving him. So, could he think that Boris hadn't been involved in that failed execution? Could it have been only Silver Star? Two equations and one light on the horizon. Geo could not say what Boris could gain from torturing Geo publicly and almost killing him. But he wasn't in the best shape now, so probably his mind wasn't as clear as necessary.

The woman's chest was rising and falling slowly in the rhythm of deep sleep. Was she the doctor? Should he wake her up and ask her about his condition? Watching her entire body moving with her breath, he felt his eyes closing, lulled to sleep. It was getting hot. Sweat trickled down his temples and his nape. So hot and he was so tired…

"I'd like to hear a real conclusion, doctor!" That was Boris's voice, tinged with irritation.

"I'm sorry, sir. He's still in danger. I can't—"

"He's awake!"

Boris smiled at him with a worried frown. "Hey Geo, so nice of you to wake up in the presence of your sovereign!" Boris laughed loudly at his own joke.

Geo smiled weakly. He felt less pain, but he was so very tired. He could barely keep his eyes open. They smarted. And his lips were by now just dried up flakes of skin.

The doctor was an old Corrosive with most of his forehead gone, but otherwise in pretty good shape. He gave Geo some water to drink. It felt good, yet his throat remained parched.

"What's…going on…Boris?"

"Well, my friend, it's not good."

"Ah…" Geo encouraged him to talk faster, as he didn't know how long could he stay awake.

"You see, your brother's corpse bit you and that brought on infection. And we don't have the medicine you probably have in the Cave. We tried to treat you, but your body is reacting poorly as it is."

"Your body is still fighting the gelled water. You got infected while turning into…us," said the doctor.

"Which, apparently, is not an ideal situation, my friend," said Boris quickly. "We *Corrosives*," he added, grinning as if at some private joke between them, "don't get infections. It's one of the perks. But you're not completely…turned."

"Ah." Geo nodded, or thought he nodded, and hoped Boris took the hint.

"We cannot save you. We don't have the necessary drugs that could help you," said the doctor, and under Boris's withering look, retreated from the room with his head bowed in submission.

"My doctors cannot do anything else. And your infection has spread. It's—you're beyond saving."

Geo shut his eyes and smiled. He felt sad for having to leave before he'd succeeded in his plans. Before he'd secured the future for everyone that mattered to him. But he was so tired. Too tired to keep going.

"Oh no, my friend." Boris put his hand on Geo's shoulder and squeezed. "I'm not yet ready to give up on you."

Opening his eyes again, Geo looked at the prince. If he didn't know that Boris was doing all this because he needed Geo and what he was bringing to the kingdom from the Woodman Clan, he'd be moved by it. "I'm ready, Boris," Geo said with effort.

"I'm not. There's a theory that metamorphosis purges your body and soul. We'll do the ritual tonight and I'll save you."

Geo needed a minute to process all that. The ritual. And Boris would save him. That was the most terrifying thing he'd faced in a long time.

"So you see, my friend, I'll be with you to the end. My

friendship is forever. I promised you. I always keep my promises."

Boris *helping* him meant he was going to take control of Geo's mind and turn him into whatever the prince felt could serve him best. The image of the whining mastiff that once had been the bright and warm Lukas was seared in his brain.

The prince talked some more, but Geo didn't hear him anymore. He needed help. He needed a way out. He…

"Apparently, there's a way to command your brain that's more direct than just willpower, but only if you're a Corrosive. Only if you've left the gelled water to take control of your DNA." Bree's voice poured over his heated body like crystal clear, cold spring water. They had a spring in the Cave and the water was so cold that touching it felt as if you'd been cut to the bone. He yearned for that coldness right now. But the memory of Bree's voice had a very intimate effect. Soothing and calming.

Yes, Boris had threatened to take Geo's mind away from Geo. But Bree's voice was bringing hope back. And strength. He needed strength to stand against Boris's will and go through the ritual at the same time. Go through the ritual and follow the plan he'd put together with Bree.

"You're not alone, Geo. You're my family. We're in this together."

The Ritual Hall was sunk in a dance of darkness and flame. The incense and the smoke from the torches overwhelmed any other bodily odor from the mass of Silkers present for the ritual. Boris presided from his princely throne on his mayoral dais. Lady L and Lady S stood behind him. All the commanders and the ministers and other important dignitaries of the Silker Court waited all around the dais. Veteran warriors from every Silker army lined the walls, standing tall and dark.

In the center of the hall there was only one stone. A ritual axe leaned against it. Geo stood there, trying not to sway or hunch. He shivered every now and then as the waves of cold alternated with waves of heat. He was burning up. His eyes were red and he saw everything around him in a golden haze.

His breath rasped in his chest. They had bathed him and cleaned his wounds, but the bite in his chest was purulent and stank of death and rot.

He paid little attention to everyone in the hall. His focused on keeping his mind as lucid as possible, on not surrendering. Intellectually he knew what to expect. In reality, fear made him shiver as much as the infection.

Boris was talking. Geo didn't want to understand him. He didn't care about their ritualistic words. What would happen to him would be brutal and deadly no matter what brave and supposedly sacred words they uttered. He was not one of them.

Boris kept talking.

"We're in this together." The memory of Bree's voice relaxed him a bit. He inhaled and visualized the anatomy of the human body he'd memorized before all this. Time to leave math behind and go on his biology quest. He began recalling the different organs and body parts he had to use in the ritual. Name, location, function, how it integrated with the rest of the amazing machine that a human body was. And Bree's voice was there, repeating with him every word in her kind, soft voice. Guiding him, as she'd guided and taught him in their hideout in the Rat King Temple.

The sound of thunder made him tremble. The ritual was already nearing the moment where Geo would discover what he was made of. Following the thunder, the sound of rain, the liquid water pouring from the heavens, filled the room and Geo felt at once his heart freezing and tears rolling down his cheeks. There was something so beautiful in the sound. And yet, that sound meant death.

The mayor prince of Torono inhaled deeply when hearing the rain's whisper filling the Initiation Hall. He closed his eyes and saw in his mind the drops of liquid water hitting the glass and draining in transparent rivulets down the window. Then, under his eyelids, he envisioned the dark gray, wet asphalt soaked by rain and the glorious liquid water frothing down the streets to the sewer drains. He'd seen battles in his time. He'd

seen tragedy and ecstasy. But these rain tableaux were by far
the most powerful imagery he could possibly see or experience
in his life. And he hadn't even experienced them. No, he'd only
seen them in an old recording. And his life had changed radically since that fateful day. He'd become the most powerful man in
the world. The prince.

He opened his eyes. His court were bowing their heads
to him. Even Silver, his irritating older brother. Boris was the
Master of the Water. The water was his mistress. And soon, the
entire gelled chain of holy water, from the Great Sea to the Great
Mountains, would be under his control. With Geo's help, Boris
would become the absolute ruler of all the land between the waters. And after that—well, after that, everything would become
really interesting.

Geo felt the hand of his Silker Guide on his back, pushing
him forward. Not hard, but with kindness. Just guiding. Not
leading. Geo took off his shirt. He knelt. There was something
disappointing in hearing the pattering of the rain and not feeling
the cold water on his skin. The world was broken and he could
do nothing to mend it.

He extended his left arm on the stone. He knew that was
somewhat against the Silkers' tradition, but he didn't want to
dispose of the right arm, the one he used for everything. For
writing. And working. And loving. He raised his head and saw
Bree standing next to the stone. Smiling. Radiant. *We're in this
together. Zzzip!*

Zzzip! The ritualistic axe fell. Geo's arm dropped in a gush
of blood. And the boy held up better than Boris had expected.
Better than most of the prince's officers. Especially considering
how sick and weak the Woodman was. That was something to
remember if Geo made it through the ritual with at least part of
his mind intact.

Lady L touched his arm. The prince startled. Her touch had

always been electrifying. He almost pitied Geo for having to deal with her. He turned and looked at those red lips and that blank black mask covering her entire face. She couldn't be read. She couldn't be measured. She couldn't be had. She was his mentor, his strength, his rock for building the empire to come. He owed her everything. And no one knew. No one knew who or what she was. His secret weapon.

Boris took Lady L's right hand between his palms. He kissed it. Smiled. And pressed it against his heart. His secret. His queen. He closed his eyes and focused. Her will was so strong. Her mind so powerful. He saw her with his mind like a beacon in the darkness of the hall. Like the lighthouse of humanity in the perpetual storm the world had sunk into. She was his savior and the last hope for humanity.

Her mind melted its liquid warmth within his brain's cir-cumvolutions. Hot, honeyed stream imbued his gray matter. He felt shiny. He felt electrified. He felt superhuman. He now could lend her abilities and use them as his own.

Boris breathed in and when he started exhaling, he began expanding his senses around him. The minds of his court were like pinpoints of light, sources of flickering light in existence. Weak and pathetic. Silver had a more impressive flame, but his fire burned with a blinding black energy. He always wondered what was wrong with his brother. What could he do to turn that dark energy into the bright one that Lady L was?

But now, his interests lay on a stone deep in the darkness, beyond his court's mortal lights. There it was—his first liquid water human. His first proto-human. Boris paused for a mo-ment, taking in the show. That was interesting. He knew that Lady L could see what he was seeing, so he stayed for a while and enjoyed it. It was like he was witnessing the splendors of the past; the force and potential that past had been and never would be again.

Geo burned with a blue liquid flame. It was like a sea of liq-uid water was burning bright and pure. Foaming waves crush-ing against the boy's cranial shores. His brain was completely enveloped in this water miracle. Gelled water! What a spectacle!

Boris felt the boy coming alive. Beginning to discover his own body, his own new gelled essence. Now was the time to act. The prince didn't want Geo completely obliterated inside a mastiff's body, like those of his unsuccessful soldiers, but he wanted to have a great deal of control over his mind. To make it his own tool. He wanted the Woodman conscious and independent, but with the right triggers in his mind to respond to Boris when pulled. There was an art to it and Boris was the only human alive strong enough to do it.

The world smelled of incense and blood. The brightness of Lady L's mind rumbled like a huge fire ready to devour its surroundings. Boris hovered his will over Geo's limp body, taking his time to approach this rare event. He felt the strong pull of the liquid water still flowing through Geo's body, like a force of gravity. To lap liquid water—what else could be more powerful than that?

Boris touched Geo's mind and shivered. The freshness. He sank slowly, slowly, as if not wanting to scare the precious liquid water so near to him. His mind enfolded Geo's brain in its entirety. Then it began closing down on his liquid resources. On his gray matter. Imbuing it with Boris's will, with Lady L's warmth and personal scent, which would entice Geo in the right direction, eliminate fear, make him comfortable and ready to be taken.

It wasn't pain so much as it was a burning sensation—instant, deep, shocking. His teeth clenched and his jaw locked. BURNING!

Geo's vision blurred even more. The hall disappeared, but Bree stood right there, in front of him, smiling. Speaking with him. Telling him what he needed to know. Transferring knowledge. The knowledge his brother had brought to him. Without even knowing he would need it. Saving him.

He grunted and thought proudly that he hadn't screamed. He hadn't shown weakness in front of the Silkers.

A storm was rising inside him. He felt his blood boiling, overwhelming him. He'd read about this. The gelled water had surged and was taking control of absolutely every function of his body, manipulating his DNA in overdrive mode, like a super-charge that coursed through him and purged him of everything old, bringing in the new—new cells, new blood, new plasma, new neurons. He now knew from Alex's research that the overwhelming pain and the loss of a limb—flesh, bone, and artery—had put the gelled water in supercharged mode and body control mode. Brain control mode. He had to take back control of his mind. That was the greatest battle he had to fight if he wanted to bring about the metamorphosis that would save him and make him a Silker. Or, in Alex's words, a chimera. A Nightmare.

Geo surfed the gelled water wave and checked his body in a way he hadn't been able to before. The pain disappeared somewhere under the rush of chasing the charge through his own veins and flesh. It remained like an unpleasant feeling, rubbing his nerves raw.

He'd reached the brain. He. Could. See. His. Brain! Intellectually, he knew he could only *see* the representation he had in his mind of his brain. But he could really *sense* his entire brain, its circumvolutions, neurons, synapses, the entire network of electrical impulses making his brain alive and—his own. He shut his eyes—or more accurately, just turned off his vision and waited for the dizziness to pass. He felt sick. Lost. With no grip on reality. He counted to twenty in darkness, then allowed his vision to return. The pink fields of his brain unfurled to the horizon. He struggled to keep his balance and grasp the reality of what he was seeing and feeling. It was so much. *"Never use 'too' in any circumstance,"* Woodman the Elder's calm voice soothed, balancing him. So much to grasp right now, but not too much. He could do it. *If "too" doesn't exist, you can do anything you put your mind to.* Right. He could do it.

A sky-wide shadow floated above his brain. It floated closer and closer, testing his mind with gentle touches, probing. Geo could physically feel the external touches. Not the gelled water, not his own will. Something else. Strange and foreign. Burning. He flinched inside his mind at the burning feeling.

The shadow engulfed his mind and pressed down. It was beginning to penetrate the brain matter, melting inside and mixing, taking control. *Boris!* Geo realized, and panicked. He turned to flee, swimming downstream the gelled water torrent, against the current. He got slower and slower with every stroke. Eventually he just let go and floated upward again, back into the brain. Where it was almost night. Darkness had engulfed his mind and was snuffing out his constellation of flickering neurons, each and every single one.

Night was falling and the searing pain had melted down to nothing. It was quiet and warm. Not cold, not hot. Just warm and relaxing. It was so good to finally let go and disappear.

"To take over your mind and dictate what your body can do, Boris needs to take control of your neurons. Actual, physical control of your neurological pathways." Bree's voice was louder than the droning sound of burning neurons.

Geo remembered the plan and the promises. The promises he'd made to Bree, and to his Corrosive friends. To Woodman the Elder. No uttered promise to Alex, and yet he felt like he owed something to his brother for his sacrifice. For his research.

The cavern of his head was getting darker and darker. Geo focused on the gelled water's fury and saw its viscous body filling all the pathways of his anatomy. *The gelled water is the best conductor of our matter and electricity.* Who'd said that?

He drew forth all the energy he could muster and conducted the electricity through his body with the help of the water. He maneuvered it up and up and upward, until it reached his brainstem and crackled nervously under his will.

The darkness was advancing unopposed. A brain was a very lethargic creature, without a consciousness to put it to work. Time to power up the weird globular organ that the brain was. Geo didn't remember where he'd heard that, but he liked it. It expressed how it felt right then and there. So much energy and one big, fat organ to put to work.

The stored electricity surged like a wave of lava and light. Pure sunlight, as Geo had always imagined it would look like. Sun! What a wonderful concept. The electricity flooded Geo's brain, lighting back up its neurons and recharging its neural pathways, sparkling at crossroads and sizzling in contact with the darkness, making it withdraw. Pulsing nervously and shuddering under the constant electrical attack.

When Geo stood on the highest peak of his brain, he surveyed his glorious domain, feeling all-powerful and crackling with energy. A last wave of electricity, like a nice, warm explosion, and Geo shuddered in something close to ecstasy. His domain was devoid of Boris's influence. There was no trace of darkness that he could sense anymore. His mind was his again. He established an electrical net around his brain, to prevent further intrusions. Now the arduous work of metamorphosis was going to start.

Glands first. Extension of the blood network second. Protein factories third. And fourth—still so much work to do.

36.
Shelter

Bree went to the market under the cover of darkness, when there were fewer people in the streets, less visibility. She'd thought she'd have to run again, but this time no one paid her any attention. She was still wearing her containment suit with the Woodman logo displayed on her chest and her protective helmet, but she covered everything with some ragged clothes found in the operation center. Geo had probably used them for the same purpose. She was tired of running for her life. She couldn't do any task if she was always in danger of being killed by the psycho with the star on his forehead.

She was still worried sick for Geo, but at least she got to see him saved by the black bowmen. Someone out there, maybe the prince, maybe someone else, was still preoccupied with keeping the Woodmans' ambassador alive. She gulped and found it hard to breathe when she remembered Alex's corpse biting into Geo's face. Those were the kinds of horrifying images you didn't expect to see outside of a book's pages. Nothing made any sense for her. There was nothing in Alex's research pointing to necromancy. How was that possible in the reality of physics and chemistry?

This should be a door. Bree knocked carefully so as not to attract attention from the street. Then she realized this was supposed to be a store. You didn't knock on a store's door. *Dammit!*

Way to stay under the radar. She turned the knob and pushed, but the door didn't open. She tried again. No luck. Shit! She'd done it again—yes, a store is open for customers, but only during the day, not at night. *Shit, shit, shit!* Bree looked around to see how many people had noticed her already. Still no one.

"We're closed," came a sleepy voice from above, at one of the windows.

"It's me, Bree," she said as loud as she dared without the entire street hearing her.

Several voices sounded upstairs, then the window closed. Two minutes later somebody opened the door carefully. Mic. Frowning and surprised. "Come on in. Quick!"

Mic took her arm and dragged her across the dark store all the way to the back, then through a door. Once inside, he lit a lamp. The entire family was there, but instead of the older brother with the weird corrosion decorations, there was a girl. She was one of the most fully formed humans Bree had seen since arriving in the city.

"Good evening, sweetie." Momma Mar smiled from a chair next to a desk. Behind the desk was the old man, Jon. "I'm sorry, but I know from Geo that there's nothing we can treat you with to be safe for you."

"It's all right, Momma Mar. Thank you."

"So, what can we do for you?" asked Jon directly in his hushed voice. He had the most inquisitive eyes. It was like he could see inside you and discover if you lied to him.

"I came to say *yes*, I'll help you."

"Why?" Jon again, in a curious voice.

"Geo told me about his plan and I realize he may not be able to help you very soon. So I might as well pick up where he left off and continue his work."

"But why?" insisted Jon.

Bree looked from Jon to Momma Mar and felt a connection for the first time since coming to Torono. These were simple people who were at the mercy of powerful men. Men who didn't see beyond their lust for power and their ambitions. Men for whom other people were only white noise. Nothing valuable. Just some annoying filling for the world that could be sacrificed for their narrow, egotistic vision.

"When Geo told me his plan to save you from what's to come, my first thought was, why would he put you first, before his own people? The people he—we—left behind, in the Cave."

Everyone sat on something and listened attentively. She felt just like Woodman the Elder probably felt when he was giving a lecture and the students listened raptly from their places in the auditorium.

"The truth is, he didn't place you first, or second, or last. He just saw you as human beings left behind by those in charge. Forgotten—or better, *ignored* by those responsible for your well-being. And the main problem is that the people who ought to be responsible don't feel that responsibility for the people they rule. We're only in the way of their ambitions. Of their dreams of grandeur. Once you realize that you're no longer the subject of the ruler, you've become responsible for yourself, your family, your community."

Jon stood with difficulty. Momma Mar smiled with what looked like happiness. The old man went around the desk and stopped in front of her. He cupped the armored glass of her helmet with tenderness, as if he were caressing her cheek. Then he hugged her; he was much stronger than he looked. When he let her go, his eyes were glistening. "You are my daughter, and I will protect you like family. We will stand together." Jon nodded, his face revealing more emotion than Bree had thought Corrosives could show.

"Let me show you what Geo and I have discovered under the city." Bree took from her knapsack the map of the possible shelters against what was to come. The map she'd drawn on a piece of cloth especially for them.

37.
The Metamorphosis of
Geo Woodman

The explosion caught Boris by surprise. He collapsed to
the floor next to Geo's bloody stump. His guards drew their
weapons and surrounded him protectively, looking around with
suspicious eyes at everyone in the hall. As far as they were concerned, any of the courtiers could have done something to their
prince. The courtiers rose and approached their fallen sovereign,
but another noise drew their attention—Lady L had also collapsed on the mayoral dais, next to the wooden throne. She was
thrashing like a possessed doll.

The court remained completely silent for a good minute.
Then Silver Star raised his axe and took the rest of the steps to
the Ritual Stone, where Geo's body lay trembling slightly while
his mind was supposedly working through the Seven Thresholds of Sleep, as the doctrine had taught them.

"No…" the prince weakly raised a hand to stop Silver Star.

Lady M and Lady Y helped Boris stand. He felt dizzy and
a little bit confused. The Ceremony Hall looked in order. No
traces of the explosion. Nothing out of the ordinary, except the
curious looks on his courtiers' faces. Not worry, not concern,
only curiosity. Like a pack of Nightmares ready to pounce and
devour. Ready to assume power and take control of his empire.
HIS. EMPIRE. Anger boiled in his chest and he felt its icy flames

purifying his thoughts.

"What happened?" Boris asked, watching their expressions.

The courtiers retreated to their seats. The princely guard kept their weapons drawn, sensing in their charge's voice that something was still amiss. That their action may be needed still.

"Nothing happened, my prince," whispered Lady M.

"There was an explosion," he said.

He saw everyone's look of confusion and wonder. So, the explosion had happened only in his mind. But his mind was supposed to be protected. He looked back to his throne. There lay Lady L, unconscious. Only now did he sense their lack of connection. Only now did he realize her absence. He gasped. How could one regular boy have this much power? No, that was not even the first thing of importance. The first one was *how could a liquid boy have the presence of spirit to* know *when his mind was invaded?* And furthermore, *how could one liquid boy* know *how to resist such an invasion?* He needed answers, but right now, Lady L was more important than any of that.

Boris rose and ran to the dais, refusing anyone's help. Lady L was still breathing, but barely. He couldn't sense any cerebral activity anymore. She was a dark spot. Her bright sun had turned into darkness in just an instant. Her power had always been a source of wonder for him. How could that kind of power be switched off so easily?

"Take her to my rooms," he murmured.

Then he turned to the Ritual Stone. Geo was still lying there, alive, breathing, his expression calm, as if he were sleeping. *Actually* sleeping, Boris reminded himself. His eyes moved quickly under his closed lids. His arm—his arm was still just a stump. Cleanly cut with only one stroke. Bloody and messy. The Silkers' best officers had their first flesh buds out in less than an hour, thus preventing rot and deterioration of any kind. His weakest had their first buds out in several hours—already too late to prevent spoiling of the flesh and corruption of the spirit. What would it be for Geo, the Woodman ambassador? Even more important, with that kind of power, would it be wise to allow it the possibility?

"Sire?" the captain of the guard asked.

"Put him on ice," said Boris. Then he breathed easier. That had been a gut decision. No thinking, just ordering. The best kind. His court murmured approval.

The guard lifted Geo carefully, keeping his stump elevated. They silently left the hall. The prince watched his court. All of them were loyal to a fault. As long as he was alive, they'd be there at his beck and call. Well, except his brother. But the moment they thought he was incapacitated, the ascension war would start. And to be incapacitated could be so easy.

Lady M wrapped a fur around his back. It was frigging cold in the ice room. Boris took her hand and kissed it. She was one of the kindest souls in his entourage. She was the balm he needed when he was hurt or worse, defeated. Because, yes, he'd been defeated numerous times. He had known how to display the defeat as just a delay, or an insignificant victory, so his commanders would not doubt him, and continue fighting. And Lady M had always been the balm to soothe his wounds and give him the courage to continue fighting.

This was not a defeat, he told himself. Geo's body lay still on a bed of ice. Two hundred meters underground, in what once had been a frozen hall, now turned ice room for the Silkers. A place where ice was eternal, even in the hottest summers.

Geo's stump looked fresh. No rot, no infection. The ice helped with that. It also helped keep his temperature low, so his mind wouldn't overheat and fail. In a way, he was helping the boy. Even if in the end he'd have to kill him. Or more appropriately, destroy him, if things went the way everyone supposed they'd go. With each passing hour, even Boris couldn't see a happy ending for Geo. Well, his plans would suffer a slight alteration, but in the end, he'd get the Woodmans' labs and their research. They would be his no matter what.

"How's Lena?" he said, holding Lady M's hand in his and rubbing it to keep it warm.

"It's still uncertain, my love."

"Any…any mental activity?"

"Not yet. It's not a lack, it's just…"

"I know. It's withdrawn and we don't have the tools to dig deeper."

"She'll be fine, love. If I learned one thing from Lena, it's that she'd never die. She'd never disappear. Her light shines too brightly."

Boris smiled and kissed her. His balm.

Geo was reaching a limit. He felt tired. He hadn't had a break in more than twelve hours. At first his body temperature had risen alarmingly, making his job difficult. But then it started to slow down, then drop lower and lower, and now it was actually so cold that it made him slumber.

He had everything organized in systems, and the systems branched out and evolved in subsystems. All the details had been worked out with Bree, and put in the proper order and sequence. It was a lot of work, he'd known that even then, but now he was actually realizing that they may have been too ambitious. He knew that the Silker officers had a limited time at their disposal for metamorphosis. Otherwise they would be taken over by Boris. Well, in his case, Boris had tried to take him over without giving him the opportunity to perform his metamorphosis. He'd managed to reject that attempt. But what would happen when the time was up and Boris had no access to his brain? Would they just discard him? He hadn't thought this through. They hadn't accounted for the process taking this long. Truth be told, they had no previous experience with how metamorphosis worked.

Well, he'd rested enough. Back to work now, and maybe he'd better change some of the priorities, as he'd have to show some external changes to Boris to prove he was not lost, that it was only taking a bit longer. He had to give the prince enough to keep him going.

All right then, finish the skin job and then move directly to flesh budding. Grow some shapes and then get back to functions. The most complex job was actually the hormones, creating new types of hormones and the entire system to produce them on cue and at more accelerated rates than the body was used to. Not to mention the entire mechanism that would keep the body from rejecting the new hormones and the manufacture of new hormones. That would take hours more to design, and then days to make the body accept them and integrate them into its system.

To put a face to the guiding voice, he visualized Bree's face explaining the entire process. Yes, it was better than just consulting a drawing of the systems. She could be his guide and his companion. He felt she was one with him. It was the most intimate thing he'd ever felt, especially in this bodiless state of simple will and spirit.

Bree was his North Star, he thought, remembering the expression. Of course he knew what that was, even though he'd never seen any star. Ever. Nor would he. But that didn't mean it didn't exist or didn't have the same value. She was his North Star. She was the flame to keep his mind warm enough to continue working. She was the reason he was still alive.

38.
Secrets

Jon sat down on the stone seat. The little girl approached and deposited on his stone a cup of tea. Silk dusk tea, which he'd always ordered since the first time he'd discovered this little gem of a teahouse in the west end of the city. They'd opened it in the melted-down ruins of a brick house. He remembered when this house was a restaurant, in the times before the Black Rain. A restaurant in a row of restaurants, pubs, and clubs, on a famous street of the city. Now all just former shapes of what it had used to be. Shambles of memories. He'd shed tears, if his tear ducts would still work the same way. But now, his tears could not flow anymore. If they could not flow anymore, they could not express his pain, his distress, or simply his sadness. They'd lost their function so they just vanished and left their ducts viscous. Once people had lost the ability to cry, they had lost the ability to openly express their feelings. That had a deep impact on how people expressed their feelings nowadays. A deep and tragic impact.

But Jon didn't like this place for the memories it brought forth. He liked it because it was one of the very few splashes of color in an otherwise gray city. The owners had painted the teahouse façade in a mad mix of pink, yellow, and crimson. One could see it from the other end of the city. Sadly for the business, the people of the Corrosion Age didn't much like colors. They preferred black and blue, for the nostalgia for lost blue skies and the longing for a truly dark night of rest without fear of turning into a Nightmare.

The little girl smiled and he deposited a coin in her out-stretched palm. She was a little piece of human, probably not older than ten. Her face had been savagely gnawed by the corrosion and her little body was twisted and deformed by a lost battle with the gelled water. She was beyond any human shape, yet her eyes—her eyes were shining with the innocence and cheerfulness of a child. A child who still didn't know what life had brought upon her. A child who maybe didn't have a full decade left in her ravaged little body. So, she was still enjoying life and took it one day at a time with its daily moments of pure, unadulterated happiness. She was the main reason he had kept coming to this little corner of heaven. Jon longed for innocence. He longed for the rare glimpse of humanity's lost soul in this bleak world of seething green.

He watched her hop away from his stone, mumbling a little song only she could hear. He smiled and breathed with ease. His tea was steaming in the porcelain cup. They'd somehow man-aged to find a porcelain tea service of unbroken cups, allowing them to serve their clientele in such a luxury. He dropped a wedge of bitter bark into the tea and mixed it with the metal stick that had replaced the spoons. Silk dusk was a very sweet melange of herbs and silk that not only had a wonderful taste, but offered some mental stimulation to tired brains, like his old brain. The best energetic stimulation, after real black tea and coffee had disappeared from their world. Jon was probably the last one to still remember coffee.

"Good morning, Jon," Lir's voice scraped his ears. He opened his eyes and sighed, resigned. Yes, he was here to meet her. Not the main reason he visited the teahouse today, but cer-tainly the opportunity to do it.

Lir was a hulk of a woman, taller than him and broader in the shoulders. Her face was still untouched by corrosion, though her body was beyond stocky; it was bulbous in some parts, and a bit twisted. She was quite an impressive presence. The strength that radiated from her kept everyone at bay. Her eyes were dark brown and incisive. She always looked suspicious of everyone around her and liked digging into their minds to find a shred of evidence against them. She was not a pleasant person, Jon decided for the hundredth time.

"Good morning, Lir."

"I don't know why you make me come all this way to this silly shop. It's not like it's closer to your neighborhood."

"It gives me the opportunity to walk. To exercise my aching body."

"You always sound weird, Jon. A man from a different time."

Jon chuckled and looked for the little girl. She was approaching them to take Lir's order. He had an urge to keep the girl away from this unpleasant woman. The presence of innocence in proximity to Lir screamed danger. And that was something he should consider for the sake of his community. If Lir sent so many perilous signals, why did he keep working with her? He'd done some background research on the woman, but couldn't find much. She was a mystery to him. Which triggered his common sense as danger. Yet his common sense had never been in tune with this new reality.

"Whatever he drinks," Lir ordered, and the little girl ran back into the teahouse with the order for her mother.

"What do you have for me today, old man?"

"We need six diggers."

Jon noticed the flash of wonder on Lir's face. Just two seconds, then she was back to her usual grumpiness. "What do you need them for, Jon?"

"The ambassador showed us where to dig to find a deep enough place to hide from the coming Rain."

"You really believe that Liquid's words?"

"If there's a 10 percent chance for the next Rain to come soon, would you just sit and wait because your source is a Liquid?"

"Hmm," grumbled Lir. "Ten percent seems to me a pretty small chance of getting the Rain."

"How about those six diggers?"

"That's a tall order, old man. I mean, it's not like you're asking me for a sewerer. Diggers are kept under tight security."

"I'm sure you can divert a few to us and put them down as part of a delivery," said Jon.

The little girl brought Lir the tea in a stone mug. She placed the mug on the stone in front of her. "Are you, now?" said Lir, and caught the little girl's arm in a flash.

"What are you doing?" said Jon, feeling his heart pumping harder. Maybe it hadn't been such a good idea to expose the teahouse to his underground movement and its brutish conspirators.

"Why does he have that and you brought me this?" the woman asked the little girl, pointing to her ugly stone mug.

The girl shook away Lir's fingers and glared at the woman. "That's why."

"That's why what?"

"Because you can do these violent things and we don't trust you not to break our cups. But the old man is always so gentle." The girl turned on her heels and ran back into the teahouse.

Lir looked at Jon with something like incredulity on her face. "Did you hear that little shit?"

"Yeah. Loud and clear," confirmed Jon.

"Where you wanna dig?"

"Not far from here. Apparently, there's an undiscovered network of tunnels."

"Hmm," grumbled Lir. "I don't know. Kind of risky."

"How much?"

"I'll see what I can do first, then send you a message."

"Good. Thank you, Lir."

The woman spat and rose. She left without a word. Her tea wasn't even steaming and it had a certain unclear look to it. The water was half-gelled. The teahouse owners didn't like Lir much. Jon sympathized. He grinned and sipped from his tea. Delicious.

39.
Hyalophora

Geo opened his eyes and stared at the ceiling. He was not in the old refrigerator room he called the Woodmans' operation center. And he was not in his room in Silkers Tower. The ceiling was raw gray concrete. There was a strong, sharp smell in the air. Something unpleasant. Something that stank like a warning. He wrinkled his nose and grunted, trying to rise. The air was dense and so, so humid. He was—

Someone vigorously rang a bell. Gelling wood, that was a terrible noise! His head hurt like hell.

Geo heard footsteps. He rose with an effort and rested on the edge of the bed. More a cot, like a prison bed: a thin, dirty mattress on top of a rusty metal frame. The bed was in a very large, dark, and empty hall. Not far from his bed, right at the edge of darkness, a number of soldiers stood with their nocked bows trained on him.

What happened? He saw flashes of a wet, red world and an expanse of bright lights in a deep field of darkness. A network of liquid channels—Geo groaned. His head was splitting and everything seemed to be spinning around him at the speed of sound. He fell back on the mattress. The bowmen tensed, adjusting their arrows. *What the fuck!*

"Look who's up!"

That voice was familiar. Boris. The flashes began to make

sense. The ritual.

Geo rose again and looked at his arms. He gasped in shock. He remembered, yet the reality was beyond what he was prepared to accept. He choked. His trachea was constricted. It wouldn't allow the air in or out. He shut his eyes and struggled, grabbing at his throat with his right hand. The archers stepped closer, their bowstrings squeaking.

"Easy!" Boris placed a palm on Geo's back, helping him to remain upright on the edge of the bed. "Breathe."

Geo opened his eyes again and exhaled with a long hiss. He noticed that Boris held out his hand to the archers, signaling them not to shoot him. They were afraid. They were afraid of him!

"Yes, that's it. Breathe. Easy. Focus on the floor. Nice floor."

Holy Wood! He'd pulled it off. He actually did it. Geo Fucking Woodman went through the entire corrosion metamorphic process and exited at the other end conscious and aware. So far, it felt like he was still the same old shitty Geo.

"Good," said Boris. He stepped back and grinned. The archers stepped back with him. Geo rose on uncertain legs. It still took effort to breathe. It was an effort to move his muscles. He felt as if every muscle needed a separate command, like he couldn't just move them automatically, as he was used to. His body felt like a battalion of untrained soldiers, each waiting to be addressed individually. And from what he remembered, that was not good. At all! He had to regain control of his own body. Fast. Or Boris would—what would Boris do?

"Nothing exists except atoms and empty space," the prince said gravely, his expression solemn.

Before Geo could think of anything, he heard himself utter distinctly, "Everything else is just opinion."

"Welcome, my Hyalophora," said Boris, grinning wider than Geo had ever seen.

"Nothing but atoms and empty space!" repeated the soldiers in a single voice. They'd taken the arrows from their bows, and formed a living wall all around Geo.

"What's going on?" murmured Geo.

"You are now truly a Silker. You are now our brother in spirit," said Boris.

"Nothing but atoms and empty space!" thundered the soldiers again.

"This is the Silkers' core philosophy. And this is how your spirit recognized ours and entered Silker holy communion." The prince beamed with enthusiasm.

Geo kept quiet. He slowly realized he'd known the quote from his days of study, but he would never have remembered it just like that. He couldn't say right now who had said it, but he was certain it was an ancient Greek philosopher. So, the Silkers' core philosophy was the cosmological perspective of the universe of whoever had said that thousands of years ago. Obviously his brain was currently working in slow motion, but somehow he'd replied without thinking to the Silkers' pass phrase of acceptance into their ranks. What the fuck was happening?

The warriors retreated. Only the prince stayed. He approached Geo again and still beaming with satisfaction he bent and levelled his eyes with Geo's.

"Now, you're truly one of us."

"I don't understand how this happened…"

"Don't fret now. In time, you'll understand everything. Right now, you need to step into your new role."

"My new role?"

"You are the Silkers' Hyalophora. You are now truly our man."

"All right…"

"Show me," said Boris.

The prince's grin had started to irritate Geo. One could grin when given reason, but then it needed to stop. Who would freeze their expression into a grin for hours? It was not the first time Geo had felt tired of the prince's…sign of madness. Yes, that was it. Boris was probably mad.

"Well?"

"What?" snapped Geo.

"Your Silker's arm!"

Oh, shit! With all the weird things, he'd forgotten what all this was about. He looked at his bandaged arm with fear. What would be hidden under the bandage? He'd designed very specific plans with Bree, but it was one thing to draw theoretical things and another thing to actually produce them inside your body. To use your body like a factory and your mind like a computer and…

That's exactly what they are, Geo. You need to step into that frame of mind. Your brain is an ultrafast supercomputer. You just have to find the conscious interface and start using it as such to its full capacity. Bree's voice calmed him. Hers had become the voice of reason. His anchor into what was happening. He had to keep a grasp on reality and manage his situation. Because right now he was at Boris's beck and call in the bowels of the prince's tower.

"Right," said Geo. "Right. My arm."

He unwrapped the bandages layer after layer. Clean and professionally done. He probed for pain. But there was no pain, no discomfort. He could move his arm freely, flex his muscles; everything seemed in order. Only it didn't move as fluidly and naturally as he was used to.

He unwrapped the last layer and let it fall on the floor.

"Rust!" Boris's grin twisted with fury.

Geo's arm looked normal. He remembered the searing pain when the axe had sliced through his flesh and detached his arm at the elbow. Now his arm was back in its entirety. Pink, fresh, and alive.

"What the gel did you do?"

"Relax," said Geo. "You'll see."

He flexed his fingers, one at a time, which looked weird as hell. Had he somehow scrambled his connections? How could he get back into moving more than one muscle or one group of muscles at the same time?

"How are you doing that?" said Boris.

"I don't know. I think I'll need some time to adjust to this new reality."

"And what reality is that?"

"Gelled water inside me and post-metamorphosis."

"I don't think it has to do with any of that," said Boris.

"I have difficulties moving more muscles at the same time. Isn't this normal for—"

"Post-metamorphosis?" the prince mocked.

"Silkers. For Silkers."

"No. I've never seen anything like this before. Probably it's because you didn't know how to properly build and connect an arm to your body."

"It's not just my arm, Boris. It's my entire body."

The prince paced through the empty room. Geo tried to order his body to move more at once. He felt like a broken robot.

"Rebuilding your arm as it was is not part of our metamorphosis goal. It is not part of our philosophy. This is…"

With a huge effort, Geo stood. Boris looked at him curiously. Then he went on: "Doing this means insult. It means capital offense. Anything milder than this takes you to having your head chopped off and a dog head regrown onto your shoulders."

"Would you do that to me?"

"Happily," said Boris, dead serious.

Geo stared at him. Nothing to be said after all. Not that he had ever considered the prince his real friend. But he'd hoped for some bonding over time, with all they'd been through.

"After all that has happened, you deserve worse."

"What has happened?"

"I staked my throne on your metamorphosis when everyone asked for your head."

"Why would they ask for my head?"

"It took you two weeks to get out of the nine thresholds process," said Boris.

"Holy Wood!"

"Yeah, and Lady L has been in a coma ever since."

"Lady L's in a coma? Why?"

"Because of you."

"I don't understand."

"During your ritual you did something that—that…"

"How was that possible?" Geo couldn't stand anymore. He crumpled onto the mattress. The prince seemed to be really upset. He'd never seen him that angry. Lady L! Coma?

"The more I think about it, the more I realize that I'd like very much to chop off your head," said the prince.

"This." Geo held up his right arm with his left hand. "This is not all, Boris. You have to trust me."

"Trust you?"

"Let me show you what it is."

Geo scrambled back to his feet. He exhaled and focused. Focused on his right arm. His Silker's arm.

"Really? I allowed you two weeks for metamorphosis when my weakest Silker gets twenty-four hours at the most and now you're not even able to—whatever it is you want to show me."

Geo closed his eyes and tried to bring back the experience he'd had during the ritual. He tried to visualize inside his body, to check that everything was in place, everything was working, everything was...

"I've seen enough. Guards!"

Boris hurried to Lady L's apartment. The doctor's assistant ran in front of him as if leading the way. The prince sorely needed to just push the annoying kid aside and run too. But he had to maintain an image. The prince, and even more so the mayor, didn't run. Even when in a hurry, he had to walk majestically toward his goal.

But more important right now was the fact that Lady L had awakened. Finally, good news in an otherwise shitty day. Who was he kidding. A shitty week.

His plans were completely derailed by Geo's fuck up. What were his options now? With the ambassador condemned, he had no alternative but to give free rein to his brother.

"My lord," a child yelled breathlessly, cutting him off. "The Morpho Master sent me to fetch you."

What was with youth and lack of discipline? Etiquette, you gelling idiots! That's what will elevate us. Not bumbling imbeciles thinking they can do whatever they want, whenever they feel like doing it. The prince grabbed the yelling child by his scruff. "Never. Ever. Use fetch in the same sentence with me." He pushed the boy down the stairs and turned back. The boy would recover. He was young. They always recovered. But that might teach him to at least pause before an outburst.

The doctor's assistant again bustled in front of the prince to lead the way. Boris grabbed a handful of his shirt and stopped him. He tried to tell him something, to teach him a lesson, but no words found their way out of his mouth. He realized he didn't care to teach that fool anything. So he tossed him over the stair railing. The young man fell with a short scream that ended in a sick, fleshy smack. Well, that one wouldn't recover. He'd seen people get back on their feet even after breaking their necks, but this time he doubted there would be any recovery.

The corridors fell silent. Everyone retreated out of his way. *That's right. You're learning.* Boris felt good. Lesson well done. People learned when given concrete examples.

He resumed his majestic walk to Lady L's apartment. His personal guard reformed behind him and followed. That was the key behavior Boris was looking for in any of his subjects. Any breathing, corroding, gelling subjects in his kingdom—FOLLOW. No need to make any effort, like thinking, choosing, deciding. Their prince did all that for them. All the effort for his unworthy subjects was on his shoulders.

Boris entered the apartments like a thunderstorm. Hurried, yet displaying leadership and restraint. The guards remained outside. The door shut behind him with a big bang worthy of the type of monumental door he'd had installed for every member of the royal family.

"Your Highness," said the doctor, and bowed.

Lady L was sitting next to the window. She turned her head and smiled. Her plump red lips spread joy. A joy that her black mask could not render otherwise.

"She's still weak, but fully recovered, Your Highness," murmured the doctor.

"Does she still need you?"

"I don't—I hope not."

You don't offer much confidence as a doctor when your professional opinion contains hope rather than concrete information. Then leave."

The doctor bowed again and left. The prince looked at Lady L for a few moments. She'd been so close to leaving him. That was a terrifying thought. He stepped closer and knelt next to her chair: "Oh, Mother, you scared me so."

The prison cell was an improvement to the room he'd awakened in. It was smaller, colder, and he was alone. Unfortunately he only had a few hours in front of him. By nightfall, he'd probably be dead. Silkers liked to be swift when administering justice. That was, when getting rid of enemies. And that's what he was right now—enemy. He'd put Boris in jeopardy and the prince would have to take stern measures to prove to his court that he was always acting to their benefit. To the Silkers' benefit.

Two weeks in a self-induced coma. That was a lot. How did they keep him alive? Boris was right. He had to not only keep everyone from murdering Geo, but take active measures to take care of Geo while he was in a coma. That was commitment. Dedication. And that was where math had to intervene and keep everything ordered and neat.

Boris was not Geo's friend. He'd known that despite the prince's repeated declarations. He'd said clearly now that friendship was not part of the deal. So, first equation—Boris was not Geo's friend. Shit, it still hurt.

But—but Boris had saved Geo repeatedly. At least three times so far. And the last time had been the most serious one. He'd gone against his court's murderous ways to keep Geo alive, despite the unprecedented happening. No Silker officer had ever stayed in the Nine Threshold Sleep, which practically was a coma, more than twenty-four hours. Which made Geo a unique case that had broken all the unwritten rules of the Silkers Law. Although they'd never thought of that—their law was based on tradition and tradition meant twenty-four hours. But there had been no precedent. So practically, there was nothing against a coma longer than twenty-four hours. Nothing but their own murderous intent.

So, the second equation was that the court wanted him dead while Boris wanted him alive. Were these one or two equations? Let's make it two and have a three-equation system. The Silker Court wanted Geo dead out of fear or simple blood lust. Second, Silver Star wanted Geo dead because of his hatred for liquid people.

Anyway, more importantly, the third equation, Boris wanted him alive, although the prince was not his friend and didn't care about Geo as a person. That meant he only cared about Geo as political potential. Would the result of this system be that the prince wanted a peaceful relationship with the Woodman Clan? He wasn't afraid of the Woodmans. He'd expressly stated that. He didn't have much use for wood, no matter the prestige that brought. After all, Boris had already seized power in Torono. He was the *de facto* ruler of the entire Ont kingdom. With his wooden throne he didn't need more wood to impress an already submitting kingdom.

The only mathematically logical conclusion was that Boris was after the Woodmans' science. The only thing that they had more of than anyone else in this part of the world. That and clean, liquid water. But the prince was a Corrosive through and through. If he had the possibility, he'd destroy all sources of liquid water and force the entire human population to submit to the Corrosion.

Well, that was an interesting thought. But if Geo wanted to entertain that idea, another culprit rose to the front of his equations system—Silver Star. That psycho was definitely the one who would want to not only destroy all sources of liquid water, but wipe out all Liquid people, as they referred to them.

Hmm, interesting. Geo was the tool to be manipulated in Boris's hands to get to the Woodmans' science. Geo was also the abomination to be erased, in Silver's eyes. The court seemed to lean more toward Silver's position, rather than that of their prince. Which was weird, considering that until a few weeks ago, Silver Star had been the enforcer of the opposition. He'd played the strong arm of the Silkers' enemy, the former mayor of Torono. The late de facto ruler of the kingdom.

So, his entire equations system placed Geo on a sand foundation. To stay alive, he would need to convince Boris's court he was worth saving. That he was now a real Silker, like them. That he was now part of their tribe. That the Woodman Clan was now his enemy too. Because even though they entertained the idea of trade with other clans, everyone outside the Silkers Clan was automatically an enemy. They were very much the embodiment of xenophobia.

He'd have to examine each equation separately and come up with individual solutions. And just in case, have a fourth solution as a backup plan. Think quickly, before they came after him.

Right—

The cell door opened and a couple of warriors looked at him from the corridor. Shit! Geo stepped back and stared at the two men. Armed to their teeth—professional warriors. Death was their trade. He needed a backup plan.

"You're free to go," said one of the warriors.

Geo continued to stare at them. The words didn't process well.

"You're free to go, sir," added the second one.

"Go where?"

Was that the first thing he was asking? Why did he feel like this was an out of body experience?

"Wherever you like, sir."

40.
Diggers for the Revolution

The night was quiet. Humid and fragrant. The air trembled in waves of liquid heat from the torches. Jon rested his legs on a piece of concrete, close to a building still standing tall, but only glass and steel, hard to keep cool in the summer, impossible to warm during winter. No use for Corrosives. It was uninhabited and had succumbed to dereliction. Jon supposed it had been a business building before the Rain. He couldn't remember. It had been so long ago. Sometimes it almost felt like the memories were from a fictional life. Too good to be true. Too long ago to be clear. Lifting a finger, he traced the path that tears had once followed down his cheeks. He missed them. He missed crying so much, it hurt.

He had so much to teach young people, yet there was no one left to teach. Life was so hard in the Corrosion Age that they barely had time to learn to read and count. With no more books to read, he knew that his death would not only mean his death, but the final death of Pythagoras, Aristotle, and Plato; the death of idealism, pragmatism, of nihilism and existentialism, stoicism, and every other human idea and intellectual thought. He was the last professor of philosophy in this part of the world. After the death of the written word and the disappearance of every other type of historical account, Jon's knowledge was the last bastion of human knowledge. Everything would be forgotten.

Everything would be new, freshly discovered. New, but not innocent. Night could bring such thoughts upon the former academic.

Jon heard shuffling and heavy breathing. He rose from the concrete slab and stretched his back. A few silhouettes detached from the darkness. Lir led a group of diggers, their bodies undulating while they walked, as if they were swimming through the dense air. Jon shivered at the sight of them. He'd never seen one, just heard of them. They were real giants in the world of humans, with heads like enormous pumpkins, small, double-lidded eyes, no nostrils, and mouths collapsed inside the head and protected by tightly interlocking, scaly lips. Their arms were longer than normal and ended in huge, fingerless palms that looked more like shovels. Jon knew that the external appearance of the diggers was the least important genetic transformation. The drastic changes were inside, in the new organs and the new functions of those organs that no human could perform.

Lir had brought him three diggers. That was awesome! Now their plans would have a real chance of success.

"Old man," said Lir.

"Lir." Jon nodded in greeting.

"Here's your request."

"Thank you. I really appreciate it," said Jon.

"Where's my payment?"

Jon swept his arm sideways and watched the street behind Lir and her diggers. A light flickered two blocks down and vanished. Then again. And a third time. Jon smiled and turned his eyes to the diggers. "Are they locked?"

"First my payment, then you can have your keys," said Lir.

Worried, Jon again looked down the street.

"Really, old man. You think that I brought the Blues on you?"

"You can never be too careful."

"True, that. But I worked with you for years."

Indeed, Lir had connected with the underground movement about three years ago. Who had introduced her? No one he could remember. Had there been anyone? As far as he could remember, Lir had seemed to suddenly operate inside the move-ment. Jon's movement. Which felt odd. But yes, she was right—she'd always delivered.

"Stev," said Jon.

The young man came out of the darkness carrying a bag. He offered the bag to Lir, but she stepped back. "Drop it." Stev dropped the bag on the cracked pavement. Then he took a step back and waited.

"So, here's the entrance to those unknown tunnels?" asked Lir nonchalantly.

"Maybe." Jon smiled.

"I'd like to see where you plan to dig, old man."

"Why?"

"You know that you have to return these diggers to me in the same condition. That is, almost new and undamaged."

"Yes, I know that, Lir. It's part of the contract."

"Then you understand I need to make sure that where you want to use them is compliant with the terms of the contract. I don't like surprises."

"I don't like surprises either," said Jon.

"Meaning?"

"Meaning you seeing the digging site is not part of the con-tract."

"You don't trust me," Lir stated.

"No."

"Open it," Lir said to Stev.

The young man looked at Jon. He nodded. Stev untied the mouth of the bag and opened it carefully, then tipped it toward Lir. Jon offered his torch to illuminate the bag's contents. There was slow movement under the torch's flame. Lir bent over and opened the bag's mouth wider. A wet slapping sound made Jon jump. Lir yelped in pain and retreated, shaking her right hand. A dark shape clung to her skin, despite her violent movements.

"Stay still," growled Jon.

Lir grunted in pain and stopped shaking her hand. She extended her right arm. Jon touched the flame to the dark shape. With a jolt, it detached and fell, leaving a purple mark on Lir's trembling hand.

"The poison will dissipate in a couple of hours," said Jon. "Until then, try not to use your hand."

"Motherfucker!"

"Yup," agreed Jon. "A bag full of kissing mushrooms, as requested. Now I need those keys, please."

"Motherfucker!" repeated Lir, holding her right hand with her left.

"I think we already agreed on that."

The woman took out a small pack made of leaves and interwoven blades of devil's grass. She threw it to Stev. "You'll find everything you need inside." Then she turned to Jon. "You never warned me."

"Anyone who requests such a payment must know what it is they asked for."

"I won't forget this." She spat on the pavement, grabbed the bag of kissing mushrooms, and walked away.

The diggers waited with vacant eyes. Jon felt a twinge of sadness. He took the pack made of devil grass from Stev.

"Wow, three diggers!" said Stev, visibly impressed. "You said one is enough."

"Yes, I like to ask for more and see what happens."

"We'll be ready way ahead of time."

"This time we really have a chance," said Jon.

41.
The Bastard's Recourse

Doc looked from Momma Mar's chest to Jon and back. He sighed.

Jon knew what he was going to say, but as always in life, one needed the certainty of words. "What is it, Doc?"

"I'm sorry to be the bringer of bad news, but…"

"The suspense is killing me faster than the corrosion," said Momma Mar, covering her chest.

Of course she knew as well. Jon had no doubt that Mar had known for a while now. Yet it was the kind of subject they'd always avoided.

"The treatment is not working as it should. That means that in a very short while, it won't make any difference anymore."

"That would be the end of the line," said Momma Mar, smiling.

"Only if you have a flair for drama." Jon grinned and patted her hand.

They both knew that it may well be the end of the line, if the gelled water decided that. Or the water may keep her alive for another hundred years. But those could be very tortured years for Mar. Jon didn't know what to hope for. A swift death would mean he'd lose her. Forever. But if she survived his last years next to him, she may become a breathing sponge with the functionality of a stone, yet with her consciousness intact, and suffering every moment. Or she may retain some functionality and live an almost regular life. That was the thing with the gelled water—it was unpredictable. He was supposed to be long dead. He was probably the oldest Corrosive in the city, and he was still functional and living as close to normal as possible.

"I'm sorry, my friends," said Doc.

Jon's grin slipped a bit. Their friend wasn't melodramatic. He was just very sensitive. Quite emotional. He'd always been that way and that was what had made him so endearing, despite working for the enemy. "Doc, you've been visiting with the mayor's scientists. No word yet of a new treatment?"

"I wish my clearance was that good, my friend," said Doc.

The door opened and Ton entered, trying to avert his eyes. Doc laughed. "Don't fret, young man, we're done."

"Dad," blurted Ton, "the Hyalo Warriors—they're here with Pi."

Jon opened his mouth to ask "what?" but realized it was useless. It was too late to repair past mistakes. He nodded to his son and offered his hand to Mar. "We need to go, love."

"No!" Doc was beyond indignation. "No, you don't need to go because of that squirt Pi!"

"You could come with us, Doc."

"No!"

Doc stormed out of the room and Jon could hear his heavy footsteps going down the stairs. He helped Mar stand and followed Ton toward the back door. They moved as quietly as possible. Jon couldn't help but hear the exchange downstairs, in the shop.

"What do you think you're doing here, Pi?"

"Where's the bitch without tits, Doc?"

"You impertinent prick!"

"He's giving treatments for free! He's stealing from His Highness!"

"No, I'm not! Hey, take your hands off me! Get off —"

The words ended with a gurgling noise. Jon could very well imagine the cause of that. "Goodbye, my dear friend," he whispered, trying to keep up with his son and Mar.

"Let's check upstairs for the thieves."

Di was keeping the back door open for them. Jon followed everybody out the door and Di closed and locked it behind them. The backyard was dark. No light to detach the ghost from the bottomless emptiness of the city. There was a trapdoor ten feet from the door. It led to the sewers—their only way out of the Hyalo Warriors' claws. That and a good measure of luck.

The sewers were not only dark and stinking of feces, they were full of the groans and grunts of the sewerers. Those miracles of bioengineering could not pass through their section of the sewers because of the two gates installed years ago on both ends of the waste tunnel, just for a time such as this.

Di opened the secret door leading to a smugglers tunnel, dug years before the corrosion. They had discovered the door by accident when they'd tried to dig a panic room for themselves. After that, they had explored the tunnels at their leisure and years later had finally emerged in the Lakefront Tribe's palace across from the station. A mere fifteen-minute walk on the surface, but quite a convoluted and arduous underground road. Obviously, they hadn't opened it at the other end, as they hadn't wanted to reveal it to the Frontlakers.

Now, though, it would be different.

42.
The Circumvolution

Bree touched his face. Geo was thin, with heavy, dark circles under his eyes, and he hadn't shaved since she last saw him. He didn't wear his helmet anymore, only his visor. And his left arm was bandaged up to his elbow. She cringed when seeing that— she'd remembered what Geo had told her about the Silkers' barbaric ritual. So, he'd gone through that and survived.

His skin was wet with sweat. *So he can still sweat and lose water.* He was probably only half Corrosive. Not long now before he reached the final stage. Would he still be the Geo she knew?

Geo took her hand and kissed her palm. She shivered. He smiled his usual warm, childish smile. He was still himself. Her Geo. But for how long? She leaned over and kissed his lips. They were cold and wet. She sensed him hesitating for a second before kissing her back.

The freezing room was dark and cold, the mattress dirty, and she'd had only ultrasonic showers for the past weeks, yet this was perfect. This was all she'd dreamt of lately. This was their first and last love. Sadness settled in her mind and as he removed his protective suit she hugged him desperately. They collapsed onto the mattress. He helped her get rid of her t-shirt and her underwear. When they were both naked, skin against skin, Geo helped her climb on top of him and guided her gently. He was hers now and she was his. Before he'd become something else.

The secret door opened into a dark cellar. It was musty and draped in spiderwebs as thick as wool. Ton started a torch. The flame flickered, undecided. Sparks jumped and touched the spiderwebs and the flames spread languidly on the walls, crackling and smoking. He stepped carefully aside, making room for the others to enter as well.

The cellar was abandoned, full of dusty bottles and cans. Dust—something they hadn't experienced in half a century. That's when Jon realized that the air was dry and stale. That room had been perfectly isolated since probably well before the Black Rain. He chortled.

"What's wrong, Jon?" asked Mar.

How could he explain his delight in breathing some dusty, stale air? They wouldn't understand. "Nothing's wrong. It's just…"

Everybody looked at him expectantly. He'd been the classic *pater familias* for his family not out of his love for patriarchy, but because he'd been more the teacher, not only for his children, but for his wife as well. Everyone expected him to always have solutions to everything.

"We may find it difficult to get out of this room," he added, still smiling.

"Nothing funny about that," said Mar, puzzled.

The room's door was bricked in. There was no visible vent, yet although the air was stale, it was still breathable. So, the insulation hadn't been perfect. Somewhere, the room was exchanging air with the outside world. They just had to find the way out.

"All right, everyone, new plan," said Jon. "Move the furniture. Bring it to the center of the room."

"Tell me everything." Bree felt choked with expectations. She'd understood Geo's motivations and the real necessity of subjecting himself to the Corrosives' cruel rituals, but—There would always be a *but*.

"I always imagined that when death came, I'd be cool and dignified," said Geo.

"What? You imagined when your death would come?"

"Well, yes. Out here, that's a big certainty."

"You never said anything."

"What could I say, Bree? 'My dear council, I fear I may die on the next mission. And here is how I'll die'?"

Bree knew he wanted to make light of a grim situation, but she couldn't smile, let alone laugh at his joke. Why did boys always have to believe that they bore the weight of the world on their shoulders? They always needed to pose and play the brave and unflinching. She tried to imagine how it must be to leave home every time with the thought that it was your last time. She could never...

"Not to the council, dummy. To me."

"You were not mine to burden you with this."

"I've always been yours, Geo."

"Then it's better I didn't know that."

"Why?" Bree stared at him, fascinated. It was like discovering a complete stranger behind the façade of her old friend.

"If I knew..." he sighed, "if I knew, I-I probably wouldn't have had the strength to go through with this."

And *that* was the difference between Geo and his brother. That right there was why she'd always loved Geo.

"So you know, not when you die suddenly, but when you know and you're waiting for the final blow. When you realize that's it, it's all ending, no more days, love, family—it's all coming to the final end. That's what went through my head before they chopped off my arm."

"Oh, Geo..." Bree's eyes filled with tears. "I wish I could've been there with you, holding your hand."

"So, the sound began, they actually have a recorded rain, pre-corrosion. You know, like a normal, liquid rain. Drops of water splashing on the asphalt, on the window's glass; you feel it pouring, draining—you kind of feel its liquidness, the chill feeling of it washing down your face. It is eerie. It's a good and a bad feeling all at once."

Geo gulped and closed his eyes. A teardrop formed at the corner of his eye. It oscillated between its liquid state and the new gel state, like water freezing in front of her eyes. *His last tear*, Bree realized and started crying. He'd surprised her, surpassing her cry like boys do. Like the boys doing it to protect the other's feelings. To present the others with an always happy state, so they wouldn't burden anyone. She was doing it without realizing it. And weirdly enough, she felt guilty for crying now, when he was going through this horrific experience of becoming a Corrosive and she was the one expressing her horror, not allowing him his last tear in peace.

She felt his palm caressing her face. His eyes were moist, fighting their last chance at crying.

"Thank you," he said.

"Why?"

"For caring. It's been so long since anyone cared about me enough to allow me to feel it."

That was it right there. No more guilt. Just normal human instincts. Bree smiled sadly. She kissed his palm, salty and wet with her tears.

Jon had been right—behind a rack filled with cans was a small door opening to a passage inside the wall. It was no more than a few steps long before ending at another bricked-over opening. Only the construction of this one was shabby, the mortar cracked, barely holding. It was obvious that it had been only a disguise meant to trick strangers. It should be easily dismantled. Indeed, it proved a small job for Ton, who kicked it open.

They passed through the tunnel one by one into a kitchen, where cooks looked at them emerging with expressions of alarm and curiosity. It wasn't every day that someone broke into your kitchen through a wall, filling it with dust and cottony spiderwebs.

They tried to run through the kitchen and out of the building, but when they ran out the back door to the alley, guards surrounded them, their spears pointing at their hearts. They'd just broken into the Lakefront Tribe's palace and probably ruined the lord of the Lakefront's meal in the process. Jon knew nothing of the lord. Nothing to give him leverage. No one had ever seen him outside the palace. He was one of the urban legends of Torono.

"Lord Lakefront awaits you," said the captain of the guard.

"You make it sound easier than what I imagined," said Bree.

Geo smiled and rose. He stretched and she could see his restlessness. Some things had happened these last weeks that he didn't want to share. But it was obvious they weighed on him and he needed solutions. Well, she couldn't force him to talk, but she could coax him.

Bree smiled in her turn and rose as well. "Well, let me tell you about my adventures."

"Oh, you had adventures?"

"Real exciting adventures, mister."

"Pray, tell—"

The security alarm burst to life, emitting low buzzes inside the room, followed by the flashing red light. Somebody had broken into their security perimeter.

"There's no one that—"

"We expect?" said Geo. He grinned and pressed a button in the wall.

"What did you do?"

"I disabled the system that keeps the rats away from the inside of the temple."

Bree smiled. She should've guessed there was a system to defend this place. Geo continued to surprise her. If only her grandfather had known how thorough and smart Geo was. Maybe, just maybe everything would have been different then. No use thinking of that now. They had to survive out here, and right now.

"Come on. Get dressed and let's go," said Geo.

"But..."

"Well, even if the rats will keep them away for now, this

place is now compromised. So we need to relocate."

"Relocate?" She said, pulling the protective suit on.

"Less talk, more action. I'll explain everything on the way."

Behind them, the things that they couldn't carry burned furiously. Geo led her along the walls of the King Rat Temple, keeping to the shadows. They activated their suits' ultrasounds against the rats, so no rodent approached them. Instead they swarmed the main hall of the temple, where a detachment of soldiers was fighting them off. No small task, considering the size of the rats and their fangs. And their sheer number. The rats were legion.

Geo stopped and studied the men battling the rodents. He swore.

"What?" Bree asked.

"They're Luna Warriors."

"I don't know what that means, Geo."

"They're Boris's warriors. He tricked me. Again."

"Oh," said Bree and grabbed his arm. "I say let's escape while we can. It seems to me these Luna Warriors are quite efficient."

"Let's go," acknowledged Geo. He took her hand and guided her away from the battlefield, toward the back of the building, straight into the Rat Fields. He ran crouched low, trying to stay undetected while moving quickly.

They soon left the Rat Fields behind and entered the Nightmares Esplanade. But not for long. They took the first street on the right and returned to the city proper.

Geo looked like a man on a mission. Like he'd found his new purpose. Bree didn't know if she should relax while being guided by him, or if she should be scared and careful. Because he looked now like he had too much purpose. They had to talk.

Luna Warriors! If she'd heard that name in a story, back in the Caves, she'd have romantic notions about them. The name alone was wonderful. But then she'd seen them, their horrific masks, their methodical hacking of the rats, blood splattering their uniforms. They were perfect killing machines: cold, calculating, efficient. Butchers. Nothing romantic about them.

Geo had just returned to her and now their world had collapsed around them once again, and monsters were hunting them. Was there no respite in this new world?

The Lakefront Palace was ridiculously beautiful and perfectly preserved. Here, people moved with purpose. It was like they'd stepped into a different era. Music flooded the antechamber where the guards had brought them. Jon stiffened. Everyone else looked around with big, round eyes.

"What is that?" whispered Mar.

Jon watched them. If he could still cry, he'd cry right now. Instead, he smiled and cupped Mar's cheek in his hand. "This is a miracle."

"Never heard anything like this," said Mic, his skin collar ruffled.

"It's magic," said Di.

"It's music, but not as we know it now," said Jon, happy to see his family so entranced by classical music.

"No, you said it's a miracle, so it must be magic," insisted Di.

"Yes, my dear, it's magic. This is Chopin."

The guards opened the doors and pushed them into a grand room. The walls were painted in dark blue and gold. There were still carved wood panels where the walls turned into ceiling. A huge chimney rose in the middle of one of the walls. And a piano stood in one corner of the room—a real, shining, grand piano. A huge man sat playing the piano, his lower body a mass of throbbing, pulsing flesh, his upper body still normal, save for his hands. They had already turned into tentacles, which moved gracefully over the piano's keyboard. The half Nightmare played Chopin.

43.
The Pits of Madness

The tunnel was pitch dark. Iron tracks ran along its bottom and wiring, along the walls. He hadn't been here since the first time he'd set up his backup camp in the bowels of the city. It wasn't a pleasant journey and last time, he'd encountered some lost sewerers. They had forced him to mount a different kind of defense than he'd used in the Rat King's temple. He'd still created an ultrasound barrier around it, but more important now was the electrical barrier. Which was down at the moment so he could get back to the place, and would go up as soon as they stepped inside.

So much effort…it had seemed like madness at the time, but this was his underground fort and he'd known it would come in handy one day.

The torch lit their way down the Pits of Madness. That's what the Toronions called the underground tracks. The expeditions that ventured down there had turned back with madness in their eyes. The underground track had remained unclaimed territory. Not even the sewerers had managed to claim it.

This had been Geo's first option for operations center, but the thought of spending so much time in darkness and silence had convinced him to make it his second option. The backup. And now it couldn't have been at a better time—he was not alone anymore. He had Bree.

A tiny voice crept into his head. *What about Bree?* What about Bree? Bree had him. He was going to make sure Bree would always be safe. Geo smiled and caught Bree's hand and squeezed it.

"Are we there?" she asked in a tiny voice.

"Not yet. Just wanted to—you know," he said.

"Yes," she said and squeezed his hand back.

"Keep close, and if you want you can keep your hand on my shoulder."

"Sure," she said and placed her right palm on his shoulder.

What about Bree? What about her! He was a bit annoyed. Just a bit, because he remembered his first days here, in the Pits of Madness, and that had not been a normal experience. Yes, he was here now with her, but the darkness and the silence eventually got to you. This was a bad idea, he realized. He could not keep Bree here while he was out doing his…duty. And that turned into a second equation: what was his duty, anymore? Did he still have a duty to the Woodmans? Well, he'd always be a Woodman, but that was not what the second equation was about. It was about the danger that had taken a turn and went away from the Woodmans and encircled the Toronians.

The first equation was Bree's life and safety. The second was—well it had to be the Toronians' survival. The third equation was the Woodman Clan's continued independence and freedom. It all rested on his shoulders to solve this system of equations and keep everyone alive and safe. He'd failed his brother, but that should be his last failure. He'd made too many mistakes so far and that had to stop.

Suddenly he stopped walking. Bree stumbled into him. "What—"

"Ssh." He put a finger on the visor in front of his lips.

Yes, he could hear hushed voices. Very hushed, which meant they were close by. The torch he carried had probably given them away already. So, they were exposed, but no one had attacked them yet. That was strange. Plus, everyone being here was even stranger. He wouldn't put it past the Luna Warriors to follow them here, but the voices were coming from in front of them, so someone had arrived here earlier than Bree and himself.

Or could this all be in his mind? Was he so weak that the darkness had gotten to him so quickly?

"Who's voice is that?" whispered Bree, her voice coming over his helmet's speaker.

So, it wasn't his mind crumbling to bits. The voices were real. Geo took out his gun and aimed it in front of them with his right hand. Holding the torch with his left hand, he advanced. Ten steps away he encountered a huddle of bodies. He approached it carefully. Two, three, at least four bodies huddled together, palms raised to protect their eyes from the strong torchlight.

A shriek filled the deafening silence of the underground tracks. It washed over them like a rain of pain and terror. Bree grabbed hold of Geo's gun arm. The bodies formed a real live bundle, shaking and moaning in despair. A second shriek made them all grunt in pain.

After the shriek came the stench. The unbearable death stench that only a shrieking Nightmare could produce. That told Geo it was close and it was coming. They didn't have time to hide.

"Geo!" A voice he knew called to him.

He looked around and recognized one face in the huddle on the floor. It was Jon, the leader of the underground resistance. Then other faces looked at him and he recognized all of them. And that filled him with dread—the hope of Torono's resistance and future was all here, very close to its demise.

He focused on his memories. They were less than thirty steps from his hideout, yet the Nightmare would catch up with them before they could get inside. There was the electricity panel several steps closer, still too far from them. And then…there was the changing room.

"Quick, follow me!" he said loud enough for everybody to hear and ran, pulling Bree after him.

Five steps farther he jumped on the raised concrete ledge, grabbed the knob, twisted and pulled. The door opened with a deep creak and a wave of stale, musty air made him gag. He pushed Bree inside, then helped each of the others climb up onto the threshold and enter the room. The Nightmare's stench was closer and denser than he'd ever experienced before. He was dizzy and bile rose in his throat. He staggered into the room, heaving a trail of vomit, just as the Nightmare slapped the air in the spot where he'd just been. Ton slammed the door shut behind him and Bree locked it. Geo wiped his lips. The vomit had left a sour taste in his mouth and burned his throat.

The room was small. They stood shoulder to shoulder. In a corner was the mummified body of someone in uniform. The walls were brown with ancient blood. Geo hadn't wanted to have anything to do with the ghoulish room, but special circumstances now made it their little paradise.

The Nightmare bumped into the door. More like a knock, Geo reckoned.

"What are you two doing here?" said Jon.

"We're so happy to meet you here," said Mar at the same time.

Bree smiled behind her visor and the entire room seemed to lighten.

"We're glad to have bumped into you too," said Bree. "We're looking for something."

"Well, aren't we lucky!" mumbled Mic.

The Nightmare crashed into the metal door and its hinges creaked ominously. It obviously wasn't meant to take that kind of pressure. Everybody fell silent. Geo nodded and bit his lip. The distance should do. They were close enough to the hideaway for his defenses to work. He just needed to get into the electrical room, twenty feet away. Past the Nightmare.

"Bree, put my helmet on," he said and turned his back to her.

"Why?" said Bree.

"What's he doing?" murmured Mar.

"Just do it, Bree."

She reluctantly complied and attached his helmet to her suit, connecting it with the suit's system.

"Just recapping for you," Geo said, hoping his voice sounded casual enough.

"Yes?" Bree pushed aside the others and made some room

around Geo.

"These suits are armored to withstand a bullet."

"And yet, Alex's armor couldn't stop a spear."

The Nightmare crashed against the door and the metal buckled inward. One hinge partially loosened.

"That was a special case, Bree. I know now why it was pierced."

"How do you know this is not a special case too?"

Geo ignored Bree's question. "As I recall, Jon, a shrieking Nightmare is mostly made of gelled water."

"*Poisonous* gelled water and AnJie skeleton. Not even your suit could face the AnJie."

"Thanks, Jon." Geo grinned. He wasn't an adrenaline junkie, but had learned how to get his adrenaline pumping when needed to help him overcome a violent situation. In other words, he wasn't his brother, but could manage any situation for which he had some control over the information. And now he was informed.

Another crash. One hinge popped free and the metal split.

Geo counted to three. Then he turned the doorknob and opened the door. The Nightmare was right there, withdrawn to the opposite wall, preparing for another attack. Seeing Geo, it released a shriek. He felt the sound filling his chest and his mind, leaving him trembling in horror. But instinctively he slammed the door behind him and heard them locking it from the inside.

The Nightmare attacked.

Geo dropped to the concrete ledge and rolled over onto the tracks. The Nightmare smashed into the door, missing Geo by a hair. In a flash of movement the AnJie ribcage extended from the gelled water body and caught Geo as if in a real cage. Then it pulled him into the gelled water body, keeping him from falling back down.

The Nightmare shuddered and turned. It had its prey, so it ceased the attack. It went back the way it had come. Toward Geo's hideout entrance. Geo moved his hand slowly, not only because the gelled water offered resistance to movement, but he also didn't want to trigger the AnJie skeleton's reaction. He extended his left arm, still bandaged. He could see the electricity switch next to the electrical room. They were getting closer.

The movement was lethargic now. He felt as if he were floating in suspension. Ten more steps to the switch. His arm was almost in position. He closed his eyes and focused. Time to test his Silker's weapon.

He emptied his mind and tried to visualize his target. His nervous system connected to the weapon's system. He imagined a red bull's eye in front of his closed right eye. The red bull's eye moved and everything became aligned around him. He could visualize with his weapon's optic system the walls, the concrete ledge, and there—he identified the switch. He could feel his glands producing bullets. The bull's eye overlapped with the switch. He waited for a couple of seconds to compensate for the movement, then ordered his weapon to fire.

The electrical grid came alive like a bright cubic sun around him and he had to blink in his mind to adjust to the switch in the visual system. The Nightmare stopped shuddering. Its shriek came from somewhere in the middle of its ribcage. Geo gulped for air and felt his heart stop.

Lady L was resplendent in her Crawling Nightmare dress. The polluted gelled water stones around her neck and wrists reflected light in small iridescent rainbows. She placed her right hand on Geo's chest and her left hand on his right hand on the tabletop. The table was made of a rusted metal. The metallic odor was strong in the air.

The sky was a deep cyan, no traces of clouds. Just a vast expanse of blue. The sunlight was blue, everything was so blue around them that it made his heart cry. Lady L's plump, deep red lips parted in a smile, revealing two rows of sharp teeth. Her hair cascaded down her shoulders. He'd never seen her hair. He looked at it in wonder. Her hair was like a sea of thin and delicate antennas. Millions of sensors waving gently in the morning breeze. The blue light at her back reflected through two pairs of transparent butterfly wings, shining like they were made of crystal. Lady L was magnificent.

"Breathe through me…" she said in her smooth voice. Her hand on his chest passed through his flesh. She grasped his heart in her palm. "Breathe through me," she said again.

Geo breathed in the rhythm imposed by her palm massaging his heart. The more he breathed, the more his mouth tasted like metal.

"Feel through me," Lady L whispered in his ear. "What do you fear?"

"Losing you," he said back into her lips. He kissed her.

She squeezed his heart and the pain made him wince. She squeezed again and he groaned in pain.

Geo opened his eyes and choked. He turned on his side and coughed. His chest hurt. His entire body hurt. He rose tentatively and checked his suit. It held against the poisoned gelled water and the AnJie's pressure.

He was alone in the underground tunnel, between the train tracks. No cyan sky, no metal table, no—Lady L.

It was pitch dark in the tunnel, but with his special Silker vision he could still see the electricity in the walls. His defenses were up and that would make it impossible for Bree and the Corrosives to pass.

Geo walked slowly to his hideaway and typed the code to open the door. Stale air, but at least not carrying a death stench. He entered and switched on the light. On one of the walls was the security panel. He switched the electricity off in the security perimeter and sighed. He was so tired. He sat on the only chair in the room and his helmet hit the table like a rock.

Bree didn't know if she liked Jon. But she liked Mar. Mar seemed the embodiment of a grandmother—kind, patient, understanding. And she also seemed smart and knowledgeable. Which made Bree ache for her mother. She missed her so much.

But the fact that Mar was Jon's wife and the love between them was so visible, made her give Jon some leeway. Despite his controlling and contradictory nature. Also Geo trusted him, so in a way, Jon presented all credentials Bree needed.

"You better think about it and decide to be on the right side of history," said Bree, studying him.

Jon sniggered.

"What?" she snapped.

"That's a presumptuous statement."

"It's not. I know that what we're fighting for is the right thing. There's no doubt in that."

"That's good, but not enough," said Jon.

"I don't understand. What more could there be besides the rightness of our cause?"

"Historically speaking, the right side of history was given by the victors. They get to impose the new order and write the history we know. So, your cause may be right, even moral and just, and you may still end up on the wrong side of history."

She kept still, looked at Mar with a disappointed expression. "So, you're saying that nothing matters. It's all in vain."

"Well, that depends."

"On what?"

"If you win this fight or not. The way I hear it now, you're sure you'll lose it."

"I didn't say that."

"You don't need to."

She sighed and all the huff and puff melted from her demeanor.

"Look, all I'm saying is, don't fight for a cause on principle," said Jon. "Fight because you believe in it and you want—*want, desire, believe*—you can change things. Then and only then will you win."

"But what if…" she said, frightened.

"And that has been the question for centuries. Don't think of what if, think of what you really, really want, deep inside your soul."

"We'll win this fight."

"Geo!" Bree turned and looked at Geo.

He was sitting on the edge of the mattress, grinning. "Jon likes to prod and push you to think deeper and further than you may feel comfortable. It's the professor in him."

"So all this has only been academic debate?" Bree felt frustration.

"I'm on your side in this, Bree," said Jon gently. "There's no other side for me, for us, to be on. And I believe, really believe, that we'll win this."

Bree sighed and felt like crying. This was their resistance cell. Their last hope. And yet Geo and Jon were smiling and so calm, they might be talking about abstract things, not the survival of the people of Torono.

"And I know how," added Geo.

"Finally," said Jon.

"There's an underground place north of here as big and deep as the one here, where the former mayor had built his bunker. That would fit a lot of people. Maybe everybody; I don't know. And it's connected with this underground railway."

"Subway," said Jon.

"Sorry?"

"It's called a subway. And I do have a vague recollection of what you talk about."

"I'll give you a map and if you follow it, it should lead straight there."

"We'll manage without the map," said Jon.

"I don't think we should take the chance," said Geo.

"Listen, what's more important is how to get people there. We cannot return. The prince's men are hunting us."

"I'll take them," said Bree.

"Then you take the map. You'll need the help of my disciple, Stev. He knows everything and knows how to begin the exodus."

"I'll need Bree for a different plan. I'll talk to Stev and put things in motion. Bree will go with you."

"You'll also have the help of Lord Waterfront."

Geo looked at Jon in wonder. He'd heard the rumors about the reclusive lord. How did someone like Jon get the ear of Lord Waterfront when not even Boris had managed that? "How…"

"Let's say that while being hunted by the Silkers' Luna Warriors, we were offered asylum by Lord Waterfront. And when he heard our plea for the people of Torono, he opened the access to these subway tracks and told us this is the way he can help us save as many as possible. We'll just have to bring them down here. But it's so dark and there are the Nightmares...I don't know anymore."

"Yes, they proved to be in the Pits of Madness, as everyone calls them," intervened Mar. "I don't know how you can convince anyone to come here."

"We can walk above ground," suggested Ton.

"We'll be exposed up there," said Jon.

"Given a choice between a Nightmare and Luna Warriors, I'd prefer to face the warriors," said Ton.

"You mean between the two, you prefer to die at the hand of men rather than a Nightmare."

"It's just the darkness talking," said Geo.

Jon nodded. He smiled sadly.

Bree thought hard about how she could help them. She knew nothing of these Pits of Madness. But the darkness could really get to you and nightmares could swallow you even when they were not real. Even when they were only in your mind.

"And I have a solution for that too," said Geo.

"Aren't you a wonder today?" Jon grinned.

"You can disperse the darkness?" asked Mar.

"Yes, I can light your way in your trek to the north ruins. And give you a fighting chance against the Nightmares, if there are more."

"Then the plan is set," said Jon. "Geo finds Stev and tells him the plan. Stev gathers the people and starts the big exodus. Being underground, we may evade the Silkers' attention and succeed in moving greater numbers than we thought previously."

"And I'm coming with you to help you and help Geo with his other plan."

Everyone looked inquisitively at Geo. What other plan could he have? Bree didn't know what to believe. They were here, they were on their way to a safe place. What else could Geo want?

"My other plan..." Geo hesitated. "We're all in this together, so you may as well know everything."

"Shit," said Jon, "it does sound bad."

"The prince is hunting us too. And I know with definite certainty that the prince will not allow the people of Torono to escape. He wants his experiment. He wants to see how the new Rain will transform the people further. Even if that would mean killing 90 percent of you."

"You think he'll hunt us down in the underground?"

"He'll hunt you down anywhere you go. And he won't allow you to escape."

There was silence after that statement. Bree didn't know much about the damn prince, only what she'd caught from Geo. He had three armies and was the most powerful man this side of Ont Lake. He could be the most powerful man on the continent, as far as Bree's small world was concerned. And if Geo started fighting openly against him, the Woodmans would eventually have to face him. She shuddered.

"I have to take him down," said Geo.

No one said anything. It spoke to the enormity of the statement. Prince Boris was not only the leader of the mightiest army of their time, he was also a legendary Silker with a secret weapon no one had survived to tell about.

"And I have a plan on how to do that. I just need Bree's help and my plan aligns with the execution of your plan, so don't worry. I'll keep the prince busy while Torono's people escape."

44.

Last Train Out of Torono

Cecropia Mori Commander Damial approached and glowered at Silver. "My warriors are on the train."

"Good," said Silver.

He turned and saw his brother, up on the dais beside the railway. The prince looked resplendent, surrounded by his Luna Warriors and his court. He was like a shallow dream. And his commanders were as empty as him. Empty, but dangerous. Silver knew that Boris had sent Damial on this mission to keep an eye on him. The prince trusted Silver up to a point. And he wanted to make sure that the particular point of trust was where he wanted it, not where Silver saw it.

The morning was greener than usual. The sky looked charged, full of electricity. There was a veiled threat in the atmosphere that Silver didn't like. *Move onto the train, Worm,* he messaged. The crowd gathered to see the army departing withdrew with a fearful roar as his first Nightmare snaked its way toward the train. It climbed in through the last car and moved forward.

"Mantis," Silver said, and his lieutenant stepped forward. "Get our men on the train. First car, separated from Damial's men. And make sure all our supplies are loaded."

Prince Boris was giving a speech for the crowd. Silver knew that he too was supposed to take position and listen. The speech was about the brave Silkers army and how it would go now to defend the independence or freedom of Torono's people, or some such dumb things. Liquid things, he thought, disgusted. The only things that mattered in the world were fear and necessity. Nothing else. The honor and freedom rhetoric was such a thing of the past. All Liquid values should be nipped in the bud.

Night, on top of the train, he ordered, frustrated. Their world was so wondrous, full of magic and power, and they still had to deal with the perverse, weak, craven Liquids. And his brother, Prince Boris, was one of those perpetuating such feeble behavior, all in the name of diplomacy and state interests. More Liquid values.

Night flew over the crowd and landed majestically on top off the train, like a strip of night sky darkening the early hours of the morning. Even Boris silenced at its sight. Silver felt pride fill his chest. That was real power—having Nightmares at your disposal. He grinned as the thought popped into his head.

He'd lived in his brother's shadow, in his brother's mythology, when the perspective, if noticed, offered such vast possibilities. What he could be, with an army behind him—what he could be, with an army of *Nightmares* behind him! The world would tremble at the sound of his name. He'd be the Nightmare Prince.

Silver clambered up the ladder on the side of the train and hopped on top of the train. The people could stay on the train. He was the Nightmare Prince and he'd ride this train of horrors high, next to Night, his most fearsome Nightmare warrior.

Boris watched him in silence. Silver had managed to silence the prince for once. The train whistled and started moving. Silver stood, gloriously surrounded by the ethereal wings of Night. The train caught speed and he felt relief at leaving all this behind and moving toward his future. His own terrifying future.

45.
The Other Side of the Night

The two Luna Warriors stared at him with contempt. Wearing their chitin armor, they looked triple his size as he stood in his own insulation suit. They didn't even bother to answer him. Just crossed their spears and forbade him passing.

"I'm the prince's hyalophora, one of the Seven," said Geo, flustered.

"It's actually the Six, and you're not in it, my friend," said a voice behind him.

Geo turned and saw Hymenoptera Jodi, or the Wasp, as he was known to everyone. The Trade Minister of the Silkers. His neck flesh was overflowing, and his left hand looked like an uncooked meatball, plump and raw. His Silker's weapon, visible hovering above his sleeve, was a gigantic wasp—except its stinger protruded from its mouth, thick and sharp, dripping venom.

"The prince said…" Geo left the sentence unfinished. The prince had said a lot of things, most of them lately proven lies.

"Yeah," said the Wasp.

"I need to see Lady L. Could you help me?"

"Need is such a strong word."

Geo looked down to his feet. Need *was* a strong word and he was becoming careless. He'd learned quite early that even when in a desperate situation, you needed to take your time and think, not act impulsively. That was why he was a good ambassador and not a good soldier, as Woodman the Elder had told him so many times.

"You're right." Geo nodded. "I'm young and thoughtless. I have so much to learn from you, and from the rest of the Six, if I am to be of any value to the prince. I'm sorry."

"Why do you *need* to see Lady L?"

"She's become sort of a friend. She's my…guide here, at court. I *need* her counsel."

"Lady L is a bit fragile at the moment. Anything I can help you with?"

"Sorry, it's—we're not yet in that kind of relationship. I need a friend."

"And I thought you *were* my friend," said Wasp.

"Thanks for listening." Geo turned to leave.

"Let him pass," Wasp told the guards.

"What?" Geo turned back.

"Go, but don't stay long. We need her restored to her former glory."

"Thank you," said Geo and for a second he was tempted to extend his hand for a shake. Then he recalled Boris warning him against shaking hands: *"That's a Liquid custom."*

The room was dark. Heavy curtains covered the tall windows. Someone was humming a sad lullaby in a hoarse voice, filling the room with regrets.

"Mr. Hyalophora?" Lady L's voice was as erotic as ever. Geo felt warmth wash through him, hearing her. He sighed and smiled. He'd felt guilty after Boris had told him that he'd apparently attacked Lady L with his mind during the Rain Ritual. He didn't know what that could mean. As far as he could tell, he'd felt Boris trying to invade his mind, and he'd fought against that invasion. What connection that was with Lady L, he had no idea.

Geo walked around the big bed and approached its head. He could see what he guessed was Lady L's head supported on a pillow. A flame flickered into existence on the nightstand. The light shone on Lady L's masked face. Geo fell to his knees and took her left hand in his. "I'm so sorry," he mumbled.

"Ela, leave us," Lena said in a low voice.

The lullaby stopped and a shadow rose from the other side of the bed and left. After he heard the door close, Lady L put her left hand over his and smiled. "What are you sorry for?"

"Boris told me that I did this to you."

"Nonsense. The prince is overly dramatic."

"How do you feel?"

"A bit weak. That's all. Just need to get my strength back."

"Anything I can do to help? I mean it."

"I know you mean it, Mr. Hyalophora. But don't worry. In a day or two I'll be like new."

Geo smiled despite himself. Lena had always been so formal. Even when they—well, even when intimacy was expected. And that was something so *Lena* that he'd missed it.

"Now, why are you here, Mr. Hyalophora?"

"Courtesy visit, Lady L."

"Come now, Mr. Hyalophora. I think we've reached a point in our relationship where we can be honest with each other."

He'd wanted so much to believe her. He knew that she hadn't lied to him directly, but omission and diversion were in the same category as lying. There were so many things he wished he could ask her, but...

She took his silence as hesitation, which was not far from the truth. She pulled him closer and kissed his hand. "You're special, Mr. Hyalophora. Believe me, you're so special. I'd like to help you, but you need to let me."

"I'm here to say goodbye, Lena."

"What's going on?"

"Remember when I told you about the Rain to come?"

"Yes. I remember you told the prince as well."

"Right, I told him. Only he doesn't want to do anything to help the people of Torono."

"What?"

"I told you, he said he had no interest in helping them."

"But that was then and now is—have you told him again?"

"Yes. With no success."

"I'm so sorry, Mr. Hyalophora. Let me think how to help you with that."

"I actually found a solution."

"I see…"

"I found a place where most of the people of Torono could hide during the Rain. Shelter."

"I thought we knew of all the underground places in the city," said Lady L. The flame flickered and went out. Geo found himself staring into utter darkness where before he could see Lena's exquisite mouth.

"Not here, but up north, Lena. I found a place where they used to have shops and restaurants. Deep enough, and really big."

"Yonge and Bloor," murmured Lady L.

"How do you—yes, that's the name on the map."

"That's dangerous territory, Mr. Hyalophora. The Yor Tribe owns those lands and they're savages. Cannibals too. I wouldn't drive Torono's people straight into their hungry mouths."

"Don't worry, I have it all planned carefully. And it's done anyway. They're on their way already."

"*Planned carefully*? Like the attack on the mayor's lair?"

Geo was startled. He let go of her hands and rose. What could he say to that? What could he say now to that?

"I'm sorry! I'm sorry, Mr. Hyalophora, I didn't mean it."

"No worries, Lena. I just wanted to see you one more time and have a chance to say goodbye."

"Is there nothing I can say to stop you?"

"I'm sorry, but somebody has to step in and help them. No one deserves to be left out in the Rain."

"My sweet Ambassador."

The candle flame came back to life. Lady L's mouth smiled sadly at him.

46.
The Pioneers

The last two hours, they'd walked in silence. The tunnels seemed to go on forever, and the tracks made it difficult for them to keep the pace. The mother of the group, the one they called Mar, was clearly sick and barely able to keep up, and the father, Jon, was even sicker, but he hadn't complained once. Grunting and puffing, he'd stayed next to Mar and helped her. As for their youngest, Mic, the one with his corroded layers turned into an intricate lace around his neck, he was all nice and big words, smiles and jokes, but nothing other than a huge asshole.

Bree was amazed how similar they were to their human counterparts. Although human was not exactly the differentiator. Corrosives were nothing but mutated humans, so in the end, humans too. What was that term they used once—Liquids? Yeah, it was a Corrosives world where Liquids like her were tolerated.

She looked at the ragged group of Corrosives in front of her and wondered if that was what the humans—the Liquid humans—had become: a tolerated species. Like the Neanderthals before them. On the brink of extinction and seen as an oddity by the species more adapted to the new environment. Now that she was living out here, she saw it was obvious. She needed an envirosuit to survive the Exterior conditions, while the Corrosives were in their natural habitat.

So, was saving them the right thing to do for her species?

She felt the hair on her nape stand up as a chill drained through her spine, despite the humid heat that her suit could barely keep at bay. The simple fact that she asked herself that question meant that this world of kill or be killed had affected her. That was not acceptable.

"We're almost there," she said.

"That's what you told us an eternity ago," said Di. She was walking almost beside Bree. She'd tried to make conversation, but the subjects they had in common were so few and the walk through darkness was so exhausting that she'd quickly given up.

"This time will be a quicker eternity." Bree couldn't help smiling.

"We are getting closer," she heard Jon's raspy voice confirm. "I can feel a draft and it smells different than the tunnels."

"Pops the stench-tracker." Mic chuckled. Nobody else reacted to his joke.

"No, he's right," said Ton. "It smells bad!"

They soon exited the tunnel into a wider space that opened to their left. They climbed up onto a platform above the tracks and Jon counted them all there. "Stay close together. Bree, do you have the plans for this station?"

Not only didn't she have the plans, but she had no idea that it was called a station.

"Let me remember, then," Jon said and sighed. Everyone looked at him in wonder. For all of them, the station was part of ancient history, some period kept alive only through stories told generation to generation. To have a person alive *remembering* it was close to a miracle.

"We're coming from the south, so this would be the upper platform. We're close to the exit here. Bree, do you have any landmarks on your map to help us find the underground structure?"

"Geo marked a couple of landmarks."

"All right, considering that everyone else will come through this tunnel as well, we should leave a burning torch at its mouth to show them where they exit the tunnels."

"Excellent idea, dear," said Mar.

"As far as I remember, we can get back on the streets in that direction." Jon pointed in front of them.

"I see some stairs there," confirmed Ton.

"Let's go." Jon took Mar's arm and led her forward.

Bree followed them. She was as lost as they were here. She knew what to look for once they were back on the streets, but down there—she just hoped Geo would manage to find them by himself.

When they reached the top of the stairs, they stopped, breathing hard—their exit was blocked by a forest of impaled skulls. Most were mummified or fleshless, but some of them looked quite fresh.

"What's this, Pops?" whispered Ton.

"The locals want to keep us out of their territory," said Jon, swallowing dryly.

"I don't like this," said Mar.

"We're only six and by the number of skulls, the locals could be in their hundreds," Mic observed.

"We are on a tight schedule," Bree reminded them.

"You can go on to help your boyfriend," sneered Mic. "We'll stay here and wait for the others to come. You know, strength in numbers."

"Mic, don't be callous!" Mar's voice was harsh.

"But that's the reality, Ma," said Mic.

"We *are* on a tight schedule here and we don't have time for fear." Jon lit another torch. "Mic, mount this torch somewhere here to signal those coming after us of the direction. Ton, let's clear a path through this skull forest."

"Why are we on a tight schedule, Pa? Because they said so. The Liquids. Are you really going to put us all in danger for them?"

"Mic! All this ends now. Help us or just keep quiet and wait here."

"Pops!" Mic placed a hand on Jon's shoulder to keep him from advancing. "We're not doing this! It's madness!"

Bree grabbed the first metal rod holding a head and yanked it from the ground. The skull fell and clattered on the floor. Mar followed her and grabbed another rod. Ton and Di followed.

"Are you all crazy?" cried Mic.

"Get a grip on yourself, Mic. Compared to what's coming, confronting a strange tribe is a small task."

"Pops, I'm going up those stairs to keep watch. I wouldn't want to be caught by surprise by whoever erected this forest." Ton waited for his father's approval.

"Good thinking, Ton. We'll follow you shortly."

Bree avoided looking back to see what Mic was doing. She didn't want to add to his frustration, but she guessed that soon they'd have to deal with his narrow-mindedness and egotism. She just hoped it wouldn't be in the middle of an important event that their lives depended on.

Nothing else to do now but clear the way for those coming behind, and preparing the battlefield for Geo. If his plan worked. If he'd survived the long trip before the battle. As for the battle itself—there were so many *ifs*. Geo had grand plans and few resources. No, that was not fair, she corrected herself. He'd proven to be more resourceful than people gave him credit for. Woodman the Elder was the only one who'd seen Geo's full potential and believed in him. She had to believe in him too. Because if he didn't succeed…

47.
Exodus

Geo slowed down. He noticed warriors at the entrance to the tunnels. He approached carefully, but without hesitation—after all, he was still one of the prince's top ten. He was not yet officially a rogue agent. Then he saw the insignia on their clothing— they were the warriors of Lord Lakefront and Jon had vouched for him. Apparently Lord Lakefront was a former professor, Jon's colleague from university.

He saw giant Stev talking to one of the warriors. Everything seemed to be going according to plan. Although the line of people fleeing the city was sparser than Geo had imagined it would be.

"Hey Stev," Geo said tentatively.

"Geo, this is Lar, Lord Lakefront's captain. He and his warriors will help us lead the people through the tunnels and his master and his household will be the last ones to follow."

"That sounds good, Stev. Captain, I didn't have the pleasure of meeting Lord Lakefront. We are grateful for his help."

Lar nodded, studying Geo from head to toe. His eyes lingered on his Silker's arm. It looked almost normal, if you ignored the holes in the forearm and the sievelike skin on his upper arm.

"Right," said Geo. He turned to Stev. "Any problems so far?"

"A lot of people dropped out. They…"

"Don't want to come?"

"Yes. Something changed their minds."

"We did all we could. Now is too late to—"

"Friends and neighbors, Geo. People I care about."

"I'm sorry, Stev." Geo started to lay his hand on the big man's shoulder, then thought better of it. He'd always felt Stev was withdrawn in his presence and not as forthcoming in their relationship as Jon was. Stev didn't trust him.

"Let's make sure that those who chose to come travel safely," said Geo. He turned to the captain. "You may encounter Nightmares on your way. I hope your men know how to fight them."

"I sent my two Nightmare hunters ahead to clear the tunnels."

"Perfect. How long until everyone is down in the tunnels?"

"Why, is the prince on your tail?" said the captain.

Geo grinned at Lar. "Yes. But I'll make sure he follows me on the streets. We need to be careful, nonetheless."

The captain stared intently at Geo. Then he exchanged a look with Stev and turned away, sneering, "*Nonetheless*—I don't like the way you talk, Silker. I don't like the way you look or smell. I suggest you go do your business with your prince and leave the people to us. This is not your problem."

Stev looked down at his feet. Geo could almost feel the big man's embarrassment crushing him.

Well, Woodman the Elder always said that it's wise to choose your battles rather than just going blindly from one to the next. On one hand was the exodus of people from the city to the north. On the other hand was his plan to trap the prince. Really simple math here. He'd done everything he could to make sure that the people of Torono would be safe. With the clock ticking, what else could he really do? It seemed that those who wanted to be saved were on their way into the tunnels and professional armed men were there to make sure they were safe. What else was there for Geo to do? Other than pissing off the very people dealing with the escape?

"You're right, Captain," said Geo. "Good luck to you. We'll meet on the other side."

Geo walked away, feeling weird. He'd warned them about everything. He'd given them the solution. And they didn't want him there with them, saving the people. First they had a problem with him being a Liquid. Now they had a problem with him being a Silker. But no one thought of him as being their savior. And that hurt more than he'd thought.

He stopped in front of the train station. People milled about, as usual. Fewer than usual, though, so maybe he'd saved more than Stev claimed. Yet more people had stayed behind than he'd hoped. He looked around. No soldiers. No Silkers, no mayoral forces. Something was off. Where could they be? Something was happening and Geo had no idea what. The prince had always been two steps ahead of him. Sometimes even ten steps, if Geo admitted how stupid he'd acted in several crucial moments.

Geo had a bad feeling. Was it possible that while he thought he'd set a trap for Boris, the prince already had a bigger trap in place? One that would condemn not only Geo, but the people of Torono as well? And Bree with them. He remembered the walking dead his brother had become at the hands of Silver Star and shivered, imagining Bree instead.

The streets seemed normal, but that didn't say much. The feeling of dread stuck in his throat like a lump of gelled water. He knew the direction, he'd even memorized the streets he'd have to take. Bree was already there, setting up the scene. And he was so far from her. He started running north. Straight along a boulevard called Blackthorn Way, formerly know as the University Avenue. Originally he'd wanted to avoid such a straight road with such an open vista for the Silkers to hunt him. But now he didn't care anymore—the bad feeling smoldered in his belly like hot coal and he wanted to get there quickly to protect Bree.

In the distance he saw the ruins of the former seat of power, like a skeletal hand holding up the sky. He knew that was the Nightmares killing field, but he didn't care. He could avoid the area when he got closer.

He attached his visor while running and switched it on. He ordered a scan of the area. There were still people along this route, this was still a habitable part of the city. But only some of them were also running. Coincidence? Woodman the Elder didn't believe in coincidences. He had taught Geo that it's better to always act like there were no coincidences. The bad things that could happen from ignoring a coincidence were less grave than ignoring a planned evil deed as a coincidence.

So, he was jogging along the Blackthorn Way and Boris's men were following him at a safe distance. Were they only the trackers or the force meant to stop him? Or probably the prince was already north, preventing the whole trap.

The distance melted away and the ruins grew closer. Ethereal Nightmares filled the sky above their killing field. A Dream floated alongside him for a while, likely trying to stop him, but he ignored its transcendent beauty and forged ahead. And now his scanner picked up an entire army behind him. And in the middle of that army was the prince's cavalry with him in the lead. Gaining. Coming up way faster than Geo could manage.

48.

The Trap

Geo settled into a steady pace, his feet banging the road in an almost calm rhythm. His breath was under control and he wouldn't sweat anymore, thanks to the gelled water inside him. As far as he could see on his scan, the prince and his cavalry were pursuing him on a parallel street, another large boulevard. And they were not just gaining on him. They were already in front of him, probably waiting for an opening to cut over his way. As for the ones behind him, the foot soldiers, they were keeping their distance. Either because they couldn't outrun him, or because Boris wanted to deal with him personally.

The problem was that the cavalry had already cut off his way north, toward the setup Bree was working on. And then he felt like smiling—if Boris was here, Bree was free. Out of danger. If the prince was following him, the people of Torono had a chance to escape. So, he'd better make it good and give them as much time as possible.

The cavalry was clearly gearing up to intercept him before the seat of government. And while he wanted to get as close as possible to the ruins, he was not crazy enough to try and cross the Nightmares' killing fields. He only hoped that his strength would get him as far as those ruins and that he'd be the first one there.

He pounded the broken asphalt for fifteen more minutes,

then the scanner showed him the cavalry approaching from an intersecting street. He veered left just in time to see the prince in the distance, riding a gelling motherfucking *monster* at high speed. From the speed and Boris's position in the saddle, it was clear that he was in attack mode. In his calculations, this would end now, in less than a minute.

Geo slowed down, mesmerized by the army of monsters attacking. It was utterly terrifying. Silker Nightmares—probably former Pupa training recruits who had gone through the Silkers' ritual and either it went wrong for them and the prince had turned them or that had been their goal from the beginning. Long, multiple articulated insectile legs; translucent wings to give them speed and help them perform miraculous jumps, maybe even fly; huge carnivorous heads with mandibles and fangs like swords. And their eyes, their eyes were the most unforgettable. Insectile multifaceted eyes with a 360 degree vision. This was the secret of the Silkers' rapid expansion and invincibility in a world with no mechanical vehicles still working and no more live horses.

The prince's monster shrieked, waking Geo from his trance. He turned left and ran as fast as he could, adrenaline pumping through him and giving him wings. He was aware that he wouldn't be able to maintain that speed for long, but he didn't need it. There was a stone building still standing and he was perhaps five hundred meters from it. The riders were farther away, but closing the distance faster than he'd anticipated.

Worn stone steps, overgrown in brambles. Geo skipped one in two steps. He heard the clicking of the monsters' claws on the stone behind him. He jumped the last step and saw a doorway in front of him, its door missing. Before he could choose it a strike in his back threw him through the dark entrance. He slid over the floor, twisted, and saw Boris trying to fit his mount through the small entrance. The row of doorways darkened with the monsters carrying their riders up the stairs, ready to enter after him.

Geo turned and noticed that the stairs going up were almost gone, their metal rusted away. But there were concrete stairs going down. He rose and made for the downward stairs, skidding in his panic. He knew he was trapped and couldn't offer the refugees more than the fifteen minutes he'd gained for them in running and a couple of minutes now, as he descended into darkness followed by the Silkers' monsters. He'd failed everybody. Why had he thought he could outsmart Boris?

49.
The Jaws of Darkness

Stev kept his daughter between him and Sara. They were the last in the column of refugees advancing silently and slowly along the tunnel. The darkness was punctured by the torches' flames. The exodus looked like an enormous snake slithering through the city's bowels.

He knew that somewhere behind them, Lord Lakefront and his people followed. He felt safer knowing that warriors were a stone's throw away and ready to protect them if necessary.

Magi stumbled. He caught her before she fell, cursing. This road was too difficult for a child. Yet it was a price worth paying if that meant their survival. Although, he'd had a discussion with Jon about it, and Jon had confessed that he believed the new Rain would not only bring death and destruction but, like the first one, the Black Rain, it would bring transformation. Metamorphosis. Evolution.

Terrifying word, evolution. Yeah, they were the product of evolution through the gelled water, but look how different they were from the Liquids. This was not your usual form of evolution. This was explosive evolution. Did they need another such explosion? What would the new people be like? And after a run of a few decades, would the Corrosives' reign already be over? That was absolutely terrifying.

Stev despised the Liquids, but now he knew how they'd felt

when the new species had appeared on the world stage. They had been terrified. They felt outdated. Even more, extinct. He wouldn't like to feel extinct.

So, in this light, would it be wiser to stay and face the Rain? Confront your destiny? Yes, there was a greater chance you'd end up dead, but there was also that slim chance you'd be the new species.

Now, evolution doesn't necessarily mean it's upward. It could be sideways, or even downward. Depends on the point of view of the observer. If I am the genes of Jon and the next evolution replaces my brain with a new organ that makes me tougher to kill, then the evolution was upward. I'm now in a position to offer a better survival to my genes. Genes are selfish. But if I am Jon's consciousness and I'm suddenly left without a brain, then my evolution has been downward. I've been degraded, reduced, lowered on humanity's evolutionary scale. People are selfish too.

Stev had remembered Jon's words and played them continuously in his head. He had to consider Magi's future. Would she be better hiding and surviving as she was, or facing the Rain and fighting for her chance as a newer species?

Shouts and screams from ahead of the refugee column made everyone stop and look ahead, frightened. Sara looked at him with big eyes. Her normal joyfulness had deserted her face. She was totally scared. She gathered Magi to her and kept her tight against her body, as if she'd be the wall to protect her daughter, if necessary.

"Go back?" Sara asked him quietly.

But Stev knew there was no going back. "There are warriors protecting us. Don't worry."

"Then why are the screams going on?"

"People get scared. People scream."

Sara smiled a little bit. She kissed Magi's hair.

"Stick to the wall!" Lar, Lord Lakefront's captain, ordered in his strong voice. "Stick to the wall, people. Now!"

A handful of warriors followed the captain. Something dark and big marched after them.

Stev pulled Magi and Sara to him and helped them clamber

onto the ledge running along the wall. The others followed his example and climbed onto the ledge, pressing against the wall when they saw what was approaching.

The warriors passed them by and a huge shadow covered in darkness stamped after them. It repelled the torchlight. It looked like a dark cloud of thick smoke contained as a mountainous shape that moved deliberately after the warriors. They seemed to be opening the way for it.

Stev shuddered. That was a Nightmare if he'd ever seen one. Lord Lakefront's warriors were—what? Working together with a Nightmare to fight other Nightmares? Using it like a weapon because it was their hostage? Or—no, he couldn't possibly go there. This Nightmare seemed tame, not an immediate danger to the refugees, but— He knew that it was too late now to turn back, but by the Holy Rain, what deal had Jon made with Lord Lakeshore?

Stev had never seen the lord. No one had seen him. He was a legend, an urban ghost story. But Jon had seen him and vouched for him. So Stev had to trust him and their deal as well. That is, if that damned Liquid Geo hadn't betrayed them. But why would he? Well, because now he was a Silker and everyone knew that Silkers wanted to see what became of Torono's people after another Rain. So they would be the most forceful opposition to this exodus. Stev's head hurt. He hated politics and it seemed that was one of the ugly practices the Corrosives had inherited from the Liquids.

A thunderous roar shook the tunnel. Screams were continuous now, and shrieks rose between the roars. The earth shook and dust filled the air, extinguishing the torches. This looked and sounded like the end of the world, or at least the end of their journey. Stev took Sara and Magi in his big arms and hugged them ferociously.

50.
The Empty Cage

The room was large, full of dust and spiderwebs, broken plastic mannequins, and hardened piles of sawdust. She gave the plastic mannequins a wide berth. Those could be extremely dangerous. But then she realized they were underground, quite a ways from the streets, so probably untouched by the gelled water. Maybe this plastic was the old, dead plastic. Maybe not.

One wall was mirrored from ceiling to floor. Bree couldn't imagine what the purpose of such a room might be. The people before the Black Rain were into all sorts of extravagances. Waste and greed, that was how Woodman the Elder used to describe the previous era. But that extravagance was now so helpful for them—how do you catch Medusa? Yeah, that's right—classic education proved to be useful even in barbarian times. Or especially then.

She saw the canvas that Geo had brought here rolled up in front of the mirror. There was also rope on top of it. Bree looked at the chronometer on her visor screen—it was getting close to the time scheduled to spring the trap. The heat was oppressive. Sweat ran in rivulets down her neck and back. Luckily, her suit captured every drop of moisture and converted it to drinking water. She could survive with this suit for at least a week without any supplies.

She missed Woodman the Elder. She missed her laboratory.

Her colleagues. She smiled and sighed. Melancholia—that was the worst enemy in gelled water country, she remembered Geo telling her once. Shaking free of nostalgia, she began working on setting the trap.

Jon surveyed the scene. The room was large, but not large enough. He'd put everyone to work to empty it of all the garbage from before the Black Rain, to maximize the space. But they would need a lot more room to accommodate the entire population of Torono. Geo had told him there was room enough for the entire city to fit. *Deluded young man.* Jon was frustrated that he'd fallen for it and taken Geo at face value. He walked out and checked for other potential hideouts. There were other rooms like caves beaded along the corridor. They needed to empty all of these.

A draft caressed his face and a humid, stale stench hit him full force. He gagged and waited for the nausea to pass. A draft here could mean one of two things—either the exterior was closer than they expected, in which case it was bad. Or there was another underground space nearby, one that was bigger and connected with a lot more underground. In which case it was good. Really good.

There was a larger room where the corridor turned right. Jon lit a torch. He was pretty far now from the initial room they'd started cleaning and the light was not enough to see inside this one. The flame detached the details from darkness. The floor was partially collapsed and apparently it had taken half of the back wall with it.

The light revealed footsteps in the thick dust covering the floor, made by heavy soles, like those made by special boots no Corrosive had. They were traces of Geo, Jon realized. This was where Geo had led them. Not the small rooms along the corridor, but this one.

Jon reached the edge of the broken floor and brought the torch forward. There was a rope still knotted to one of the rebars twisted out from the floor. There wasn't enough light to pierce the darkness beyond the demolished part. He threw the torch with all his might into the hole. It flew for about twenty steps and fell to the floor. It revealed a limitless space. No edges, no walls, no ending. This. Was. It. And then he saw the walls. He gaped, mesmerized. It was a miracle. It was water.

This was the hideout they'd come here for. Now the people of Torono could come. They would all be saved.

Di and Mar had completed weaving almost four rungs of a rope ladder. The lights were focused on a point beyond them. Not the one she'd left them in before. She entered the room and gasped. There was a hole in the floor, but the back wall and beyond—well, beyond there was a vast expanse of space and the walls were wet. Liquid water ran down them in rivulets. How could that be?

This was one of the very few liquid water oases! And it was untouched. No one had discovered it until now. Or at least until Geo had found it. This was an incredible gift for the people of Torono. With this discovery, Geo could have been the richest Silker in the hierarchy of the kingdom, yet he'd chosen to give it to the people.

And that was the difference between him and Boris, the mayor and prince of Torono. Life was more precious than riches. Saving the lives of the city's people was more important for Geo than securing a place at the power table. Woodman the Elder's teaching was behind all this.

"Can you believe it?" Jon's raspy voice startled her.

"This is…" She couldn't finish. She didn't have words. She blinked back tears.

Jon looked at her in wonder. She smiled, embarrassed.

"I'm sorry I'm staring. But I haven't seen tears in decades. You, my dear, you and Geo are our miracles. Not this hideout, not this water. You two are our miracles."

"You'd have done the same in our place."

"I don't know about that. And I'm not saying I'm ill-intended or greedy, but you helping us now takes a certain kind of courage and selflessness that I don't know I possess."

"Any word from them?" Bree changed the topic. She felt good but also embarrassed. This was all Geo. She'd arrived later in the game and she was only doing backstage things. No courage needed. Just commitment.

"No. I sent Mic ahead to see what was happening and guide them here."

Bree nodded. What now, then? The trap was set, it seemed that Jon had everything under control here, everything looked good, yet…

"Geo?" asked Jon.

"No sign of him. And he's one hour late."

"I'm sure it's all part of his plan," said Jon.

Bree smiled bitterly. She didn't need reassurance. She needed purpose and direction. "He's already one hour late," she repeated, wishing she could just shut up and keep up morale.

"I see. What now? Do you have a fallback plan?"

"Geo probably had one, but we didn't have time to share it. So no, I'm useless."

"Well then, you wouldn't mind helping me," said Jon.

"What can I do?"

"Would it be too much to ask for you to go back in the tunnels and help us bring the people here?"

"Didn't you send Mic to do it?"

Jon sighed and looked away. "I know he's my son, but I'm afraid he'll failed me. Again. I'd feel safer if our people's fate lay in your hands."

"I won't fail you," said Bree.

"I know."

When Bree reached the tunnels, the first Toronions were exiting. Mic was leading them to the hiding place. It looked like a trickle of refugees, not the flood she wanted to see.

"Faster, faster, people! The Rain is upon us." Bree began pulling and pushing them to speed up the exodus.

Two soldiers approached her with a threatening air. "We

need to hurry. There's no time!" she told them.

"Another Liquid," said one of them, his tone disdainful. The way the other deferred to him, Bree deduced he was their boss.

"If the Rain catches you in the streets, it will melt you down where you stand," she told him. She thrust her arm skyward. "And look at the sky. It is almost upon us."

That made them look up. The sky was boiling, green clouds bubbling and exploding menacingly as if a war raged there. In no time the sky would erupt and let out all the puss it contained.

The soldiers turned to the people. "Let's move! Faster! Faster!"

The column of refugees began running after Mic. And kept running.

Bree exhaled with relief. She couldn't know if all of them would make it before the Rain started pouring down, but at least she'd prevented them all from falling victim to the fury.

51.
The Holy Water Crusade

They had tracked the former Liquid ambassador to the point where he had stayed for a couple of hours before disappearing. When they probably had discovered the tracking paint and cleaned it. Which would mean that the Liquid settlement should be around here. What was it that Boris had said? *"It is a subterranean river so their settlement must be underground. A cave or something similar."*

They had stopped on a mountain, in front of a peak that could be a mountain in itself—stone all around them, no traces of vegetation, no signs of life. A desert. Nothing to indicate a cave.

Cecropia Mori Commander Damial stood fifty paces away, in front of his troops. His face was inscrutable. Mantis was next to Silver Star, and Silver's hunters were all gathered behind him. Not in an orderly fashion like the Mori Warriors, but twice as fearsome. Night was floating above them, and Worm—well Worm was nowhere to be seen. Worm was doing reconnaissance.

Silver felt a ping in his mind. Worm! He signaled Mantis to follow and Damial to wait. His hunters extended their spears to full length and followed. They went around the peak's base, their movements silent and deadly, and stopped a hundred steps away from a man dressed in an isolation suit, like that dumb fucker Geo and his zombie brother. That was definitely a Liquid.

And that told him all he wanted to know—Geo's people were here and he only had to find the entrance to their underground hideout.

He signaled for his people to lie low and wait. They watched the man doing all sorts of nonsensical things, like collecting rocks and dust, and scraping moss from the mountain's stone. He collected them all in different small bags that he would then seal and hide in a big box he was carrying around. Finally, after a lot of fooling around, the man went to the stone face of the mountain and placed his palm on its surface. A door opened where before there was only stone. Tricky Liquids!

Silver nodded to one of his hunters. He crawled to the front. He had a crab arm with very prominent muscles. It was thrice the size of his left arm. He grabbed his spear with his right hand, rose, aimed, and threw. His spear soared at an incredible speed and impaled the man on the threshold, its end impeding the sliding door's closure.

"Call the Mori Commander. We have a way in now," said Silver.

They approached the secret entrance into the mountain. The man was dead, his face frozen in an expression of shock. Which was weird, since Crab's speed should had taken his life so fast that his brain didn't have time to process and register what had happened. So, he hadn't died instantly. Silver grinned. None of the Liquids would die instantly. He would make sure of it.

He studied the space that had opened in the mountain. If he had to guess, it must be an elevator like those he'd seen in the buildings in the city. But they needed something called electricity to make them work, something that they had lost decades ago. It seemed the Liquids still had it. This would be a secret he'd want for himself. One day he'd be the Nightmare Lord, and he'd have in his power toolbox the electricity thing. He'd need to keep one of the Liquids alive to give him the secrets they held. Wasn't that what Boris wanted as well? He'd sent Silver to bring back all their secrets.

52.
Luk

The basement was certainly part of a bigger structure. This was a corridor with a lot of doors on both sides. To his right, the corridor ended at a door. Maybe that was another exit. Geo ran that way. His flashlight revealed a room with old machines on the walls, but no exit. He heard a growl behind him.

Three huge silhouettes advanced along the corridor toward him. Wide shoulders, big heads, sharp fangs, enormous paws ending in claws like knives—Boris's hellhounds. Unfortunate kids who hadn't pass the Water Passage Ritual that Boris then twisted into beasts to serve him.

Geo retreated inside the room. He only had a knife on him and knew that wasn't enough to keep the hellhounds away. He looked around and didn't see any hiding place, or anything to use as a weapon against them. End of the line, Geo thought, though it wouldn't be at the end of Boris's hand.

He withdrew until he felt the wall at his back. Then he realized he was a Silker now and that his right arm was a weapon, and a mighty one, at that. He didn't want to give away what he had, but there were only the hounds there.

The hounds entered the room growling and slowly advancing on him. Suddenly, one of them sniffed the air, took two steps forward ahead of the other beasts, and sniffed again. It barked and wagged its tail. It took another step, while the other two stayed behind it, confused.

Geo turned the flashlight on it and saw the crucifix on its neck. Luk! He dropped down and extended his hand, palm upward. The hound came, its tail wagging, and licked Geo's hand.

"Luk, am I glad to see you!"

The other two hounds growled again then pounced on them. Luk took one down, biting its neck. Geo kicked the other hound and withdrew again. He focused on his right arm—*bullets, charging weapon, aiming*—he kicked again and withdrew to gain more room between him and the beast. He aimed and fired. The bullet hit the hound between its eyes. It fell, instantly dead.

The other hound was whining on the floor with Luk chomping down on its neck. Could they all be like Luk, if given the chance? He bent down and stretched his hand toward the second hound's muzzle. It tried immediately to bite and started fighting against Luk with all its might.

Geo loaded another bullet, aimed, and fired. Silence fell as the hound died instantly.

"We need to go, Luk," Geo said and ruffled the fur on Luk's head.

They exited the room and ran up the corridor. They needed to find another exit before Boris decided to come in person, followed by his warriors. How could he attract Boris alone to a secluded location? It seemed madness to think of something like that, but Geo needed Boris by himself. Well, maybe there was a way.

He reached the end of the underground corridor and saw some stairs going up. That was it—his way out of this trap. At the other end, Boris had managed to get his mount inside the building and was coming after him.

53.
Reconnaissance

There was nothing else to do. The trap was set. The time had passed. Bree could admit that while they were on a tight timetable because of the approaching Rain, it was difficult for Geo to put things in motion with somebody like the prince at the exact moment he wanted. Unless—no it would be dangerous to go there. She had to think positively.

And the Torono people were late too. Coincidence? There were no coincidences, but for lazy minds, Woodman the Elder used to tell his students. Jon's family was doing wonderfully at preparing the refuge. The place was absolutely miraculous. Geo had outdone himself.

There was nothing else she could do to help Geo. If he didn't come, she'd know that the prince had won before the battle had started. And that she'd be alone in the new world after the Rain. What would be her chances of getting back to the Caves? Better not think of that yet.

Bree took out the map and opened it. Geo's route leading the prince to the trap was clearly marked in red. In retrospect, how childish to think you could lead someone with an army down a particular route. She traced the route with her finger and looked around to get her bearings. The route went through an area dense with exceedingly tall buildings, like this, back in Torono. Possible places for the Skull Tribe settlement.

Her suit system was optimal. The air scrubbers worked exceedingly well. The water filtration system was at 100 percent. Bree activated the scanning system and saw only Jon's family as activity in a five hundred meter radius. She began walking. Carefully, so she wouldn't bump into any Skull tribesman. But the road was clear. She picked up the pace.

The road was full of obstacles. There had been no authority here interested in cleaning up the roads and accessways. The former buildings, all in complete ruin, formed shady canyons covered in moss and vines. The rust-colored grass on the road was almost as tall as her. Advancing was difficult. The possible Rain the Woodmans had predicted was due anywhere between five and twenty-four hours. She broke into a jog. The scanner impeded her vision so after checking that there was still no one in the vicinity, she deactivated it.

She had to go a kilometer down that road, then make a right and after five hundred more meters enter the Dark Forest. Cross the Dark Forest and take the Main Road down to Torono. The route was simple to follow. Perhaps too simple and straightforward. What chance did Geo have to keep a safe distance between him and the prince's army?

There were easier ways to go to Torono, but she had to keep it to the trap route, or she wouldn't have a chance to meet Geo, or find out about his fate. The first kilometer went fast. There among the ruins to her right was the Dark Forest. As she got closer, the tortured tree trunks grew taller, darker, the stench more fetid. How could a putrid forest survive and thrive? The stench was almost unbearable.

The tree trunks were not close together, but their branches formed a wooden labyrinth with the wood the consistency of mushrooms, either oozing sticky drops, or pulverizing on contact, like an explosive charge. And the noise—it was like the dead forest was still evolving; no animal noises, just a lot of cracking, rustling, and swishing. Bree shivered and stepped into the darkness.

Her progress was amazingly slow. She had to duck under limbs, sidle around branches, or climb over fallen trunks. She tried to maintain a direction, but it was difficult with all the acrobatics she had to do. Although her suit was working overtime, the humidity was becoming unbearable even inside the suit.

Something tripped her. She fell hard, and then something landed on her back, the weight crushing her. She fought panic. Hands lifted her helmeted head and put a bag over. *Fuck! The Skull Tribe has caught me!* was her last thought before losing consciousness.

54.
The Attack

First, Woodman the Elder heard the screams and the battle cries. Then the terrible shrieks. His students were already up, their interest in his class lost. And why not—this was a first. There had never been screams and battle cries in the Caves. Woodman shivered—had Geo's fear come to fruition?

"Stop!" he shouted after his students. They all stopped, fear on their faces. They had never seen him lose control of his temper.

"Go to your homes. Nowhere else. HOME!" He had no expectations that they'd listen, but at least he tried.

He ran toward the screams, then remembered the security center. They had cameras everywhere, remotely controlled from there. He cursed their lack of military practice. Because there had never been an attack on their Caves, they had never trained for it. Decades of peace had made them complacent.

Most of the security center was filled with screens monitoring the entire cave system. Two security specialists were standing and looking at two of the screens with perplexed expressions. He saw what had caused that. A huge snake with wings had passed their decontamination area and was attacking people in the hallways. Another—thing—was floating down the hallways. So far it hadn't attacked, but— There were no words to describe what it was; who knew what it was capable of. A man in a silver helmet was advancing behind the monstrous serpent, hacking his way into the complex.

And, on a third screen, he saw an armed group descending into their complex. Somehow the Corrosives had discovered their elevator and how to hack it and had descend into their world. They were as smart and cunning as Geo had warned.

Woodman went to the main desk and pressed a red button. The deafening alarm shrieked throughout the complex. Lifting the microphone, he announced, "We are under attack! All security forces to their posts. All security forces to their posts!"

"What are our orders, sir?" asked one of the two security specialists, looking at him with guilt in his eyes.

"You two direct everyone who is not a combatant back to the living quarters, as far as possible from the areas under attack."

They scrambled to fulfill their mission.

Woodman squinted at the command panel. He used to know every little button there. But that was thirty years ago. Now he struggled to remember. Yeah, that panel. He began reading the numbers under the keys and correlated those numbers with the area numbers on the screens. That was one of them, he'd found it! He turned the key and saw on the screen a reinforced wall sliding down and isolating the rest of the complex from the area where the man with the silver helmet was advancing.

He now needed two more keys to completely isolate the areas under attack from the rest of the complex. That's when he saw that the other monster, the one he could not relate to anything known, the one that hadn't attacked anyone yet, had made it beyond the isolation wall.

He'd have to search through the Corrosion Lab's research to see if there were some methods of combating the Black Rain's monsters. He knew that Alexandre was studying the Corrosion's specific transformations that were triggering these monstrosities. He returned to the keys and began comparing numbers again. The second wave of invaders had killed anyone in their way and were almost past the borders between decontamination and security. The Woodman troops were there already and engaged. *Come on! Which one is it?* He cursed himself for being old and unprepared.

He finally found the second key. He turned it hastily and watched on the screen as the wall came down in the middle of the fight between the Cave's security and the invaders. A third wave of invaders had just arrived and were making their way toward the third breach into the complex. Right, so now the third key.

"Stop right there!" Greg Rumi's voice was commanding.

"Give me a minute, Greg," said Woodman.

"Arrest him!"

Woodman turned in confusion. What was going on? Two security people stepped forward and put their hands on Woodman's shoulders. Greg Rumi was followed by a bunch of fellow councillors.

"Are you mad?" said Woodman the Elder.

But all councillors kept silent and made room for the security people to place Woodman under arrest and take him from there.

"There's one more door to lock, Rumi. Give me a minute! Please!"

"Take him to the Council Room," ordered Greg Rumi and walked away, not looking at Woodman the Elder.

"You've been found guilty of treason. Your entire family has been found guilty of treason. You will be incarcerated awaiting the sentence. Probably prison for life, or execution, even. Depending on how severe the treason evidence is."

Rumi stopped and stared at the old man. He was the only one in the room looking him in the eyes. All other council members were avoiding looking straight at him and taking responsibility.

"Have you stopped the attack?" asked Woodman the Elder.

"That's a security issue that is not to be discussed with a traitor," said Greg Rumi, watching his fellow councillors.

"This is a farce, Rumi. Instead of addressing with what's really important, you conduct this farce and waste the Cave's defense time. You're the traitor!"

"Take him to jail," ordered Rumi.

Two security officers helped the old man to stand and led him out of the room.

"Are you all right, sir?" the voice stirred him from his thoughts. It was one of his students. She placed a tray with food on the cell's table.

"I'm fine, Elsa. Thank you for asking."

"I'm sorry for all this, sir. We all think this is bullshit."

"We?"

"All the students. We want to protest against this."

"What's the situation with the attack, Elsa?"

"We stopped it, sir. The enemy is still here, but no longer a threat."

"How much—how much have we lost?"

"A third of the Caves," said Elsa in a trembling voice.

Woodman the Elder sighed and lowered his head. "And lives?"

"Sixty-three confirmed dead. Over a hundred lost to the conquered parts of the Caves."

"Goddammit, Rumi!"

"Is this his fault, sir?"

"As much as mine, Elsa. As much as mine."

55.
Bree

He burst into the building and stopped in awe. Now, that was a real amphitheater. Fifty times larger than that in the Cave. Luk barked furiously. Geo took another step inside and heard the whistle. He jumped aside as a cloud of arrows slammed into the massive door, walls, and floor where he'd been standing a fraction of a second ago.

He turned, aimed, and fired. A Silker fell before drawing his bow again. He found cover before the next wave of arrows could touch him. The amphitheater was huge, so it certainly had another way out of it. A backstage door, he thought, remembering the term.

The arrows came through the open door, so Geo stepped sideways, aimed, and fired. A scream told him he'd hit another target.

"Stop shooting!" he heard Boris shouting. No volley of arrows followed. His men maintained army discipline.

"Come out, Geo!"

"I'd rather not," Geo shouted back.

"I have a surprise for you here. And if you don't come out to face me, the surprise will die."

Geo looked at Luk. The hound was with him. And Boris wouldn't touch one of his Butterflies, one of his ladies of the court. So it couldn't be Lady L. Of course, that was Boris's crass sense of humor. The surprise was his right arm, his Silker's arm. Medusa.

"Nice try, Boris! I'm sure she won't die."

"I mean, it sounds cold to sentence to death one of your own so easily, but at least take a look when I kill her. She deserves that much."

Wait! What? *One of my own?* Without thinking he peeked out through the doorway. Bree was in front of Boris's mount. Her hands were tied at her back. Most of the prince's men were aiming their bows at him, but a couple aimed them at Bree. Goddammit!

"Let her go!"

"Ah, not so cool anymore," said Boris, dismounting. He took out his sword and came up next to Bree, the blade aimed at her body. "You've kept secrets from your sovereign, Geo. Political secrets. Her presence is the proof of espionage on your part and your tribe's part. That's a punishable offense."

"This is between me and her. Let her go and I'll come with you willingly."

Geo noticed eight men, six with their bows trained on him, two relaxed, now that their boss had taken the prisoner's matter into his own hands. No more hounds. Only the warriors and their beasts. Then he remembered that he'd seen additional troops that were not cavalry. He couldn't see them, but no doubt they were hidden somewhere close. Otherwise how could they have caught Bree?

"Oh, believe me, it is between us, but she's as involved as you. She's one of yours and that's something we can no longer tolerate. Your clan is done. Your people are already dead."

"And that's just because I wanted to save your people," said Geo, hoping for a glimmer of sympathy from the warriors.

"Oh no, my friend. That was amusing. No. This is for caring and using a firearm when you know the law prohibits them. Just as she had one on her. Your clan is openly breaking our law. This is punishable by death. For the guilty party and their family."

Holy Wood! They didn't know about his weapon arm! His Silker's arm. They thought he'd used a real firearm on them.

Boris still thought his Silker's arm was lame, useless. He had to test this theory.

Geo raised his right arm and pointed it at the warriors: "You all believe these lies? That your master's actions are not related to me saving your own people?"

None of them flinched. Their ignorance was obvious.

"Don't bother, Geo. They're not so easy to turn. Now, step forward."

So, not only doesn't he know about my weapon, but his Medusa doesn't work from a distance. He needs a certain proximity. Geo's mind started working on overdrive. Keeping his body from overheating when producing a lot of bullets at once—coolant in his blood stream—gearing up his weapon for repeat—

"Why don't you and I settle this like men, and like the friends we once were?"

"I don't need to. I'm the ruler of everything. You have two choices: either come out, or I order my men to kill you."

"And if I come out, you kill me and then you kill her."

"You will never know." Boris grinned.

The bullets were being produced. Geo felt a little bit feverish. He started panting. He was trembling with effort. "Then I see two choices for you—either release her immediately and I will surrender, or don't release her and I will continue to fight."

"It seems we are at an impasse," said Boris, his grin wider.

A few more minutes, just a few more bullets. "Then let's talk about it. Remember our talks? We can discuss anything. We can solve any difference." Geo tried to focus on his production at the same time he focused on Boris's every move.

"Well, the time to talk is over. Let me make it simple for you." Boris raised his left arm holding the sword and pressed its point against Bree's ribs.

"No, wait!" Geo shouted, raising both arms.

"I'll count to three. At three if you're not right here with me, she's dead."

Geo kept his arms up. He needed just two more minutes for a full load of one hundred small bullets. But he knew he didn't have two more minutes. His time was up.

"One."

Geo stepped over the threshold, his hands still up, though he lowered them a bit. He stopped the production short of the hundred mark and started his target scanner.

"Two."

Geo took one more step and then another one. He was still out of Boris's range. It was clear from his attitude. Geo now knew that Boris first needed to give his men the order to close their eyes, then he'd expose his Medusa.

"Two and a half…"

Geo began walking toward Boris, arms lower, almost aiming his right arm at the prince's warriors. He now could clearly see Bree's face, and hurt inside. He'd never imagined he would see that kind of expression on her sweet face—halfway between fear and resignation. She knew she was going to die.

"All right, now we understand each other," said Boris and sheathed his sword.

Geo slowed down as he approached the prince. The warriors kept their bows trained on him and now, at this range, they had deadly accuracy. What if Boris didn't want to use Medusa?

"*Ex nihilo…*" Boris grinned madly. He knew that Geo knew the password and he was toying with him.

Bree's legs buckled and she fell to her knees. Geo aimed and his internal target made his shot accurate.

"*Nihil…*"

His warriors started lowering their bows. Geo stopped ten feet from Boris.

"*Fit!*" shouted the prince.

His warriors turned as Boris took the hood off his Medusa. Geo fired one shot that penetrated the prince's Silker's arm. He grunted in surprise and lowered her Medusa. Geo then started shooting on repeat, round after round, taking the warriors out one by one. Luckily they hadn't gotten the order to open their eyes and, knowing Medusa was out, they were afraid to look.

Boris raised his arm again and Geo shot wildly in his direction. One bullet grazed the prince's ear and one went through the Medusa's head. Then Geo turned his back and stopped shooting, afraid he'd hit Bree. He tried walking with his back to Boris.

He heard the prince grunt, and then a scuffle. Geo risked a look and saw Boris throwing Bree down and unsheathing his sword again. He aimed and shot in less than a second. The bullet took Boris through his head. He fell heavily over Bree.

Then Torono's ecological alarm sounded, covering everything else. Heavy drops of rain were falling.

56.
The Rain

Geo kicked Boris's corpse aside and dropped to his knees. He checked Bree. She was breathing hard, looking at him with wide, frightened eyes. He pulled her to his chest and hugged her hard. She was all right. She was all right.

He felt the raindrops hitting him hard. The drops of water were pink. It was still the beginning, not a heavy rain, and he knew that their suits would protect them for at ten to fifteen minutes.

"We need to go. We need shelter," he said, looking at Bree. She was crying. But she nodded her understanding and rose with him.

He pushed her toward the amphitheater. "Run into that building."

"What about you?"

"I'm coming. I'm right behind you."

That's when they heard the screams from the dead forest. The Rain had caught up with Boris's men. Bree turned and ran.

Geo picked the Medusa's hood from the ground. Without looking, he covered Boris's right arm and secured the hood in place. Then he took out his blade and started hacking at the arm. The Rain was getting heavier. He felt a little burn on his left shoulder. The suit was not as good as he'd thought. With a few more strokes he managed to hack off Boris's right arm at the elbow. He picked it up and started running.

Bree was waiting for him on the threshold. They both got inside and pulled the heavy door shut after them. It was mainly just the steel frame and some metallic plating; the wood had deteriorated since the Black Rain.

"Where to now?" Bree asked.

He looked around the amphitheater. The chairs and the wooden stage had melted during the last Rain, so the room offered no protection. It would be completely flooded in two days, at most. They didn't have time to check another building—his suit was already compromised and his skin burned on his left shoulder and back.

He ran to the backstage area. There were stairs downward. He took them without considering. No more time to waste. He heard Bree's footsteps behind him, and turned on his flashlight.

"Oh my god, Geo, you're hurt!"

"I'm good! Keep running!"

At the bottom of the stairs, a corridor led to their left. After fifty steps it branched into three corridors. On the walls he could see signs of the Black Rain. They still hadn't reached safety. If the room upstairs was flooded, this corridor would be as well. They needed to keep searching. Left, right, or middle?

"Take the left," said Bree.

Geo made a left and ran. Seeing stairs descending on his right, he scrambled down them to a narrow corridor with pipes of all sizes running along its stone walls. Rats were also running down this corridor. He followed them. The rodents always knew which way to run from danger.

Ten minutes later, after a few staircases up and down, they were in a round, windowless space with stone walls. More importantly, they were above ground and the roof was solid steel. If this didn't keep them safe, then nothing would.

He collapsed on the floor, breathing hard. That's when the pain hit him. He groaned, surprised. He'd forgotten about his burns. He let go of the Medusa and curled up in pain. A couple of rats made an attempt to steal Boris's arm. He shot both instinctively.

"Hey, relax," said Bree.

"We need that thing. We must hold onto it."

"All right, I'll take care of it," she said and took the wrapped Medusa head and attached it to her belt. "Now let me see your back. You're hurt really bad."

Geo took off his helmet, then the upper part of his suit. It was damaged beyond repair. Useless. Bree washed the wounds with some clean water from her suit. Then she sanitized the wounds with some alcohol swabs. Finally she stuck some gauze on his back and shoulder and gave him two pills from her first aid kit. "These will take care of the infection and the pain. At least for a while."

There were hundreds of rats everywhere around them, eyeing them with curiosity. Or hunger, Geo told himself, and sighed. Fortunately these were not the monster rats from the temple. They certainly weren't as small as ancient rats, but they were no bigger than a cat. Still a danger, yet also a source of food for them if they were forced to stay here longer.

"How did you know to take a left there?"

"I remember the maps you had in your op center. You know, from when we studied possible places for Torono's people."

"You're awesome!"

She blushed, but smiled. "By the way, we found the underground place you located for them. It's perfect."

"So they should be safe now."

"The family I traveled with, yes. I don't about the rest."

"What do you mean?"

"They were late. You were late."

"That's why you didn't stay put."

"I couldn't—"

"No, no, I'm just saying. I am glad you're now here with me."

"Me too." Her smile grew bigger and she met his gaze.

He rose and looked around. If they were going to wait here for a week or so, they'd need to prepare some sort of accommodation and protection from the rats.

"What now?" Bree asked him.

"Now we find ourselves a place where the rats cannot touch us."

"How long do you think we'll stay here?"

"It could be a week, or two."

Bree sighed.

"Well, it doesn't matter. We have food, we'll make water, and more importantly, we have each other."

"I'm not eating rats."

"We'll see about that, Ms. Fancy."

Bree grabbed his arms and pulled him to her. She smiled shyly. He kissed her lips lightly.

"I love you, George Woodman."

"I love you, Bree Rumi."

TABLE OF CONTENT

Born in Tomis, **Costi Gurgu** grew up in
Bucurcity. He is the author of many
acclaimed science fiction short stories,
the award-winning novel *RecipeArium,* and
the novel *Servitude.*